STATE FAIR

Earlene Fowler

BERKLEY PRIME CRIME, NEW YORK

THE BERKLEY PUBLISHING GROUP
Published by the Penguin Group
Penguin Group (USA) Inc.
375 Hudson Street, New York, New York 10014, USA

Penguin Group (Canada), 90 Eglinton Avenue East, Suite 700, Toronto, Ontario M4P 2Y3, Canada
(a division of Pearson Penguin Canada Inc.)
Penguin Books Ltd., 80 Strand, London WC2R 0RL, England
Penguin Books Ireland, 25 St. Stephen's Green, Dublin 2, Ireland (a division of Penguin Books Ltd.)
Penguin Group (Australia), 250 Camberwell Road, Camberwell, Victoria 3124, Australia
(a division of Pearson Australia Group Pty. Ltd.)
Penguin Books India Pvt. Ltd., 11 Community Centre, Panchsheel Park, New Delhi—110 017, India
Penguin Group (NZ), 67 Apollo Drive, Rosedale, Auckland 0632, New Zealand
(a division of Pearson New Zealand Ltd.)
Penguin Books (South Africa) (Pty.) Ltd., 24 Sturdee Avenue, Rosebank, Johannesburg 2196,
South Africa

Penguin Books Ltd., Registered Offices: 80 Strand, London WC2R 0RL, England

This is a work of fiction. Names, characters, places, and incidents either are the product of the author's imagination or are used fictitiously, and any resemblance to actual persons, living or dead, business establishments, events, or locales is entirely coincidental. The publisher does not have any control over and does not assume any responsibility for author or third-party websites or their content.

STATE FAIR

A Berkley Prime Crime Book / published by arrangement with the author

PRINTING HISTORY
Berkley Prime Crime hardcover edition / May 2010
Berkley Prime Crime mass-market edition / May 2011

ISBN: 978-0-425-24155-4

BERKLEY® PRIME CRIME
Berkley Prime Crime Books are published by The Berkley Publishing Group,
a division of Penguin Group (USA) Inc.,
375 Hudson Street, New York, New York 10014.
BERKLEY® PRIME CRIME and the PRIME CRIME logo are trademarks of Penguin Group (USA) Inc.

PRINTED IN THE UNITED STATES OF AMERICA

10 9 8 7 6 5 4 3 2 1

Acknowledgments

For the eyes of the Lord range throughout the earth to strengthen those whose hearts are fully committed to Him.

2 Chronicles 16:9

Praise always to you, Lord Jesus Christ.

Also my grateful heart (alphabetically) thanks:

Charlotte "Bunny" Brown—for your friendship, for always being right there to answer any questions I might have about ranching or horses and for kindly inviting me to tag along on your fun adventures.

Katsy Chappell—talented actress, comedian, quilter and beloved friend who not only loaned me her name but also opened her heart and gave me insight into the African American world. You are one very fine and funny lady!

Tina Davis—dearest and wisest of friends and dedicated Webmaster who is always there for me and, without intending to, gives me some of my best opening scenes.

Jo Ellen Heil, Christine Hill, Lela Satterfield and Laura Ross Wingfield—who patiently listen to me whine and kvetch—you, my dearly loved sisters, are the best!

Jo-Ann Mapson—whose thoughtful critique

of this manuscript helped me tremendously—my friend, I dearly miss our shopping trips and our literary lunches at Chester's.

Pam Munns—who keeps me on the straight and narrow about law enforcement details—your friendship is a treasure.

Jo Ann Richardson—who asked me to speak about quilts at the Mid-State Fair many years ago, thus giving me the idea for this book.

Vivian Robertson—CEO of California Mid-State Fair—thanks for allowing me access to the best county fair on earth. I assure everyone who reads this that my fair and its often dastardly characters are entirely fictional and don't reflect anybody at the real Mid-State Fair!

Kate Seaver—a wonderful and thoughtful editor whose insights I always appreciate—it is a pleasure working with you!

Jane Tenorio-Coscarelli—a brilliant artist, writer and quilter—thanks for your personal insights, your enlightening stories and your friendship.

Kathy Vieira—Western woman extraordinaire who shared all her years of fair stories and experiences. I picked your brain like a vulture, and good friend that you are, you never once complained. Any mistakes are mine, not yours!

My husband, Allen—who has had a starring part in my story since we were fifteen years old—the best is yet to come!

A Note from the Author

Just so you don't get confused, *State Fair* takes place in August 1997. While only a little less than five years have taken place in my characters' lives in San Celina, I actually have been writing the Benni Harper novels for almost seventeen years.

I suppose they are now considered (semi)historical fiction. It is a challenge to try to remember what things were like back in the 1990s, but I'm doing my best!

Though there is an actual Mid-State Fair in Paso Robles, California, this book is about a fictional fair in a fictional town. Back in 1992 when I wrote *Fool's Puzzle* I never expected it to be published, much less that I would write (so far) thirteen more books in the series. In the first book, because I didn't know what else to do, I fictionalized all the towns Benni actually went to in San Celina County (inspired by San Luis Obispo County). The towns she just mentioned in passing . . . well, I used their real names not guessing I'd ever actually have to write about them. So I'm stuck with a fictional county with half "real" names and half fictional ones.

Just in case anyone was wondering . . .

State Fair

The English word *fair* comes from the Latin *feriae*, meaning "holy days." Fairs in America first started in the 1620s with the Dutch settlers in New Amsterdam. The Berkshire County, Massachusetts, fair is widely considered the first county fair. It took place on September 24, 1811, and three thousand people attended. Since then, state and county fairs have become a beloved tradition for millions of Americans. For a few days or weeks once a year exhibition halls are filled with the pickles, cakes, pies, pottery, steers, lambs, hogs, giant pumpkins and quilts of hopeful competitors. After their win (or loss), there are then the midway carnival rides and games, fried foods, cotton candy and the ubiquitous commercial buildings selling everything from waterless cookware to genuine Native American turquoise rings.

There is not much history about the State Fair quilt pattern. There are actually five patterns recorded in books that claim the State Fair name. One is a Nancy Cabot pattern. The others were created by unknown quilt makers. Perhaps these anonymous quilt designers were inspired by a local county fair where they showed their first lamb or entered their special chocolate-chip cookies or received their first kiss atop a Ferris wheel. Like so many quilt patterns, its origin will be a mystery. But we can be assured of one thing. Fairs will spin their enchanting dreams for generations to come, because, after all, who doesn't love the fair?

CHAPTER 1

𝓜Y DAY DIDN'T START WITH A DEEP-FRIED TWINKIE,
although the thought crossed my mind.

"Benni Harper Ortiz, step away from that counter," said
my best friend, Elvia Aragon Littleton. "It is only eight
o'clock in the morning. It's too early for anything fried in
that much fat."

"Fat grams don't count with fair food." I gazed at the
photo menu of Mustang Sallie's Fried Food Emporium
and plotted my snacks for a day I knew would stretch long
into the night. Deep-fried artichoke? Or maybe the fried
avocado, which I'd tried yesterday. It was tastier than it
sounded, kind of like hot guacamole dip. And definitely
the fried Oreos again. I'd become addicted to those. They'd
tasted like a gooey chocolate cake surrounded by a fresh
doughnut. "Besides, I'm only contemplating future meals.
They don't open until eleven a.m."

Mustang Sallie's, a mind-throbbing magenta-colored
building accentuated with rainbow polka dots and a pink

and orange fiberglass pony perched on its roof, squatted in the center of the San Celina County Mid-State Fairgrounds in the North County town of Paso Robles. It was one of the fairground's oldest structures, and for as long as I could remember the garish snack building had been used as a central meeting place for folks during the fair's twelve-day run.

The building, along with the fair, held a bittersweet nostalgia for me. Too many times to count I'd met Jack, my late first husband, in front of this very building after showing our 4-H cattle and later, when we were adults, after helping kids in my Gramma Dove's 4-H club wash and primp their hogs, steers and lambs for a run at that coveted blue ribbon. Back in the 1960s and '70s Mustang Sallie's sold grilled hot dogs, skin-on French fries, oak-grilled tri-tip steak sandwiches and onion rings, but in the last few years, they had expanded their food selection to more exotic fried fare. They were locked in a never-ending quest to top themselves. Last year's fried Coca-Cola was proving hard to beat, at least in terms of originality and sugary "ick" factor.

Elvia leaned down and checked on her seven-week-old daughter, Sophia Louisa Aragon Littleton. My goddaughter was carefully swaddled and tucked away in her fancy silver and blue top-of-the-line Graco stroller. "All I know is I cannot even peek at anything fried for the next six months. I'm still fat as one of your 4-H hogs."

I laughed right in her face. "What are you a size six now?" I mimed holding a phone to my ear. "Calling Richard Simmons for an emergency intervention."

Elvia laid her freshly manicured hand across her stomach. It *was* still a little pudgy from childbirth, but she was by no stretch of anyone's imagination *fat*.

"I'm still a size eight!" she cried. "Honestly, what do movie stars do to get their figures back so quickly?"

I'd already turned my attention back to the painted

menu. "Hey, look, fried pickles! That's new." I turned to gauge her reaction. Her lips, painted a shiny pomegranate red to match her nails, were scrunched up; her black lashes glistened with tears.

"Movie stars?" I said, swatting a fly that hovered over Sophie Lou's stroller. "Oh, they live on lettuce and laxatives. The photos you see of them? Totally fake and touched up by experts trained by the FBI. I read that in the *National Enquirer* so it must be true."

"Emory practically force-feeds me! Says his daughter needs hearty milk to drink. I informed him that he gets to breast feed the next one."

"Good luck with that, *mamacita*."

THE TRUTH WAS MY COUSIN EMORY, WHO ALSO HAPPENED to be her husband, wouldn't or couldn't ever force Elvia to do anything. He was, however, not above tempting her by having all her favorite foods readily available. Foods cooked by her own mother who made the best green chile enchiladas, sweet corn tamales and killer flan on the Central Coast.

"You've read every prepregnancy, midpregnancy and postpregnancy book written in the last twenty years," I said. "Don't they all agree that it takes a little time to lose your baby weight?" I stooped down and ran my finger across my goddaughter's creamy golden cheek. She didn't even stir. "Ah, sweet Sophie Lou, what're we going to do with your *mami grande*?"

Elvia shot me an irritated look. "Sophia! I told you to call her Sophia. You and Emory are going to drive me loco."

After much back and forth about their daughter's name, Elvia and Emory had finally agreed on Sophia Louisa, which seemed to fulfill both her Mexican and his Southern requirements . . . and let Sophia share a middle name with her adoring godmother—me. Elvia even reluctantly agreed that to honor our Arkansas roots, Emory and I could call her Sophie. That was until we actually started doing so.

"You promised Emory." I stood up, shifting my leather backpack from one side to the other, my shoulders already aching. It felt like I was carrying ten bricks.

"Don't you have to judge something?" Avoidance was always Elvia's method of dealing with something she didn't like.

"Not judge, help control. I'm going to be a pig wrangler for Novice and Intermediate 4-H Hog Showmanship. I don't have to be there until nine a.m. Plenty of time." I stretched out my arms and yawned. "I'm starving. I rushed out of the house with only one cup of coffee in my system. I cannot spend the next three hours chasing gilts and barrows . . . not to mention tiny humans, without sustenance."

"Gilts and what?" She tilted her head, confused.

I smiled, having forgotten for a moment that my best friend since second grade and I had always had huge parts of our lives that were totally foreign to each other. She spoke Spanish. I spoke Ag. "Gilts are female pigs and barrows are castrated male pigs."

"So what are uncastrated male pigs then?"

I grinned at her. "Boars."

She returned my smile. "I dated a few bores in my time."

I nodded, making one last note of Mustang Sallie's menu. Deep-fried tomatoes. Wasn't that actually kind of healthy? "I remember every one of them. Aren't you glad you took my wise advice and married my adorable cousin?"

"Humph," she said, still refusing to admit I'd picked the best man in the world for her and nagged her until she finally married him.

"Without him, there'd be no Sophie Lou," I reminded her.

She gazed down at her sleeping daughter. "Sophia, Sophia." Her voice was more gentle and tender than I'd ever heard it. "I'll owe you forever, *mi amiga buena.*"

"Care to put that in writing?"

She rolled her black eyes. "Don't you have some gilteds to push around?"

"Gilts," I corrected. "Yes, but I have just enough time to sneak over to the Kiwanis booth and buy myself an eggs Kiwanis." My stomach growled in anticipation of the traditional fair breakfast favored by the locals—crisp bacon, a fried egg, cheddar cheese and mayonnaise between two squished hamburger buns. I added Tabasco sauce for extra kick. Eggs Kiwanis had been my preferred fair breakfast since I sprouted teeth.

"A bowl of oatmeal would be much better for you," she said, pushing the dark blue stroller down the carnival midway. All the colorful game stands and rides were closed, but a few carnies were starting to wander in, looking bleary-eyed, wild-haired and like they'd just gotten out of prison two minutes ago.

"You sound like Gabe," I said, falling in beside her. My health-conscious-when-it-suited-him second husband was always nagging me about my vegetable-starved diet. "I will eat oatmeal at the fair the very minute someone deep-fries it and puts it on a stick."

"Hey, Robbie!" I waved at one of the fair security people, dressed in a bright red polo shirt with Security in white letters across his chest. He drove by in one of the fair's official yellow and red golf carts hauling a utility trailer filled with empty trash cans.

"Hey, girl!" Robbie called. "You stay outta trouble!" He was one of the woodworkers from the Artists' Co-op affiliated with the Josiah Sinclair Folk Art Museum where I was curator and manager of the co-op. Many of our artists worked the fair either selling their products in a booth or taking one of the numerous temporary jobs like security detail or ground maintenance.

"So, what's on your agenda today?" I asked Elvia.

"I promised Emory I'd check on the new hospitality

suite. He wants to make sure that everything's perfect, but between opening the new chicken restaurant in Santa Maria, all his civic volunteering and being president of the fair's Booster Buddies, he's scheduled to be in five places at one time."

Emory and his father, my uncle Boone, owned Boone's Good Eatin' Chicken, a smoked chicken company based in Sugartree, Arkansas, Emory's hometown and where Uncle Boone still lived. When Emory came west to pursue Elvia, he talked his father into opening up a restaurant selling their chicken in San Celina, gambling that Californians might enjoy the taste of real Southern-style smoked chicken. To support his adopted state, Emory bought chickens grown in California but used the smoking method perfected in Arkansas. The business became more successful than he'd anticipated, which was great in terms of money, but bad in terms of time, especially now that he was a husband and a new father.

Elvia reached over and tucked Sophie's green and yellow Birds-in-Flight quilt a little closer around her. My gramma Dove and I pieced the quilt the minute we found out Elvia was pregnant. "I just need to show up, make sure the smoked chicken sandwich platters are there and that there is plenty to go around. Then it's back to the bookstore." Elvia owned Blind Harry's, San Celina's only independent bookstore.

"Did the decorators finish in time?" I asked, walking past the giant Ferris wheel. Before the fair ended, in memory of Jack, I'd have to ride it. "Did they take your suggestions? I've been so busy getting the folk art museum's fair booth set up and helping with 4-H, I haven't even been up to see it."

In appreciation for how well his business was going, Emory had donated half the money needed for the Booster Buddies' new Western-themed hospitality lounge. The nondescript green building was located in front of the Sierra

Vista Grandstand Stage and Arena where the most popular musical stars performed and where the country rodeo took place. The spacious and even more important during the fair, air-conditioned, hospitality suite was located on the second floor of the building. Not only was it a comfortable place for the Booster Buddies and their guests to relax, it also had some of the best concert seats. Located off the hospitality lounge's balcony, the padded seats reserved for the Booster Buddies and guests had a dynamite view of the stage and arena. It was a small compensation for the thousands of volunteer hours members put in every year, not to mention the five-hundred-dollar-per-person annual dues.

"Yes, they finished last week. It looks wonderful. I'm glad Emory reconsidered the Pendleton furniture and went with my suggestion to hang Pendleton blankets on the walls instead. Can you picture beer and wine stains on ten-thousand-dollar sofas?" She gave a horrified shudder. "We went with navy corduroy sofas from JCPenney."

I nodded in agreement. I'd enjoyed access to the Booster Buddies' old hospitality suite for many years because my dad Ben and my gramma Dove were charter committee members. Twenty-seven years ago, forty-two people formed a group whose primary reason for existing was to promote what was then called the San Celina County Fair. (A few years back the "powers that be" decided to fancy it up and rename it the Mid-State Fair, thus confusing folks ever after.)

The Booster Buddies now had 150 members. Membership was supposed to be purely altruistic, but like most groups it had its political side. A lot of deals, both pertaining to the fair and other economic concerns in the county, took place in that spacious room nicknamed appropriately "the Bull Pen." Still, even with the wheeling and dealing, the primary activity in the hospitality suite seemed to be drinking too much, eating too many sweet and salty snacks and more than occasionally, exaggerating everything from the size of your cattle herd to the return on your favorite mutual fund.

"Will I see you at the Bull Pen and concert tonight?" I asked. We'd turned around and were walking back toward the center of the fairgrounds. "Kathy Mattea is performing."

Elvia narrowed one dark-lashed eye at me. "Can't we rename the hospitality suite something a little classier?"

"Traditions are mighty hard to break round these parts."

She gave an exaggerated sigh, conceding the truth of my statement. "I'll probably drop by tonight since it's the only way I'll get to see my husband before one a.m. Luckily, Sophia's taken to the bottle almost as well as to me, so I can express some breast milk and leave her with Mama."

We parted ways at the hospitality suite. Amazed, I watched Elvia flip a few switches and turn part of Sophie's stroller into a carrier. Holding the carrier on the crook of her arm like a purse, she punched the code on the locked door and headed up the stairs to the suite.

My thoughts were on my upcoming breakfast when my cell phone rang—"Happy Trails to You."

"Ah, get lost, Dale," I said out loud, fumbling through my leather backpack. I'd already started regretting the ease with which people could reach me on my cell phone. In the good old days, I could use being someplace like the fair as an excuse to be out of contact with people and their problems. But, since I was curator of the folk art museum, wife to San Celina's often controversial police chief, with all its myriad and pain-in-the-butt social obligations, and granddaughter to Dove Ramsey Lyons, one of the busiest women in the county with her agriculture committees, homeless shelter and historical society meetings and way too many church activities, I felt obligated to be available.

"She's back," the gravelly, old voice whispered. It sounded like a tin cup of rattling quarters.

"Who is this?" I demanded. "Is this a prank call? How did you get this number?"

The voice took on its normal, scolding tone. "I'm the woman who paid for all your fancy prom dresses with her chicken money, that's who."

"Hey, Dove." I smiled, knowing all along it was my gramma. "What's cookin', good lookin'?"

"No time for jokes. She arrives this evening on the Amtrak and I'm thinkin' about just leaving her at the train station."

I didn't have to ask who "she" was because we'd been through this scenario countless times in the last thirty-something years since Dove moved in with Daddy and me right before Mama died of breast cancer. *She* was Garnet Louise Wilcox, Dove's only sibling, with whom I and Sophie shared a middle name. Dove and Garnet got along, as Daddy liked to say, like two bobcats trapped in a burning outhouse.

"You knew she was coming," I said, waving at acquaintances every few steps. There was no such thing as privacy at the fair. "Why are you panicking now?"

"I know she *said* she was coming, but I thought . . . well, to be honest . . . I prayed that she'd get sick."

I stopped dead in my tracks next to the red, yellow and blue Hot Dog on a Stick kiosk. A young girl in blue shorts and a tricolored jockey cap was making lemonade by vigorously pushing a plunger up and down in a large barrel. "You prayed that God would strike your sister sick? Dove, I'm pretty sure that's *not* what Jesus would do."

"Oh, pshaw," she said. "Just because Jesus was the Son of God, you can't tell me his brothers and sisters didn't annoy the heck out of him sometimes. It no doubt took great restraint on his part not to lightning bolt them once in a while. Besides, I only prayed that she'd get a head cold. Just a little sinus infection, not the bubonic plague.

The Lord obviously didn't answer me." Her voice sounded more than a little put out.

"Or maybe your answer is you're supposed to entertain your sister like an angel unawares and show her a good time."

Her voice grew sly. "I think I'm getting a message from our Lord right now that you haven't spent near enough time with your beloved great-aunt . . ."

"What? What?" I yelled into the phone. "I'm losing our connection!"

"Don't you dare turn me . . ."

"Out of range! Goin' through a tunnel! Bye!"

I hit the end button and shoved the phone deep into my backpack. I'd pay dearly for that little rebellious act later, but I wasn't up to hearing her complaints about Aunt Garnet. Dove knew good and well my plate was full during the fair. Right now, I had no time to referee the contentious relationship of my gramma and her prim and proper sister. I'd worry about Dove's sibling rivalry problems later, once I had a full stomach and finished my pig wrangling.

It took me another twenty minutes to make my way over to the Kiwanis booth mostly because I was forced to stop every few steps to shoot the breeze with someone I hadn't seen in months. The fair was like a huge family reunion for San Celina County's shrinking agriculture community. I'd been attending it since the early sixties when my family moved to the Central Coast of California from Arkansas. My daddy and mama, Ben and Alice Ramsey, bought our original five-hundred-acre ranch and started their dynasty with only one Hereford bull of dubious lineage and two healthy heifers. Right before Mama died when I was six, my gramma Dove Ramsey came out from Arkansas to live with Daddy, the oldest of her six children, to help him run the ranch and raise me. She arrived in San Celina's California mission-style train station armed with her favorite cast-iron frying pan, a stash of quilting fabric, her much envied recipes for cheesy corn bread and chocolate-coffee icebox pie and my twelve-year-old uncle Arnie, Daddy's youngest brother. Arnie had long ago left San Celina for Montana where he now worked as a ranch foreman for their sister, Kate, but Daddy and Dove still raised cattle—232 head now, not counting my 58—and were a beloved part of the Central Coast agriculture community.

I started walking toward the Livestock Show Arena with my eggs Kiwanis sandwich half devoured when I heard my name called for the umpteenth time. It was Maggie Morrison, my husband Gabe's extremely capable assistant. Since it was Friday, she must have taken the day off from her never-easy duty of keeping Gabe's complex schedule running smoothly.

Maggie was a young African American woman who lived with her older sister, Katsy. They raised a small but excellent herd of Herefords on a ranch outside the town of Santa Margarita, not far from the rough and rowdy Frio Saloon. She was twenty-six, twelve years younger than me, though so mature for her age, I often forgot our age difference. Gabe constantly sang her praises, claiming he'd drown in an ocean of paperwork and never get anywhere on time if it wasn't for Maggie. She was organized and discreet and understood his often delicate position of being a minority in a powerful position in a county that was and always had been primarily Anglo.

I'd known Maggie from the time she was nine and I was twenty-one. Her mother, LaWanda, an emergency room nurse at San Celina General Hospital, had been one of Dove's closest friends. They'd bonded years ago when Dove brought one of our ranch hands into emergency to have his broken wrist set. Dove and LaWanda discovered their common Arkansas background and understanding of all things Southern, which they claimed rural Californians, who often had Southern roots a few generations back, never really "got."

LaWanda, a champion reined-horse competitor, died in a riding accident when Maggie was eighteen and Katsy was twenty-four. The two women still lived on the hundred acre ranch LaWanda had leased. With her insurance settlement, they bought the ranch and were trying to carry out their mama's dream of a rural lifestyle.

"Wait up," Maggie called, quickening her step to catch up with me. She was taller than me by seven inches and had long, coltish legs that I envied with all my five-foot-one heart. She wore her hair in a close-trimmed Afro-style, complementing her oval face, and had almond-shaped brown eyes and skin the color of Karo syrup. She could have been Natalie Cole's younger sister. Today, rather than in her normal business attire of a jacket, silk blouse and slacks, she wore tight blue Wranglers, a grass green snap-button Western shirt and black round-toed roper boots.

"That sandwich looks killer," she said. "I have to sneak over to the Kiwanis booth."

I held it out to her. "Want a bite?"

"Don't mind if I do." She took one, wiping a drop of mayonnaise off the corner of her mouth then fell in beside me. "Yep, that's definitely my next stop."

"You left my sweet husband on his own today? I bet he'll be crazy *loco* by the time he gets home tonight." I popped the last bite of my sandwich into my mouth. "Thanks loads."

She laughed, waving a hand. "He'll be fine. Jim's there and Bambi can handle any photocopying emergency. There's always my voice mail if he really doesn't want to deal with someone. He won't even know I'm gone. Thank goodness, the only thing that is really causing him any extra stress lately is that rash of stolen trucks and SUVs. I guess the thieves have moved into Santa Barbara County."

"Gabe told me. Glad my truck is purple. Bet nobody's gonna want to steal it. I still can't believe Gabe hired someone named Bambi."

She gave another deep laugh. "It's even harder to imagine someone naming their daughter that. But she is super-organized and isn't a bit rattled by any of the trash-talking cops, which is one of the most important requirements of our job. Don't worry, I made sure that this would be a light day for Señor Ortiz."

"Smart lady. Fewer problems for you to handle Monday."

We walked into the swine building, already teeming with hundreds of nervous kids dressed in their white 4-H shirts, white Wranglers, bright Kelly green kerchiefs for the girls and neckties for the boys. Their chevron-style caps always reminded me of old-time gas station attendants. Adding to the melee were their equally agitated livestock and sleep-deprived parents and leaders trying to French braid hair, clean spots off white shirts or jeans, slick down cowlicks with parental spit and bring some kind of order to the whole crazy scene.

Nostalgia enveloped me when I smelled the familiar scent of animal manure, fresh hay, toasty popcorn and a sharply sweet, medicinal scent I'd always associated with the fair—sort of a mixture of eucalyptus and cotton candy. The county fair—*this* county fair—had been a part of my annual schedule for as long as I could remember. Though I hadn't shown cattle or sheep for over twenty years, I still looked forward to the fair—its crazy foods, its competitions, its familiar rituals. And, in the last few years, for the painfully sweet memories it brought of a more innocent time of my life.

"What are you doing today?" I asked Maggie. "I've agreed to help wrangle pigs for Novice and Intermediate Hog Showmanship. Then I think I'm going to check out the new Bull Pen. Elvia says it looks like a million bucks."

"You haven't seen it yet? God bless your rich cousin. Without him we'd still be sitting on plastic patio chairs and eating frozen pizza rolls."

I waved at Marguerite Zechiel and her now grown

daughter, Laurie. Laurie had once been in Dove's 4-H club. They sat behind a battered card table outside the large saw-dust-covered pen filled with nervous nine- and ten-year-old youngsters trying to keep track of their squealing hogs.

"C'mon," I said, "it wasn't that bad. Those old plastic chairs had a lot of interesting graffiti on them—kind of an oral history. Besides, he didn't pay for it all himself. His donation just got the ball rolling. That hospitality suite has needed renovation for years."

"Grab yourself a pig board, girls," Marguerite said, patting her silvery bob, her sky blue eyes twinkling with patient humor. "We need all the wranglers we can get out there."

"Ladies, choose your weapons." Her slim, dark-haired daughter, Laurie, pointed to the pile of two-by-three-foot rectangular plywood boards painted green and designed with hand holds, sort of like a huge painter's palette. They'd been spruced up by Marguerite and Laurie, both talented tole painters who belonged to the Artists' Co-op. One side of the boards depicted bright pink pig faces, their snouts open in exaggerated screams. The other side boasted in large white letters—Swine Escort.

Unlike lambs and cattle, there was no way pigs could be trained to stand still long enough for the judge to consider conformation and the finer points of porcine excellence. Photos of pig judging were the ones that often made the local newspapers because there was a good chance something funny happened when you had twenty 4-H kids wielding "pig sticks," twenty hogs avoiding said sticks and as many wranglers as you could, well, wrangle into being there to shove their pig board between two agitated pigs.

"I'm taken," Maggie said to Marguerite. "I have a two-hour stint as docent in the Family Farm exhibit building." She turned to me. "Have you seen the exhibits yet?"

I grabbed a pig board. "Haven't seen anything yet. I've spent most of my time getting the museum booth ready."

"The judging's been quite . . . uh . . . controversial this year."

"When isn't it? I'll come by when I'm through here." I glanced over at Marguerite for confirmation. "When am I free?"

"We should be done by noon," she said.

"See you later," Maggie said, with a wave.

I tucked the Booster Buddies all-access pass hanging from a lanyard around my neck inside my Josiah Sinclair Folk Art Museum T-shirt and spent the next few hours doing enough aerobic exercise chasing after swine to qualify me for a couple more days eating off Mustang Sallie's menu.

After my hog-wrangling duty, on the way to agriculture building no. 1 where the Family Farm exhibits were displayed, I decided to check out the situation at the folk art museum booth. It was twelve thirty and the fairgrounds had been open to the public for a half hour. Since it was Friday, we expected a larger and hopefully more shopping-inclined crowd than on the fair's first two days when a good part of the fair's visitors consisted of frugal, retired folks or summer camp kids on field trips. The fair officially opened on Wednesday, so this was our first weekend night. Kathy Mattea's long-anticipated concert would kick the fair into high gear.

The folk art museum's booth was located on Artisans' Row, next to Bears Quilt Shop, a new quilt store that just opened in the seaside town of Cayucos. I took special pride in our museum and co-op's booth because I'd talked the Booster Buddies and the city of San Celina into cosponsoring it. Most folk artists barely made enough money to eat and pay rent, so the expensive retail space at the fair was beyond their means. This access to the public both provided them a little more income and advertised our museum. Constance Sinclair, the wealthy, longtime resident of San Celina County who donated her family's adobe ranch house and stables that housed the folk art museum, had given her seal of approval to my suggestion, thus convincing the city officials who held the purse strings that the money was being put to good use.

We'd worked hard at making the booth both fun and educational with a varied representation of our artists' work—quilts, wood carvings, tole, acrylic and watercolor painting, greeting cards, duck decoys, fiber arts, leather carving and horsehair hitching, the art of braiding horsehair into intricate patterns that were then fashioned into key chains, belts and hatbands. This year, to complement the African Americans Settle the West exhibit in the creative arts building, we had a section devoted primarily to African American–inspired quilts and wall hangings.

"Hey, boys!" I called to one of the guys who owned Bears Quilt Shop.

"Hey, Benni," answered Vivs, the shop's computer guru and a talented long-arm quilter. "Got some great new Western fabric from Alexander Henry. Check it out." He held up a bolt of fabric showing cowgirls and boys on horseback talking on cell phones.

"Cool! Save me a couple of yards. You know, we did try to use cell phones to talk to each other on our last roundup, but way up in the hills the reception was real sketchy."

"There goes all my romantic Western fantasies about rounding up little dogies," said Russ, also dynamite on a long-arm machine. Many quilters in our local guilds hired him to machine-quilt their pieced tops.

"You know, Russ," I said, "it would take about two seconds at a real roundup to shatter any city person's romantic fantasy about what goes into providing them with that juicy sirloin steak or stir fry. There is more manure and blood involved than most people realize."

He put his hand over his ears. "No, no, don't tell me any more. I want to enjoy my tri-tip breakfast burritos."

"My lips are sealed," I said.

The museum booth was so busy it took me a few minutes before I could talk to Jazz Clark who was in charge of the cash register during this four hour shift. Jasmine "Jazz" Clark was the perfect example of what I'd been writing about in my grant proposals pertaining to the future of our folk art museum. She was nineteen years old and a talented painter and fiber artist whose story quilts were already starting to catch the eyes of local collectors. She was a sophomore at Cal Poly with a major in art and minor in African American studies.

We'd become unlikely friends in the last few years despite the almost twenty years' difference in our ages. We both lost our mothers when we were very young girls. Our relationship started one winter afternoon at the museum when she was sixteen. She'd become a member of our Artists' Co-op because her "adopted" aunt and uncle, Jim and Oneeda Cleary, had recommended it to her dad, Levi, as a way to keep her busy. She'd taken to quilting like she'd been doing it all her life. She was hand-stitching a quilt in the large craft room and I walked by on my way to make some hot chocolate. I asked her to join me and over our cocoa in the co-op's tiny kitchen, after a casual comment from me about how whipped cream on cocoa always made me miss my mother, she opened up her heart about how hard her dad tried to be both mom and dad to her, but how she always felt something was missing.

"You're so lucky to have Dove," she'd said, sitting across from me at the round wooden snack table. She was dressed in jeans, hiking boots and a gray sweatshirt she'd hand painted with bright Van Gogh–style flowers. There was always something unique about the clothes she wore, some bit of lace or embroidery or grouping of antique pins that turned her simple clothing into little art pieces. "Both my grammas are gone. Bad hearts, just like my mom." She sighed, poked a nail-bitten finger into her whipped cream.

Jazz's mother, Ruth, a red-haired Irish woman, died of

congestive heart failure when Jazz was four years old. I'd met Ruth a few times but didn't remember much about her. Jack and I had been in our twenties, newly married and didn't hang around the same young parents' crowd as Jazz's mom and dad.

I reached across the tiny table and patted her hand. "Yes, I was lucky. But you've got a wonderful dad and lots of other people who care about you."

She gave me a wide, heartbreaking smile. Her oval face was perfectly formed and her downy milk chocolate hair twisted into two pig tails. "Yeah, I know. I have Dad and Uncle Jim and Aunt Oneeda and all the ladies in the Ebony Sisters Quilt Guild. I shouldn't whine, I guess."

"Oneeda adores you. She always talks about what you're doing. And Jim's just as proud of you as if you were his own grandchild."

Jim Cleary was one of Gabe's captains at the police department, the one with whom I had no doubt Gabe would trust his life. I'd met Jim and Oneeda when I started dating Gabe. She and I immediately took to each other. More than anyone else, she helped me understand what it would mean for me to marry a police officer. She'd had multiple sclerosis for as long as I'd known her but never let it stop her from enjoying life. Her flannel lap quilts, given to anyone who came across her path whom she felt needed comforting, were that much more beautiful because of the effort it took her to make each one.

"Aunt Oneeda's the best storyteller," Jazz said. "She tells stories about back in the day when white people made her drink from a different water fountain than them. She said even I wouldn't have been able to just drink anywhere and I'm half white!" She wrinkled her nose. "Not that I'd drink from any kind of fountain. Think of the bacteria! Gross! Thank goodness we have bottled water now."

"It *is* hard for us living in the '90s to imagine."

Jazz stared down into her half-finished cocoa. "Do you think my mom and dad had it hard here in San Celina?"

Her father, Levi Clark, was the county fair's general manager, the first African American to hold that position. He'd started out cleaning restrooms at the fair when he was eighteen, a Cal Poly college student studying business administration. Now he was in charge of the entire Mid-State Fair.

I wasn't certain exactly how to answer her. "I don't really know."

"Dad says Mom really had a temper and wasn't afraid to tell people what she thought."

I smiled at her. "She and I would have gotten along just fine."

Behind the cash register at the folk art museum booth, I wasn't surprised to see Jazz had everything under control. She'd been essentially running the household for her and her father since she was tall enough to turn on the oven.

"I came by to see if you need help," I said, "but looks like you are doing fine."

She grinned at me, took a woman's fifty-dollar bill, made change and handed her three red and black Drunkard's Path pot holders. "Thanks," she told the customer. "Please, tell all your friends! Get your Christmas shopping done."

"How are sales," I asked, "or is it too early to judge?"

"They're super! We might have to ask the artists for more things if this keeps up. Items under ten bucks are selling fastest, but I sold three fifty-dollar crib quilts today. And the black cloth dolls? Totally flying off the shelf."

"The Ebony Sisters will be happy to hear that."

All the money earned from the dolls was going to a rural charter school they'd adopted in Mississippi. Even the artists' co-op, which normally received 10 percent of whatever the artists sold to help with operating expenses, was donating their profits from the dolls to the school.

"So, where are you headed?" she asked, restacking some fabric eyeglass cases.

"To the Bull Pen and then over to the Family Farm exhibits. I'm dying to see what the families have come up with this year."

The Family Farm exhibits began years ago as a good-natured competition between the farm and ranch families in San Celina County. Each family was given a hundred-square-foot area to decorate and promote their farm or ranch. It was intended to be a fun competition primarily for kids, but the tone gradually changed when adults started becoming a little too involved in creating the exhibits. The last few years it had evolved into a somewhat silly, egotistical contest of one-upmanship. It was amazing what people dreamed up every year and even more amazing how whoever won or didn't win caused such resentment. First prize was a picture of your exhibit on the front page of the *San Celina Tribune*, a dozen free passes to the fair and a two-hundred-dollar Farm Supply gift certificate. The winners also won bragging rights, which meant a lot in the ag community.

"Did you enter?" Jazz asked.

I shook my head no. "Too many other irons in the fire this year. Besides, it's really more fun if there are kids involved."

"I helped Maggie and Katsy with their exhibit," Jazz said. "We made papier-mâchés of a bull and two cows. Maggie and I machine-quilted a Hen and Eggs quilt and draped that over the bull's back. Then we painted a big wood board with all these old African American cattle brands, including their own great-grandpa's."

I smiled at her enthusiasm. I'd been working with Katsy on the African American quilt exhibit at the museum for almost a year. When she wasn't ranching or managing a clothing store in San Celina, she taught two classes of American history at San Celina Community College. We combined the quilt exhibit with a smaller exhibit of rare black cloth folk dolls from the nineteenth and early twentieth centuries in our smaller upstairs gallery. They were on loan to us from a collector in Oakland who was a friend of Katsy's.

"How's your dad doing?" I asked. "I really should drop by his office and cheer him on."

There had been a fierce competition for the fair's general manager position. Though many people applied, some not even from our county, Levi got the job. But even though Levi was immensely qualified with his long years of experience and MBA in business, there'd been uneasy murmurings that a little unspoken affirmative action had taken place.

"I guess nothing bad enough to tell me about," she said, placing her hands on her hips. "But you know my dad. He tries to protect me too much."

"A daddy's prerogative."

"I'm nineteen. According to the law, that's a grown-up." Her bottom lip stuck out in a pout that made her appear about fourteen.

"He knows that. Let him baby you a little longer. Otherwise, he's going to have to admit to himself that he's trotting briskly into middle age."

"He's forty-eight," she said, her tone practical. "That's only middle age if you live to be ninety-six."

"I suggest you don't voice that particular observation until after the fair. Right now, he likely feels closer to ninety-six."

I glanced at my watch as I headed toward agriculture building no. 1. It was almost 1 p.m. My eggs Kiwanis sandwich had been hours ago and my stomach was primed to partake again of fair food. I stood in line at Mustang Sallie's trying to decide between deep-fried artichoke hearts with ranch dressing or just jump ahead to dessert and buy a fried Snickers.

"That stuff'll kill you," a male voice whispered in my

ear. I turned to face my friend and nemesis, Detective Ford "Hud" Hudson of the San Celina Sheriff's Department. He wore faded Wranglers, black cherry–colored cowboy boots and a gray fitted T-shirt that asked in red lettering Who's Your Crawdaddy? Born and raised in Beaumont, Texas, he was proud of his half-Cajun, all-Texan heritage.

"Turn blue," I replied in my perkiest voice.

He removed his white Stetson and placed it over his chest. "Ranch girl, that'll be what happens to you if you continue eating that crap."

I turned back to the menu. "Gabe's nagging I have to endure. Yours, no."

"So, how's the old chief doing these days?" he asked. "Emphasis on old." He and Gabe had grudgingly become civil to each other over the last year, but Hud could never resist a poke at my more serious-minded husband.

"Too busy, but aren't we all? What's new with Maisie?" Maisie was Hud's eight-year-old daughter and the reason he left his beloved Texas to live in California. Despite their divorce, he and his ex-wife, Laura Lee, were on amicable terms. She'd moved here to be near her family and he followed. Hud could be irritating as a rope burn, but he was a dedicated father.

"She's showing her first chicken," he said proudly. "Not officially, of course, since she won't be nine until next January."

You had to be nine years old to be an official 4-H member and show your animals, but she could be in mini 4-H, where they let kids experience the process without being eligible for either a ribbon or to sell their animal. "What kind of chicken is she raising?"

One of his brown eyebrows arched with contempt. "It's some kind of fancy rooster or something. A Frizzled Coachman?"

"A Frizzle Cochin," I corrected him, laughing. "Those are real pretty birds. What color?"

"Plain ole white. Ugly as a rotten tree stump, if you ask me. A chicken is a chicken. All it makes me want to do is dig out the frying pan. Let me tell you, I have *sacrificed* for this bird. First, he cost me an arm and two legs from some loony-tunes chicken breeder in Bakersfield. Apparently this baby rooster—"

"Cockerel."

"What?"

"That's what young roosters are called."

"At any rate, this cock-in-the-rail apparently has a royal bloodline, which is why he cost so dang much. Second, he conveniently can't live with Laura Lee and Maisie because of their neighborhood's zoning laws. So he and I are roommates. I swear my house is full of bird mites despite the fact I built him a fancy-pants chicken coop at the very back of my yard. After the fair, that cockamamie bird is history."

"Really? You realize that she can show him again next year when she can actually win a ribbon?"

"No way. Another whole year with Mr. Prickles?"

I laughed. "Mr. Prickles?"

"She thought he looked prickly. I tend to shorten his name by a few letters."

He groaned just as I reached the front of the line causing the kid behind the counter to give him a confused look.

"Ignore the crazy man," I told the kid. "I'll take one deep-fried avocado and a lemonade, please."

"Good girl," Hud said. "Eating your veggies."

"Mind your own," I said without turning around. After he ordered a raspberry lemonade, he fell in beside me while we walked toward the agriculture buildings.

"So, ranch girl, what should I do?"

I took a bite of my fried avocado, burning my tongue. "Ow."

"Serves you right."

We passed in front of the row of instant-picture booths, which, I noticed, now cost three dollars and were in color.

I had dozens of the old black-and-white strips, the kind
that cost a quarter way back when, tracing Jack's and my
courtship from age fifteen to right before he was killed in
an auto accident at age thirty-four. The fair always made
me think of Jack.

"Hey, we've never had a photo together," Hud said,
grabbing my hand and pulling me into one of the booths.

"Hud! I don't have time . . ."

"Hush and smile," he said, slipping bills into the slot.
"Or you're going to look like a fish."

Humoring him, I'd found, was the quickest way to shut
him up. As we waited for the photos and I ate my fried avocado, I brought up Mr. Prickles again. "I think you're going
to have to just be the great father you are and suffer with
Mr. Prickles until her interest moves on to something else."

The photo machine beeped and coughed up the photo
strip. In the third photo, he had given me devil horns.

"You are so predictable," I said, punching his upper arm.
"Gotta run. I want to see the Family Farm exhibits."

"I do want to be a good father," he said, sticking the
photo strip in his shirt pocket. "Why couldn't Laura Lee
encourage her to make a quilt or jam, something less
noisy?" He scratched the side of his sunburned neck, his
face miserable.

"Walk with me to the agriculture building and I'll tell
you a story that'll make you feel better. My first 4-H project was a sheep. I named him Moses."

"Moses? What kind of sheep name is that?"

I waved my hand at him. "That's who we were studying
in Sunday school. Anyway, keep in mind that I was raised
on a ranch. I knew before I even acquired Moses that a
castrated male sheep served no purpose except for being
on someone's dinner plate. Moses won Grand Champion
Market Lamb that year. When it came time for him to be
auctioned off with the other lambs, I ran to Daddy, crying hysterically. It suddenly dawned on me what was going

to happen to Moses. I couldn't bear for Moses to be lamb stew. So, with me hanging on his arm bawling, he started bidding."

Hud listened intently, for once his dark brown eyes serious. "Then what happened?"

We reached the front door of the agriculture building. A small crowd of children wearing bright orange Beth David Preschool T-shirts stopped us.

"Sorry," said a frazzled young woman trying to maneuver them into two lines. She wore a T-shirt identical to her charges. "We're three parents short."

"No problem. We're not in a hurry."

"Moses," Hud prompted. "What happened?"

I turned back to him. "Oh, Daddy bought him for an exorbitant price, mostly because his Farm Supply buddies saw what he was doing and kept jacking up the bid. We brought Moses home where he lived for sixteen more years. Dove said I should have named him Methuselah. And Daddy got razzed every week of his life of those sixteen years, not just because he was feeding a basically worthless animal, but also because it was a *sheep* and Daddy's a cattleman. But he took it on the chin." I cocked my head. "Because he's a good daddy and I think you are too."

The children had finally lined up, locked sticky hands with their partners and were being led inside.

"Great," Hud said, walking behind me into the cool, cavernous building. His voice echoed slightly. "What if she never wants to let Mr. Prickles go? He will live out his life waking me at five a.m. every dang morning."

"Talk to Dove," I said over my shoulder. "You annoy her, but she loves Maisie. I bet for the right price—possibly a generous donation to the San Celina Food Pantry—you could convince her to let him board at the ranch and Maisie can visit him. Dove keeps a small group of fancy chickens and other animals for Cattlewomen Association school tours."

"Thank you, ranch girl. You are my savior."

"Nope, Jesus is your savior, but you definitely owe me one, Inspector Clouseau."

"And I won't forget it."

Suddenly the amusement in his face turned to concern. I turned around to see Maggie walking quickly toward us, her mouth tight with anger.

"Benni, you aren't going to believe this," she said, taking a deep breath. "Someone's stolen the Harriet Powers quilt."

CHAPTER 2

"WHAT?" I SAID.

"When?" Hud said a nano-second later.

"No one knows." Maggie frowned at Hud. "Aren't deputies supposed to be patrolling the fairgrounds?" She blinked her eyes quickly, fighting for control.

Hud lifted an eyebrow and glanced at me, his mouth twitching. I shook my head slightly, willing him not to react. Maggie was just letting off steam. She worked with law enforcement and knew that they couldn't be everywhere.

"Jazz and Katsy are in the home arts building," Maggie said.

We followed her out of the agriculture building's front door to the home arts building next door. It was a long, flat-roofed structure with shiplap siding painted a glossy sunflower yellow. Hundreds of multicolored pansies, gerbera daisies and marigolds were planted in the brick-lined beds surrounding the building. No doubt it would be a favorite spot for people taking family photos.

The African American quilt exhibit sat directly inside the front door.

It was obvious where the replica of the famous Harriet Powers quilt once hung. There was a conspicuous blank spot in the middle of the dark brown velvet backdrop. The quilt had been bordered by sepia photographs of sober-looking pioneers who settled the West.

Katsy stood in front of the exhibit, her hand on Jazz's shoulder. Jazz's cheeks were glossy with tears. Next to Jazz stood a thin young man with a peeling, sunburned nose. He was not much taller than her—maybe five six or so. His clothes were typical North County rancher—pigskin-tight Wranglers stacked in denim wrinkles over his dusty roper boots, a black T-shirt advertising last year's National Finals Rodeo in Las Vegas and a sweat-stained straw cowboy hat with a braided leather hatband. His arms were as wiry and hard as old rake handles, which told me he was probably an actual working cowboy. He looked like any number of young men prowling the fair, jeans slung low on their hips, drinking beer out of plastic Budweiser cups and paying five bucks to take their chances riding the mechanical bull.

"Hey, Benni," Katsy said, nodding at me.

Though the family resemblance was obvious, she was a few inches shorter than Maggie and six years older. Her eyes were hazel, a jewel-like silvery green with dark flecks. Her shoulders were wider than her younger sister's, her face rounder, but with the same sharp, dignified cheekbones as Maggie. She wore black denim jeans with silver stitching and a lacy red tank top. Her shiny boots were needle-toed and high-heeled, a fashionable contrast to Maggie's practical ropers, not surprising since Stylin', the clothing store she managed in San Celina, was popular with all the affluent Cal Poly girls.

"Hey," I replied. "I just heard about the quilt. That stinks." Katsy's major in college had been African American history, and this exhibit, as well as the two at the folk art museum, had been special to her.

"Who would do something like that?" Jazz asked. "We worked so hard on that quilt."

"When did you notice it was missing?" I asked Maggie.

"Shawna, the building superintendent, noticed that the space was empty when she opened up this morning. But she also knew that we'd been working on it off and on last night, taking it down and putting it back up. She assumed one of us had it. When Katsy came by a half hour ago, she realized it was stolen."

"Maybe it's a prank," Hud said, studying the blank space on the velvet wall.

"It's not a prank," Katsy said. "But I'm not entirely surprised. After Levi told me about those letters . . ."

Jazz stepped back from Katsy. "What letters?"

Hud looked equally surprised.

Katsy held out her hand. "Look, honey, I'm talking out of school here. I shouldn't be the one . . ."

Jazz scowled at her. "Just tell me, okay?"

Katsy glanced uneasily at her younger sister. Maggie nodded. "Jazz is right. Levi shouldn't hide things like that."

I could tell Katsy was uncomfortable by her conflicted expression. She and Levi had been dating for a little over a year. It didn't surprise me that Levi confided in her about something that sounded serious, though doing so without telling his daughter also might not help her and Jazz's new relationship.

A small crowd started milling around us, staring at the place where the quilt once hung. Maggie gestured at us to follow her. Once we were away from the gawkers, she said in a low voice, "Katsy, tell them about the letters. There's a Log Cabin quilt I can use to fill the spot. That was a popular pattern during the settling of the west. I'll write up a quick display card. It'll have to do until the quilt shows up." She fiddled nervously with one silver hoop earring. "*If* it shows up."

Hud, Jazz, the silent young man and I followed Katsy to the relatively quiet walkway between the home arts and agriculture buildings.

"What's going on?" Jazz said, crossing her bare arms over her chest. Her young friend moved protectively closer.

Katsy stuck her hands into the back pockets of her jeans. "In the last few weeks, Levi has received a few repulsive letters about him being appointed fair manager."

Hud murmured, "Shades of the sixties."

Jazz's young face looked puzzled.

"Has he reported it to law enforcement?" I asked.

Katsy nodded. "The Paso police are aware of it, but I don't know about the sheriff's department."

Hud's scowl informed us they weren't. His Texas accent was cool. "Y'all might remember that the sheriff's department has legal responsibility for the fair. We should have been informed."

Katsy gave him a long look. "It didn't occur to us that they wouldn't tell you. Seems to me that would be an issue between you and the Paso police."

I'd observed conflicts like this more than once since marrying Gabe. Like most people, Katsy wasn't aware that often there was a rivalry—sometimes good-natured, more often acrimonious—between many police agencies. Because of Gabe's position as chief of police, I was often privy to the carping that went on between various city police departments and the county sheriff. The fair would be a particularly touchy situation, Gabe told me. The actual fairgrounds were state-owned property, which, in some convoluted way, put them under the jurisdiction of the county sheriff, but the fairgrounds were technically located inside the Paso Robles city limits, which made the city police feel proprietary.

When no one responded to his comment, Hud waved an impatient hand. "Tell me about the letters."

Katsy looked irritated. "First one came through the regular mail to the office two weeks ago. Another to his house a few days later. The third one was dropped in the suggestion box outside the administration office the day the fair opened."

"What did they say?" Jazz demanded.

Katsy studied the pavement. "No direct threats, just innuendos about whether he'd gotten his job fairly. One said that he might have bitten off more than he can chew." She looked back up. "Levi didn't want the media to hear about the threats so he asked that the police keep a low profile and they have. He is determined not to let anything overshadow the fair and ruin it for people."

"Do the Paso police have any ideas who it could be?" I asked.

"No," Katsy said. "The Paso detective told Levi that there was a good chance it was just some nutty individual who was reacting to the stories the *Tribune* ran last month about Levi being the first African American fair manager in San Celina's history."

"There are a few white extremist groups on the Central Coast," Hud said. "We keep a pretty close eye on them. Mostly it's just dirtbags who have nothing better to do than get together and whine about how life has crapped on them. So far we haven't caught them doing anything illegal."

Jazz put her hands on her hips. "I'm so mad that Dad didn't tell me."

"Cut him some slack," Katsy said. "He was trying to protect you."

"I'm not six years old!" The young man inched closer to Jazz, but he didn't touch her.

Katsy reached over and patted Jazz's shoulder. "That's between you and your daddy. But let's not overreact. That's exactly what people like that are counting on."

"I'm not overreacting. C'mon, Cal," Jazz said to the young man. "We're going to talk to my dad right now."

Hud, Katsy and I watched the teenagers walk toward the fair's administration buildings.

"That poor girl," Katsy said, shaking her head. "If she ever leaves the Central Coast she's going to get a rude awakening."

Though Katsy had lived all of her life here on the Central Coast, unlike Maggie, she'd gone away to college, a full scholarship to Emory University in Atlanta.

"Who's the kid with Jazz?" I asked.

"Her latest boyfriend," Katsy said. "Calvin Jones. Goes by Cal. Nice young man. He's done some work at our ranch. Works part time in Paso at the Mobil gas station over by Walmart. Don't know much about him except that he's a hard worker and doesn't seem to have any family. They just started dating about a month ago. Not a real go-getter, but he's miles better than her last boyfriend."

"Who was that?" I asked.

"Dodge Burnside," Katsy said.

"You're right. Anyone's an improvement over him."

Dodge was one of many young men who hung around the ranch with my stepson, Sam. Usually I liked his friends, but I'd taken a dislike to Dodge after an incident at our roundup last year. My neighbor, Love Johnson, and I had walked into the barn to let the young men gathered there know that the food was ready. Dodge had been in the middle of telling a crude joke about women using language that would have caused Dove to smack him with a broom. Red-faced, Love had cleared her throat to let him know there were women present. He looked directly at us and kept going until Sam hit him with his hat and told him to shut up.

"Why's that?" Hud asked.

"You fill in the deputy," Katsy said. "I'll see if I can help Maggie fix the display."

I nodded. "Since I'm technically in charge of the exhibit, I'll make the police report. Let Maggie know I'm taking care of that."

"Thanks. By the way, Levi knows about the theft."

"Got it."

On the walk over to the fair's administrative offices where the sheriff's department had set up a command post, I told Hud about Dodge Burnside.

"He's a local boy. He hangs out with Gabe's son, Sam, though I wouldn't mind if Sam found a little more high-class company."

"What's the kid's problem?"

"Smart-ass, disrespectful to women, always looks like he's hiding something not quite legal. Gets away with it because he's way too good looking. We're talking soap opera star handsome."

He grinned. "Hey, that's a hard row to hoe. You have no idea how difficult it is."

I ignored his remark. I didn't feel like going into the story about walking in on Dodge telling the crude joke. "His dad, Lloyd, has a real successful house and fence painting business in Atascadero. He does a lot of work for local business and ranches. He's belonged to the Cattlemen's Association for as long as I can remember. Dodge worked for him for a while, but from what I heard, even his dad got fed up with his attitude. I think Sam said that Dodge got kicked out of college and that he works for Milt Piebald now. You know, the guy that owns those used car lots with the cheesy commercials?"

"Piebald's Awesome Autos," Hud said. "I love those commercials. Especially the one where he wears that yellow cowboy suit with the cabbage-sized roses on the lapels."

"That's an original Nudie suit," I said. "Supposedly worth thousands. He claims he bought it from Porter Waggoner. Anyway, Justin, Milt's son, also hangs out with Sam. Justin's a San Celina cop. Gabe says he's a good officer."

I wiped the back of my hand across my sweating forehead. The heat was starting to become unbearable. "I can't believe Jazz ever looked twice at Dodge Burnside. He doesn't seem her type. Then again, I suppose at some time every girl falls for a bad boy just for his looks. Even smart girls like Jazz."

"Sometimes they even marry them," Hud said, shooting me with a finger pistol.

"And if I were a *bad girl*," I replied, "you'd be getting a certain one-finger salute."

He threw back his head and laughed. "Please, please, be bad, ranch girl. Just for a minute. You'll like it, I promise."

"Seriously, this particular quilt being stolen has a lot of bad connotations. I hate to think about what it might stir up." I chewed the inside of my cheek.

"No worries. We'll catch the big bad quilt thief. You have my word."

While we walked to the administrative building where the sheriff's department had a command post, Hud told me that this year he was in charge of security at the fair. It explained why he was particularly annoyed that Levi or the Paso police hadn't told him about the letters. Hud normally worked cold cases so his commanding officer thought they could spare him rather than any other detectives working current crimes. We entered the building and walked down the long hallway past Levi's closed door. I wondered how Levi would handle the media once the quilt theft was public knowledge. Chances were that some people knew about it already, so he couldn't keep it quiet like he had the threatening letters.

The sheriff's department had been given an empty back room for their command post. Hud sat down behind a battered gray metal desk and pulled an official-looking form from a side drawer.

"Pull up a chair and rest your weary boots," he said, taking a gold Cross pen from his shirt pocket.

"I really want to believe the theft isn't about race," I

said, sitting in one of the plastic visitor's chairs. On the desk there was a black phone, a metal filing tray and a yellow legal-sized tablet. Behind him were a small beige filing cabinet and a plastic trash can. A metal-framed bulletin board and a fair poster from last year decorated the tan walls. Two folded notes were thumbtacked on the cork board with "Bob" written in felt pen.

Hud started filling out the report. "Wish away, but though we'd like to believe all of that is in the past, it isn't." He looked up from the report. "Let's look on the positive side. Maybe it's a jealous quilter."

"Quilters aren't like that," I said, nibbling on my ragged thumb nail.

"Yeah, right," he said, his brown eyes mocking.

"Frankly, it would be a lot less frightening if it was just some whacked-out quilter who was envious of the quilt."

"Whatever." He went back to writing.

"What're you going to do?"

"Give me a description of this quilt."

I leaned back in my chair, causing it to emit an ominous creak. "It's a copy of Harriet Powers's first story quilt. It's an appliquéd quilt."

He looked up at me, his face blank.

"Appliqué is a technique. You take small pieces of fabric and sew them onto a larger piece of background fabric. Harriet Powers's quilts show biblical stories like Adam and Eve naming the animals and Cain going to the land of Nod in search of a wife. Harriet Powers is probably the most famous black quilter in history. The quilt that the Ebony Sisters copied was Harriet Powers's first known story quilt. The original is at the Smithsonian."

"The Ebony Sisters? That some kind of singing group?"

"It's the quilt guild that Maggie and Katsy belong to. They formed a smaller quilting group out of our bigger San Celina Quilt Guild. I mean, anyone can join them, but they like having, you know, their own . . ." I let my voice trail off. It was often hard to explain why the Ebony Sisters wanted to have their own group.

"I get it," Hud said. "Is there a photo of the quilt? That would make it easier."

"I can find you a photo. The quilt is double bed size. There are eleven panels. I could describe each panel, but a photo would probably be better."

He nodded and continued filling in blanks.

"So, what now?" I asked.

He signed the bottom of the form with a flourish. Then he opened a drawer in the desk, took out a manila file folder and, his eyes not leaving my face, dramatically slipped it inside, and then placed the folder in the vertical metal file holding a few similar folders.

"Not funny. This quilt really is special. One of the contributors died a few months ago so they'll never be able to duplicate it exactly."

The Ebony Sisters Quilt Guild had started this quilt over a year ago in preparation for the museum exhibit. Hundreds of hours of work had gone into its making.

He leaned back in the old office chair, locking his fingers behind his head. "I'm just messin' with you, Benni. I do understand how important this quilt is and I wish I could say you have a tinker's chance in Hades of getting it back. But if it *was* one of these hate groups, believe me, you might not want it back. If it's just a person who wanted the quilt, chances are it has already gone to wherever stolen quilts go. The quilter's pawnshop?" He laughed at his own joke.

I sighed and stood up. In terms of being a significant crime against humanity, this wasn't even close. Still, it was important to some of us. "If there's anything I can do, let me know."

"Find me that photo and then I suggest you make up

some posters, offer a reward. If it was some carnie taking it on a lark, you might actually get it back."

"That's not a half-bad idea. I'll tell Maggie and the others."

Back outside, the fairgrounds were elbow to elbow with people and the temperature was pushing 100 degrees. That actually wasn't too bad for an August afternoon in Paso Robles. I could recall Mid-State Fairs where the temperatures soared to 115 degrees, though the heat had seemed easier to take when I was younger. A thin stream of perspiration trickled down the side of my neck as I walked back to the home arts building.

I felt sick for Maggie, Katsy, Jazz and the rest of the Ebony Sisters who met at the folk art museum every other Tuesday night. I'd watched this quilt's birth from the initial bantering over fabric choices to practically the last binding stitch. Before the fair, it had been displayed at the folk art museum. The Sisters had seriously debated whether they should take a chance on showing it at the fair whose security didn't match ours at the museum. It was Jazz who had been the driving force for it to be shown at the fair. It wasn't surprising that she'd taken its theft so personally.

"Hardly anyone will see it at the museum," she'd said at the quilt guild meeting eight months ago when we first discussed the fair exhibit. She glanced at me, blushing slightly. "No offense, Benni."

I held up my palm. "None taken. I'll be the first to admit our museum's viewership is limited." I was attending this particular Ebony Sisters guild meeting because I was Oneeda Cleary's ride. After the meeting, she and I were meeting Gabe and Jim, her husband, for chicken pot pie night at Liddie's Café.

"It could be damaged," Katsy had argued. "People can be so careless. I hate the thought of any food or drink being near it."

"But isn't it more important that people see it and learn about Harriet Powers?" Jazz insisted.

"She's right," said Flory Jackson, her white hair a striking contrast against skin the color of burnished copper. "It's just fabric and thread, ladies. Both are replaceable. It's more important for us to tell Harriet's story to as many people as we can. The fair does that in a way this lovely museum cannot, despite how hard Benni works to entice folks in here." She smiled at me.

"Agree," said Oneeda Cleary, sitting next to me in her wheelchair. Because of her advanced MS, her words were garbled, but we'd all been around her long enough to understand her. She took a deep, labored breath and slapped one hand down on the armrest of her wheelchair. "Folks . . . need . . . to know."

So, the African American quilt exhibit at the fair, co-sponsored by the museum and the quilt guild, was centered on the replica of the Harriet Powers quilt. The exhibit at the museum was running concurrently and had been a huge success. It had been Katsy's idea to ask her friend in Oakland to loan the museum some of her collection of black cloth dolls, African American dolls made from 1870 to 1930. She and I had worked together on the brochure using information we gleaned from a similar exhibit curated by Roben Campbell of the Harvard Historical Society. We mailed out our brochure to both local and out-of-area newspapers and magazines.

Black cloth (as well as white cloth) dolls are a folk art tradition that came about because of newly available low-priced factory-made fabric. In 1822, Lowell, Massachusetts, factories started producing inexpensive cotton cloth which, along with the newfangled sewing machine patented in 1847, made it possible for women to stitch quilts, dolls and clothing with relative ease. Black cloth dolls followed the natural progression of many folk arts—an early period of original work, a second period of prolific output and great popularity and a declining third period that eventually ended the craft altogether. With black cloth dolls the three periods follow the African American struggle for equal rights and freedom. The early dolls (1870–1890) are finely stitched and hopeful; the middle dolls (1890–1910) are more neutral, not as optimistic and the later dolls (1910–1930) show a decline in the craft and seem to wear expressions of patient fatigue. Most dolls proudly show the loving care of the creator as well as the adoration physically bestowed by the child who played with them.

The museum had received more media attention for these exhibits than any other except for the time we showed some original, previously unseen photographs by my famous stepgrandpa Isaac Lyons. When the media got wind of the theft, it would bring publicity of a different kind.

Before facing the anxious faces of my friends and informing them that it was doubtful the sheriff's department would be doing much to recover the quilt, I decided to fulfill the request of the San Celina Historical Society secretary and head nagmeister, Sissy Brownmiller. She wanted photographs of the Family Farm exhibits.

According to the fair program, there were fifteen Family Farm exhibits this year. That was down from a high of thirty-seven in 1968, because, sadly, a lot of our county's family farms no longer existed. San Celina County was definitely changing and every year it was never more apparent than at the Mid-State Fair.

Inside the agriculture building the swamp cooler unit chugged hard keeping the room fairly pleasant. The damp, cool air felt luxurious on my skin after the blistering temperatures outside. I pulled out my camera. Snapping photos of the Family Farm exhibits would relax me.

This fair competition had always been one of my favorites. When I was a little girl, Dove, Daddy, my uncle Arnie and I planned and worked all year on our exhibit. In 1972 we actually won Grand Prize. We'd made a detailed diorama of the Ramsey ranch and I personally painted thirty-five heifers myself—their markings exactly matching some of our actual cattle. Arnie, who'd just gotten his own camera, made us dress up like ranchers circa 1880 and took surprisingly realistic photos that he enlarged in his high school photography class. I surrounded them with frames made from corn cobs cut in half.

These exhibits revealed our county and its incredible variety of agriculture to a section of our population who didn't always remember what county fairs were originally about—a way for the everyday farmer and rancher to show off their produce, animals, or expertise in quilting, woodcarving, jam making or leatherwork. County fairs were as much a part of the American lifestyle as apple pan dowdy and the right to vote. And nothing shouted county fair more than these homemade exhibits. This year's theme was "Cow Town Boogie."

I laughed at the Vieira Family Farm exhibit where the kids showed Mom and Dad (in Wranglers and old checkered shirts stuffed with hay—their faces painted on pale pink fabric) dancing in front of a thirties-era radio while the kids did all the work of gathering eggs from hens made of calico fabric and chicken wire, feeding papier-mâché calves and pulling weeds in a garden showcasing the Vieira ranch's carrots, corn and giant pumpkins. "Ranch kids boogie hard for their money" was their motto. The exhibit's homespun look hit just the right note. The crooked printing and offset eyes painted on the mannequins revealed immediately that the ranch family's children had participated in the exhibit's creation and construction.

I took photos of the exhibits, attempting to capture the uniqueness of each one, recording something that I suspected might not be prevalent in ten or fifteen years—the family farm. Change was inevitable, and sometimes even good, but a part of me was saddened as every year I observed hundreds of acres of San Celina ranch land sold for wineries or developed for tract homes. The best I could do was record what San Celina County once was.

When I reached the Piebald Family Farm exhibit, like everyone else around me, I momentarily gawked. It had won the huge Grand Prize blue ribbon and it was obvious why. On one side of the large coveted corner booth, there was the rusted shell of an old 1940s pickup truck. Crowded into the truck's bed were boxes of huge Golden Delicious apples, giant-sized avocados, perfect bales of alfalfa and two smiling, one slightly panicked-looking cow made of cow-print fabric with a leather face. Inside the cab, a grinning stuffed sheep sat at the wheel wearing a red gimme cap that said Eat More Beef. The banner across the front of the truck proclaimed Templeton Cattle Auction or Bust.

On the other side of the booth sat a realistic-looking fabric rancher sitting on a hay bale staring at a splayed deck of cards while a bunch of intricate topiary calves watched him over a wooden fence. Professional caricatures of the Piebald family members—Milt; his young second wife, Juliette; his sons, Justin and Billy—looked out of frames shaped like playing cards: heart, diamond, spade and club. They were colored with red, black and white flower petals and looked as professional as a Rose Parade float. A king-sized quilt—Hole in the Barn Door pattern—made of fabric printed with fruits, vegetables, cattle and horses bore the bold, black machine-embroidered phrase "Ranching is a gamble—but what a way to live!"

It was certainly the cleverest and most eye-catching exhibit. I also noticed they didn't actually incorporate this year's theme. But to be fair, a lot of the other exhibits didn't either. The Piebald exhibit technically deserved the blue ribbon attached to the front of the pickup, but I and probably a lot of ag people had mixed feelings about it winning top prize.

The Piebalds lived on a fifty-acre ranch just barely inside Paso Robles city limits complete with a half-dozen horses and a sprinkling of cattle, chickens, goats and sheep. Milt Piebald actually made his money not from ranching but from the five used-car dealerships he owned in Salinas, King City, Paso Robles, Nipomo and Oxnard. But I suspected that wouldn't be what bothered most of the ag community.

The Piebalds had probably hired professionals to design their booth. They took a competition that was supposed to be a fun activity for kids and turned it into an adult contest. Still, it was a committee of ag people who judged this competition, which made me wonder what Milt might have on some of them.

Everyone knew that Milt Piebald liked winning. His story was well known in our community. Though he was fifteen years older than me, I remembered Daddy and the other ranchers talking about Milt when he played football for Cal Poly back in the sixties. A big-chested, beefy guy, he'd also been a champion steer wrestler on the college rodeo team. He dropped out in his junior year and after a year in pro-rodeo, he came back to San Celina and, with a small inheritance from his grandpa, bought his first used-car lot. Milt Piebald found his niche.

"Piebald's Awesome Autos—gallop on over for the best deals in pre-owned cars" was notorious for selling flashy cars and trucks to people whose iffy credit precluded them from buying from more reputable dealers. He'd made, as Daddy liked to say with a sardonic half smile, a "shipload of money" selling used cars and trucks to suckers. The problem was that some of those suckers had been his friends and neighbors. But he was also an enthusiastic and generous booster for 4-H, Little League teams, both the high school and college rodeo teams and many other community activities. Feelings around town about Milt were mixed.

Milt's first wife, Marlene, had been the daughter of a respected old family who'd once owned the largest grocery store in the county. When she died of renal failure, Milt mourned for two months, and then married another local girl, Juliette Baxter, gifting the snippy society ladies of San Celina County (and, admittedly, the rest of us) with no end of gossip and speculation.

Juliette was also a local celebrity of sorts. She was seventeen years younger than Milt's fifty-three years and gorgeous, a former Miss San Celina Rodeo Queen. She'd been nominated a record eight times for princess on both San Celina High School and Cal Poly San Celina homecoming courts. She was infamous for the quote "It's a real, true honor to just be nominated." She, Elvia, Jack and I had all gone through high school and college together. By the time she'd repeated those same words in her senior year in college when Sarah Rodriguez won homecoming queen, they were coming out a little pinched and she'd become a popular person for local comedians to parody.

With a marketing degree and beauty queen looks, she'd gone on to become a KSCC weather girl, then after marrying Milt, landed her own local television show called *The Juliette Piebald Show* (Piebald Awesome Autos was the show's first sponsor). It featured local artists, businesses and events, whatever caught Juliette's interest. She'd given our museum some much-needed publicity early in our inception, so I had a bit of a soft spot for her. I'd even felt bad when her show got the ax only a year after it debuted. The story was she couldn't attract any sponsors other than Milt.

I studied the professional photos of the Piebald family. They all gave wide smiles except Justin, who appeared to be staring at something over the photographer's shoulder.

Justin, Milt's son by Marlene, was a quiet young man, with neatly trimmed dark hair and wary gray eyes. He surprised everyone a year ago when, a week after he graduated Cal Poly, he applied at the San Celina Police Department and was accepted at the academy. Gabe had confided to me that he'd had some reservations about employing him because of Milt Piebald's shifty reputation, but the young man's dedication and hard work had impressed him.

Billy Piebald was Milt and Juliette's son. It was Billy's first year in 4-H. I'd watched him show his first hog earlier today where he'd won second place in showmanship. He had a cotton-top, freckled, Huck Finn cuteness that invariably made people smile.

I snapped a few more pictures, thinking the whole time how the fair rules should state that the exhibits be made exclusively by the families, not a professional designer, when a silky voice behind me said, "You have to admit, it's the best one."

I turned to face Juliette Piebald and was mesmerized, as always, by her perfection. She stood five foot ten, with glossy, shoulder-length chestnut hair, not a strand out of place. Her complexion was as smooth as a hen's egg. Some of it had to be makeup, but she'd also been blessed with silky skin. Emerald eyes straight out of a romance novel gazed down at me. She wore thigh-hugging maroon Wranglers, a pristine white Western shirt, a galloping horse rhinestone belt buckle and an expensive straw Stetson. She was so perfect that you wanted to hate her but couldn't because her perfection was so incredibly fascinating, like a *Vogue* magazine photo come to life.

"It's real nice, Juliette," I said. My voice went high and chipper, making me a little sick by my duplicity. Though I hadn't entered the competition this year, the fact that she and Milt used professional designers kind of bugged me. I rubbed my sunburned nose, feeling like the country mouse. "I'm taking pictures for the historical society."

"Good," she said, touching a painted nail to lips that

were the exact shade of Pepto-Bismol. On her, the color actually looked good. "Will it be in a book or something?"

"No, we don't have that much money. These photos will probably just go into the permanent records. For future historians."

"Darn." Her glossy mouth turned down into a pout that was so attractive that it had to be rehearsed. "I'm so proud of Billy and Justin's exhibit. They worked awfully hard on it."

Was she serious? The only thing Billy and Justin likely contributed to this exhibit was posing for the professional pictures displayed in the playing card frames.

She sighed, looking vulnerable for a moment. "I'm donating the gift certificate to the battered women's shelter. Billy and Milt are mad at me, but I told them that we need to share our good fortune."

This was the kind of thing that always made me feel a little ashamed by how I immediately judged Juliette whenever we met at some society function. Yes, she was a bit of a plastic beauty queen, but she also seemed to have a good heart.

"That's really nice of you, Juliette," I said.

She flashed her sparkling rodeo-queen/talk-show-host smile. "What's two hundred bucks anyway? Wouldn't even pay for a set of earrings. Tell Gabe I said hi." She loved flirting with my husband, who took her silly flattery with a good-natured laugh and much ribbing from Emory. But I'd known Juliette since high school when she moved here with her newly divorced mother. Flirting had always been her favorite sport. Shoot, I remember her flirting with Jack when we were all teenagers, which made me feel more than a little old.

It was almost 5 p.m. by the time I left the agriculture building and since all I'd eaten was that deep-fried avocado—an appetizer, really—I decided to grab something to eat on my way home. I wanted to shower and change clothes before coming back for Kathy Mattea's concert in the Sierra Vista arena at 8 p.m.

I checked the schedule I'd typed up a week ago. Tomorrow was the cattle drive, an event that ranchers both complained about and looked forward to every year. The antics of both the cattle and the locals who watched or participated in the drive gave Daddy and his coffee-drinking cronies at the Farm Supply something to moan and groan about all year. Reliving last year's mini stampede was a favorite pastime around the never-empty coffeepot at the Farm Supply. Some newcomer's yappy little mixed-breed terrier had discovered some long buried herding dog roots, leaped out of his owner's arms and charged the placid cattle herd. The startled bovines, alarmed by the fuzzy, barking rat, veered off course, in the process trampling the fancy lawns of a couple of Paso's new million-dollar homes. We still heard occasional grumbling about that, despite the fact that the county repaired the damages and gave all the homeowners and their guests free fair passes. On the other hand, people would gripe if we didn't do the traditional cattle drive, so there really was no winning.

I faced a dizzying array of choices for my snack. Garlic fries and a hot dog on a stick or a tri-tip steak sandwich with salsa? A deep-fried burrito or a giant barbecued turkey leg? Australian battered potatoes or pan-fried chicken? I could eat tri-tip steak or fried chicken any time so I sprang for the hot dog on a stick. Besides, it was the easiest thing to eat while walking back to my truck. On the way to the parking lot, I noticed the cinnamon-scented funnel cake stand. Tomorrow would definitely be a funnel cake day.

One of the best things about being a Mid-State Fair Booster Buddie was our access to the preferred parking lot right across the street from the entrance. That meant I didn't have to search for a space in the crowded public lot a block away and made my truck easy to find. Not that my truck was ever really difficult to spot. The Barneymobile is what everyone at the folk art museum called my little Ford pickup, which was painted Ford's idea of sapphire blue. Sapphire blue might be its official moniker, but in the bright Central Coast sunlight, purple it was.

Just as I opened my truck, my cell phone rang. At the same time, I heard the sound of a male voice raised in anger. I turned and looked across the preferred parking lot to the back row. It was Dodge Burnside and Jazz Clark. He loomed over her, jabbing a finger in her face. Amazingly, people walked through the parking lot, close enough to intervene, but no one even turned a head. I threw my backpack in the truck, locked it and jogged quickly toward the couple, shoving my cell phone in the back pocket of my Wranglers.

"I mean it," Dodge said, when I was within ten feet. He grabbed Jazz's upper arm. "If you see him again, I'll—"

"Hey!" I cried out in my deepest, most authoritative voice. "Is there a problem here?"

"Get lost," he said, without even turning to look at me. "This is between me and my girlfriend."

"I am so *not* your girlfriend," Jazz snapped, jerking out of his grasp.

I walked up next to her, crossed my arms over my chest and gazed up at the young man. Even scowling, his looks were striking, magazine perfect with sculpted features and blue eyes that glowed on his suntanned face like pieces of turquoise on a desert floor.

"What's going on here?" I asked in my best annoyed schoolteacher-librarian voice.

"Nothing." His jaw clenched so hard it seemed he'd break a tooth.

I looked over at Jazz. Her cheekbones were flushed and shiny. "Are you okay?"

"I'm fine. We're so done," she said, her upper lip slightly lifted. "Dodge's just acting like a crybaby."

He lifted his fist.

Gabe's voice echoed inside my head. *If you're being threatened, speak with authority. Use their name. People respond to tone of voice.*

I stepped between them. "Dodge, cool it. Now!"

White flashed around Dodge's eyes. My heart thumped in my chest. Had I miscalculated? His anger felt like a physical presence, like a hot Santa Ana wind. I pulled out my cell phone. "I'll call the police."

"Dodge, you idiot!" Jazz said. "She's a police chief's wife. If you hit her, you will *so* go to jail."

His arm slowly dropped to his side. "This isn't over." He pushed past us, dust kicking up from the heels of his boots.

We watched him walk toward a white Chevy truck and climb inside.

Jazz let out a shuddering breath. "Wow, thanks. You came along just in time."

"What was that all about?" I asked.

"Dodge Burnside is a jerk," she said, studying her nails. "We hung out, but it wasn't serious." She shrugged, seemingly unconcerned about someone who I felt was one second away from assaulting her.

"Looks like you were right to break up with him," I said, shading my eyes against the bright afternoon sun. "If he doesn't leave you alone, let me know and I'll talk to Gabe."

"No worries," she said, her voice breezy. "I've totally got it under control."

Apparently not, I wanted to say. She seemed already past it and ready to move on. Her expression brightened and she lifted her hand at someone behind me. "Sam! Justin! Over here!" She raised her arm and waved.

I turned around, relieved to see my stepson, Sam Ortiz, and Justin Piebald stride toward us.

Sam's face was tanned deep mahogany from his daily surfing schedule. He smiled and called out, "Hey, *madrastra*. What's up?"

"Not much," I replied. "What's up with you?"

Madrastra was his name for me from almost the first time we met, not long after Gabe and I eloped to Las Vegas. It meant stepmother in Spanish, but was considered an endearment, almost like "second mother." Just seeing him made my spine relax. Sam was a perpetually happy young man who didn't seem to have one single enemy. He had not inherited either his father's sober intensity or his attorney mother's focused ambition. Instead, he slid through life on his good looks, laid-back personality and ability to get along with anyone.

"Me and Justin are on our way to the beach. I have a new long board."

"It'll definitely be cooler there than here. How're you doing, Justin?"

"Fine, Mrs. Ortiz." He ducked his head, flushing slightly. I'd given up trying to convince him to call me Benni.

Justin was a few inches shorter than Sam's six feet, his frame more square and solid than Sam's lanky swimmer's body. He had his father, Milt's, prominent jawline, though it seemed less jutting and belligerent on Justin.

Justin looked directly at Jazz. "Want to come with us?"

"Sure." She turned back to me. "I'll see you later, Benni. Thanks, again." She linked arms with both young men.

"Bye," I said, watching them walk away, Jazz chattering like she didn't have a care in the world. Where was that Cal Jones I'd seen her with earlier—the kid who Katsy said Jazz was dating now?

The three kids were gone before I was able to gauge whether the young men had seen her encounter with Dodge. Dodge was one of their surfing buddies. What would they think of the way their friend treated Jazz? And why wasn't Jazz more concerned about Dodge's temper? What was the deal with kids today?

I laughed at myself. Maybe my questions meant I'd officially passed into middle age, though thirty-nine still felt just this side of it. I wiped the back of my neck, sweaty from the heat. When I reached my truck, I sat inside for a moment waiting for the air-conditioning to cool off the cab.

On the radio, KCOW, our local country station, was broadcasting from the fairgrounds by the midway. In the background, you could hear people screaming from the carnival rides.

"Win an all-expenses-paid weekend at the Flamingo Hotel and Casino in beautiful Las Vegas, Nevada!" yelled Brahma Bob, a popular local DJ. "Come on down to the booth and enter. Grab yourself a free boot-shaped human-powered fan to keep yourselves the cool cats that you are!"

I pulled slowly into the street in front of the fair behind a blue two-tone '96 Ford pickup I recognized because it had been out at our ranch numerous times. Justin Piebald manned the driver's seat with Jazz sitting between him and Sam. She playfully grabbed Justin's cowboy hat and stuck it on her head.

Poor Cal Jones, I thought. Looks like he's already history. Still, Jazz could do worse. Though Milt was a loud-mouthed bragasaurus, somehow he managed to raise a really nice son. At least, Justin seemed that way to me. Gabe said that he was well liked by the other cops and did his job diligently and without flash.

Cal certainly had some formidable competition for Jazz's affections—Dodge's model looks and overt sexuality and Justin's dependability and easygoing nature. Cal didn't have particularly great looks or even a good job.

The whole situation made me grateful that I was no longer in my twenties. As much as I missed the stamina, the sheer joy and hope of youth, not to mention (already regretting my hastily eaten hot dog on a stick) a young person's cast-iron stomach, I did not miss the drama and heartbreak.

The traffic light two blocks from the fair turned a quick red, causing both Justin and me to stop abruptly. Out of habit, I glanced up in my rearview mirror, dismayed by what I saw, a frowning Dodge Burnside whose eyes burned right through my vehicle to the one ahead of me. When the light turned green, he floored his truck with a screech and cut in front of me.

"Watch it, you jerk!" I yelled in vain. With both our windows rolled up, it was doubtful that he heard me.

He squeezed his truck behind Justin's, turning right when they did, both trucks heading downtown. I shook my head and kept driving straight until I came to the Interstate 101 on-ramp. Not my problem, I thought. Doesn't have a thing to do with me. I am *so* staying out of this.

Words, Gabe always swore, that he was going to have engraved on my headstone.

CHAPTER 3

"AREN'T YOU GLAD WE'RE TOO OLD FOR ALL THAT nonsense?" Gabe said, kissing my neck while I stood at the kitchen counter mixing dog food for Scout's dinner. I'd just finished telling him about Jazz, Dodge, Justin and Cal. "By the way, Dove called. Three times. She wants to know if there's something wrong with your cell phone."

"Not a thing. Do you think I should mention Dodge's behavior to Levi?"

"Not our business," Gabe said. "Dove sounded awfully annoyed."

"Aunt Garnet arrives today. Still, don't you think he should know that some guy is threatening his daughter?"

Gabe leaned back against the kitchen sink and crossed his long legs at the ankles. "I distinctly remember you saying the last time you got involved with someone's love life that it would be the *last* time."

"You're a dog," I said to him, then looked down at my gentle-faced brown Lab-mix, Scout, whose tail waved back and forth, a perpetual metronome of goodness. "No offense, Mr. Scout. You are the most true-blue man in my life." I placed his dinner on the floor. "A young woman's safety could be at stake."

Gabe scratched the side of his jaw with his knuckles. Through the kitchen window behind him, I could see our across-the-street elderly twin neighbors, Beebs and Millee, watering their rosebushes with identical old-fashioned watering cans. "So, tell him. We'll probably see him at the concert tonight."

"We could mention it. Casually. Just in passing."

He held up his hands. "This is your deal. Leave me out of it."

"Fine," I said, poking him in the chest. "By the way, you'll have a certain wild-eyed, ex-rodeo queen waiting for you tonight. Mrs. Juliette Piebald sends greetings."

He laughed and pushed himself away from the counter. "She's . . . quite something. But you have nothing to worry about. I'm just one pearl in a very long strand of men in her life."

I shot him a baleful look. "Who's worried?"

"I'm crushed. So, how're things going at the fair?"

"Same as every year. I have a list of things to do during the fair's run that would rival the president's schedule. But it's pretty quiet at the folk art museum, so I'll be okay." I washed my hands, then dried them on a kitchen towel. "We have a little while before we need to leave for the fairgrounds, so I'm going to rest my bones."

He joined me in the living room where we sat in matching leather chairs, sipped iced tea and watched the neighborhood through our picture window. The last thing I remember was Beebs and Millee practicing their Tae Kwon Do moves under the towering valley oak tree in their front yard.

I jerked awake when the phone rang. The mantel clock said 6:40 p.m.

I simultaneously picked up the phone and shook Gabe's shoulder.

"Sergeant Friday, wake up!" It was a nickname I'd given him when we'd first met because of how much he adored rules. "We're going to be late for the concert."

It was Dove on the phone.

"Get out your checkbook and look up a bail bondsman," she declared. "I'm ready to commit murder." Her voice was loud enough to assure me that Aunt Garnet wasn't in the immediate vicinity.

"Are you going to the concert tonight?" I asked.

"Did you hear what I said?"

"Yes, ma'am." There was obviously no way I was going to dodge this conversation. I gave a loud dramatic sigh, hoping it was audible over the phone. "Gramma, she's your sister . . ."

"She's already dusted my house—twice! I swear she's rubbed the coffee table down to bare wood. She says my chicken feed is too fancy. She told your daddy he needs a haircut . . . well, he does . . . but that's beside the point. She says her *corn bread* is better than mine!"

Oh dear, that was truly throwing down the gauntlet. Dove's three-cheese corn bread had been a church potluck favorite and a Mid-State Fair prizewinner for years. It had won dozens of blue ribbons. Out of good sportsmanship, she didn't enter it in this year's fair.

"Can't we talk about this tonight?" I said, leaning against the fireplace mantel.

"I'm not going."

"But Kathy Mattea is singing. You love her song about the eighteen-wheeler and a dozen roses."

"Sister says she's too tired to go to the fair tonight and I'll be darned if I'm going to leave her here alone to poke around and find more things to nag at me about. I tell you, she's already driving me crazy! She follows me everywhere. I think she's trying to steal my corn bread recipe."

I managed to soothe Dove's agitation by promising her I'd think of something, though I had no idea what.

After splashing cold water on my face, rebraiding my hair and changing clothes, I gave Scout a biscuit and a perfunctory belly rub. "Guard the house. I promise to make it up to you after the fair is over." Scout licked my hand, took his treat and lay down in the middle of our cool, polished oak living room floor.

"You look great," Gabe said, running his hand down my hips. I wore black Wranglers, a long-sleeved turquoise Western shirt and my best Lucchese cowboy boots. Though it was blazing hot during the day, the evenings in Paso could get chilly, especially in the arena.

"You look pretty fine yourself, Chief." Though normally he wore conservative Brooks Brothers suits with pristine white shirts, tonight he looked like a real rancher in Levi's, a deep blue pearl-buttoned Western shirt and polished black cowboy boots.

Minutes later we were in his '68 Corvette speeding toward Paso. For once, his love for speed came in handy and we made the normally half-hour trip in twenty minutes. We parked, maneuvered our way through the crowd and were at the entrance to the hospitality suite just as the opening act, a local band called Rifle Shot, started singing their first song.

"You go on up," I said. "Rifle Shot will be on at least forty-five minutes. I want to check on the quilt exhibit." I'd told him about the quilt theft earlier and he'd agreed with Hud that it was doubtful it would be found.

"My money's on one of the carnies," he'd said.

"I'm hoping to find Hud. I have the photo he requested of the quilt." Luckily, I'd had some color flyers made up a few weeks ago advertising the quilt exhibit at the museum. I'd used them in press kits and had about ten or so left. The photo of the quilt was crystal clear. "Save me a seat."

"I'll try, but I can't guarantee your seat won't be grabbed by some hot rodeo queen with the initials J. P."

I smacked his butt, making him laugh. "I'm not above a cat fight, Friday."

He bent down and kissed the hollow of my throat. "I like the sound of that."

I ruffled his black, shiny hair. "In your dreams. The only thing I'd fight Juliette Piebald for is the last Krispy Kreme doughnut."

Maggie and Katsy had done a wonderful job rearranging the exhibit. Anyone viewing the display would never have known another quilt had been there before. The log cabin quilt that replaced it, made with deep brown, blue and black flowered fabrics to suggest the types of leftover fabric available to slaves, fit perfectly in the spot where the Harriet Powers Bible quilt once hung. They'd also hung a poster of the Harriet Powers quilt so the information on the display cards made sense. I was flipping through the pages of the guest book, skimming the comments when I felt a hand on my shoulder.

"We've received a lot of positive remarks," Maggie said, smiling at me. "It doesn't make up for the quilt being stolen, but I'm happy that the exhibit has gone over so well."

"Me too," I said, setting the guest book back down on the wooden pedestal. "Are you going to the concert tonight?" I glanced at my watch. "It starts in about a half hour."

She shook her head no. "Wish I could, but I'm exhausted. I've been here since this morning and I plan on riding in the cattle drive tomorrow so I'd better get some sleep. Besides, someone has to go home and feed the critters. Katsy's staying. She's trying to support Levi as much as she can."

"I haven't seen him all day. What did he say about the quilt?"

She reached up and tugged at the silver hoop earring in her right ear.

"He was angry, of course. But he's also trying to keep it quiet so people don't start running off at the mouth. Controversy is something he definitely would rather avoid."

"Hud said it could be as simple as one of the carnival workers taking a shine to it. Gabe agreed with him."

"Has Hud come up with anything?"

I shrugged. "Have no idea. Last I talked to him, he'd made the report and filed it away. Oh, I forgot, he said it would help to have a clear photo to show the security staff and he suggested offering a reward. I have those flyers we used for press kits. We could print up some lost quilt posters."

She cocked her head. "But Levi said he wanted to keep the theft low profile."

"You're right. So, why don't you and Katsy discuss it with him? Maybe we can wait until after the fair ends." Though, by that time, I thought, the chances of finding it might be close to zero.

"Okay, but if you see Levi at the concert, feel free to mention it." In the distance, we could hear Rifle Shot's loud thrumming bass. She gave a wide yawn.

I fought the urge to mimic her. "Stop that right now. You know yawns are contagious and I still have to survive three more hours."

"Did you ever make it home?"

"Yes, and I even took a little nap, but that just seemed to make me more tired." I hesitated a moment. "Something happened with Jazz this afternoon and I think I should tell Levi about it."

"What?"

I described the incident in the parking lot between Dodge and Jazz. When I finished, she waited a moment before speaking.

"That is touchy territory," she said, smoothing down one black eyebrow. "Jazz is an adult, even if she seems like a kid to us. She has the right to see whomever she wants."

"But Dodge Burnside is big-time trouble."

"Still, I'm not sure it's our place to tattle to Levi. It's not like she's under age, which would be an entirely different story."

I nodded my head, wishing she wasn't right. "I guess I'm being overprotective. Maybe she'll tell Justin and he can talk to Dodge. So tell me, what's the deal with that? I thought she and Cal—"

Maggie held up her hands. "Girlfriend, don't even get me started on this younger generation and their capricious dating habits."

I laughed. "Younger generation, my foot. You're not that much older than Jazz."

Maggie joined my laughter. "I can't imagine trying to juggle dating three men. I'd have enough problems with one."

"Amen, Sister Maggie."

We parted ways at the entrance to the hospitality suite.

"I'll see you at the cattle drive tomorrow morning," she said. "We're supposed to meet at the Golden Hill Auto Center on Highway 46. You know, the GMC dealer."

"That's where Daddy bought his last truck. Mark gave him a good deal. He's a nice guy, though more than once he's tried to talk me out of my little Ford pickup. I'll be there with my spurs on."

The security guard at the door to the Bull Pen, used only on concert nights, nodded at my all access badge and waved me through. Upstairs, the hospitality suite was hat to boots crowded with people, most of whom I knew. It took me almost ten minutes to cross the room to the bar and order a Coke. There was no sign of Gabe, but the suite had three rooms, not to mention the outside patio where padded seats overlooked the Sierra Vista arena. People's loud laughter, the buzz of shouted conversation, the stifling heat, mingled perfume scents and Rifle Shot's bone-rattling drums and bass guitar were already starting to make my head throb. I contemplated my options. The air would be fresher on the patio, but the band would also be louder.

"Hey, Benni! Here's a spot." Levi waved me over, pointing to an empty bar stool at the curve of the long bar. I inched my way over to him.

"Hey, Levi," I said, hopping up on the bar stool. I felt a whoosh of cool air and looked up. The stool was situated right underneath an air-conditioner vent. "Wow, coolest seat in the house. Literally. Thanks."

He smiled down at me and sipped at some kind of clear drink. "Yes, it is. I figured that out right off. How's the fair treating you so far?" His mouth turned down naturally at the corners, usually giving his resting expression a hint of sadness. But tonight he was all smiles.

"I pig-wrangled this morning. Brought back lots of memories. Can you believe how long we've been coming to this fair?"

He shook his head, running a hand along the side of his short, graying hair. He wore creased dark slacks, a white short sleeve Western shirt and a Western string tie made from a shiny chunk of obsidian. A splattering of tiny dark freckles dusted his light brown cheeks.

He said something, but Rifle Shot had apparently decided to close their set with a spirited rendition of "The Devil Went Down to Georgia." He leaned closer and said in my ear, "Don't tell anyone, but I'm exhausted already. I'm looking forward to the fair being over."

I put my finger to my lips and smiled. "The music lineup is great!" I turned up the volume in my voice, trying to be heard over the crowd. Any thought I had of telling him about his daughter and her confrontation with Dodge Burnside wasn't going to happen here. Maybe I'd drop by his office tomorrow and talk to him under quieter circumstances.

"Thanks!" he yelled back.

It was impossible to carry on a decent conversation, so I waved good-bye and went outside to find my seat on the terrace. Gabe was already there, sipping bottled water.

"Crazy in there," he said, draping his arm around me.

"Pretty crazy out here too," I added.

Eventually, Rifle Shot finished their set and Kathy Mattea took the stage. She performed many of her hits and most of my favorites, but I especially loved it when her songs became more bluegrassy, her lyrics a tribute to the coal-mining part of Kentucky. They always touched something inside me, especially her rendition of the haunting "You'll Never Leave Harlan Alive." The song always brought tears to my eyes, reminding me of the pain and exhilaration of being young, of Jack's strong, beautiful forearms and how life never stays the same. Before we knew it, the concert was over. We wandered back inside the hospitality suite, talking to Emory and Elvia. It was a little past ten o'clock.

"Great show," I said, yawning. "But I'm ready to call it a night."

"Me too," Elvia said, catching my yawn. "I can't believe we used to stay out until one or two in the morning."

"Me neither. I'm going to hit the ladies' room before we drive home."

"Good idea."

After I washed my hands, I told Elvia I'd wait for her out in the hallway. It was quieter there and I was enjoying the respite from the noise when I overheard Milt Piebald's voice. It was sharp and low, coming from the partially open door leading to a set of outside stairs that ended inside the arena.

"Yeah, well, he was never my choice. He may be *real* sorry he ever got the job."

My heart beat faster at his words. My first thought was of Levi. Milt had been appointed by the governor to the fair board five years ago and so had been involved in the hiring of the fair manager. Who was he talking *to*? I inched closer to the door, hoping to hear more when Elvia came out of the restroom. She looked around, then spotted me at the end of the hall. When she started walking toward me, I held up my hand for her to stop and hurried over to her.

"What were you doing over there?" she asked.

"Tell you later," I whispered, looping my arm through hers and pulling her back into the noisy hospitality suite. In the ten minutes we were powdering our noses, our husbands had been shanghaied by one slightly tipsy ex-talk-show host and rodeo queen.

"Hey there, girls!" Juliette's voice trilled when we walked up. "I've been telling your gorgeous husbands here how much I loved Kathy's show." She placed her hand on Gabe's shoulder. Her heels were so high she actually looked down into his eyes. She wore glittery silver eye shadow that should have made her look cheap but didn't. "Didn't you just *love* Kathy?"

Milt walked up next to her, his red cheeks shiny in the room's bright can lights, an ingratiating smile frozen on his face. He wore a black cowboy shirt with black piping, black slacks and gray sharkskin boots that probably cost more than a good ranch horse. He was one of those thick-necked men who looked like they've never eaten anything but blood rare steaks their whole lives.

"Ms. Mattea was great," Gabe said, winking at me before ducking away from Juliette's hand and deftly moving out of her range.

"We met her before her show," Juliette said. "She's just a little thing. But celebrities always look so much smaller in person. She was just as nice as could be. If I still had my television show, I'd've asked her for an interview." Her usually well-modulated voice was shrill. She flashed an irritated look at Milt, who seemed to be ignoring her.

"She's quite a gal," Milt said. "Worth every penny." He gave a husky laugh. "Well, maybe not every penny."

Juliette pushed her face close to mine. "Milt wanted to pay her less. Her agent almost canceled. So embarrassing." I moved back slightly, trying to be polite, but getting a sour whiff of whatever it was she'd been drinking.

"Well, I'm bushed," I said, coughing. "Guess we'll

see you all tomorrow at the cattle drive." Or maybe not. *Somebody* might be waking up with a big ole hangover tomorrow.

"We're riding our new cutting horses," Milt said. "Bought them in Wyoming last fall. Cost me almost as much as Juliette's spa treatments in Jackson Hole."

"Milt, shut up," she said, her voice sharp, like the alcohol had suddenly dissipated. Just as quickly, her tone became neutral again. "I love my new horse, Sugarpie. I swear she reads my mind."

Milt gave a loud snort. "Short trip."

Juliette's face turned scarlet and there was an awkward silence.

I glanced at Elvia whose expression was blank, but I was sure she was thinking the same thing I was: *Let me out of here!* Though Juliette wasn't exactly a friend, I didn't like seeing her humiliated.

"We'll see you all tomorrow morning bright and early," I said, keeping my voice light.

At the bottom of the stairs, in front of the grandstand stadium, Gabe and I parted ways with Elvia and Emory. Though Elvia and I were dying to talk about what just happened, we agreed to rehash it tomorrow.

"I want to check on the museum's booth again," I told Gabe. We passed by Mustang Sallie's, which, though it was ten forty-five, still had a long line. "If it wasn't so late I'd get a fried Oreo. I used to be able to eat stuff like that any time of day or night. Now I'd be awake until three a.m. mainlining Pepcid AC."

"Welcome to adulthood," Gabe said.

At the museum's booth we were surprised to find only Jazz working.

"What're you doing here alone?" I asked. It was absolutely against our co-op rules.

She rang up a purchase, thanked the customer, then

turned back to me. "Marnie was supposed to work with me, but her boyfriend wanted her to go to Salinas with him. They're picking up some part for his truck. A door, I think. No worries."

No worries, indeed. Obviously the incident in the parking lot this afternoon hadn't rattled her as much as it had me. "We'll stay with you and help you close up," I said, glancing at Gabe, who nodded in agreement.

"Don't need to," she said in a brisk tone.

I ignored her irritation. After what happened this afternoon, there was no way I was going to let her walk to her car by herself at midnight despite the fact that hundreds of people would be leaving at the same time.

"We don't mind—" Before I could finish, I heard Gabe greet Justin.

"Why aren't you working, Officer Piebald?" Gabe's baritone voice was low and businesslike.

In the bright lights of the booth, we watched Justin's face turn a dull red. "Uh, I . . . have the night off? I could . . . I mean if you need me to . . ."

"Oh, stop it, Gabe," I said, lightly smacking my husband's upper arm. "He's teasing you, Justin."

Gabe grinned, corroborating my words.

"See, you guys can go home now," Jazz said. "Justin will stay with me until the fair closes, won't you?"

His adoring expression told us that he'd stay with her for the entire month if she'd let him. "No prob. I'll make sure she gets to her car safely."

"Good man," Gabe said, clapping the young man on his shoulder. "Carry on."

On our walk back to his Corvette, I teased Gabe. "Good man? Carry on? What, are you studying to be Prince Charles? You're watching way too much PBS."

He grabbed my waist, tickling me until my screams for him to stop made people start to look strangely at us.

"You're ruining your reputation for being a staid, up-tight police chief," I said, still laughing while he unlocked the Corvette's passenger door.

"For tickling my wife? I'll take that risk."

By midnight we were in bed with Scout happily snoring at our feet. Six a.m. was going to come way too early.

"Any news about the stolen quilt?" Gabe asked, as he punched his pillow.

"Now that you mention it, I didn't see Hud at the concert. He's the one who would know. I'm sure glad Justin was there to walk Jazz back to her car. That Burnside kid worries me."

Gabe lay back on the cool sheets, stretching out his naked body. Though San Celina was usually twenty degrees cooler than Paso, it was still August and warm. I had also shed all of my clothes and lay next to him on the pale blue sheets.

"It's just kids being kids," he said. "Remember how we were at that age? Every relationship seemed so important, so intense. They'll work it out."

I contemplated his answer, not certain I agreed with him. He hadn't seen how angry Dodge had been.

"I've decided to tell Levi about it tomorrow, even if Jazz gets mad. I mean, it's really my responsibility, not Katsy's or Maggie's, because I was the one who witnessed it."

"Your call," Gabe murmured, almost asleep.

I stared down at our legs resting next to each other. It had always amazed me how opposite our skin colors were—his copper-colored legs covered with black hair and my pale, almost translucent skin. For some reason I loved looking at the contrast. I turned on my side and ran my foot down his leg, feeling the coarse hair under my foot.

"I'm tired," he murmured, his eyes closed. Then he smiled. "But not *that* tired."

"Friday, I'll save your pride. I *am* that tired. Besides we have an early morning cattle drive."

I pulled my foot back and turned on my back, staring at the intricate patterns the moon made shining through our lacy curtains. As I listened to his breathing slow down and move into sleep, I lay awake, suddenly fearful, though I didn't really understand why. I stared at the spiderweb patterns until the moon moved on and the ceiling disappeared into darkness. It was only then that I realized I'd forgotten to tell Gabe about Milt's ominous words.

CHAPTER 4

THE NEXT MORNING—SATURDAY—WHILE WE GRABBED a quick breakfast of cereal, coffee and juice, I told Gabe what I'd overheard Milt say in the Bull Pen hallway last night.

"I bet he was referring to Levi," I said. "Remember how he was against Levi getting the job?"

"He's a jackass," Gabe said mildly, not as upset about the remark as I was.

I poured maple syrup on my oatmeal. "I wonder who he was talking to."

Gabe sipped his coffee, his expression mild. "Who cares?"

"I thought you'd be more upset. When you add that to the letters Levi received—"

"What letters?"

"Levi received some threatening letters. Do you think Milt might be behind them?"

He was still calm, surprising me again. "Sweetheart, I've listened to idiots like Milt Piebald my whole life. I'm sure Levi has too. You can't let people like him pitch a tent in your head. The only thing it does is keep you from doing what you have to do to succeed. Levi made it to where he is today because there's no one better qualified *and* he worked his butt off. Milt can't do a thing about that so he's just shooting off his mouth to make himself feel more powerful than he actually is." He looked back down at the newspaper folded next to his plate. "Wonder how many rat dogs are going to charge the cattle this year?"

"Okay," I said, doubtfully. "You would certainly know better than me about how much credence to give Milt's remarks."

Since we knew we'd likely want to leave the fair at different times, Gabe and I took separate vehicles. We parked in the Booster Buddies preferred lot and were lucky enough to catch a ride with a rancher who was also heading to the Golden Hill Auto Center on Highway 46. The dirt parking lot next to the auto center was already crowded with dozens of trucks and horse trailers. For a moment I just stood and listened. The sounds of snorting horses, clinking spurs, loud masculine laughter and the high murmuring of women's words as they calmed their mounts composed a symphony I never tired of hearing.

Daddy's truck and trailer was parked over by a back fence. He was unloading Tanya, a new ranch horse he'd bought from his good friend Charlotte Brown over in Riverdale. Rooster, my little brown quarter horse who was as solid as a gold brick, and Badlands, the big sorrel gelding Gabe liked to ride, were already saddled and waiting for us.

"Thanks, Daddy," I said, kissing him on the cheek.

"What'd you two lazy birds do, sleep in this morning?" he said with a soft drawl that revealed his Arkansas roots.

"We got up at six a.m.!" I said, reaching into my pocket and giving Rooster pieces of carrot. The other two horses nickered for their share. I promptly heeded their commands.

Daddy chuckled and checked my rigging. "I'd eaten breakfast, plowed a field and done my taxes by then."

"Ha-ha," I said, drying my damp palms on the sides of my jeans. "You ready to ride?"

"Ready to watch a bunch of yahoos try to kill themselves or someone else," he grumbled. Every year he carped about this cattle drive and every year claimed it would be his last. Every year for the last thirty years.

After everyone saddled up, we rode over to the portable corrals next to the dealership where the cattle, already agitated because their routine had been broken, were bawling to beat the band. The route chosen for the cattle drive this year was one we'd used the last few years. It had proven to be the safest route for the hundred or so head of cattle that were driven, Old West–style, to the fairgrounds.

Even over the bawling cattle I could hear my cell phone, which I'd stuck in my shirt pocket. I ignored it since I had a good idea who it was and I wasn't up to hearing what Aunt Garnet had gone and done this morning.

"Same thing as last year," yelled Cody, whose parents owned a ranch out near Parkfield. He was cowboy in charge since it was his family's cattle. "We'll be driving them down Golden Hill Road, right on Confederate Road, left on North Salina, left on Crestline, over the bridge then right on Creekside Avenue past the Pioneer Museum and into the fairgrounds. We'll be going through some crowded neighborhoods and we're expecting a lot of spectators so be extra careful. Go slow and pay attention."

"I hope the horses and cattle are paying attention," I said to Gabe. "Because the riders who should be listening sure aren't."

"Paramedics are standing by," Gabe said.

Of course, the usual new-to-the-country-life folks showed

up for this traditional event with their green-broke horses
and fringed and spangled outfits that resembled something
you'd more likely see on Hollywood Boulevard rather than
a cattle drive.

"For Pete's sake, look at that one," I said.

A thirtyish woman in Daisy Dukes, a paper-thin white
T-shirt stretched tight across her impressively enhanced
chest, bright pink straw cowboy hat and neon green and
blue boots rode by us on a wild-eyed paint controlled only
by a braided halter. It was a spectacular wreck just waiting
to happen.

"Howdy, cowboy," she said to Gabe, giving him an ap-
preciative look.

Gabe grinned, touching the rim of the white straw Stetson I talked him into wearing. "Ma'am."

She giggled and blew him a kiss.

I rode up next to him, took off my Ramsey Ranch cap
and smacked his Levi's-clad thigh. "I'll ma'am you, Chief
Ortiz."

He laughed and adjusted his seat in his saddle. "Hope
she doesn't fall off her pony. She might experience road
rash in some mighty delicate places."

"Hope she has her plastic surgeon on speed dial."

Of course Miss Daisy joined the other inexperienced
riders at the front of the herd completely ignoring the
shouted suggestions of the real cowboys that if you didn't
have much experience herding cattle to please stay at the
side or back of the herd. Oh, no, these dudes and dudettes
wanted to be at the front so their friends and family could
snap pictures and take movies of them leading a "real" cattle drive. The fact that half of them were sneaking sips of
beer at nine in the morning made me wonder why the city's
insurance gurus allowed this event to continue every year.

Still, despite my complaints, I'd be as disappointed as
anyone else if they ever stopped it. As big a pain as these
crazy, half-drunk wannabes were, they also gave us some-

thing to laugh about up in the Bull Pen. I saw Daddy on the other side of the herd and I waved, then circled my temple with my finger. He saluted me and shook his head. This cattle drive wasn't exactly a reenactment of the Old West, but more like a scene from the editing floor of the movie *City Slickers*.

At the start, the inexperienced riders always became overly excited, like a bunch of sugar-high toddlers, and did way too much yeehawing, making the already skittish cattle a bit wild-eyed. But once the cowboys yelled at the riders to shut up and slow down, they usually relaxed and went with the flow. We were moving along nicely with no incidents, slowly maneuvering the cattle down Confederate Road, the longest stretch of the drive. The connecting street's intersections were blocked off by Paso Robles police cars and the closer we moved to the fairgrounds, the larger our audience. People lined the street with their lawn chairs and coolers, snapping photographs and taking home movies of something most of them had only seen in television Westerns.

Crossing two bridges—one over the river and one over the 101 freeway—was the next challenge. By this time the cattle were relatively quiet considering all the new sights and sounds they were experiencing. But some of the horses, as well trained as they were in ranch work, were getting spooky. The echoing sound of their hooves on the concrete bridges and the rumbling sound of trucks roaring underneath them as we crossed over Interstate 101 was enough to make all the sensible riders keep a close rein on their mounts. Halfway across the bridge over the Interstate, I felt Rooster tuck his tail underneath him, his front end coming up off the ground a little while he danced a nervous two-step.

Once we made it over the bridges, I let out a sigh of relief and felt Rooster start to relax under me. Only a few more blocks to go. Once we turned right on Creekside Avenue, we were within spitting distance of the fair. I could see the top of the midway's giant Ferris wheel. So far, things were going okay. The city slickers had listened to the cowboys and were riding nose to tail, keeping the cattle in line, resisting their urge to shout "yee-haw." My phone rang twice during the ride and finally I'd turned it off. I'd pay big-time for that later.

I was riding along just fine, keeping an eye out for any recalcitrant cattle when Rooster tensed beneath me, started tip-tapping. I tightened his reins, murmuring, "Ho, boy, ho."

"Heads up!" a woman yelled behind me. Hoofbeats clattered on the pavement. "Loose horse!"

A riderless horse dashed past me in a flat-out gallop, reins dragging.

My heart tumbled like a bucket of rocks. The call "loose horse" reverberated down the line of riders like an electric current. A steer bolted in front of me, swerved a sharp right trying to break from the herd.

"Hup!" Gabe yelled, touching his heel to Badlands, who immediately did what he'd been trained to do. Badlands cut off the steer, expertly pushing it back into the forward-moving herd.

"Yeah!" Gabe lifted a fist in triumph.

I laughed at his excitement. Gabe had grown up in Kansas working his grandpa Smith's wheat farm, but everything he knew about cattle he'd learned from Dove, Daddy or me. He'd been a good student, easy to teach, because he was a natural on a horse, one of those riders who just relaxed and trusted the experienced animal underneath him.

"Good job, cowboy," I said, riding up next to him. His lean, long-legged body looked sexy on horseback. Then again, to me, almost any man looked sexier on the back of a horse.

"Thanks, but you trained this old guy," Gabe said, patting Badland's glistening neck. "So most the credit goes to him . . . and you."

That was another thing I found sexy. He wasn't afraid to let me be the smarter one sometimes. "To be fair, I started the training. Daddy finished it. Despite his name, Badlands is a darn good cowpony."

After our little excitement, we stayed even more vigilant. No one could really relax until the cattle were inside the fairgrounds, in the pens. This group of cattle was better than last year's wild bunch. This year they were spicy enough to make it fun, but not too dangerous. Good thing, since it seemed we had twice as many weekend riders. Word came up the line that the thrown rider was okay and someone had caught the horse.

"What are your plans after this?" I asked my husband, our shins occasionally bumping as we rode next to each other.

He readjusted his Stetson. "Thought I'd catch some of the animal judging. Maybe watch the cutting horse competition this afternoon, then head over to the wine pavilion."

We drove the cattle into their final pen near the beef barn where they'd stay until the country rodeo the second to the last night of the fair. While waiting for Sam to bring the horse trailer from the GMC dealer, we let tourists take photos of the horses.

"Want to meet for lunch?" Gabe asked, loosening Badland's cinch, then tying up the saddle's rigging for the trip back to the ranch.

"How about Mustang Sallie's at noon?"

"I'll meet you there, but I refuse to eat that crap."

"How about the Kiwanis stand?"

"Deal. Their cheeseburgers are worth risking my arteries for."

After we loaded the horses back into the trailer, Daddy and Sam headed back to the ranch.

On my way to the museum's booth, I cut through one of

the commercial buildings to cool off. I'd gotten caught in a human traffic jam between the spiel of a waterless cookware salesman and a slice-and-dice demonstration, when, over the din of voices, I heard someone yell my name. The voice carried a distinctively familiar timbre that instinctively made me want to bolt in the opposite direction.

"Young lady, you freeze right there!"

Dove's voice and personal charisma were powerful enough to make the crowd part like Moses did the Red Sea. She marched up to me waving her shiny blue cell phone. "What, pray tell, is the use for this contraption if you never answer your phone?"

"Hey, Gramma," I said in my most conciliatory voice. "I was on the cattle drive and you know how nervous those cattle can get at the least little noise . . ."

She grabbed my upper arm like I was six years old and maneuvered me through a side door to the concrete walkway between buildings.

"You have to do something," she said, once we could hear ourselves talk. "Seriously, honeybun, I think I may kill her. I caught her snooping through my books this morning. I'm sure she set her alarm to get up early. She is dying to sink her claws into my corn bread recipe. Bet she thinks it'll get her a blue ribbon at the Arkansas State Fair."

I held back the urge to laugh at the mental picture of my great-aunt Garnet tiptoeing down the hallway carrying her house slippers so she wouldn't wake up Dove. Since Dove habitually rose at 5 a.m. that meant Aunt Garnet had to get up pretty darn early. Dove's cheesy corn bread was good, but it wasn't *that* good.

"Isn't there a two- or three-hour difference in Arkansas and California time? Maybe she got up early because it felt later to her. Isn't five o'clock here like seven or eight o'clock there?"

Dove was silent a moment and I realized that hadn't occurred to her.

"Nevertheless, I caught her going through my cookbooks."

I lifted up my hair, trying to catch a breeze and cool my sweating neck. "Aren't your cookbooks in with all your other books?"

"What difference does that make?"

"Maybe she was just looking for something to read."

"Something to read like notes that would give away my corn bread recipe."

"I think you're being . . ."

Dove narrowed her eyes, placing her hands on her plump hips.

I was going to say paranoid, but my gramma didn't raise no dummy.

"Where is Aunt Garnet anyway?" Changing the subject sometimes worked.

Dove pointed her thumb in the direction of the home arts building. "Watching the cake-decorating demonstration. Probably telling them how they're doing it all wrong."

"So, she's out of your hair for a little while. Why don't you go watch the 4-H kids show their lambs? You know how you love that."

Dove was a sucker for a cute kid in a green-and-white 4-H uniform. She'd spent a good part of my youth hauling around a "bag of whites" to supplement the uniforms of her 4-H kids whose sizes seemed to change by the hour.

"Well . . ." she said, contemplating my suggestion.

"Change of subject, just for a minute, okay? I need your advice."

She gave me a suspicious look, certain that I was making up an excuse to stop her complaining about her sister. Then again, she could never resist giving her opinion. "About what?"

I quickly told her about the letters Levi had received and what I'd overheard Milt say last night.

Dove tsked under her breath. "Lord, Lord, some things never change."

"Gabe thinks that Milt's just a jerk saying stupid things, but I'm worried they might be connected. Should I tell Levi about what Milt said? And there's something else." I told her how Dodge Burnside threatened Jazz in the parking lot yesterday. "Should I tell Levi about that too? Maggie and Katsy say that Jazz isn't a kid anymore and that it might not be our place to tattle on her. Do you think I'm just being a busybody?" I leaned against the wall of the warm building.

Dove patted my cheek with her soft palm. "Of course you're being a busybody, but only because you care about this girl. Try to convince Jazz to tell her daddy herself about what happened with this Burnside boy. She might surprise you and agree. But if she doesn't want to, you'd best stay out of it since it'd be better for her to stay speaking to you than not. As for what Milt said, well, I'm not sure it would do any good to tell Levi about that. This isn't likely the first time Milt has talked trash about Levi and probably won't be the last. Right now, Levi doesn't need more things to fret about. He's got a full enough plate."

I hugged my gramma, inhaling the sweet scent of her Coty face powder. "You are so wise."

She gave me a little push. "Now, back to me. What am I going to do about Garnet?"

"Why don't you let me be her chauffeur for the rest of the day? That'll give you a break. How long is she supposed to stay anyway?"

Dove gave a little growl. "She will not give me a going home date! That woman is up to something."

"Maybe it's not your corn bread recipe she's after. Maybe it's something else entirely." The minute the words were out of my mouth, I tried to grab them back. I slapped the side of my head. "Crazy me, what am I saying? She's just here to visit you and—"

"You're right," Dove said, her voice pitched low with realization. "The question is what? You keep her as long as you can, honeybun. I'm heading back to the ranch to phone WW back in Sugartree, see if I can pry anything out of him. I'll bribe him with my snickerdoodle cookies."

I watched her stride away, as much as a five-foot-tall woman with a twenty-eight-inch inseam could stride, and wondered if somehow she'd again outfoxed me. Maybe the whole story about Aunt Garnet wanting her corn bread recipe or going through her books was just a ruse to trick me into entertaining Aunt Garnet. If it was, it had worked. Which left no doubt that Dove Ramsey Lyons was still the smartest hen in the chicken coop.

I called Gabe on my cell and told him that now that I was Aunt Garnet's escort, we'd probably leave the fairgrounds for lunch since I was pretty sure a cheeseburger at the Kiwanis booth wasn't up to her persnickety standards. With the heat, I couldn't imagine that she'd want to stay around the fairgrounds the entire day.

According to the daily fair schedule, the cake-decorating demonstration had another forty-five minutes to go, so I walked back into the commercial building and wandered the aisles looking at turquoise jewelry from New Mexico, magic mops, sewing machines that could practically drive your car, American flags from every time period in our history, fireplace mantels, CDs from the All American Boys' Choir, rhinestone cell phone accessories, ladders that looked like you'd need a degree in engineering to fold and unfold, Jacuzzi spas, the ever-present Gilroy garlic products, a man selling honey who wore a hat shaped like a beehive and, my personal favorite, the Electronic Personality Handwriting Analysis. Jack, Elvia and I never could resist this booth, doing it three or four times each fair when we were teenagers just to prove that it was fake. One time Jack and I got the exact same "analysis."

"See," he'd said. "We're perfect for each other."

"Get your personality analyzed," the twentyish-looking man with a ring in each nostril announced in a bored voice. He handed me the blue and white form with a space to sign my name. "For three dollars our supercomputer will reveal who you are."

"What a bargain," I said. "Except it used to cost me fifty cents to find out who I was."

His expression slid from bored to apathetic. I was only thirty-nine, but to him I was a boring old lady.

"Shoot howdy," Dove used to say when I read them out loud to her. "I could tell you the same thing and I'd only charge you a quarter."

It was silly, but it was also a tradition so I signed my name with a flourish—Albenia Louise Harper Ortiz—and gave it to the hawker. The "supercomputer" with its flashing lights and tinny sound track spit out my "analysis" in about a minute.

Your persuasive manner enables you to often get your own way. You have an extremely generous nature. You have definite ideas, but you're open to others' opinions. Once your mind is made up, you do not hesitate to move forward. You are independent and tend to rely on yourself. You have a special way of influencing others. You are intrigued by the mysterious. You have highly evolved investigative abilities. Your lucky numbers are 7, 19, 25, 47 and 84.

I smiled to myself. They hadn't changed. The one thing you could count on was the "analysis" could really apply to anyone's personality. The line about my highly evolved investigative abilities pleased me. That would give Gabe a laugh. I stuck the paper in my backpack and grabbed a free cup of icy water from the Arrowhead Spring Water booth before heading over to the home arts building.

The cake-decorating demonstration lady was squeezing

the final bit of red piping on a dark chocolate cake when I slipped into the empty chair next to Aunt Garnet.

"Hey, Aunt Garnet," I said, putting my arm around her knobby shoulders and giving her a hug. "Are you having fun?" She smelled like fresh mint leaves.

"Where have you been hiding?" she asked. "I arrived a good twenty-four hours ago and this is the first I've seen hide or hair of you."

Two seconds in her presence and I was getting scolded. I was already regretting my offer to relieve Dove. I sat back in my chair and faced forward, trying not to let her see that she'd ruffled my feathers. The trick with Aunt Garnet was to feign complete neutrality so she couldn't ferret out your weak spots.

"I'm here now," I said cheerfully, "and I'm going to be your personal chauffeur for the rest of the day." I didn't glance over to gauge her reaction but concentrated on the Martha Stewart clone showing the audience how to make perfect-every-time frosting roses. How did she get the frosting that deep dark red? It kind of reminded me of blood.

"Where's Dove?" Garnet asked. "What does she have to do that's more important than visiting with her only sister?"

I turned to look at my great-aunt, amazed as always, at how physically different she was from her only sibling. Dove was short, plump and had white hair that she wore in a long braid down her back, while Garnet was taller by a vast three inches, thin to the point of gauntness and had short, tightly curled hair that reminded me of a poodle. Only their hair color was the same—the silvery white of former redheads. I mentally put that on my to-do list—find a beauty parlor for Aunt Garnet. Dove wouldn't have the first clue about hair salons—I trimmed her hair when she needed it, as she did mine—but Aunt Garnet was definitely the weekly wash-and-set type. Maybe one of the docents at the folk art museum could recommend one that specialized in helmet-haired ladies.

I ignored her question and opened up my fair program. "There's lots of stuff to see at the fair. Plus I want to take you by the folk art museum and you've always liked the chicken and dumplings at Liddie's so I thought we'd go there for lunch and, of course, there's Blind Harry's bookstore. I know you want to see Emory's baby. I'm sure Dove told you her middle name is Louise like yours and mine. Actually Sophia Louisa, but Emory and I call her Sophie Lou. She's as beautiful as an Italian painting, but, of course, I'm a little partial—"

"You know," Aunt Garnet said, abruptly standing up. "I'm not ignorant. I know my sister pushed me off on you. You can just take me back to the ranch. You don't need to force yourself to entertain me." Her voice, normally sharp and demanding as a mockingbird's, sounded a little . . . hurt.

I stood up and took her arm in mine. "Nonsense." I cringed at my choice of words. I sounded like . . . well . . . Aunt Garnet. "It was my idea. You and I have not spent enough time together and I thought it would be fun. You and Dove will have plenty of time to visit."

I think her face actually softened and her thin, tangerine-painted lips turned up into a hint of a smile. "Why, Benni Harper, that sounds real nice."

"It's Benni Harper Ortiz now," I said, patting her dry, powdery hand. "Did Dove tell you I took Gabe's name?"

Aunt Garnet gave me a wider, approving smile. "No, she didn't. I'm so proud of you. I have prayed and prayed for your stubborn heart to soften toward that dear, patient husband of yours."

The smile on my face felt frozen. I gritted my back teeth. Be nice, I told myself, be understanding. "Yes, Gabe is a good man. He's here at the fair. Maybe we'll run into him."

She continued smiling, clueless about how her words had sounded. She grasped my hand and I could feel a small tremor. Guilt pushed aside my irritation. Okay, she was old and cranky and certainly judgmental. But she *was* my great-aunt and I *did* promise Dove.

"Let's go see the Family Farm exhibits," I said. "They are something I think you'll enjoy. Then, unless you want to eat here at the fair, we can drive into San Celina and have lunch there. I'd love to show you the improvements we've made at the folk art museum."

"Lead the way," she said.

Fortunately we didn't have to walk far in the hot, sticky air since the agriculture building was right next door. The blessed swamp coolers were valiantly doing their job. While we wandered from exhibit to exhibit Aunt Garnet gave a running commentary on how each one reminded her of something about the farm where she and Dove grew up in Sugartree, Arkansas. The land had long ago been sold out of the family and Aunt Garnet and Uncle WW lived in town. But whenever Dove visited Arkansas, she and Garnet drove the twenty miles out of town to visit the old barn they played in as girls.

It was the only thing left of the farm.

"Oh my," Aunt Garnet said when we came up to the Pie-bald Family Farm exhibit. "I reckon I can see why this one took the grand prize."

"I suppose," I said, still rankled by the award. "Actually, there's some controversy about it. Some people think they might not have designed the exhibit themselves, which kind of ruins the whole point of the competition."

Her face looked thoughtful. "Yes, that would bother folks. I suppose there are people like that everywhere, just have to win no matter what it takes."

I looked at her in surprise. It sounded so unlike her. The observation was actually *nice*. Maybe Aunt Garnet was softening in her old age. I could hear Dove's voice murmuring, "And I've got some beachfront property in Little Rock I'd like to sell you for a wooden nickel."

"Look at that old pickup truck," Aunt Garnet said.

"Daddy used to call them pick-me-up trucks. He had one just like that, only it was dark blue. I remember many times taking cold lemonade out to him in the barn when he was working on that truck. Just like that there dummy. Seeing those legs sticking out like that just brings back Daddy like it was yesterday."

I heard her sniff and turned to witness a tear running down her wrinkled cheek. Aunt Garnet crying? I'd never seen her cry.

Not wanting to embarrass her, I turned back to look at the Piebald exhibit, studying the truck that had made her so emotional. I stared at the crazy grinning stuffed sheep, the panicked cows, the sign—Templeton Cattle Auction or Bust. Something looked different. I glanced down at the jean-clad legs sticking out from underneath the truck's shell. Legs. *Legs?* Legs that hadn't been there yesterday. It felt like the blood in my temples had suddenly doubled.

I cleared my throat. "Aunt Garnet, why don't you sit over here on this bench and collect your bearings. The air in here is kind of close."

"Thank you, dear, I believe you might be right."

I helped her over to a bench in the center of the exhibition hall, then strolled casually back to the Piebald exhibit. I sidled close to the white picket fence enclosing their exhibit, trying not to appear suspicious. Unless the Piebalds had decided since last night to add something extra to their bucolic barnyard exhibit there was something dreadfully wrong.

I reached over the short fence and poked the leg, hoping to feel the give of hay or polyester stuffing. It was solid as a wood beam. My heart did a loopy dive, like the first twist on a Tilt-A-Whirl.

I pulled out my cell phone and dialed Hud. He answered on the second ring.

"Detective Hudson." His husky voice sounded bored.

"Where are you?"

He laughed, his voice turned intimate and teasing. "Why, want to meet at the Ferris wheel? I'll bribe the operator to stop it at the top so we can look down on everyone else. Do you think the chief will mind?"

"I need you in the Family Farm exhibits."

His voice immediately sobered. "What's wrong?"

"I think . . ." I inhaled deeply and lowered my voice. How many more times in my life was I going to have to say these words? "I think I've found a body."

CHAPTER 5

"*I*'M TWO MINUTES AWAY. HOLD TIGHT." HE CLICKED off and I stood next to the exhibit, unsure what to do next.

Aunt Garnet was occupied, searching through her tan pocketbook for something, so I decided to stay put until Hud arrived. Should I call Gabe? Dang, should have called him first, I thought, instantly feeling guilty.

But it *was* Hud's jurisdiction. Gabe was a civilian at the fair. Still, I knew he would be annoyed. Then again, what if this wasn't a dead body? Maybe it was a joke, a man-nequin someone had slipped into the exhibit to tease Milt and Juliette.

Minutes later Hud came through the building's double doors. His face was composed and expressionless, but I could see the agitation, even anticipation in his face. He was beside me in a minute, close enough that I could smell his Juicy Fruit gum.

"Show me the body," he whispered into my ear, then chuckled.

Of course, at that moment Aunt Garnet chose to look up and, by the expression on her face, didn't like what she was seeing. She pursed her lips and frowned.

I elbowed Hud in the chest. "Step back. My great-aunt is watching."

He turned and nodded at Aunt Garnet, sliding a finger across the rim of his Stetson.

Her frown deepened and she shook her head like she used to in church when she caught me swinging my legs and flipping pages in the Baptist hymnal, not paying close enough attention to the preacher.

"Legs," I hissed, hoping none of the people milling about looking at the exhibits could hear. "Under the truck. They weren't here yesterday. Maybe it's a practical joke, but when I touched one, it felt"—I took a deep breath—"real."

He patted my shoulder. "Ranch girl, go pacify your uptight auntie and I'll check out Mr. Legs. It's probably a joke. Milt Piebald's annoyed a few folks in his life and this is probably righteous payback." He looked back at my aunt and grinned at her.

"Quit making eyes at my aunt. You'll only give her fodder to lecture me on how married women shouldn't be flirting with other men."

"If you want, I can assure her with complete honesty and disappointment that you never, ever flirt with me." He made an exaggerated sad sack face.

"Check out the body," I snapped.

I began defending myself when I got within five feet of my aunt. "That wasn't what it looked like. Ford Hudson is the sheriff's deputy in charge of security here at the fair. There's something . . ." I sat down beside her, considering my words carefully so she wouldn't be too shocked. "The Piebald exhibit. There might be a body in it."

She stared at me, the mention of a possible homicide the only possible thing that could keep her from commenting on Hud's flirting. "As in a *dead* body?" Her blue eyes were grave; her voice held an odd-sounding tremor.

"Yes . . . well, maybe. It's probably a joke, but those legs you saw under the truck shell? They weren't there yesterday and when I touched one, it felt . . ."

"Cold? Clammy? Was there rigor mortis?"

Wait. That wasn't a frightened tremor in her voice. That was . . . *excitement.* And the expression on her face was somber, but not swooning like one would think of a proper, dyed-in-the-wool, Southern Baptist lady whose favorite authors were Jan Karon, Janette Oke and Matthew, Mark, Luke and John.

She dipped her head and whispered, "Are they sending for the bone wagon?"

My mouth literally dropped open. "What?"

She looked at me like I was the one talking crazy. "You know, the morgue van. Y'all have one, don't you? What is the forensic team's ETA?"

"I suppose they'll send one. If it's actually a . . . wait a minute. How do you know a term like bone wagon?"

She sat up straight, settling her handbag in her lap. "I watch a little television. And I read."

"What do you read that talks about bone wagons?"

"A little of this, a little of that."

"Who?" I demanded, keeping my eye on Hud who'd climbed over the fence and was pretending to rearrange the display. The look on his face and how quickly he opened his phone and started punching numbers told me I hadn't been wrong.

"James Lee Burke," Aunt Garnet confessed. "Though I'm not sure I learned that particular phrase from him."

I turned to stare at her rosy cheeks. "You read James Lee Burke?" He was one of Gabe's favorite authors, mine too, but there was no doubt his books were pretty violent and often more than a little crude. Definitely not what I'd expect my straitlaced aunt to read.

"And a few others."

I didn't have time to quiz her any further about her surprising reading habits because Hud was standing in front of us.

"Ranch girl, you sure know how to find 'em. I think we got ourselves a genuine homicide here. Unless, of course, some poor fella just up and had a heart attack underneath the Piebald's truck shell, which seems a might unlikely."

"Who is he?" I asked.

"Couldn't exactly pull the old boy out and look at his face," Hud said. "Besides, it might be a *she*. Before we do anything, we need to secure the building, interview everyone we can." He glanced over at the double doors that suddenly opened. Levi, followed by three security guys, entered. Behind him—my stomach lurched—was my stone-faced husband, whom I still hadn't called.

Gabe moved around them and reached us with three long strides. Levi was seconds behind him.

"Are you all right?" he asked me, completely ignoring Hud.

"Yes, I'm fine. It's just that—"

"We'll get your statement in a minute. First we need to secure the building." He turned to speak to Levi but was stopped by Hud's exaggerated throat clearing.

"Excuse me all to heck, Chief Ortiz," he said, his Texas twang deliberately exaggerated. "But I reckon that, despite your outranking me in, say, the general law enforcement world, this here, well, it's pretty much my little rodeo." He smirked at Gabe.

If Gabe were a cartoon character at that moment he would have been one of those bulls with the steam coming out of his nose. I looked at Gabe, at Hud, then back to Gabe. I could see my husband almost literally counting to ten in his head.

"Absolutely, Detective," he said stiffly. "My apologies."

Aunt Garnet's eager eyes took all of this in like she

was watching an episode of *Law & Order.* Or a James Lee Burke book come to life.

"What do you want us to do?" I asked, not looking at either of them. I wasn't about to get in the middle of that little testosterone battle.

"Just relax," Hud said. "We'll take your statement, but we need to get the forensic team here without causing a huge amount of panic."

"Fat chance," Levi said, speaking up for the first time since they'd walked in. His expression was a composite of anger and frustration. "This will be the headline story for the next month. And *that's* going to make a lot of people really happy." The bitterness in his voice caused us all to look to the ground, knowing that he was right.

"But Detective Hudson is right," Levi continued. "We need to secure this building and make things as easy as possible for law enforcement to do their job." He turned to Hud, his face all business. "What else do you need me to do?"

Within a few minutes, Hud called more sheriffs' deputies to the scene, a couple of highway patrol officers, and a good half-dozen Paso Robles police officers. He stationed officers at each of the building's two entrances to keep people from entering and used the rest to quietly ask people to follow them over to a back room normally used to store maintenance equipment. Sheriff's detectives would take down their contact information, ask a few questions, then let them go on and enjoy the fair. Even Gabe would have to admit that Hud expertly coordinated all the agencies to initiate the investigation without too much hullabaloo.

Aunt Garnet sat next to me on the bench, her moist blue eyes animated, absorbing everything. "It's just like *Hill Street Blues,*" she whispered.

"They can't really do much," I whispered back, "until they identify who was under the truck and what happened to him."

"Or her," she corrected. "There's no confirmation about whether the victim is male or female. I hope they remember to look for latent fingerprints."

I tried not to laugh. A nutty picture popped in my head of Aunt Garnet wearing a houndstooth Sherlock Holmes hat and holding a magnifying glass.

After the building was emptied of curious fair attendees, the investigative team carefully moved aside the white picket fence surrounding the Piebald exhibit. Supervised by Hud, six officers placed themselves on both sides of the truck shell. On the count of three, they lifted and pushed it over on its side, promptly wrecking Milt and Juliette's winning display. The blue ribbon flew off the front of the truck's hood and landed on the concrete floor.

"What the—?" one of the forensic people said when they saw the body.

"Hey, Ryan, get a photo of this! He looks like a mummy!"

There were so many officers standing in front of the body I couldn't see what they were gaping at.

"What is it?" Aunt Garnet said, standing up. "What does he mean he looks like a mummy?"

"I don't know," I said, jumping up on the bench to see over the people crowded around the body.

"Oh, crap," I said, catching a glimpse of the victim. "Double crap." I didn't even care that Aunt Garnet might smack me or quote Bible verses about using crude and foolish speech.

"What is it?" she said, stretching her neck to see. "What?"

"I think they've found the missing Harriet Powers quilt."

CHAPTER 6

"*T*HE HARRIET WHAT?" AUNT GARNET TUGGED AT the leg of my jeans.

I stretched myself taller trying to see more. Please, please let me be imagining this. But, no, there was no doubt. The victim's upper body, hidden before by the truck shell, was wrapped in the Ebony Sisters' beautiful replica of the Harriet Powers story quilt. I could see one edge, the square that showed a spotted animal resembling a donkey and the blue-gray crook of a figure's arm—Adam and Eve naming the animals.

I got down from the bench. "It was a copy of a famous appliqué quilt made by this African American woman who was born a slave. The original hangs in the Smithsonian. The copy was part of an exhibit over in the home arts building. Someone stole it last night." I pulled out my cell phone. "I have to call Maggie and Katsy."

I tried Maggie's number first. She answered on the first ring. In the background I could hear the sound of clippers and blowers, the muffled squawk of the PA system announcing some event. "This is Benni. I have some news about the quilt."

"What?" she yelled. "You found the quilt! Hallelujah!" The background noise made her next words undecipherable.

"What?" I yelled.

"I'm helping at the Beef Barn," she yelled back. "Let me move to somewhere quieter." Her breathing was audible as she walked, the sound of the agitated cattle and the crackly PA voice retreating further in the background.

"There," she said with a loud sigh. "I'm far enough away to actually hear you now. Where is the quilt? Is it okay?"

I was silent for a moment, wishing I didn't have to be the one to tell her.

"It's not good, Maggie. They found it . . . wrapped around a body. In the Piebald Family Farm exhibit."

She was quiet for so long that I thought we'd lost our connection.

"Maggie, are you still there?"

"Yes," she said, her voice tired. "I'm just trying to absorb the information. Wrapped around a body? A *dead* body?"

"I'm so sorry. It was under the truck shell in the Piebald exhibit."

"The quilt was under a shell?"

"The body was wrapped in the quilt and it was under the truck shell. You couldn't actually see the quilt until they moved the truck. I found the body." I glanced over at Aunt Garnet, who was listening avidly to every word. "Actually, it was my great-aunt Garnet who noticed it first."

Aunt Garnet beamed at my words.

"She and I were looking at the exhibit and she was mentioning how her father used to work under trucks just like this dummy under the Piebald truck. Except I didn't remember the dummy being there yesterday and it wasn't because it . . . wasn't a dummy." I heard my voice wind down.

"Who is it?" Maggie asked.

"They haven't identified him. At least they haven't told us. They parked Aunt Garnet and me kinda out of the way. Let me see if I can wiggle my way in and see what's going on. I'll call you right back."

"Levi knows?"

"He's here right now."

"I'll call Katsy. She's working at the museum booth." There was a long moment of silence. "You know the people who are against Levi being the fair manager are going to be celebrating tonight."

"There's no way he could have prevented something like this."

"Tell that to the voracious media. They are going to be all over this. See you in a few."

I closed my phone and turned to Aunt Garnet. "I'm going to see if someone will tell me who the victim is."

"It's someone named Cal," Aunt Garnet said. "One of the security boys in the red shirts recognized him."

My head felt like it was filled with buzzing bees. Calvin Jones? Jazz's new boyfriend? This was getting crazier by the minute. Who in the world would kill that quiet, unassuming young man?

A scowling face suddenly came to my mind. "Dodge Burnside."

Aunt Garnet stared at me. "Who's Dodge Burnside?"

"Be right back." I walked over to where Gabe was talking to Miguel, one of Elvia's younger brothers and a San Celina police officer.

"Hey, Miguel," I said. He wore one of the red Fair Security polo shirts, so he was obviously moonlighting, something a lot of the young officers did. "Gabe, I need to talk to you."

He nodded at Miguel, then walked with me away from the crowd. "What's up?"

"I heard that Calvin Jones is the victim."

"They don't have a positive ID yet, but one of the security guys recognized him from working at the Mobil station."

"Did you know he and Jazz were seeing each other?"

He tilted his head. "No, but how is that relevant?"

"The fight between Jazz and Dodge Burnside," I reminded him. "I never told Levi about it. I don't know if Levi is even aware she was dating this Calvin Jones."

Gabe thought for a moment. "Right now I think the more information Levi has about all this, the better he can decide what to do. But I'm not sure you're the right person to tell him."

We glanced over at the doors where the sound of a very unhappy woman's voice was arguing with one of the security guards. It was Katsy. Maggie stood behind her, resting a hand on her sister's arm.

"Young man, I need to see Levi Clark now." Katsy's strong, contralto voice carried across the room. "Let me by or I'll report you to your superior." The security guard looked around as if he were debating whether it might be prudent if *he* fled the scene. "Detective Hudson. DETECTIVE FORD HUDSON!"

Hud's head jerked up. When he saw who was shouting, he called over to the security guard, "Let them in."

Katsy headed straight for Levi who was standing next to Hud. Maggie walked over to Gabe and me.

"This is unbelievable," she said, her eyelashes glistening.

I stood up, put my arm around her shoulders and gave her a quick hug. "Has anyone gotten in touch with Jazz?"

Maggie shook her head. "She isn't answering her cell phone. No one has seen her all morning."

That made me more than a little nervous, though there was no reason to believe she was in danger. "Maggie, someone has to tell Levi everything. He needs to know about Jazz and Cal and about the fight she and Dodge Burnside had yesterday. We have to find Jazz and make sure she's okay."

"I know, I know. Katsy and I discussed it on the way over here. She's going to tell him everything."

I breathed a sigh of relief. At least it wasn't up to me. Since Katsy was practically Jazz's stepmother, the information seemed more appropriate coming from her.

"Do they know how the poor boy died yet?" Maggie asked. "Oh, I feel so bad for him. He didn't have a soul in the world. Both his parents died before he was fourteen and he was in nine foster homes before he aged out of the system. He was trying so hard to make a life for himself." Her dark eyes filled with tears. "Cal Jones had had some problems with alcohol and some petty crime, but he really was a good boy at heart. Hardest working hand Katsy and I ever hired." A tiny sob caught in her throat. "That poor, poor boy."

Gabe put his hand on her shoulder and patted it gently. "Let me see what they've found out."

"At least he had you and Katsy," I said while we watched Gabe walk over to Levi who was talking into his walkie-talkie for the tenth time in the last five minutes. "And he had Jazz. He didn't die without people caring about him."

We walked back over to join Aunt Garnet who sat perched on the edge of the wooden bench writing in a small leather notebook. I sat down next to her and said in a low voice, "Aunt Garnet, *what* are you doing?"

"Making a list of things we know. It's so easy to forget the details. We need to establish who had access to this place during the probable time of the homicide. Then we need to find out who saw him last. Then . . ."

Before I could sputter any kind of answer to my aunt's crazy ramblings, Gabe came back, his face sober.

"Looks like someone whacked him in the head with a board or maybe a baseball bat."

"Blunt force trauma," Aunt Garnet murmured, nodding her head and writing furiously in her notebook.

Maggie's face scrunched up, tears only seconds away.

"Mags, you know that the sheriff's department will do their best to find out who did this," Gabe said, resting a hand on her shoulder. "Detective Hudson is in charge and he's an excellent investigator."

I tried to hide my shock. Fortunately, Gabe was looking at Maggie, not me. Gabe giving Hud any credit for being a good detective was one miracle I thought I'd never see in my lifetime. Especially after Hud just embarrassed Gabe in public. Then again, my often arrogant husband kind of deserved it. He'd do exactly the same thing if Hud tried to take charge of a crime in Gabe's jurisdiction.

"What's going on now?" Maggie sniffed loudly and started digging through her purse. "Why don't I ever have tissue when I need one?"

"Here, dear," Aunt Garnet said, handing her a neatly ironed, lace-trimmed cotton hankie. "You sit down here next to me and pull yourself together."

"Thank you," Maggie said, dabbing the hankie under each swollen eye.

"They're getting the path behind the building cleared so the body can be removed with as little fanfare as possible." Gabe grimaced. "No pun intended. This is apparently the first homicide they've had in the fair's history. It's a delicate situation."

"Political backlash will be a problem," Aunt Garnet said, nodding. "They'll likely have to form a task force after establishing firm jurisdiction, of course. No one's going to want this hot potato."

Gabe's eyebrows rose in surprise. He glanced at me. I shrugged. Apparently my aunt's body had been taken over by Jessica Fletcher.

Levi and Katsy walked up, both their faces unemotional. Levi's walkie-talkie crackled loudly and he turned the volume down.

"Benni, may we talk?" Levi asked. "Alone?"

"Sure." We walked over to the other side of the building in front of the Vieira Family Farm exhibit.

He stuck his hands in the pockets of his creased slacks. "Katsy tells me you saw what happened with my daughter and this Dodge kid. Tell me everything."

After I told him what I saw yesterday, he stared silently at the Vieira exhibit. "What is wrong with kids today?" he finally said.

I didn't answer because, one, it sounded like the question was rhetorical, and two, if it wasn't, I sure wasn't qualified to give any insights into late-twentieth-century teenage psyches.

I stared at the all access badge clipped to his shirt pocket. His photo showed the wide, friendly smile, something he'd always been known for. That and for never being rattled by any situation no matter how crazy or dire. From the first years he worked at the fair, when something went wrong whoever was in management grew to depend on Levi's opinions and solutions. With his cool-headed, organized personality and his knowledge of every aspect of the fair's inner workings, he was an invaluable employee. Those traits were, no doubt, why he got the manager's job. Mishaps, big and small, were a guarantee with the fair and Levi expertly handled it all. Except murder. Like Gabe said, this was a first.

"I knew she'd been seeing this Burnside kid," he said. "I didn't like it and I told her so. I also knew she'd run around with Justin Piebald. He's a nice young man, but . . ." He left the rest unsaid, letting me fill in the rest. Justin was okay, but his dad was another story. "But this Calvin Jones. Who in the world is he? I know absolutely nothing about him except what Katsy told me five minutes ago. And the Burnside kid threatening her? How could my daughter keep something like that from me?"

Before I could answer, there was another ruckus over at the door.

"Let me in now!" Jazz demanded.

She pushed past the young security guard who'd tried to keep Katsy out and who now wore an expression that seemed to say—maybe working at McDonald's wasn't so bad. Hud went over and assured him it was okay to let her through.

"Where's Cal? Someone told me that Cal was hurt." Her voice rose into a hysterical soprano.

Levi started toward her, moving quickly across the hall, trying to intercept her before she reached Calvin's body. But he wasn't fast enough. He and I came up behind her seconds after she pushed her way through the forensic team to where they were now carefully untangling Calvin's body from the bloodstained quilt.

Her scream echoed through the building's high ceiling. She turned to Levi, her face glossy with tears.

"Daddy," she cried, collapsing into his arms.

CHAPTER 7

$\mathcal{A}$FTER LEVI CALMED JAZZ DOWN, HE BROUGHT HER over to the bench where Aunt Garnet sat. My aunt spoke softly to the young girl, rubbing her back with small circles in the way you might calm a toddler. She seemed to be able to soothe Jazz when no one else could.

Hud came over to where we stood. "Levi, I'm sorry, but this building will be off limits until tomorrow. Maybe longer."

Levi nodded, his expression resigned. "We'll do whatever we can to help your investigation." He kept giving his daughter worried glances.

"Can we look at the quilt?" Maggie asked Hud.

He nodded. "Just don't get too close or touch anything."

The forensic team had spread the quilt across the hood of the truck shell. The sisters' heads touched as they bent over surveying the damage, their hands clasped behind their backs.

"Would you like me to take Jazz home?" I asked Levi.

He shook his head. "Thanks, but Katsy said she'd take her out to their ranch. Better chance of avoiding the media." He ran a hand over his perspiring face. "This is going to be a nightmare."

Gabe placed his hand on Levi's shoulder. "You'll get through this. No reasonable person can blame you."

Levi's face remained sober. "Reason never has anything to do with what the media pounces on. Controversy is what sells papers."

Gabe nodded without answering. He knew Levi was right because he'd experienced it. Anytime something happened with the San Celina Police Department that was the least bit controversial, there was always someone who questioned whether Gabe actually "earned" the right to be chief through his abilities or whether he was an "affirmative action" appointee.

"Let me know if I can help," Gabe said.

A young uniformed sheriff's deputy cleared his throat behind Levi. "Uh, Mr. Clark? Detective Hudson would like to speak to you."

Levi glanced over at Jazz.

"Don't worry," I said. "Aunt Garnet and I will stay with her until Katsy or Maggie takes her out to the ranch."

"Thank you," he said.

He bent over, whispered a few words in his daughter's ear, then kissed her on the head.

"Guess I'll go on home," Gabe said to me. "Are you going to be all right?"

I stood up on my toes and kissed his cheek. "I'm fine. I thought I'd take Aunt Garnet to Liddie's for dinner. Want to join us?"

"If you don't mind . . ." His expression was apologetic.

"Go home, Friday, and put your feet up. Don't forget to feed Scout."

"I'll keep the home fires burning. Change that to I'll keep the air-conditioning on."

I joined Aunt Garnet and Jazz, whose quiet crying had turned into an occasional shuddering hiccup. Her cheeks were stained with dots of mascara; her eyelids pink and swollen.

I sat down next to her. "Your dad told you he wanted you to go out to the ranch with Katsy and Maggie, right?"

She threw up a hand in frustration. "I don't need to be protected! He's just afraid I'll fall apart and the newspapers will see it."

"Sweetie, I think he's just trying to keep you safe. I know about overprotective daddies. They can't help themselves. He's under a lot of pressure right now so why don't you humor him and stay under the radar tonight? This'll all look a little less daunting tomorrow."

"She's right," Maggie said, walking up to catch the last of my sentence. "We'll reconsider everything tomorrow, okay?"

Realizing she was outnumbered, Jazz nodded mutely and gave a loud, wet sniff.

"You keep it," Aunt Garnet told Jazz when she tried to return her hankie. "I have a hundred of them. Apparently people think old ladies do a lot of nose blowing."

After saying good-bye, Aunt Garnet and I walked over to where Hud watched the forensic team bag evidence. She peered over the shoulder of one gloved technician. "Careful now, young lady. Don't want to contaminate the evidence."

The frizzy-haired woman who looked to be about my age gave her a bewildered look. "Are you with one of the other departments?"

"Independent investigator," Aunt Garnet said curtly. "Carry on."

Hud slipped a hand up to his mouth, hiding his smile.

"Can we leave?" I asked him, feeling my face turn warm. "Aunt Garnet needs some supper." And, apparently, a reality check.

"Sure," he said, winking. "I'll call you if I need to ask

you anything tonight. Otherwise, just come over to the office first thing tomorrow morning. I'll take an official statement."

"No problem," I said.

"We'll be there," Aunt Garnet said, settling her leather purse over her arm.

There'd be no "we" about it, but I wasn't about to rain on her parade right now.

Aunt Garnet and I slipped out a back door to avoid the journalists already hanging around the front entrance. A couple of security guys were sneaking a smoke in the small, secluded patio. When they saw us, they dropped their cigarettes and stubbed them out with their steel-toed black boots.

"Lung cancer is very painful," Aunt Garnet said, breezing past them.

"Bite me, old lady," one guy said in a low voice.

"I'd rather eat dirt," my aunt replied primly over her shoulder.

He'd obviously miscalculated her hearing capabilities. And her chutzpah.

Her quick retort caused me to giggle.

"Cancer isn't a bit funny," Aunt Garnet said. "Those foolish young men should heed my words."

"No, ma'am. Yes, ma'am." Then I immediately sobered. Was she trying to subtly tell me something? "Aunt Garnet, are you all right?"

She glared at me. "Whatever do you mean? Of course I'm all right."

She pulled her purse close to her body and marched away. I double-stepped to catch up with her.

"Follow me," I said. "I know the shortcuts." Utilizing the secret paths I'd learned as a child, Aunt Garnet and I made it through the fairgrounds without any reporters seeing us. Though I was beginning to wonder if giving an interview that would show up on the front page of the *Tri-*

bune might actually be what Aunt Garnet was hoping for. This new Aunt Garnet was kind of kicky, but also nerve-racking because she was so unpredictable. I was beginning to appreciate Dove's suspicions about her sister. There was definitely something going on with her, though I doubted that it had anything to do with stealing Dove's much envied corn bread recipe. Aunt Garnet's sharp comments about cancer had unnerved me.

"Tell me all about the crime scene," Nadine said, once we sat down in the spongy red leatherette booth at Liddie's Café. (Open Twenty-Five Hours a Day! its sign proclaimed.) Her brown eyes were magnified behind the bright pink cat's-eye glasses perched on her bony nose. I wasn't surprised she had already heard about the murder. Nadine had been pouring coffee, serving pie and keeping tabs on folks in San Celina County since long before I was born.

"Give me a break, Nadine," I said, perusing the big plastic menu I knew by heart. "You already know every detail of what happened."

"I know some of 'em," she said, taking a pencil out of her pinkish teased hair. "But there's nothing like an eyewitness." She was counting on us giving her some tidbit that would give her street cred with her next fifty customers.

"It was quite something, Nadine," Aunt Garnet said, sipping her iced tea. Since Aunt Garnet had visited San Celina at least once a year for the last thirty years, she and Nadine were old friends. "I think they needed more forensic investigators. They should have fingerprinted everyone present, but they let us go without taking prints. A bit incompetent, if you ask me. And not nearly enough photographs were being taken of the crime scene. Their cameras seemed a bit outdated. One would think they'd have more advanced technology seeing as this is the West Coast. They ought to look into that newfangled digital photography."

"Tragic," Nadine said, shaking her head. "Who's running the show?"

"Benni's young man, Detective Hudson."

"He's not *my young man*," I said.

"He's all right," Nadine said. "Kind of a smart-mouth but sharp as a new razor. Usually works cold cases."

"Well," Aunt Garnet said, "let's hope this doesn't become one due to his incompetence. There was much at that investigation scene needing improvement. Maybe I should write the sheriff a note."

I looked over the top of my menu. "In case anyone's interested, I'll have a cheeseburger and strawberry malt."

"You know our sheriff's a woman, don't you?" Nadine said to Aunt Garnet. "Women always take constructive criticism better than men. What'll you have, Garnet?"

While Nadine reeled off the night's specials, I excused myself to call Dove. "If she hears about this from the Sissy Brownmiller grapevine, there'll be a second murder—mine."

Outside to the parking lot, I tried the ranch's land line first.

"You just caught me," Dove said. "I'm on my way back to the fair. What's my sister been up to?" Obviously no one had told her about the murder yet. I said a silent thank-you.

"We've been pretty busy. Right now we're at Liddie's having supper. There's some news you need to hear so Sissy Brownmiller can't hold it over your head."

"Spill the beans."

I quickly told her about the last few hours, leaving out the part about how Aunt Garnet seemed to thrive in the atmosphere of the murder investigation.

"Poor Levi," Dove said. "They're going to really go after him for this."

"I know. I wish there was something we could do."

"Stand by him is what we can do. Shout down anyone who tries to besmirch his good name."

"The fact that Jazz was seeing Cal is going to make things complicated."

I heard Dove sigh over the phone. "I'd only met that young man a few times. He did some work for your daddy, but he seemed like a nice boy. Very polite. Somewhere in his life someone taught him manners."

"I wonder what's going to happen to his . . . him . . . after the autopsy."

"Ask your friend Hud. By the way, he practically got on his knees begging me to take in that rooster of Maisie's. I'm charging him by the day."

"He can afford it."

"I'm donating the money to the animal shelter."

"To answer your question, your sister seems to be enjoying herself. She . . ." I could see Aunt Garnet bobbing her head as Nadine talked. Nadine pointed her pencil at Aunt Garnet; they both laughed.

"She what?" Dove demanded.

"She had fun at the fair, well, until the murder, of course. And I haven't found out anything yet about why she's here. She seems . . . almost . . . happy." I said the word with a bit of surprise.

"I know! I know!" Dove shouted. "That's what I mean. She's *never* been happy in all the years she's been alive. There's something up, I tell you. Keep on the job." She hung up before I could answer.

After supper, since it was still early, I asked Aunt Garnet if she'd like to take a tour of the folk art museum.

"You know I'd love that," she said, "but I'm getting a little tired. Maybe another day?"

"Sure, we have plenty of time. Let me take you back to the ranch."

At the ranch, Aunt Garnet said good night and went into the guest room. Before leaving, I poked around the walk-in pantry to see what goodies I could steal to take home to my patient husband. I found a cherry pie with one piece missing, a large plastic container of oatmeal-raisin cookies and under a clear glass domed cake plate a magazine-perfect black walnut cake with maple icing. It hadn't been cut into yet and I was contemplating whether I should take the chance. Dove might have made it for something special.

"Caught you." A deep voice startled my contemplation of the cake.

It was my stepgrandpa, Isaac Lyons. Because of his broad face and wide-set, calm eyes, his surname always amazed me with its appropriateness. He had long white hair, pulled back in a thinner version of my gramma's braid, a deeply tanned face from his years taking photographs all over the world, a gold stud earring in one ear. But it was that famous voice, like the roll of a kettle drum that drew people to him like children to an ice cream truck jingle. A man-of-the-world who had never stayed in one place for longer than a few months, he changed after marrying my gramma Dove. His home became the Ramsey Ranch, San Celina and most of all, Dove. To the world, he was the celebrity photographer who'd taken portraits of five presidents and has his work hanging in hundreds of prestigious galleries and museums. To us, he was simply Isaac, the man who loved Dove.

"Hey, Pops," I said. "Do you have the 411 on this cake?"

He grabbed the cherry pie and sat it on the breakfast counter. "I've been eyeing that cake for the last four hours. I desperately want a piece. But, no, I have no idea what it's for. We could call her." His expression was hopeful.

"It's probably for one of her meetings. Best we stick to the cookies and pie." I pulled out a quart-sized plastic bag and stole six cookies. "How are things going so far with the sisters? Dove seems more agitated than usual."

He leaned forward, resting his forearms on the counter's red and yellow calico patterned oilcloth cover. "It's like watching two jungle cats circle and eyeball each other." Spiderweb lines radiated from his eyes. "The tension is great. I'm tempted to do a pictorial. At any rate, while

Garnet's here, I'm determined to take that sister portrait whether they like it or not."

"You may have to slip some Valium in their morning coffee." I leaned over the counter toward him, keeping my voice low. "What do *you* think is the reason Aunt Garnet is visiting?"

"I have no idea and I don't have to tell you, it's driving your gramma nuts. She tried calling WW this morning, but old William Wiley is living up to his middle name. He's a cunning old coot, not about to be the Greek messenger. All he'd say is Garnet has something personal to talk over with Dove, but he wouldn't give a hint what it was."

"Personal? That doesn't sound good."

Isaac scratched his weathered cheek and winked at me. "I think the girls just like to keep things interesting."

I rested my chin on a palm. "With what is going on at the fair, things are interesting enough, thank you kindly."

His face grew serious. "I heard about the young man being killed. Any suspects yet?"

"If there are, Hud hasn't informed me. It's bound to get thorny. The murder happened on Levi Clark's watch and his daughter was dating the victim."

"Sounds complex. Who do *you* think might have done it?"

"There're actually a couple of suspects." I hesitated, not sure I should voice my suspicions despite the fact it was only me and Isaac in the room.

"You can't stop there," Isaac said.

"Okay, but this is only between us. First is Jazz's ex-boyfriend, Dodge Burnside. He of the volatile temper." I told Isaac about Dodge's behavior in the parking lot. "Though as Jazz so graphically stated, they never actually hooked up, he apparently considered them a couple. Then there's Milt Piebald . . ." I told Isaac what I overheard Milt say. "Maybe he did it to discredit Levi."

The wrinkles radiating from Isaac's eyes deepened. "Could be."

I picked at a small hole in the red table cover. "I'm going to phone Hud later tonight to see if I can pry any information out of him, but I'm guessing he'll keep the investigation pretty close to his vest."

Isaac mulled over my words. I wondered what he was remembering that caused him to look so pensive. He'd marched to Selma with Martin Luther King Jr. A photo he'd taken of Dr. King touching the blond head of a little boy whose father, a car mechanic from Detroit, had taken vacation time to march with Dr. King, made the pages of *Life* magazine. The original print, hand developed by Isaac himself, hung in the Smithsonian.

"Are you taking any photographs of this year's fair?"

"Already started," he said. "I'm thinking about doing another book on fairs. I may attempt talking your gramma into taking a road trip, visit some of our country's state and county fairs."

"That's a great idea. Your first county fair book is one of my favorites. Dove does need to get out of town . . . and I mean that in the nicest possible way."

He chuckled. "I agree, but there's no way she'll leave while Garnet is visiting."

"Maybe her visit will be a quick one." I walked around the counter and slipped my arms around his waist, giving him a warm hug. "I imagine I'll see you at the fair . . . if not sooner."

Before going home, I dropped by the folk art museum. Since I started working there almost five years ago checking on the museum daily had become second nature. The day didn't feel right if I didn't go in at least once and make my rounds of the premises, like a Great Pyrenees dog checking its flock. Saturday was usually our busiest day, both with artists working in the studios and patrons visiting our exhibits. Since the quilt and doll exhibits opened three weeks ago, they'd received rave reviews and visits from many local and out-of-state quilters, folk art lovers, doll lovers and African American history buffs. Though the museum had been closed since six o'clock, and it was now almost eight, a few docents were still working at the boutique and artists were still back in the studios. Every month a different co-op member had responsibility for locking up.

Behind the counter, Kay Pulcini, one of our long-time docents, was dusting the shelves.

"Hey," I called. "Need some help?"

"I'm almost done," she replied, running a hand through her short, silvery bob. She held up a drink coaster made in the geometric style of the Gee's Bend quilts. "These are flying off the shelves faster than the Ebony Sisters can make them."

"That's great!" We planned for the exhibits to continue until the end of September when the quilt exhibit would move on to the Rocky Mountain quilt museum in Golden, Colorado, and the dolls would return to their owner in Oakland.

In my office, I called Hud on his cell. I still hadn't told him about Milt's remarks. The sooner I dumped the information into Hud's lap, the sooner I could check it off my mental list.

"What's shakin', Inspector Clouseau?" I said.

"Just sitting here in my office at the fair contemplating the mysteries of the universe. Think I almost have them figured out. What's up with you?"

"Any suspects for Calvin Jones's murder yet?"

"A few."

I waited, hoping he'd elaborate. No such luck. "I had to try."

"Would have been disappointed if you didn't, my nosy little beignet. Anything else?"

"Actually, there is. So much was going on at the crime scene that I didn't want to bother you, but there's a conversation I overheard last night that I think might have some significance." I repeated Milt Piebald's words. "I'm guessing he was talking about Levi."

"And you might be guessing right. What a jackass. Have any idea who he was talking to?"

"Not a clue."

"I appreciate you telling me this and it certainly makes him a *bourriquet,* but I'm not sure it makes him a suspect."

"A what?"

"A stupid man."

"He could be trying to sabotage Levi's job."

"Believable, though killing someone to do so is—hate to use a bad pun—overkill."

I groaned. "That is bad. I know you're probably right. It was just a thought."

"Maybe a wish?"

"The thought of Milt doing jail time does bring a smile to my face."

His heavy sigh filled the phone's earpiece. "Justice is a long and winding road. And there are lots of potholes that never get filled."

"On that truly dried-up old metaphor I will say good night."

"*Bon soir, catin.*"

After giving my inbox a sincere promise that I'd revisit it on Monday, I headed for home. While Gabe took Scout for his evening walk, I made one last call to Maggie. "How's Jazz?"

"She's finally sleeping, poor girl. I didn't think she'd ever stop crying. This boy must have really meant something to her."

"No sign of any reporters sneaking through the woods?"

"Not so far. With Bess and Harry on the job, we'd know in two seconds." Bess and Harry were two rescue German shepherds adopted by Maggie and Katsy. The dogs, no doubt sensing their great fortune at being adopted into the Morrison clan, had instantly bonded with the women and with the ranch. No one would sneak past their vigilant guard.

"Jazz will need all the rest she can get," I said. "Eventually she'll have to go back out in public and face people's questions."

"That's what Katsy and I figure. I know Levi can't come all the way out here during the fair, but I wish he could sneak out for a break. The poor man is probably sleeping only two or three hours a night and Katsy swears that dang walkie-talkie is surgically attached to his hand."

"I tried squeezing some information out of Hud about who they suspect, but he's keeping things pretty much to himself."

"Yeah, I know."

"I'll see you tomorrow. Let me know if I can do anything."

"We're such a boring old married couple," I said to Gabe a little while later when fluffing our bed pillows. He was brushing his teeth. "Going to bed early on a Saturday night." It was ten thirty and though cooler than in North County, it was still too warm for me. I was thankful for the air-conditioning system we'd installed last year.

"Want to go back to the fair?" Gabe called from the bathroom. "It's open until midnight."

"No, but I feel like I *should* want to go."

He walked back into our bedroom. "Why?"

"When I was a kid, we would go every day the fair was open. We almost always stayed until it closed. And I loved it." I sat down on the bed, running my bare toes across Scout's exposed stomach. He was sprawled across the oak floor trying to soak in every inch of coolness. I could relate. I lifted up my hair, holding it on top of my head.

"There're other entertaining things to do on a Saturday night," he said, smiling at me.

I wrinkled my nose. "Oh, please, it's too hot for that."

He walked over to our new thermostat and turned it down.

I laughed and let my hair drop. "Okay, but no matter what the environmentalists say, we're not doing one single thing until it is at least sixty-five degrees in here."

"I won't tell if you won't," Gabe said, slipping off his boxer shorts.

CHAPTER 8

"LOCAL MAN KILLED AT THE FAIR" READ THE SUNDAY *Tribune* headline. Beneath it was a color photo of Jazz, her face buried in her father's shoulder. They were surrounded by sheriff's deputies and fair security people.

In the caption under the photo the reporter wrote, "Levi Clark, controversial new manager of the San Celina Mid-State Fair, comforts daughter when she hears of her fiancé's alleged homicide. Sheriff's department homicide detectives are investigating."

"Controversial?" I said, looking across the kitchen table at Gabe. "Is that another word for black? And since when was Cal her fiancé?"

Gabe reached for the coffeepot. "Since when has that birdcage liner ever told the truth?" The *Tribune* had often misreported, exaggerated and even ridiculed Gabe in the years he'd been San Celina's police chief, so there was no love lost between my husband and our local newspaper.

I scanned the article. It didn't say much because there

really wasn't much to report yet. Calvin Jones had been killed by blunt force trauma, and the case was under investigation. According to the paper, Cal didn't have much history in San Celina—in foster care in the Central Valley until he aged out of the system, lived alone in a rented room in Atascadero. He worked odd jobs around the county, at the Mobil station part time for the last year. All of that I knew from Katsy and Maggie. The paper said the police were searching for next of kin and that any help from the public would be welcome.

I pushed the paper aside and stared down into the steel-cut oatmeal Gabe cooked for us. Tiny bits of brown sugar floated atop the steaming, nutty-scented cereal, but the sparse facts about Cal's short life dulled my appetite.

"It's always sad when a kid is murdered," I said, resting my chin on my hand. "But when it's someone like Calvin Jones, who has no family, no one who will really miss him. It makes me wonder if . . ."

Gabe looked up from the sports page. The wire-rimmed glasses perched on his nose made him look like a sexy professor. "If what?"

"If maybe I've lived too sheltered a life. That I don't spend enough time getting to know and care about people who are alone. People like Cal."

"You can't befriend the whole world," he said practically, looking back down at the paper.

"I know." I stared at the photo of Jazz and Levi. Levi's face was stoic, his eyes unreadable. What *had* he thought about Cal? What did he think about the statement that Cal was his daughter's fiancé? "At least Cal had Jazz." I stood up and carried my uneaten cereal to the sink. "What's on your agenda today?"

"Some paperwork I brought home. Thought I'd wash the Corvette. Maybe take Scout for a run before it gets too hot."

I stooped down and scratched behind Scout's velvety ears. "Sounds like a nice day. Scout could use some fresh air and exercise."

"What're you going to do?"

I straightened up, stretched out my arms. "Go by Blind Harry's and visit Elvia. Then back to the fair. I promised Mac I'd attend Cowboy Church this afternoon."

MacKenzie "Mac" Reid was an old friend and the minister of the church my family belonged to—San Celina First Baptist. A local boy whose late grandmother had been one of San Celina County's ranching icons, he had special sermons and music that he provided for rodeos and fairs.

I started upstairs to get dressed, but stopped when I reached the kitchen threshold. "Friday?"

"Hmm?" He didn't look up from the paper. In the bright August morning sunlight his hair shined black and glossy as crow feathers.

"Do you think that anyone from around here would actually kill Cal because he was white and Jazz is biracial?"

Gabe's head slowly came up. "Are you serious? Reread your history books."

I felt my face turn red. "Thanks for making me feel like a total dolt."

"You are not a dolt. Just a little too idealistic about your community here on the Central Coast."

"Is it a bad thing to hope it wasn't a race issue that brought about his murder?"

"Not bad, just not realistic. I'd bet a thousand bucks that her race had something to do with it."

"Jazz told me she gets annoyed when people only see one side of her—her father's side—and completely ignore her mother's heritage. You, of all people, should understand that."

He folded the paper in half and set it next to his bowl. "And I think she's also being idealistic. When people first glance at me, I'm Mexican. In that important first five seconds when human beings classify one another, I'm a brown man. There's no getting around that. No one cares my mother was white. Trust me, even after they find out I'm from two cultures no one has yet to ask me for a DNA sample to determine which race dominates. My skin informs them which dominates, at least in their minds. The same goes for Jazz. The sooner she gets used to that, the happier she'll be."

This conversation was rapidly becoming more political than I meant it to. "I understand . . ."

He interrupted, looking straight into my eyes. "Actually, you don't."

"Let me finish. I was going to say I understand that race makes things more complicated. So do you think the picture the newspaper took exacerbates the problem? Look how Levi and Jazz are surrounded by whites . . ."

He stared at me without answering. His expression appeared impatient.

Were we arguing? I had no idea how our conversation took this awkward turn.

"It is complicated," he finally said. "But this time, despite my misgivings about this paper's integrity, I think the photo is simply the one that the photographer was able to snap. What are our plans for dinner?"

Like that, the conversation was dismissed. Somehow I felt like we hadn't resolved whatever it was that had become awkward between us, the divide that race brought into even our relationship. "I don't know yet. Let me see how things are going at the fair and I'll call you."

He looked back down at the newspaper. Uncomfortable moment over. For him, anyway.

An hour later I was sitting in my best friend's office on the second floor above Blind Harry's bookstore. "Did you see the newspaper's photo of Jazz and Levi? What do you think?"

"I think using the word *controversial* was in extremely bad taste. But, as Emory pointed out, good taste doesn't sell papers."

"Do you think they're subtly trying to make it a racial issue?"

"What's so subtle about it?"

"Gabe and I sort of argued about it this morning."

Elvia fiddled with some papers on her desk. "How?"

"Maybe it was my fault. I wondered if it were believable about whether Cal might have been killed because he was dating Jazz."

She arched an eyebrow. "I'm sure that went over well."

I nibbled at a thumbnail. "Yeah, it was stupid, I guess. But this isn't Mississippi in the 1960s."

"Still, we have our problems here."

"How come you and I never talk about race?"

"Because we've known each other since second grade," she said, leaning her head back in her high-backed gray leather chair. "Time trumps race. Bless Emory for taking Sophia for a walk. It feels so luxurious to not have to worry about her for a few hours. Am I a horrible *mama* for thinking that?" She closed her eyes and sighed.

"Call me crazy, but Cal was dating a girl who is half black, whose father is the county's first black general manager of our county fair. His body was wrapped in a replica of a famous African American quilt. In my opinion someone is deliberately making this a racial issue. Or at least look like one."

"It certainly does have those undertones. But you know how this town works. People will try to ignore that possibility because no one wants to cause any tension. We're a college town. We like to pretend we're open-minded."

"What a world little Sophie Lou is inheriting," I said, shaking my head.

She opened her eyes and sat forward. "Her name is *So-*

phia! Please, go eat a fried Twinkie. This emotional stuff is getting tiresome."

"Today is my healthy day. Only fried cheese and pickles."

At the fair, I stopped by the museum's booth before heading over to the arena. It was twelve thirty and there was still an hour until Cowboy Church.

At the Bears Quilt Shop booth next to the museum's, all hands were on deck—Vivs, Russ, William and the store's namesake, Bear himself. Right in the front of their booth was a large pickle jar filled with bills and coins. The colorful sign taped to the front read Harriet Powers's Quilt Fund—Help the Ebony Sisters Make a New Quilt.

"You guys are the best," I said, putting ten bucks in the jar.

"It's not much," William said. "But we want to help."

"We heard the quilt was completely ruined," Bear said. "What is wrong with this old world of ours? What a shame."

"Pretty much. Not to mention it'll be in the evidence locker, like, forever."

"That's why we figured we'd start this fund. We'd gladly donate the fabric, batting and backing," said William, "but we wanted to make a statement of quilters' solidarity."

"I'm sure the Sisters will appreciate it."

The museum's booth was crowded and I was surprised to see only Maggie holding down the fort. Though she'd occasionally pitched in at different co-op events, she wasn't actually a member of the co-op so had no obligation to work the booth.

"What're you doing here alone?" I joined her behind the cash register.

"Jazz didn't want to come in today and I can't blame her. There would probably be reporters all over her trying to get a statement. I said I'd take her shift."

"Not up to me, but I'm sure it's fine. I don't blame Jazz for not wanting to be within twenty miles of this fair. How's she doing?"

Maggie rearranged some fabric book covers. "Not good. You know, I think she might have had stronger feelings for this boy than we realized. She said the fiancé part was bogus, but that's all she would tell us last night."

I contemplated their relationship. "People her age are very connected to their friends."

Maggie nodded, then glanced over at a group of girls close to Jazz's age. They were perusing some sixties-style bead necklaces. "Katsy went into town last night to see how Levi was doing. She says he looks exhausted."

"How long is Jazz going to stay out at the ranch?"

"I hope until they know who's behind Cal's death."

There was an awkward few seconds when neither of us spoke.

I fiddled with the stack of fabric book covers, fanning them out in a colorful rainbow. "Anything I can do?"

"Not really. It's that old waiting game."

Maggie had spent a large part of her working career around law enforcement and she knew one of the little secrets that they didn't always like the public to know . . . that a good many crimes were solved just by some person opening their big mouth and either bragging about what they did or, in a vulnerable moment, confessing it to someone who then ratted them out. Most criminals were either stupid or vain, or both.

"Where are you off to?" Maggie asked.

"Cowboy Church. I promised Mac."

"Since you're headed in that direction, do you have time to drop these chocolate chip cookies off at Levi's office?" She reached under the table and pulled out a plastic container bulging with cookies. "When Katsy's upset, she can't sleep. So she bakes."

"I can relate." I took the container.

She patted her trim stomach. "If she keeps it up for the next three months, then we all might be in trouble."

"Let's hope Cal's murder gets solved faster than that."

Doubt seemed to radiate from her dark eyes.

Inside the administration office a young gum-smacking receptionist with shiny burgundy braids and turquoise eyes dialed Levi's extension. After a few murmured words into the receiver she informed me I could go on back. Except for her, an older woman in a flowered polyester blouse working on a computer and a sleepy-looking basset hound, the office area was empty.

"Quite the impressive line of defense you have up front," I said to Levi when I walked through his open office door.

"Why would I need protection?" he asked sharply. "I can take care of myself. And my daughter. I don't need anyone's help to protect my family."

I froze. "Uh, of course you don't . . . I mean . . ." I looked down at the container in my hands. "I come bearing gifts. Cookies. Katsy baked them last night. When she couldn't sleep." I clamped my mouth shut, embarrassed by my inane rambling. I placed the cookies on the corner of his messy desk.

He rose, ran a hand down his face, then gestured at me to take a seat. "I apologize for snapping, Benni. My nerves are on edge. Really, I'm sorry."

I almost said I understand, then caught myself.

"Forget it," I said instead, sitting down in a visitor's chair. "I can't even imagine what you are going through right now. Have you heard anything new about the . . ." I faltered, not wanting to make him feel worse. "About the case?"

He pulled nervously on his left earlobe. "Detective Hudson came by this morning. He says they have some ideas but nothing concrete so he wasn't at liberty to reveal anything."

"That sounds like Hud. Did he ask you any questions

about particular people? Sometimes you can figure out what the cops are thinking by the questions they ask."

He gave me a small smile. "I guess you'd know about that. He just asked me how long Jazz and Cal had been seeing each other. Who else had she been seeing. Had there been any threats. Was there anyone angry at me." He grimaced at the last sentence. "When I was offered this job, it made a lot of folks angry."

I nodded, remembering Milt's conversation after the concert.

"But," he continued, "I told him that I didn't know of any *particular* person who was upset with me. Frankly, I think this young man just got himself involved with some bad people, probably drug-related, and they decided to send a graphic message to anyone else who would mess with them." His lips straightened. "I told as much to the mayor and the three city council members who called me."

Again, I didn't answer, not wanting to dispute something he'd obviously thought about all night. The glaring fact remained—the body had been wrapped in the Harriet Powers quilt. That took thought and planning on someone's part because the quilt had been displayed in a completely different building.

Levi came around the desk. "I'll admit I was expecting *some* trouble because of my appointment to this job. The letters didn't surprise me. I thought maybe we'd have to deal with some graffiti. Kid stuff. But nothing like this." He sighed and stuck his hands deep into the pockets of his dark slacks. He wore a pale blue cowboy shirt today, open at the collar. "I do feel for this young man. Apparently he didn't have an easy time of it. Jazz said he was trying to turn his life around."

Again I felt helpless to do anything but fervently wish that when we did find out who killed Cal that it had nothing to do with race. But I suspected I might as well have been wishing the moon was made of string cheese.

The corners of his eyes sagged. "It will be lonely at home without my baby girl, but Jazz is safer out at the ranch for the time being."

I stood up, hitching my backpack over my shoulder. "We're all going to do everything we can to protect Jazz. And I can promise you one thing, if anyone can solve this fast, it'll be Hud." I smiled at him. "The only person who could do it faster is Gabe, but it's not his jurisdiction."

Levi gave a tired smile back. "Thanks, Benni. Tell Gabe to come on by and we can check out the fair's new wine garden. I'll treat you both to some raspberry wine ice cream."

"I'll tell him. Personally, I'll stick with deep-fried Snickers."

A small chuckle actually came from somewhere deep in his chest; for a moment, the worry lines around his eyes softened. "You don't know what you're missing."

"I'll take my chances. Watch your back."

Next on my mental list was to find Hud and see if he'd clue me in on Cal's case. I knew as well as any experienced armchair detective that most homicides were solved within the first forty-eight hours. After that, much of the evidence went cold. New homicide cases took precedence and the unsolved ones slowly worked their way down the list of importance. There was a good chance Calvin Jones would become just another name on Hud's cold case list.

The door of the sheriff's command post office was closed and locked. I'd have to try Hud's cell phone. I wanted more privacy than the administration offices provided so I left the air-conditioned building. A wave of heat rolled over me and instantly, beads of sweat dampened my upper lip. I could almost feel my naturally curly hair start to frizz. I pulled it into a scrunchie, making a high bun to get it off my neck. Then I found a quiet corner under a shady tree to phone Hud. His voice mail picked up after the fourth ring.

I leaned my head back against the tree trunk thinking about Cal's murder. I spent weeks and months of my childhood visiting Arkansas where the issue of skin color could not be ignored. A good deal of California was multiethnic— but our little county, not so much. The thing that kept bugging me was the thought that if an individual or group killed Cal because he was dating Jazz, wouldn't they have at least made sure everyone *got* that point? Wouldn't they want to claim the murder?

I dialed Hud again. This time he answered.

"Where are you?" I asked. "I need to talk."

"A very good morning to you, too. It *is* a wonderful day at the fair, isn't it? What do you have planned? Have you ridden the Ferris wheel yet? Maisie says the new Scrambler ride is crazy fun. And the Great Kansas Pig Races, don't want to miss those perky little fellows. Or maybe I should say porky." He laughed at his own joke.

"Hud, this is serious. I just talked to Levi. He's really upset. You need to solve this murder fast."

There was a moment of silence. "Doin' the very best I can."

"Can we meet somewhere to talk?"

His sigh was audible. "Nothin' to talk about, but I'm always happy to see my second-favorite girl in the whole world. Meet me at Cutie's Cupcakes. I've got a hankering for a red velvet." He hung up.

I reached the cupcake stand before he did so I bought two red velvet cupcakes and two lemonades figuring to bribe my way into finding out what was going on in the investigation. I knew that it really wouldn't make a difference, that he'd either clue me in or not. Still, you never knew. Wouldn't be the first time refined sugar was used as an inducement.

The spot I found on a picnic bench beneath a scraggly olive tree felt only slightly cooler. A few minutes later Hud slipped into the bench opposite me.

"Here," I said, pushing the melting cupcake and icy lemonade in front of him. "If you'd been one minute longer, that cupcake would have been history."

"I do not understand how you still fit in your jeans, ranch girl."

"What's going on with Cal's homicide?"

He slowly peeled the paper off the cupcake and took a generous bite. "Almost as good as my *grand-mère*'s."

"What about Dodge? Did he have an alibi? What about Milt? Did you find out who he made that snarky remark to? Maybe Dodge and Milt are in it together."

He slowly ate his cupcake without answering. He licked some stray icing off his thumb. "You realize what cupcakes are, don't you? Just a highly efficient icing delivery system."

"Hud, quit stalling."

"One, we're looking into it. Two, yes. Three, we're looking into it. Four, no. Five, I seriously doubt it, but that sure would make a stupendous episode for a TV cop show."

I jiggled the ice in my plastic cup. "What *have* you found out?"

He readjusted his straw cowboy hat, running the back of his hand across the sweaty red dent it made in his forehead. "You know I can't tell you the details. That is what we call in the crime business 'privileged information.' It's the *Rules*. Capital *R*."

"Like the rules have ever meant anything to you. I'm gonna smack you upside the head if you don't tell me something."

He grinned and leaned closer. "I love it when you get mean. Okay, here's this. The medical examiner concluded that Mr. Calvin Jones likely died between midnight and six a.m. Our boy Dodge has a rock solid alibi from nine p.m. until two a.m. because he was over at the Cattle Chute Tavern making a general nuisance of himself in front of about twenty or so regulars."

"That dive in Atascadero. I've heard of it. But the bar closed at two a.m., right?"

"Right, and a buddy dropped him off at his dad's place, about two miles from the bar. His dad, Lloyd, was home and woke up when Dodge's buddy knocked on the door. Mr. Burnside said his son passed out on the sofa and was there until he—the father, that is—left for a job the next morning at seven-thirty."

"Oh," I said, disappointed that Dodge Burnside had an alibi. It would have been so easy if it had been him. "Still, his dad didn't sit up all night, did he? I mean, couldn't Dodge have left after his dad went back to bed, killed Cal and then come back home?"

Hud shrugged. "Not likely. His friends said he was pretty wasted. And he would have had to take his dad's truck since Dodge's was still at the Cattle Chute. I imagine Lloyd Burnside would have heard his truck start and gone out to see where his drunk son was going. And I doubt that he would have let him drive if for no other reason but to keep said truck from being wrecked."

I didn't know Lloyd Burnside well. He was like many of my male acquaintances who were either ranchers or loosely connected to the ag community—polite, mostly quiet around women, more comfortable in the company of other men. Would he be the type to cover for his son if his son had done something illegal?

I slipped out of the wooden picnic bench. "I'm heading over to the arena to go to Cowboy Church. Wanna come?"

He crumpled his cupcake paper and tossed it into the rainbow-colored trash can. "Le Maître and I are doing okay without someone else interpreting for us."

"Le who?"

He gave me a half smile. "Roughly, the Boss."

"Can I assume you are not talking about Bruce Springsteen?"

"Go get regenerated, ranch girl. Let me get back to catching the bad guys."

"Good luck. I really do want justice for Cal."

He slipped an arm around my shoulders. "I can't promise that, but I can do my darndest to find out who killed him."

I arrived at the fair's smaller arena—the Wild West Stage—in the middle of the first song: "What a Friend We Have in Jesus." The lead singer from Rifle Shot accompanied the crowd on an electric guitar while a bored-looking young man in a black cowboy hat kept time on a set of sparkly red drums. There was about a hundred or so people in the audience, not a bad turnout. Mac would be pleased if only two people showed up. Glancing over the crowd, I spotted Dove and Aunt Garnet in the sixth row from the stage.

"Hey, girls," I said, slipping in next to my aunt. "What's shakin'?"

Aunt Garnet put her finger to her lips and handed me her photocopied sheet printed with the words of the song. Like any child who'd spent her formative years in Sunday school and vacation Bible school, I knew the words by heart, but I wasn't about to argue with my aunt during church. I glanced at Dove, who rolled her blue eyes skyward.

After a few more traditional hymns and a bluesy solo about faith, fishes and loaves by the Rifle Shot musician, Mac took the stage. Even though he was a good distance away, his six foot four, ex-linebacker physique was still imposing. His full, reddish brown beard, olive green Western shirt and dirt-stained boots gave him an authenticity that even the young cowboys respected.

Without any hemming or hawing, he jumped right into his message. He'd preached enough of these Cowboy Church sermons to know that the fair and all its delicious glories were an irresistible siren song in the background.

Whatever point he had to make, he had to make fast. His Cowboy Church sermons were never longer than fifteen minutes.

"Only fourteen minutes and fifty-two seconds longer than a good bull ride," he liked to say.

His Scripture was 1 Corinthians 9:24–27—one that was appropriate for the fair where competition whether in cattle confirmation, corn bread, demolition derby or saddle broncs, was foremost in everyone's minds.

"Paul was telling the Corinthians," Mac said in his melodious baritone, "that in every race there is only one winner and that they should run the race in such a way so that they will be that winner. What he was saying is not that winning was the most important goal, but that doing your best is. Keep in mind that he was speaking on a spiritual level . . ."

I'd heard this sermon many times in my life so I let my mind drift off, thinking about Dodge Burnside's alibi. If it wasn't Dodge, was it maybe a friend of Dodge's? Did Dodge hate Cal enough to pay someone else to kill him so that Jazz would be free to be with him? That seemed pretty far-fetched, and I would have discounted it had I not experienced even crazier behavior in my life with people who wanted others dead. The truth was when it came to human beings, anything was possible. I made a note to myself to hunt down Sam and see what he thought since all these guys were his friends.

Before I knew it, people were standing up to sing the closing hymn. Afterward, while Aunt Garnet went to shake Mac's hand, Dove lingered so that she could speak to me privately.

"Have you found out anything?" she asked.

I hesitated, thinking she meant about Cal's murder.

Before I could answer, she said, "I've given up on WW. No matter what I try to bribe him with, he's keeping his trap shut."

Oh, Aunt Garnet. "She hasn't told me a thing." I left it at that. I was beginning to wonder if Aunt Garnet was running a con on Dove, just trying to mess with her mind. Frankly, that would have been a brilliant practical joke. But I wasn't about to suggest that to my gramma. She was worked up enough.

"She's not getting the recipe," Dove said, patting the front of her blue and white flowered snap button shirt.

I must have had an uncomprehending look on my face, because she gave a disgusted sound and reached into her shirt and pulled a three-by-five-inch recipe card from inside her bra.

"Dove!" I burst out laughing. "Seriously, I don't think—"

"It's stayin' right here until she leaves. She can nose her way through every cookbook I own. She'll never find it."

I was actually happy to see Aunt Garnet walking toward us with Mac in tow. Dove hastily tucked the corn bread recipe back into her very personal safe.

"Pastor Mac," Dove said. "Wonderful sermon. Something we all needed to hear. Especially the part about life not being a physical competition but a spiritual one."

"Amen to that," Aunt Garnet said.

I glanced from sister to sister, then to Mac's smiling face. "You know," I said. "I really need to . . . uh . . . be somewhere . . . I think I'm supposed to help with the . . . uh . . ." I realized I was getting ready to blatantly lie in front of a minister, but really, I couldn't deal with the sisters right now.

Mac grinned as he if knew what I was doing.

"I have go check on the museum booth," I concluded weakly.

"Garnet, you go on with her," Dove said, not looking at me. If Mac hadn't been standing between us, I would have pinched her. "I have some church business to discuss with Mac." She grabbed Mac's arm and pulled him away before Aunt Garnet and I could react.

"Well," Aunt Garnet said, fanning herself with one of KCOW's boot-shaped paper fans. "Looks like you're stuck with me again."

The slightly humiliated look on her face made me feel bad enough to say, "Oh, c'mon, Aunt Garnet. You know Dove. She just has so many things going on in her life. Let's buy something to drink. Then we can check out the quilts."

We were standing in line for lemonade when I caught a glimpse of my stepson's head in the crowd.

"Could you please buy me a medium with lots of ice?" I said to Aunt Garnet, handing her a five-dollar bill. "I'll be right back. I need to ask my stepson something. Sam, wait up!"

He turned, saw me pushing through the crowd and held up a hand. Justin Piebald stood next to him.

"Hey, *madrastra*," Sam said.

"I want to talk to you about something." I glanced at Justin, who picked up on my cue.

"Dude, I'll be over at the antique tractor display." He nodded at me. "Nice to see you again, Mrs. Ortiz."

"You too," I replied.

"What's up?" Sam said, after Justin strolled away.

"I just wanted to ask you about Cal Jones and Dodge Burnside."

Sam adjusted his red Boone's Good Eatin' Chicken ball cap. Emory was paying Sam and some of his school buddies with free meals in exchange for occasionally wearing the caps during the fair. "What about them? Have they found out who killed Cal?"

I shook my head. "Not that they're telling me. The detectives pretty much eliminated Dodge as a suspect. He was apparently passed out drunk at home during the time Cal was killed."

"Yeah, he said he got really ripped last night. He's kinda made a joke about it, how for once in his life getting smashed actually did him some good." Sam's mouth turned down at the corners, his dark eyes looked into mine. "I told him to shut up, that a guy's dead. A guy I liked. He called me a dickhead and we didn't talk about it again."

I shaded my eyes with my hand. "You were friends with both of them?"

"Yeah, but not at the same time."

"What do you mean?"

"It wasn't like we were all some big happy group. I surfed with Dodge and we'd hang out and stuff. Me and him and Justin and a few others. We all go to Cal Poly. Jazz hangs with us too."

"So, where does Calvin Jones fit in?"

"He doesn't. Not with that group, anyway. Cal and I met when he did some fence work for your dad. We had some laughs. We shot pool sometimes at Triggers." Triggers was a working-class bar by the San Celina bus station. "He sometimes talked about learning how to make saddles. There was this old guy he'd written who lived up near Cardinal, you know, on the way to Mammoth? A really good saddlemaker. The guy was maybe going to let Cal apprentice."

That piece of personal information about Cal made my eyes tear up. This young man had been making plans for his life. He was a person who had had plans, hopes, dreams. And someone took that away from him.

"Yeah, it sucks," Sam said. "And I know Dodge can be a jerk, but I don't think he'd kill anyone. Besides, Cal wasn't so perfect, Benni. He could be a real ass too." His face broke into a wide smile. "Hey, Mrs. Wilcox!"

"Hello, Sam, how are you?" Aunt Garnet's voice said

behind me. "Here's your lemonade, Benni. Shall I meet you over at the quilts?"

I took the cold, sweating cup. "No, I'll be just a minute." I looked back into Sam's face. "What do you mean that Cal was sometimes an ass?"

His eyes darted over to Aunt Garnet.

She waved her hand impatiently. "You can talk straight in front of me, Sam. I spotted the body first."

"Okay, the truth is, at one time Cal had some pretty skanky friends. He was trying to break off with them, clean up his act. He was into Jazz, wanted to impress her. But he said it was hard because when he was young and had no one, these dudes took him in and gave him, you know, a place to go, people he could hang around."

"What kind of skanky are we talking about?" I asked.

"You know, skins. Heil Hitler dudes."

"Lord, help us," Aunt Garnet said under her breath. I glanced at her to see if she was being sarcastic, but her face was truly sad. "It's a failing of God's people that we aren't there for young men like him, that he's forced to find refuge with people like that."

"Yeah," I said, surprised that she and I agreed on something. Especially about the church. "So Cal once hung around some creepy people. How does that let Dodge off the hook?"

"I'm just saying that Cal wasn't pure as snow. Dodge was a little pissed when Jazz started seeing Cal. Maybe he thought she was doing it just to make him jealous."

"Jazz doesn't seem to me to be the type of girl who plays games like that."

"She's not. I think Dodge was more into her than she was him. I'm not making excuses for Dodge, but you have to look at the whole picture. The cops just want it to be Dodge because it's easy." He flipped a shock of black hair out of his eyes. "And you don't like Dodge."

"You're right, I can't stand Dodge Burnside, but it is

important to look at all the facts. Did you tell the police about Cal's other friends?"

He shook his head no. "No one asked."

"Mind if I mention it to Hud?"

He gave a casual shrug. "I got no secrets."

"Thanks, Sam. I appreciate you being honest with me." I started to take a sip of my drink, when a group of preteen boys ran by. One shoved another, who fell into me, causing me to drop my cup, spewing lemonade all over my hands and boots.

"Hey!" I cried, jumping back.

"Sorry!" they screamed and ran off, laughing.

"Hooligans," Aunt Garnet said, pulling another lacy hankie from her purse. "There's a water fountain over yonder."

When I returned from washing my hands, Sam was laughing about something with Aunt Garnet, charming her like he did every female he encountered. He'd even bought me another lemonade.

"Thanks again for your help, Sam," I said. "And for the refill."

"No problem," he said cheerfully. "Catch you later, ladies."

Aunt Garnet and I watched him lope away.

"What a nice young man," she said, with a curt nod. "Well brought up."

"Yeah, he's a sweetie."

"That was an interesting piece of information about Cal, wasn't it?" Aunt Garnet said. "The fact that he hung out with what sounds like white supremacists certainly opens up the suspect pool. Definitely something we should inform Detective Hudson about." Her face got a crafty look. "Maybe we can bargain for an information exchange."

"We can certainly try." Fat chance was what I was really thinking. I hooked my arm through hers and took a long drag off my lemonade. It felt cold and good. "But right now, let's forget about murder and go look at the quilts."

She patted my hand and gave a little laugh. "That's an excellent idea."

CHAPTER 9

ON THE WAY TO SEE THE QUILTS WE PASSED THE AG-
riculture building where a sheriff's deputy was tearing
away the yellow and black crime scene tape crisscrossing
the front entrance.

Aunt Garnet's rouged cheeks flushed a deep rose. She
grabbed my arm and tugged me toward the double doors.
"Let's take another look at the crime scene!"

"All right," I said, figuring, what could it hurt?

What was the reason behind this new-and-improved
version of my aunt? Had she always had this side to her or
had something radical happened in her life that caused this
change? Before the day was over, I was going to just flat-
out ask Aunt Garnet what the heck was going on.

Inside, a few people meandered around the room pretending to look at other exhibits while trying to sneak
peeks at the exhibit where Cal's body had been discovered.
The Piebald exhibit was being dismantled by two brawny

young men. Juliette Piebald hovered over them like a kindergarten teacher on the first day of school.

"Be careful of those photographs!" Juliette Piebald yelled as the young men pulled down tissue paper-covered plywood. "Those photographs cost me a thousand bucks."

Her voice was an octave higher than normal and a little screechy. Otherwise she looked runway ready in her narrow-legged black jeans, pink gauzy tank top, diamond earrings the size of hummingbird eggs and bright pink ostrich cowboy boots.

Aunt Garnet said out of the side of her mouth, "Her lipstick matches her boots. How Miss America."

I glanced up at my aunt, amazed. She was making a joke. Sort of. Something was definitely wrong.

"Where's the truck shell?" Aunt Garnet asked.

"I bet the sheriff's department removed that last night. Since Cal's body was found under it . . ."

"DNA," she said, nodding. "Where's y'all's crime lab located?"

"We don't have one."

She tsked under her breath. "Shocking. What do y'all do then?"

"We send stuff either to a lab down in Santa Barbara or one in Bakersfield. It's pretty expensive to maintain a crime lab and our county just doesn't have money in the budget for it."

"They *are* extremely expensive." She stated it with such authority I wondered if she'd actually done research into the cost of building and maintaining one.

We watched silently as Juliette, like a border collie with OCD, circled the young men, directing them exactly how to place the stuffed sheep and cows in the big wooden boxes, what to do with the colorful tissue torn off the backdrop and where to stack the bulky sheets of plywood.

At one point Juliette turned, scanned the room with a

frown before spotting us. Her frown morphed into a practiced smile and she waved at us.

I waved back. "Do you need any help?"

"No, thank you," she called. "But thanks so much for offering."

Even from where we stood, I could see her bottom lip tremble. Though I hadn't agreed with how she essentially cheated to win the Family Farm exhibit grand prize, I couldn't help feeling sorry for her. From a back door emerged Justin Piebald and Dodge Burnside. They were deep in conversation, only stopping when they reached Juliette.

"Seen enough?" I asked Aunt Garnet, after a few minutes.

"Just a minute," Aunt Garnet said, tapping her bony knuckles on my forearm. "I think something interesting is about to happen."

"What could possibly happen now?" It felt wrong to stand here and stare, like we were rubbernecking a gory highway accident.

"Shhh," she said, her eyes glued to the scene. "Look."

The moment she said it, a large piece of plywood backdrop, held precariously by two young men, teetered a half second, then fell forward.

Juliette screamed. "Dodge, watch out!"

Dodge jumped back, the board missing him by inches.

"Are you guys crazy?" Dodge Burnside yelled. "Watch what you're doing!" He turned to Juliette, who stood a few feet behind him. "Are you okay?"

She nodded, her eyes wide.

Excitement over, I turned and started toward the exit, but Aunt Garnet grabbed my arm.

"Wait," she murmured. Then, after a few seconds, "Okay, we can go now. I saw what I needed."

I followed her out of the building, confused. "What do

you mean you saw what you needed? What are you talking about?"

"In good time, my dear," she said.

I felt like bopping her one.

Inside the building where the quilts were displayed, the air was cool and damp, the atmosphere serene. People laughed, sipped their bottled waters and pointed at the intricate quilts, hand-knit sweaters, beautifully carved jewelry boxes and clever table settings for fictional dinners that all sounded deliciously decadent. Murder wasn't on the menu in this building.

"Let's start at the beginning," Aunt Garnet said. "I don't want to miss a thing."

I gave up . . . for the moment. Aunt Garnet was immune to nagging. But I'd wheedle the information out of her eventually.

We strolled around the room, studying each display. The entries had been organized by color this year, giving the room a sort of rainbow effect. We were in the oranges, about a half hour into our tour and her comparison of every quilt with one she'd made and entered in the Arkansas State Fair, when I finally couldn't stand it any longer. I broke into her historical reverie of past quilt glories.

"Aunt Garnet, for cryin' out loud, you gotta tell me. What did you see over there when they were dismantling the Piebald exhibit? You're holding back on me." I wasn't going to listen to one more word about her quilting conquests until she told me what she saw or *thought* she saw.

She looked down at me, her long, even teeth and pale powdery skin as familiar to me as Dove's long braid. Her blue eyes twinkled and for the first time it occurred to me how the shape and color of them were so similar to my gramma's. The mischievous look in her eyes definitely reminded me of Dove.

"C'mon, Aunt Garnet. Fess up."

"You know when that piece of board fell?"

I nodded.

"Tell me exactly what you saw."

I exhaled impatiently. She obviously was going to make me work for the information. "Juliette was nagging the workers to be careful. She waved and I waved back. I asked her if she needed help and she refused. Dodge Burnside and her stepson, Justin, walk in. The three of them talk. Then he almost got hit by the falling board. Juliette screamed for Dodge to watch out."

"It's what happened right after the board fell that is particularly interesting."

I had no idea what she was talking about. "Excuse me?"

"Dodge Burnside," Aunt Garnet said, her voice triumphant.

I thought about it. So Dodge Burnside was there helping them pull down the display. Dodge worked for Milt Piebald, so that seemed perfectly logical. I said as much to Aunt Garnet.

"Ah, but does his job include "fringe benefits"?

"Aunt Garnet! I can't believe you even know what that means!"

She gave a low chuckle. "I have read books published in the last five years. And I watch Jon Stewart. So, my point is that in a split second Mrs. Piebald and young Mr. Burnside gave away the fact that there might be a little something more between them." She tsked primly and patted her cotton-candy hairdo.

I honestly hadn't noticed a thing. "They did?"

She leaned down close. "When the board fell, they all jumped back. But after it was obvious they were safe, Mr. Burnside touched Mrs. Piebald's waist just long enough and just intimately enough to tell me that he'd shimmied down that garden path before." Her lips turned up into a triumphant smile.

I was shocked. Then I was annoyed . . . at myself for missing it. "Wow, that certainly opens this situation up to a whole new ball game." Then I caught myself. "Wait, no it doesn't. So *what* if Dodge and Juliette are doing the horizontal mambo? What's that got to do with Cal's murder?"

Aunt Garnet's faced flushed telling me that I'd struck a nerve . . . and taken some of the air out of her investigating sails. Feeling bad that I'd ruined her moment of Sherlockian glory, I linked my arm through hers. I wouldn't take her mystery away from her. I mean, what could it hurt? It was only a conversation between my aunt and me.

"You're right, Aunt Garnet, it *is* suspicious. Maybe Cal saw them and told Dodge and he killed Cal so Jazz wouldn't find out. Or maybe Juliette killed him so Milt wouldn't find out. Shoot, maybe Milt killed him because Cal was the one having the affair with Juliette. There are all kinds of possibilities. I say we save that puzzle piece and come back to it when we have more information."

She opened her mouth and I was almost certain she was going to reprimand me, tell me not to take that condescending tone with her. But she surprised me. "You're absolutely right, niece. It's a small observation that may or may not have anything to do with our case." She squeezed my hand and smiled. "Now, what's next?"

I looked into her face, which seemed to me to look a little wilted, the area around her eyes pale. Like Dove, she'd never admit when she was getting tired or when something was too much for her. But since I didn't know yet what was going on with her, I decided to finagle her into resting a little while.

"Let's go over to the Bull Pen," I said. "That's what we call the hospitality suite. It's cool and they have a bar and always have snacks. Really good ones this year because of Emory. We can look over the fair schedule and decide if there's anything we'd like to see this afternoon."

"Sounds lovely. Will they allow me in?"

"Absolutely. You're with me and I've got connections." I waggled the all access pass hanging around my neck.

"Nice photo," she commented.

Tim, the official fair photographer, was an old college friend who also had aspirations toward stand-up comedy. He'd taunted me until he caught me with my mouth open, then snapped the picture. I appeared to be angling for bait. Then he refused to reshoot the photo.

"Trust me, I'm gonna get back at ole Tim for that."

Early afternoon was the most pleasant time to visit the hospitality suite. There were enough people in the room to chat with but not so many that it took you a half hour to get something to drink or eat. I bought myself a Coca-Cola and an iced tea with three sugars for Aunt Garnet. I brought our drinks and a plate of locally made goat cheese and whole grain organic crackers over to where Aunt Garnet was visiting with Emory on the sofa.

"Aunt Garnet, you have to see the Great Kansas Pig Races," he was saying. "If you're tempted to bet—mind you, it's a tad illegal, but it happens—go for Sukie, the black-and-white one with what looks like a daisy on her side." He lowered his voice. "She's a ringer."

"Shame on you!" Aunt Garnet exclaimed. "I will not be betting on pigs or anything else, Emory Delano Littleton. The Lord doesn't look kindly on gambling." The words sounded like the old Aunt Garnet, but she was smiling indulgently at her favorite nephew. In Aunt Garnet's eyes, Emory could do no wrong. If anyone could talk her into laying down a few bucks on a racing piglet, it would be Emory.

"Quit trying to corrupt her," I said, flopping down on the sofa. "What's the scoop on how the Booster Buddies are taking Cal's murder?"

Before he could open his mouth, his eyebrows went up. He stood up, a phony smile on his face. I turned around to see who would cause this quick change in my cousin. Milt Piebald strode toward us, his face definitely not in a happy place.

"Emory, have you seen Levi?" Milt demanded, his voice loud as a rodeo announcer's. His black hair glistened like the shine on his cowboy boots. "That boy seems to be a lot harder to find after this incident with his daughter. He's not answering his walkie-talkie or his cell phone. What's the use of paying for those buggers if people ignore your call? My friend, we might as well be shouting at a herd of heifers."

"Milt, shut up," Emory said. His voice drawled the words, giving them a good-natured timbre. "Levi's not answering calls because he's probably walkin' around the fair making sure everything's runnin' like it should, which is exactly his job. He's doin' fine, so just leave him be." His smile was full of steel.

Milt hesitated, recognizing that Emory was angry, something that happened so rarely that when it did, it threw people off.

Milt rolled his tongue around in his mouth. "He's deliberately trying to keep this low profile to protect his little girl. She was running around with that young man who, in case anyone is interested, already had himself a nice little criminal record."

"Hey, Milt," I said. "Did it occur to you that Levi might be trying to keep this incident low profile for the good of the fair?"

"All's I know is that we've got ourselves a peck of bad publicity and I've got myself one pissed-off wife. Juliette is not happy about having to take down our prizewinning display." He pulled a paper-wrapped toothpick out of his pocket, dropped the wrapping on the floor and stuck it in the side of his mouth. "And when the missus ain't happy, believe me, she makes sure I'm not happy."

"The sheriff has the investigation under control," Emory said, standing up. "I talked to Detective Hudson this morning and the Jones homicide has top priority. But these things take time and I'd suggest we all return to the business of making this fair as successful as we can."

Milt moved the toothpick in his mouth from one side to the other. "Easy for you to say. Your wife's not chomping on your balls every dang minute." He looked over at Aunt Garnet. Her thin lips were pressed together in a Sunday school teacher's scowl. He had the grace to look chagrined. "Sorry, ma'am. Don't mean to be crude."

"Then don't be, young man," she snapped.

Milt jerked his head back in surprise, obviously expecting her to give a polite *That's all right*. Ha, he didn't know Mrs. Garnet Wilcox. He adjusted his white cowboy hat, then marched over to the bar without another word.

"Good one, Aunt Garnet," Emory said, grinning.

"What a nasty man," she replied. Then she turned to me. "So, what now? Time's a'wastin'. Most homicides are solved in the first forty-eight hours or they are cold as a Thanksgiving turkey carcass."

Emory slipped a hand in front of his grin.

"You know, there's still so much to see at the fair," I said, picking up a program from a stack on the oak coffee table. I glanced at my watch. "It's five o'clock now. At five thirty we have a choice of seeing the Kansas racing pigs or the San Celina County Cloggers or taking in the ugly lamp contest."

"The what?" Emory said.

"It's right here. There are two categories—Made Ugly and Born Ugly."

"Definitely the lamps," Emory said. "The pigs run every day during the fair and you can see cloggers any old time in Arkansas."

"Okay, it's the ugly lamps." She pulled another hankie from her purse and patted her damp upper lip. It was downright chilly in the Bull Pen so immediately an alarm went off in my head.

Outside, I realized that the temperature had gone from

blazing hot to come-to-Jesus hot. Hot enough to convince anyone that hell indeed existed and an August day in Paso Robles might be its first cousin. There was no way I could let Aunt Garnet walk across the fairgrounds to the El Camino Real building where the ugly lamp contest was held. So I flagged down a red golf cart, flashed my badge and my most winning smile. "Official business," I said to the middle-aged Hispanic man driving. "We need to get to the El Camino Real right away."

"Ugly lamp contest?" he asked, helping Aunt Garnet into the front seat. I climbed on back sharing the space with two boxes of chicken-shaped paper fans.

"You got it," I said.

"I could've won that," he said, pressing down the accelerator. The cart started with a jerk. "My mother-in-law gave us a lamp when we got married that she said was a pair of rare black swans, but they looked more like vultures. Think she was trying to tell me something?"

"Why didn't you enter it?" I asked him.

He turned to grin at me. "Broke. It was an accident. I swear."

The ugly lamp contest was more popular than I anticipated. There were only a few seats left in the corner of the small air-conditioned building so I found one for Aunt Garnet and told her I'd stand in the back.

"Let's get a snack afterward," she said. "How about nachos?"

"Sounds good to me." Though I couldn't imagine Aunt Garnet snarking down tortilla chips, melted cheese and jalapeño peppers. Then again, this was the new, improved, throw-good-eating-habits-to-the-wind Aunt Garnet.

I leaned against the wall and watched as twenty-five contestants and the tackiest lamps I'd ever seen paraded across the platform to the song "I Feel Pretty" from *West Side Story*. A photographer from the *Tribune* was frantically snapping pictures as each lamp seemed to be more horrible than the last. This would likely be one of the human interest stories they loved to report about the fair.

Each contestant had two minutes to give his or her lamp's story. My favorite was the one about how the lamp was a wedding gift from a beloved aunt who had no taste and visited the owner regularly so they couldn't ditch it. It had a glass lampshade that changed color as the lava lamp bottom roiled and gurgled. Every time the color changed, the audience laughed. A good many of the stories involved lamps given as wedding gifts. After the stories I heard, I swore to myself that from now on I was only giving checks or gift certificates for wedding presents.

After the contest, I found Aunt Garnet.

"What now?" I asked. "Want those nachos?" It was six thirty and though we'd had snacks in the Bull Pen, we hadn't had a real supper.

"I'm a bit tired," Aunt Garnet said. "And I'd like to spend a little time with my sister. I miss her. Do you know if she's going to be home tonight?"

"Let me call her and see where she is. I'll be right back. It's too noisy to call her in here."

Okay, now I was really worried. While Aunt Garnet used the ladies' room, I told her I'd track Dove down. I knew she had to be here at the fair somewhere. I'd seen in today's program that Isaac was speaking in the fine arts building this evening. He was the featured fair artist this year since his book of state and county fair photographs had recently been reissued.

Dove answered on the third ring. "He's signing books now. Got a line clear out to the Haunted House ride."

"I'm taking Aunt Garnet back home. She looks tired." I hesitated a moment, then said. "You know, Dove, I think there's something wrong."

"You bet there is, she's always wanted—"

"No," I interrupted. "Something's really wrong. She just

said she missed you." I didn't want to scare Dove, but I had to say it. "Gramma, she might be sick or something. She's been acting real strange. I think you two need to talk."

There was silence on the phone.

"Ready to go?" Aunt Garnet asked behind me.

I jumped in surprise. "See you later," I said to Dove. "Think about what I said."

"Everything okay?" Aunt Garnet said when I flagged down another golf cart and asked them to give us a ride to the exit.

"Great," I said, silently praying, *Please, God, make that be true.* "Dove's at Isaac's book signing, but she'll be home soon." I made that last part up, but maybe after hearing what I said, she'd come right home after Isaac's event.

On the drive to the ranch, Aunt Garnet leaned back against the headrest and closed her eyes. I refrained from turning on the radio, afraid to disturb her. The quiet gave me time to contemplate Cal's murder. Though I really had no horse in that race, there was a part of me that wanted to help solve the murder. I mentally listed the suspects—Dodge or Milt seemed the most likely. There was Juliette—that was certainly possible, though that was a stretch. How would she have moved Cal's body? Unless she had help. She and Dodge? Also, if I was going to be fair, I should add Lloyd Burnside. Maybe he lied about his son not going back out after his friends brought him home. Maybe he helped Dodge kill Calvin Jones. That would make him an accessory, wouldn't it? Had Hud considered that? Of course, then there were those unknown friends of Cal's. Maybe one of them did it, using the Harriet Powers quilt as a slap in the face to Jazz and Levi. Surely Hud was looking into that possibility.

On the way down the Ramsey Ranch's long driveway, gravel pinging against our doors woke Aunt Garnet. She straightened up, flustered that she'd fallen asleep. To cover her embarrassment, she blurted, "Sam told me that Dodge Burnside told him that Justin and Cal had a fight about Jazz right before Cal was murdered."

My foot hit the brake. We jerked forward, then were caught by our shoulder belts.

"Whoa," Aunt Garnet said, reaching out to grab the dashboard.

My hands squeezed the steering wheel. "I'm sorry. You surprised me. Are you all right?"

She nodded.

I started slowly driving again. "Run that by me again. Sam told you what?"

"Justin and Cal had a fight right before Cal was killed. Dodge Burnside told Sam."

"When did Sam tell you that?"

"This afternoon when you spilled your drink and had to wash up."

We pulled up in front of the ranch house and I turned off the ignition. Daddy sat on the front porch in a wood rocking chair drinking a glass of tea. Gabe sat in an identical rocker next to him, laughing at something.

"Is that all he said?"

"Yes."

"Why didn't he tell me about it?" It annoyed me especially since I praised him earlier for being so truthful. He was a little like his father in that aspect. He told the truth . . . just left out something *significant*.

"He was afraid you'd get the wrong idea about his friend."

Add Justin Piebald to the suspect list, I thought. I liked Jazz. She was a young woman whom I thought would go far in life. She was smart, kind and talented, but it was beginning to appear she wasn't adept at choosing stable men.

I was helping Aunt Garnet out of the truck and up the porch steps when my cell phone rang.

"Benni?" Katsy's voice was an octave higher than her normal alto. "I need your help."

"What's wrong?"

"Jazz has locked herself in the guest room and won't come out. She insists she has to talk to *you*."

"Me? Whatever for? Do you think she'd do anything drastic?" I sat down on the porch steps, aware that Gabe, Daddy and Aunt Garnet were staring at me.

Katsy made a sound halfway between a sigh and a moan. "I don't think so. If we have to, we can break down the door. We have a key somewhere, but I have no idea where. We're just not in the habit of locking things up here."

"I'm at the ranch so it'll take me about a half hour to forty-five minutes to get there."

"Thanks. Honestly, this is enough to make a girl reconsider having kids."

"What's going on?" Gabe asked.

"Apparently Jazz has locked herself in the guest room at the Morrison ranch. She wants to talk to me."

Gabe rocked slowly, a frown shadowing his face. "Why you?"

I shrugged. "She trusts me?"

"We'd better get going," Aunt Garnet said. Her face sparkled with eagerness even though the tightness around her eyes had worsened. "No time to waste."

"Maybe you'd better stay here," I said. "Dove said she was on her way home and that y'all were going out someplace good for dinner." It was a blatant lie, but I'd let Dove deal with that.

"I don't like you getting involved with this," Gabe said. "You should call Hudson and have him send a detective out."

"No," I said calmly. "She wants to talk to me, not some strange detective. We don't even know if her meltdown has anything to do with Cal's death. She's probably just

being . . . a teenager. She and I have talked some about losing our moms so young." I glanced over at Daddy, whose
face still took on a tinge of sadness whenever I mentioned
my mother. I smiled at him. "Even when you have great
dads, you sometimes just need to talk to a woman."

"She has Maggie and Katsy," Gabe said. "They're family, or close enough to it."

I went up the steps, plopped a hand on each armrest and
looked deep into his troubled blue-gray eyes. "Friday, I
don't think this has anything to do with anything except
a young girl who is sad and scared because her boyfriend
was killed. Probably because of something in his past. Who
was it that said the past always follows us?"

"'The past is not dead,'" Aunt Garnet said. "'In fact,
it's not even past.'" She cleared her throat. "Bill Faulkner."

I turned and smiled at her, loving the way she said "Bill,"
as if she and the famous writer had just eaten biscuits and
gravy together that morning. "William Faulkner did have a
way with words. Don't worry, Chief Ortiz. If Jazz tells me
something relevant to the case, I'll call Hud right away."

On the drive to Katsy and Maggie's ranch, I contemplated what Jazz might want to tell me. Did she know about
Cal's troubled past? She must have. Had he truly broken
away from his old racist friends? Could a person change
so quickly, so completely? My belief in God's grace told
me that yes a person could make a 180-degree change. We
had the free will to do so. But humans were fallible. We
might want to change, but we are often lured back to the
tempting patterns of our pasts. And, sometimes, when we
are honestly trying to walk away, our past comes looking
for us. William Faulkner was right about that. The things
we do and say aren't ever really finished. If more people
understood that would they think twice before doing or
saying something cruel? Most of history revealed . . . not
often enough.

Those troubling thoughts accompanied me on my drive

down the twisting two-lane highway to the remote Morrison ranch. Their nearest neighbors, the Seavers, trained cutting horses and lived a half mile away. I passed under the bleached wood archway carved with their great-grandfather's Circle LM cattle brand and pulled up in front of the wood frame ranch house. It was painted a deep brick red with white window frames and decorative shutters with cutouts of the distinctive bulbous heads of Hereford cattle. Maggie commissioned those shutters a few months ago from one of our co-op's woodworkers. This was the first time I'd seen them on the house though I'd watched their progress in the woodshop. Maggie waited on the deep front porch.

"Hey," I said, coming up the steps. "Is Jazz still incommunicado?"

Maggie opened the wooden screen door for me. "I'm worried, Benni. She's so upset and won't tell me or Katsy a thing. We thought about calling Levi, but we wanted to see if she'd talk to you first. Levi doesn't look good. I know he's not getting enough sleep."

"Who can blame him?" I said, stepping into their living room. It was decorated with a plush navy sofa, two deep red leather chairs and a bevy of rustic antiques from old California—rusty horseshoes, Spanish-style spurs, a feed-store calendar from the 1920s. A matching red, white and navy Road to Oklahoma quilt hung over the sofa. Their mother had been born and raised outside of Tulsa.

"Last room at the end." She gestured toward the long hallway. "The one with the closed door," she added, her voice weary.

"Where's Katsy?" I asked.

"Feeding the critters. Have you eaten supper yet? We're barbecuing halibut steaks tonight."

"Let's see how things go with Jazz. If I can talk her out of her lair, maybe it would be better if I headed back home, let you all have some private time to discuss things."

"Good luck. I'll be in the kitchen making a salad."

I walked down the hallway past three other bedrooms wondering briefly if Katsy and Levi did get married where they would live—here or in Paso Robles?

There was no sound coming from behind the closed door. I knocked softly on the knotty-pine door.

"Jazz, it's Benni Harper . . ." I cleared my throat. "Uh, Benni Ortiz."

She flung the door open, took one look at me and burst into tears.

CHAPTER 10

"*O*H, SWEETIE," I SAID, ENCIRCLING HER WITH MY arms. Her sobs were deep and intense, her shoulder blades as delicate as a kitten's. Abruptly, she broke away, motioning me into the room. Once I was over the threshold, she locked the door behind us, which seemed a little over the top. And certainly unnecessary. But I cut her slack. She was only a kid and she'd lost someone close to her in a violent way.

"I really need to talk to you," Jazz said, giving a small hiccup and wiping her swollen eyes with the back of her hand.

"Okay," I said, sitting down on the double bed. "What about?"

She flopped down next to me. The bed was covered with an old-fashioned chenille bedspread the color of buttered popcorn. The headboard was an off-white Shabby Chic style that someone—likely Jazz or Katsy—had hand-painted with local wildflowers—electric blue columbine, Orangesicle California poppies and school bus yellow wild mustard.

I took Jazz's hand. "You are scaring Maggie and Katsy to death." Inwardly, I flinched at my insensitive word choice. "Anything you tell me, you can tell them."

She shook her head, her green eyes welling with tears. "They wouldn't understand. Maggie and Katsy . . . well, I love them, I do! They are . . . they're great. Like my sisters. I really, really want Dad to marry Katsy. She's awesome and Maggie . . . she's the best. I so, so admire them. But they wouldn't *get* this like you do."

I scratched my cheek, momentarily confused. "I'm not sure what you mean."

"I'm part white too," she said fiercely. "People always forget that. It's like when my mom died, that part of me died too. It's not fair. When you die, people just forget you." Her bottom lip started quivering. "Like Cal. Except for me, no one cares that he's dead."

I pressed my lips together, not certain how to answer. So I just squeezed her hand in sympathy.

She didn't speak and the expression on her face looked expectant.

"I understand it's not fair," I finally said. "I'm always telling my gramma Dove that things aren't fair and she just tells me fare is something you pay to ride the bus." I gave a tentative smile. "Frankly, I wish she'd come up with a new saying."

She didn't return my smile. I knew this wasn't a joking matter, but I was floundering because I didn't have any particularly wise words of advice. How could I tell someone almost twenty years younger than me that most of the time I was as confused by people's actions as she was? Was there really any adequate explanation for why people hate? "I'm so sorry about Cal. Is there anything I can do for you?"

She turned her head, looking out a window that still had the ancient, wavy glass of the original house. It made the olive tree outside the house resemble a surrealist painting. "Maybe I know kind of why he was killed?"

I let go of her hand and felt my spine stiffen. "What?"

She continued staring out the window. "The night before he died, we left the fair about nine p.m. It was still really hot so we decided to go swimming at my house." She started running the palm of her hand across the chenille bedspread's bumpy pattern. "We swam and then I made us some peanut butter sandwiches. When I was walking out with him to his truck, he said he was thinking about leaving town for a while." She turned her head to look at me. Her eyes were red-rimmed and teary again. "I really, really liked him, Benni. He was not at all what people thought. He wrote poems and songs. Really awesome ones. He listened to me. Not many guys ever do that. They all want . . ." She looked back down at the bedspread. She fanned her hand out, her fingers reminding me of the handprint turkeys kids draw at Thanksgiving. "He and I talked about deep stuff, like how what happens to us as kids makes us the people we are. He doesn't even remember his mom. His dad died when he was thirteen." A tear rolled down her cheek. "He spent most of his life living with people he didn't even know. He lived so many different places before he turned eighteen. Everything he owned fit in a gym bag. Isn't that just so sad?"

It was and there was not one thing I could say that would lessen the tragedy of Cal's short, troubled life.

"He was so excited about getting his GED," she continued, "and maybe going to college. He loved animals. He wanted to be a veterinarian or learn to make saddles."

Her expression was completely guileless, with the faith and hope that I remembered having at her age. It was truly a blessing to have that time in your life when anything seemed possible.

I let her talk about Cal's dreams for a few more minutes

before I finally broke in. "He sounds like he was a wonderful young man. I'm glad he had you, Jazz. He was lucky."

She gave me a surprised look. "Oh, Benni, I was lucky too."

"You're right. And finding out who did this to him would be a wonderful way to honor his life."

"That's why I wanted to talk to you. I mean, besides the fact that you kind of understand since you and Gabe are different like Cal and me. You're friends with that detective. You can tell him what I'm going to tell you."

"Why don't you just tell Detective Hudson yourself?"

She wouldn't meet my eyes. "I just don't want to."

I knew this was a traumatic event for her, but it also seemed like she was making things more dramatic than they needed to be. It really wasn't necessary for me to be the go-between for her and Hud. But if it made her feel better, I supposed it was the least I could do. "Why don't you just tell me what Cal told you and together we'll figure out what to do?"

She leaned close to me, her voice low and urgent. "For one thing, you know he once hung with some people who were kind of skinheads?"

"Yes, I heard about that. But hadn't Cal stopped associating with them?"

She nodded vehemently. "They didn't like that at all. Especially when they found out about him and me."

"How did they find that out?"

She lifted up her shoulders. "Who knows? People saw us. Maybe someone told them."

My first thought was Dodge Burnside. "So, what did they do?"

"Mostly just called him and said stuff."

"Stuff?"

"Like being a traitor to his own race. They said he'd be sorry for hanging around a half-breed. He was so embarrassed about ever being friends with them. He didn't want to tell me, but I pried it out of him." Her nostrils flared. "They said things about my dad and Katsy and Maggie. About what they'd like to do to . . . hurt us. Cal didn't want to tell me that either, but he said we should know."

"Did you tell your dad?"

"Not yet. Cal told me all this last night. Right before he was . . ." She gave a small sob. "Maybe they killed him! One of them . . . those people who said those horrible things."

"Detective Hudson definitely needs to know this."

She looked back down at the chenille spread. "There's something else."

"Yes?"

"He found out something about someone that wasn't right."

"Something illegal?"

Her bottom lip quivered slightly. "He wouldn't tell me. He just said he was going to talk to the person about it, see if they'd stop. If they didn't, then he'd tell someone because it was the right thing to do."

"Someone like the police?"

She bit her bottom lip, her teeth white against her lips. "I guess."

"Do you have *any* idea what he saw or who he was talking about?" My insides turned cold. They might be more in danger than any of us realized.

She shook her head again. "Cal didn't want me to be involved. He said he would try to make the person stop what they're doing." A small sob caught in her throat. "Maybe whoever he talked to killed him?"

A good possibility, but I didn't want to panic her. Her emotions were already in high gear. "It would be better if you told the detective all this."

"Can't you tell him? I don't want to talk to the police again."

"I can, but I'm warning you, he will want to talk to you again." I stood up, pulling down the legs of my Wranglers.

"Why didn't you tell this to the police when they first questioned you?"

Confusion and regret washed over her face. "I don't know, I don't know! I was so scared. And I didn't want people to think Cal was terrible because he hung out with those guys. Besides Cal was so serious about me not telling *anyone*. He said he could take care of it. I believed him."

Oh, the brazen confidence of the young. The minute that thought came into my mind, I wondered how many times my dad and gramma had thought the same thing about me.

"I'll call Detective Hudson," I said, keeping my voice calm. "But Katsy and Maggie have a right to know if . . ." I stopped, not wanting to actually say it out loud—they had a right to know if their lives were in danger. "You need to tell your dad about this. Tonight."

She dropped her head, studying her bare feet. Her toenails were painted a bright glittery purple. "I'll call him right now." She looked back up at me. "Could you tell Maggie and Katsy?"

I went back into the kitchen where Maggie was chopping tomatoes. Their fresh, sweet, earthy scent floated across the room. A tomato-mayonnaise sandwich eaten in front of my own television sounded so good right now.

Katsy stood scrubbing her hands in the deep farm kitchen sink. Their kitchen, one of the first rooms they'd renovated in the old ranch house, had natural pine cabinets with glass doors and pale speckled granite countertops. The pure white walls set off their collection of colorful, odd-sized folk art paintings with an emphasis on dogs, horses and cows. The paintings lit up the room with color. Bess and Harry lay on the braided rag rug in front of the back door.

"Houston," I said, folding my arms across my chest and leaning against the kitchen threshold, "we have a problem."

"Obviously," Katsy said, not turning around, "but is the problem one we can solve?"

I repeated my conversation with Jazz. Katsy and Maggie listened intently, their faces shiny with perspiration. Unlike Jazz, I don't think they much cared about Cal's love of poetry or his tenuous dreams of becoming a veterinarian or a saddlemaker.

"She's safer out here," Katsy said flatly. "We have shotguns and Bess and Harry will discourage anyone who would think half a second about breaking in."

I didn't want to contradict her, but I was afraid that being so far out in the country might be less safe. It would take law enforcement at least a half hour, maybe longer, to get here once they were called. Then again, this was their home. Their mother had leased the ranch for years and when she died, her life insurance enabled Katsy and Maggie to put a down payment and obtain a mortgage. I knew these two well. They were ranch-tough women who could take care of themselves. They would never let anyone run them off their own property.

"I told her she should talk to her dad," I said. "She's calling Levi now."

He and the Morrison women could decide whether Jazz should stay here or go back home. That was certainly not something they needed my input on.

"How about some supper?" Maggie said, holding up a halibut steak.

"Thanks, but I need to hit the road. I'll call Hud and tell him what Jazz told me. Guess we'll just have to wait for what comes next."

Maggie walked me out to my truck, Harry trotting beside us. Though it was almost eight o'clock and the sun had dipped below the treetops, the temperature was still in the nineties. Harry's tongue was rock-star long, dripping with saliva. I looked forward to my truck's icy air-conditioning.

"What's on your schedule for tomorrow?" Maggie asked.

"I'm not on the list to help anyone, but Dove will likely

drop Aunt Garnet in my lap again so I guess I'll see what she wants to do."

"It's back to real work for me. Gabe has a packed day." She made a face. "I hate Mondays."

"I'll let you know what Hud says." I leaned over and hugged her hard. "Be safe, Maggie. Don't try to do this alone."

She hugged me back. "Don't you worry, Benni. Katsy and I have no desire to be martyrs." Her tone was light, but I could hear the tension underneath, like a buzzing electrical line.

I pulled out my cell phone. No bars. "Could you call the chief and let him know I'm on my way home?"

"You bet, girlfriend."

Gabe and Scout weren't there when I walked into the living room, but I checked the answering machine. Gabe had listened to Maggie's message. A note on the pad next to the phone said they went for a quick walk. It was fifteen degrees cooler in San Celina, a relief after the North County's heat. I grabbed a Coke out of the refrigerator and dialed Hud's home phone number.

"Hud? It's Benni." I flopped down on the sofa and took a drag from my Coke.

"Hey, ranch girl. What's up?"

"I just got back from the Morrison ranch. Jazz is staying there."

"Yes?"

For the second time, I repeated Jazz's story.

After I finished, he waited a few seconds before commenting. "That is interesting, but there's really nothing that helps us. He saw *something*?"

"I know it's vague."

"Just a little."

"How much did you investigate that group he was involved with?"

"We talked to some of them. They are just a bunch of

shaved head, leather-vested, prison-tattooed losers. Their ersatz leader claimed Cal was just one of dozens of high school kids who have hung around them over the years. He made a point to say they'd not been in touch with him for over six months."

"Dozens? That's a scary thought. Do you believe him?"

"Did some background research on the group. Southern Poverty Law Center in Montgomery has a boatload of information. This group is just one of thousands of tiny hate groups scattered like rotten seeds across this fair nation of ours. Law enforcement keeps one vigilant eye on them, but this group isn't all that active on the Central Coast. Probably because we don't have that many minorities for them to harass."

I pulled off one boot, then the other, resting my feet up on the oak coffee table. "Do you think they could be behind the letters to Levi?"

"It's possible. It's a little hard to hide that he's the first black fair manager. When they were questioned, they denied it, of course. If we were a television show, we'd get DNA off the letters, run it through our lab in ten minutes and nab the bad guys before the final beer commercial. Unfortunately, this is real life."

"What about the quilt? Anything on it that helps?"

"Same thing. You know that."

"So, sue me, I'm grasping for straws. But I do think the quilt connects Cal's murder with those letters. Maybe Cal saw or heard about something that was going to take place at the fair, something to do with Levi."

"You'd best take that straw and go buy yourself a chocolate soda. Leave the detecting to the big boys."

"That is so sexist, Clouseau," I said, just as Gabe walked into the living room. He frowned in my general direction. Scout bounded past him and pushed up against my leg, demanding a neck rub.

"So terminate my subscription to *Ms.* magazine."

"Good night."

"What did *he* want?" Gabe asked. His gingery scent was strong from the heat, but he was wearing jeans so they must have only gone for a walk, not a run.

"I was reporting in on what Jazz told me. She was so upset and she . . ." I patted the sofa next to me. "Let me fill you in."

After I finished, I asked, "What do you think?"

"I think I dislike you being involved with anything to do with homicide investigations."

"But . . ." I started.

He held up his hand. "I also know you can't help but be there for your friends." He leaned over and kissed the tip of my nose. "That's one of the myriad reasons I love you."

"Well," I said, not knowing what to say. I'd expected a lecture.

"On the other hand . . ."

For some crazy reason, I was relieved. "Whew, I was beginning to think that some sweet, understanding alien had taken over my macho, protective husband."

He pulled me to him. "I wish I could lock you in our bedroom until they find out who killed this guy."

"This time, I almost wish that myself. This kind of thing is quickly losing its appeal for me. How did you do this for years? Investigate homicides, I mean? Didn't it drive you crazy?"

"Sometimes. But don't forget, I didn't *know* any of the victims. Or their families. It was easier to disconnect from the tragedy and just consider the facts."

"I'm exhausted and who knows what tomorrow will bring. I vote we hit the sack." Scout let out a loud, doggie yawn.

Gabe laughed. "I guess it's unanimous. Remember what Scarlett said. Tomorrow is another day."

"I really don't think Rhett had any intention of taking her back," I said, following him up the stairs.

"Yes, he did," Gabe argued.

"No way, Jose," I said.

We argued about it good-naturedly until we kissed good night a half hour later. Gabe went right to sleep, but like the last few nights, I couldn't seem to catch a ride on the dream train. The thought of Katsy, Maggie and Jazz out there by themselves, the reality that Cal's killer was still wandering around was enough to cause me to stare wide-eyed at our bedroom's shadows for a long time. Finally, I used the old standby insomnia cure that Dove had taught me as a child—repeating the Twenty-third Psalm.

Suddenly, it was morning and I was awakened by the intoxicating scent of frying bacon. Is there any better smell? Maybe fresh-brewed coffee, which also teased my nose. I pulled on shorts and a T-shirt. In the kitchen, Gabe was making cinnamon-buttermilk pancakes.

"Squeezed some fresh grapefruit juice," he said, turning around to smile at me. Scout sat at his feet, hopeful nose quivering. "It's in the refrigerator. How many pancakes do you want?"

I opened the refrigerator door. The cool air felt heavenly. "Three. Do you want juice?"

"Yes, ma'am," he said cheerfully.

I poured grapefruit juice into glasses and placed the full coffeepot in the middle of the table, within easy reach.

He slipped a stack of pancakes in front of me and offered me bacon, cooked crisp, just how I loved it. I took two pieces.

"Go ahead and start," he said, turning back to the griddle. "They're better when they're hot."

I didn't argue and buttered my three pancakes, taking that first bite without syrup, enjoying the first spicy taste. Then I doused them with maple syrup.

When he sat down, I said, "Who are you and what have you done with my husband?"

"Old joke," he said, smiling.

"Best I can do this early. Why the special breakfast?"

"You had a tough day yesterday."

I took another bite of pancake. "Friday, I love you and I love your killer pancakes."

While we were dressing for our respective days, the phone rang. I had a mouthful of toothpaste, so he answered it.

"Hey, Dove. Yes, she's right here, but she's foaming at the mouth." He listened for a minute, then laughed. "No, we're not fighting. Not at the moment, anyway. She's brushing her teeth."

I rinsed my mouth, then took the phone from him, kicking him lightly in the butt with the back of my bare foot. "Maybe you should change your last name to Leno. Hey, Gramma-o'-my-heart! What can I do for you?"

"Before you pick up Garnet, I need chicken feed. And dog food. And while you're there, your daddy also has a new posthole digger that he needs picked up. You may as well save him the trip."

I dabbed at a spot of toothpaste I'd dripped on my T-shirt. "Let me guess, you want me to go by the Farm Supply."

"Garnet will be ready when you get here *if* you leave right now and don't dawdle. I'm helping with 4-H market goats and then with the petting zoo." Her voice went low. "She was prowling around again last night. I could hear her opening and closing drawers. She rearranged my junk drawer."

"How can you tell?" I said. "We've been tossing things in that drawer willy-nilly for the last thirty years."

"No backtalk, young lady! Just keep her busy and out of my hair."

My life with the sisters was beginning to feel a lot like Alice through the Looking Glass. Things were just a little off—Aunt Garnet was acting like Dove and Dove . . . well,

I'd never say to my gramma's face . . . but she was starting to remind me of the old Aunt Garnet.

"I'm not backtalking. It's just that the junk drawer has never had any order so I'm a bit confused as to how you know it's been rearranged."

"Buy my chicken feed and get over here." She hung up without saying good-bye.

Normally I'd be a little peeved, but since I had a stomach full of pancakes and a husband who was in a good mood, I let it go. "I'll be there as quick as a bunny," I said to the dial tone.

"Hop to it then," Gabe said, coming out of the bathroom, tying his navy and green paisley tie.

"Ha-ha," I said, pulling on my most comfortable Justin boots. It looked like it was going to be a long day. "I swear, today I'm going to pry out of my aunt what is going on with her. Dove will have a stroke if this isn't resolved soon."

"Good luck," he said, kissing the top of my head and giving Scout a scratch underneath his chin. "See you for dinner?"

"I have no idea. I'll call you."

Mondays were always a busy day at the Farm Supply, but even more so during fair time. In the last few months, my favorite store had moved two blocks, built a huge new building and tripled their clothing and housewares department. They were doing their best to accommodate the growing tourist trade and the people retiring up here to live the "country" life. I had to admit, though the influx of city transplants often annoyed me, I didn't mind that they brought with them the money to help a hometown store like this survive and even thrive. Katey Vieira, the head buyer, said that almost one-quarter of the store's income now came from the rural-themed boutique items.

I went directly to the feed store in back. The chicken

feed, dog food and Daddy's posthole digger were ready for me. While they arranged everything onto a product truck and wheeled it up front to load into my pickup, I wandered into the clothing section to inspect a new shipment of Wrangler shirts. Most were too fancy for my taste, but I found a couple I might add to my wardrobe. I was debating between a red plaid with white snap buttons and a plain blue chambray with black buttons when a familiar throaty voice called my name.

"Hey, Juliette," I said, glancing around to see if Milt was with her. He was nowhere to be seen, which relieved me greatly. After his comments yesterday, I wasn't sure I could look him in the face without showing my disgust. A poker face was not one of God's gifts to me. "Doing some shopping?"

She lowered her voice. "Oh, I don't buy clothes here. The quality isn't quite up to par. I'm sure you know what I mean. They try real hard, but, you know . . . Well, Manuel's it isn't."

I hoped Katey wasn't anywhere within earshot. She was a nice girl and I liked many of the clothes she bought for Farm Supply. I almost told Juliette that owning a Manuel wasn't all that special. I actually owned a shirt and a dress made by the famous Western designer—compliments of my rich cousin—but what would that accomplish?

"Nothing fits me better than Wrangler brand," I said instead. "I think I'll get this blue shirt."

"Oh, yes, of course," she said, trying to backtrack. "I mean, sometimes you just like to wear something simple."

I glanced down at my watch. "Wow, look at the time. I have to go pick up my great-aunt and take her back to the fair."

She started flipping through the rack, plastic hangers clicking like castanets. "I'm already so sick of that place. Milt insists we go every night to the Bull Pen. Says it's good for business. But, honestly, most of those people buy new vehicles. I keep telling him he ought to get into selling new. We'd have a higher-class clientele."

I didn't know exactly how to continue this conversation. Though I'd known Juliette since high school, we'd never hung out with the same crowd. She'd always been a bit of a social climber, though certainly not the most obnoxious one I'd ever known. And she did have her good side, like donating her prize money to the battered women's shelter. But when she went all elitist like this, I just didn't know how to respond without sounding snippy.

"I mean," she continued, "the San Celina fair is nice, but it's not like it's the Texas State Fair or the Houston Livestock Show."

"Are you from Texas?" Her choice of comparisons surprised me. Usually I could discern even the slightest Texas accent since that was where my first husband was born and lived until he was a young teen. And I'd known Juliette since high school. Why hadn't this come up before?

"I was born in Oregon, but my heart belongs to Texas. We moved there when I was ten after Dad was killed in a logging accident. I love Oregon too, but mostly 'cause of my dad. He was once a minor league baseball player." Her eyes softened at the mention of her father. "I used to be real good at softball myself. My dad started teaching me how to hit and throw a good pitch when I was barely four. I played pony league softball until he died. Dad said I could pitch as straight as some of the pros he'd known." Her lips turned down at the edges. "Mom hated me being so tomboy, so when we went to live with her family in Texas, she put me in pageants."

"So, how'd you end up here?"

She gave a vague, half smile. "Oh, you know, Mom met some guy, married him and he was from here."

I'd seen her stepdad before at a few of the homecomings where she'd been nominated. He was a tall, thin man who worked at the Mid-State Bank. The only reason I knew that is the bank had sponsored many of her runs for Miss San Celina Rodeo. "I didn't realize your father was your stepdad."

"Lots of people say that. It's only 'cause he's tall. Actually, my real father was only an inch taller than I am now. My grandma said I got my height from my grandfather's side. I won my first queen title in Texas. Miss Santa Teresita Junior Rodeo. I was thirteen years old. Mama was so proud. She loved beauty pageants, but the only ones she could first convince me to enter were the ones where I got to ride horses. I was knobby-kneed and snaggle-toothed and there were only two other contestants, but I don't think I've ever loved a crown as much as that one."

She smiled and I could almost see the gawky, horse-crazy thirteen-year-old girl who adored her daddy. How did you end up marrying Milt Piebald? I wanted to ask.

"Say," she said, abruptly changing the subject, "have you heard anything about that boy who was killed?" Her blue eyes were bright and inquisitive behind black spiky eyelashes.

"Only what I've read in the newspaper. Why?" It kind of embarrassed me how quickly the lie tumbled from my lips.

She continued flipping through the shirts and blouses she stated moments before that she'd never considering buying. "Just curious. You know, because he was found in our exhibit and all. I heard he was into drugs."

I scrutinized her face, looking for . . . a guilty expression? "Where did you hear that?"

She lifted one shoulder and started flipping the shirts faster. "Around. You know, people talk."

"What people?"

She stopped flipping and looked at me, her jawline set. "I was just making conversation. It's no big deal." Then she smiled widely and gave a wave. I turned to see who she was greeting.

"Hey, baby," she called to Milt, who was talking to a bearded guy stocking Farm Supply T-shirts. "Did you get my sweet feed? Sugarpie needs her sweet feed."

He gave a cursory wave back, ignored her question and continued talking to the bearded guy.

"Great talking to you," I said. "See you at the fair."

She didn't acknowledge me but continued staring at her husband, her angry expression tinged with hurt. The glimpse of her history gave her a humanity that I'd not really considered before. I thought about that as I gave the counter girl my credit card for my new shirt. If we truly knew other people's stories, would we be so quick to judge them? We all are products of not only our choices, but the choices of the people who took care of us when we were kids. Was that why she married a man so much older than her? Was she trying to replace her dead father?

I walked out the large metal double doors to where my truck was parked. Cy Johnson, of the Johnson Ranch, one of our closest neighbors, passed me on his way in.

"What're you doing here?" I asked. Cy owned a small feed store in Morro Bay where Daddy bought some of his ranch supplies since it was closer to our ranch and he liked to support a neighbor.

"Just comin' to shoot the breeze," he said, giving his deep, rumbling laugh. His chestnut-colored beard always reminded me of Grizzly Adams. "Drove into town with Love. She's got an emergency Cattlewomen's Association meeting this morning. They've got some last-minute things to discuss about the Cattlemen's Lunch."

Every year the Cattlemen's Association, aided by the Cattlewomen, hosted a tri-tip afternoon meal one day of the fair. The money raised went to college scholarships for students majoring in agriculture. Love Mercy Johnson and her husband, Cy, were longtime members of both associations. His father, August, had been voted the Cattleman of the Year two years ago.

"I was going to volunteer to serve," I said. It was something I'd done at the fair every year since I could hold a platter, hand out napkins or run a cash register. "But Dove has me great-aunt sitting. I think I'll see if Aunt Garnet wants to eat there. Maybe I'll go as a guest for a change."

"From what I hear we've got plenty of help this year. You working any calves this fall?" Cy and Love often helped us brand, tag and vaccinate our calves and we returned the favor. The bulk of those chores took place in the spring, a traditional time for roundup, but here on the Central Coast, what is often referred to as "cow heaven" because the weather was so mild, calves could actually be born any time of the year.

"Not too many, maybe twenty-five or so. We should be able to handle it."

"Give us a call if you need some help," he said, touching a finger to his green ball cap printed with Cy's Feed and Seed. "Say hey to Ben for me."

Ten feet before I reached my truck, a white dually truck suddenly pulled in front of me, causing me to stop short. I didn't have to even look to see who the driver was. Dodge Burnside's laugh was audible even with his windows rolled up. He pulled slowly in beside my truck, causing me to wait. He climbed out of the driver's seat, a satisfied smirk on his face. I wondered how much his good looks had allowed him to get away with in life.

"Sorry, Mrs. *Police Chief*," he said, tossing his keys up in the air and catching them. He strode toward the feed counter, chuckling.

The passenger door opened and Lloyd Burnside stepped out, his expression grim.

"I apologize for my son," he said, his cheekbones flushed a bright red. "I'll speak to him." His voice was slightly more tenor than what you'd expect from a man who looked a little like Clint Eastwood.

I instantly felt sorry for him, even as it occurred to me that Dodge was likely the way he was because he'd been indulged by the same person who was now apologizing to me. Still, I'd known enough good, decent people who ended up with a problem kid to give Lloyd the benefit of the doubt.

"It's okay," I said, even though it wasn't. I looked up into Lloyd's face, a deeply tanned, weathered version of his son's. Lloyd wasn't as conventionally handsome as his son, but there was a rugged cast to his chin and deep-set blue eyes that told me that he probably had no trouble finding women friends. He had to be forty or forty-one, not much older than me. He'd been a few years ahead of me in high school and had belonged to the high school rodeo team. Saddle broncs, if I remembered right.

"No, it's not," he said. "Janie spoiled him, though I suppose I didn't try to stop her. We almost lost him from meningitis when he was barely born and she never got over that." He studied the tops of his beat-up cowboy boots.

I vaguely remembered the difficulty surrounding Dodge's birth twenty years ago. Probably I'd overheard Dove talk about it to Daddy. But I would have been eighteen at the time, just starting Cal Poly, and more concerned with my new classes and my romance with Jack than the health problems a young mother and father had with their new baby.

I do remember clearly when two years ago, a day after Dodge turned eighteen, Janie Burnside ran off with a John Deere equipment salesman. According to gossip, she never looked back. It was the talk of the ag community for months. Maybe that explained some of the rage Dodge had toward women.

Still, it didn't give him the right to be abusive. I wanted

to make sure his dad knew about the incident. "Did Dodge tell you why he's upset with me?"

Lloyd looked up and silently shook his head. I told him what happened in the fair's parking lot yesterday.

When I finished, he said, "Did he actually hit this girl?"

I shook my head. "But he grabbed her and if I hadn't intervened—"

"It doesn't matter what might have happened," he interrupted. "The fact is he didn't actually do anything illegal."

"No," I said slowly. "That's not exactly true. He *threatened* her."

He brought a hand up to his forehead and rubbed it. "I'll talk to him. My son isn't a bad kid. I'll tell him to stay away from the Clark girl. I was never happy about him seeing her in the first place. It was a mistake, plain as day. Just begging for trouble."

"What do you mean?"

"C'mon, Benni," he said, giving me a "just between us" smile. "They're obviously different . . . I mean, not his type at all . . . She's . . ." He stopped when he realized I wasn't returning his smile. He looked surprised, then took a step backward, shoving his hands into the back pockets of his Wranglers. "I'll talk to him about leaving her be. I doubt it will be a problem. He's moved on, got himself a new girl." Before I could answer, he turned and walked into the Farm Supply.

I sat in my truck for a moment, thinking about what had just taken place between Lloyd Burnside and me. My thoughts couldn't help but drift to who sent those threatening letters to Levi. Someone who hated the idea that his only son was dating a biracial girl? Would Lloyd go that far to keep his son from being with Jazz?

Or was it the more obvious, that someone was angry that a black man was given such a prestigious job? This was 1997, for crying out loud. Hadn't things gotten any better in the last twenty years?

It reminded me of a controversy about scholarships back when I was in college in the late seventies. Some scholarships had been allotted specifically for students of different ethnic groups and a group of the white students complained to the newspaper, threatening to bring a lawsuit against Cal Poly. The *Tribune* jumped on the controversy and ran a series of front-page stories about it despite the fact that the lawsuit never was filed. Everyone followed the debate closely. One morning Dove and I discussed it while she was making bread. I sat at the breakfast counter, the *Tribune* spread out in front of me.

"Well," she'd said, after I read her the latest episode, "I suppose it does seem unfair to some people that there are scholarships just for blacks or Mexican people, but to be honest, there're scholarships for all kinds of special folks—smart kids, kids good at sports or music, ones that help the physically handicapped."

I closed the newspaper. "One of the guys at school was complaining that he was just a normal white guy, not smart enough or good enough at sports or handicapped or a minority. He says there's nothing there for people like him."

Dove kneaded the bread dough, her face thoughtful. "It does seem unfair. But I believe in taking what you are given with a grateful heart, whether it is a scholarship or a plate of beans and then when you can, when you are doing better, you reach back and help someone else. That's what we're put on this earth for, to love God and to prove that love by serving our fellow human beings."

I cupped my chin in my hand. "What would you have said to this guy who was complaining that minorities are getting all the scholarships?"

She started kneading again. "I'd ask him if he'd trade places with any of those black or handicapped folks to get those scholarships or any other advantages they might be given. That's all. Would he take on their burden for the rest of his life? I'll bet dollars to doughnuts he'd turn that offer down real quick." She flipped the bread dough over and gave it a whack. "Everyone wants the good stuff, but nobody wants the sorrow."

She was right, I thought, inserting my key into the truck's ignition. And I supposed it was human nature, though not always the best part of our nature. I started to turn on my truck, glancing up in the mirror. I stopped when I saw Juliette Piebald walk out of the front door of the Farm Supply. She looked from side to side, then casually—too casually—strolled over to a stack of painted clay pots. She stood staring at the pots, on sale two for ten dollars. Somehow I had a suspicion that she wasn't shopping for her garden.

A few minutes later Lloyd Burnside wandered out from the feed-supply side of the store. He stopped at the pots, said something to Juliette, then seemed to slip her something. A note? I wanted desperately to turn around for a better view, but I was afraid even that tiny movement might tip them off that someone was watching. Smooth as sugar syrup, Juliette turned around and went back inside the store. Lloyd stood for a moment, staring out into the vacant field next to the Farm Supply. His face was too far away for me to see its expression. He turned and strolled back inside the feed department.

Holy cow, what was that all about? Was Aunt Garnet right about an affair, but wrong about which Burnside man it was with?

I started my truck and pulled out of the parking lot. Though the possibility that Juliette was cheating on Milt was an interesting piece of gossip, what did it have to do with anything?

Except . . . what if *that* was what Cal saw? Would Lloyd or Juliette kill him to keep Milt from finding out? But why wrap him in the Harriet Powers quilt? Why put him in the Piebald Family Farm exhibit? If they wanted him out of the picture, wouldn't it make more sense to kill him and dump his body somewhere out in the desolate Carrizo Valley? Or behind a sleazy bar somewhere? Should I tell Hud what I saw or thought I saw? I could just imagine his mocking laughter.

Maybe I'd ask Aunt Garnet her opinion. It might take her mind off whatever it was she was going through, another mystery that, hopefully, would be solved soon.

CHAPTER 11

$\mathcal{I}$ COULDN'T BELIEVE WHAT I WAS SEEING. AUNT GAR-net on the front porch. In *jeans*. Jeans? As far back as I could remember Aunt Garnet had always worn dresses. For every occasion. Everyday cotton calico housedresses. Tailored going-to-town dresses with matching belts and full skirts. Fancy Sunday dresses with lacy white collars. I think once I might have seen her in a pair of cotton slacks weeding her garden. Maybe. It might have been a dream.

"A proper lady always wears dresses," she had loved saying, especially around Dove who only suffered with dresses for funerals or weddings. I came by my dislike of them honestly.

But there stood my great-aunt waiting for me in dark blue jeans; a blouse covered with royal blue and grass green daisies and new blue Keds tennis shoes. It was, no doubt, a new day and wardrobe for my now officially un-predictable aunt.

I flipped down the truck's tailgate and started pulling out

sacks of chicken feed. "You're looking sharp. I won't be long. Have to unload these supplies."

"No hurry," she answered, descending the porch steps with careful, measured steps.

I leaned the posthole digger against the side of the porch, subtly searching her face for illness. "We don't have to go to the fair today if you're tired. We can, you know, just hang out here if you want."

She touched a finger to her upper lip. "Nonsense. I'm raring to go."

Raring wasn't the word I'd have chosen, but I wasn't about to contradict her. I gave her a big smile. "We've got dozens of fair activities to choose from today. Hope you're ready for some fun."

Her return smile was tremulous, but sincere. "Fun is my middle name."

"Do you want to drop by the folk art museum first so you can see the new exhibits?"

"That sounds delightful. I want to do as much as I possibly can while I'm here." She opened the passenger door.

"Before we go, I need to ask Dove something." Specifically, if she'd ferreted out any information from Uncle WW.

"Then you'll have to call her on that little phone of hers," Aunt Garnet said. "Sister was up and out of here this morning before I could finish my cup of tea. She's avoiding me." Her voice sounded hurt.

"It's just fair time," I said, covering for Dove who was likely doing just that. "She always overextends herself. You two will have plenty of time to catch up after the fair."

She looked out the side window. "I suppose."

On the way to the folk art museum, I told her about the African American quilt exhibit, the research I had to do and how excited I was that an old college friend of Katsy's had lent the museum part of her black cloth doll collection to complement our quilt exhibit.

"What exactly are black cloth dolls?" Aunt Garnet asked.

"Before Katsy introduced me to Rona Chappell, I'd never heard of them. Rona is an actress. She acquired her first black cloth doll about thirty years ago when she was a little girl. Her mama bought and sold antiques in Oxford, Mississippi. Rona saw the doll at an estate sale, one of those old plantations being sold out of the family. She said it was the first black doll she'd ever seen. Her mama bought it for some ridiculous amount because back in the sixties not many people recognized their cultural significance." I turned left on the highway and started toward San Celina.

"It's remarkable that any survived," Aunt Garnet said. "I'm assuming they were made for children?"

"That's what historians assume. The earliest ones were made somewhere around the 1870s. Some were definitely designed and stitched by slaves and it's a good guess they were toys for their children. But they were also made by free black women for fund-raising bazaars of the nineteenth century to raise money for antislavery societies."

"You've really done your homework," Aunt Garnet said. "Good girl."

"Thank you." I felt myself flush with pleasure. It was nice having her admire something I'd worked hard on rather than nag at me. But, again, I felt a ragged pit of worry gnaw in my stomach. People could change, but it often took something dramatic to make that happen. Something had to be really wrong with Aunt Garnet. Without warning, tears burned behind my eyes. I cleared my throat trying to control them.

"Got a frog in your throat?" she asked.

"Allergies. So, Rona got hooked on collecting them. She has one of the most extensive collections in the world. She loaned us twenty of them. We have dolls from all three periods when they were popular, from the 1870s to the 1930s."

"What happened after that?"

"Commercial doll making really took off after World

War I and handmade dolls weren't as popular. Though what Rona told me is from 1930s to the '60s the dolls made by manufacturers were mostly white. African American girls again only had the choice of dolls who didn't look like them. It wasn't until after the civil rights legislation was passed in the 1960s that black dolls slowly started appearing in the commercial marketplace. Now we have all sorts of African American dolls—Barbies, Cabbage Patch dolls and Raggedy Anns and Andys."

Aunt Garnet looked down at her pocketbook, clutched in her thin hands. "Things are certainly better now, but we've still a long way to go. Look at what is going on with Mr. Clark."

We pulled up in front of the folk art museum. The parking lot was more crowded than I expected for a Monday, the day we were officially closed. I turned off the ignition and started to open my door.

Aunt Garnet reached across the bench seat and touched my forearm.

"Benni, before we go in, I have an important question." Her face was neutral, but her pale-lashed eyes intent.

I inhaled deeply. This was it. She was finally going to tell me what was wrong. "Yes?"

"Our case. Have you found out anything new?"

A groan itched at the back of my throat. All she wanted was news on the case. "Now that you mention it, there are a couple of developments." I repeated what Jazz told me last night. "And something happened at the Farm Supply this morning. I have a feeling you might be right about there being a relationship of some kind between Juliette Piebald and a Burnside man, but it might not be the one we first suspected." I told her what I thought I saw between Lloyd and Juliette. I didn't mention Dodge harassing me at the Farm Supply. There was no point worrying her. "Now, I don't know what she really gave him, maybe a note or something, but there was definitely physical contact."

"Do you think they made you?" she asked eagerly.

"Huh?"

"*Made you*. You know, did they notice that they were under surveillance? My book says that a good way to know if they made you is if they give you the finger."

"What?" This time it came out as a squawk.

"It's a joke, Benni."

I wanted to laugh. Except I was kind of afraid to. "What book?"

"*Homicide Investigation for Dum-Dums*. I bought it in Little Rock. Are you going to inform Detective Hudson?"

"Maybe," I stuttered, still stunned by her reference book and the finger joke. "There's actually nothing concrete to tell him."

"Still," she said firmly. "We must keep him in the loop. Otherwise, he won't return the favor." She opened the truck door and swung her legs out. "I think we need to pay Detective Hudson an official visit, see if we can pump him for new info."

"If we have time." Though, I thought, it might be quite amusing watching Aunt Garnet badger Hud for information.

"The museum looks lovely," Aunt Garnet said, standing in front and taking in the white-washed hacienda buildings.

"D-Daddy's definitely a miracle worker," I said, waving at my part-time assistant who was watering the half wine barrel planters filled with San Celina native wildflowers. He was worth twenty times what we could pay him. The folk art museum and the stables that now housed the artists' co-op looked as if they were cared for by a team of caretakers, not just one dedicated ex-fishing-boat captain.

"Hello, Mr. Boudreaux," Aunt Garnet called. "How are you this fine summer day?"

"*Bonjour,* Mademoiselle Garnet," he replied in his lilting Cajun French. "*Comment ça va?*" He gave her a little bow.

She returned with a flirty little wave.

"Why, Aunt Garnet, you tease," I whispered. "I'm going to tell Uncle WW on you."

"Oh, pshaw," she said. "William Wiley wouldn't care one little bit." Her eyes moistened, and then she shook her head. "Let's go see the dolls." She walked ahead of me without looking back.

I scurried to catch up with her.

"How's it going?" I asked Kay, who was straightening up the tiny gift shop in the museum lobby, getting ready for tomorrow. She pointed up at two black cloth dolls sitting on a long, almost empty shelf. The dolls had been hand-made by members of the Ebony Sisters Quilt Guild.

"Tell the Sisters we need more dolls," she said, pushing back a strand of her short, silver-streaked hair. "We're down to our last two!"

"That's wonderful! I'll let Flory Jackson know. She's coordinating the boutique items for this exhibit."

Aunt Garnet came up beside me and picked up one of the dolls. "Jeanetta, the young woman who plays organ at Sugartree Baptist, just had a little girl. This is the perfect gift."

"It's signed," I told her, lifting up the edge of the doll's blue calico print dress and showing Aunt Garnet the signed and dated label. "Don't forget to take the pamphlet we made to go with the dolls, in case Jeanetta doesn't know the history of black cloth dolls."

While Aunt Garnet paid for the doll, I made a mental note about making a phone call to our store downtown and see how they were doing. Between both gift shops and the booth at the fair, August might prove to be our most profitable month this year. That would make Constance Sinclair, our biggest benefactor, and the woman who donated her family's hacienda for the museum, very happy. She was always threatening that she couldn't personally fund the folk art museum forever. As a group, we'd worked hard to support ourselves and, as of last month, her contribution was only 15 percent of our monthly budget, down from 30 percent a year ago.

"Let's do a quick walk through the exhibit," I said to Aunt Garnet. "It's eleven o'clock and the Cattlemen's Lunch starts at noon sharp."

"No rush, I ate a large breakfast."

"Okay, then let's take our time and eat later. They serve for four hours."

"Let's go," she said, clutching her tissue-wrapped doll.

By the time we'd toured the quilts, it was past noon. I helped Aunt Garnet into the truck. "Still not hungry?"

"Not especially."

"We could go to the pig races then. They're inside an air-conditioned building this year. The races only last about a half hour. By then the Cattlemen's Lunch two o'clock seating should be starting. It's usually not as packed."

"You're the boss," she said cheerfully. "I'm game for anything."

Again, I mentally shook my head in wonderment. My aunt Garnet had always been the one who'd plan each and every outing with the preciseness and command of a five-star general. Now she was a free spirit. Was running barefoot through a field with flowers in her hair next?

At the fair parking lot we scored big-time and found a space someone had just vacated underneath a leafy oak tree. Now the inside of my truck would only heat up to 110 rather than 130 degrees. I fit the sun shade across the dashboard, cracked my windows and surprised my aunt with a colorful parasol that I'd found at the folk art museum.

"This should make walking around slightly more pleasant."

"Why, thank you," she said, giving it a little twirl. "I feel like a character in the movie *State Fair*."

"I loved that movie! Pat Boone and Bobby Darin were great."

Aunt Garnet's face looked surprised. Then she chuckled. "I was thinking of the 1945 one starring Jeanne Crain and Dana Andrews."

I laughed with her. "That's right, there're two movies. Dove likes the 1945 one too. Can you imagine a third remake being done in the 1990s?"

Aunt Garnet gave a distinctly unladylike snort. "Starring Leonardo DiCaprio and Jennifer Aniston?"

"Pamela Anderson playing the bad girl?"

"She's no Vivian Blaine."

"Or Ann Margaret," I added.

The bleachers of the Great Kansas Pig Races were filling up fast by the time we arrived. Fortunately, I spotted Emory across the circular track. Though he was too far away for even my loud voice to reach him, I knew his cell phone number by heart.

"Emory Littleton here."

I waved at him. "Look across the arena."

He saw me and waved back. "What's up, sweetcakes?"

"Do you see any seats over there for me and Aunt Garnet?"

"She can have mine next to the announcer. You'll have to fend for yourself."

"That's perfect." I pointed at Emory. "Aunt Garnet, Emory's got a good seat for you over there."

"What about you?"

"I'll meet you at the entrance here right after the races. Now don't go betting the farm."

She arched her eyebrows. "Back at you."

I watched her push her way through the crowd toward Emory. Honestly, it was like she relearned how to speak the English language by watching second-rate television cop shows. When she was safely through the crowd and being hugged by Emory, I took a deep breath, then coughed a little. The scent of pig was already a little strong. Maybe the pig races indoors might not be such a smart idea, though it was certainly cooler than last year's outside track.

Now I had a free half hour to kill. What could I do? Luck was on my side. I looked up and saw Hud walk right in front of me. "Hey, Clouseau! Wait up!"

He didn't slow down. "What do you want?"

"Hey, it's wonderful seeing you too, Mr. Grumpy Pants. Anything new on Cal's murder?"

"Sorry. I wish I could solve this one fast for you, but it's got more tentacles than one of those Japanese monster squids."

"Squids don't have tentacles. You mean octopus."

"Whatever, *Jeopardy* girl. At any rate, we have lots of suspects, not a lot of good evidence."

"Still no forensic stuff? Can't you just make everyone that you suspect do that swab thing in their mouth?"

He snorted. "You really do watch too much *Law & Order.* There're little things like right to privacy laws. Look, I know this whole thing just rankles you. It upsets your 'life must be fair at all costs' worldview all to heck, but the truth is we may never know who killed Calvin Jones. I work *cold* cases, remember?"

I knew he was right, but it didn't make me feel any better. "That's not my worldview. I *know* that things aren't fair. It just seems like Cal never had anyone fight for him while he was a kid and I feel like . . . well, at least someone could fight to give him justice now."

He stopped abruptly, placed a hand on my shoulder and gave it a sympathetic squeeze. "Benni, I promise to call you if I find out anything new that I am allowed to tell you."

"Thanks."

His promise relieved my compulsion to *do* something. I was sitting on a bench right outside the building when Emory and Aunt Garnet emerged from it a half hour later.

"You missed a great race!" Emory said. Aunt Garnet's face beamed as it always did when Emory was around.

"I won thirty bucks!" she said. "I took Emory's advice and bet on a long shot."

"Shhh," Emory said, putting a finger to his mouth. "I told you betting was kind of not legal on these things." He winked at me.

"You can buy lunch then," I said.

Aunt Garnet waved the three ten-dollar bills. "I'll even spring for dessert."

"Okay, you can buy me a fried pie later. I hear they have chocolate ones this year."

"You got it." She looked over at Emory. "Are you coming to lunch with us, dear?"

"Wish I could, but I have to check our chicken booth and then get back to the office. I have a conference call with Daddy and Little Buck Nixon's Barbecue Sauce company at three p.m. We're thinking about adding their sauce to our menu. It won the national barbecue championship this year."

She patted his cheek like he was still six years old. "Don't forget to eat lunch. You're looking a little thin. Doesn't that wife of yours cook for you?"

He winked at me again. Though I knew I should jump in and defend my best friend who, after all, *just* had a baby, I knew that her husband was more than up to the job.

"Between my loving wife and her mama, I have more'n enough to eat. I actually weigh ten pounds more than the last time you visited."

"All right," she said reluctantly. "But you make sure not to gain too much weight. Our family has the heart troubles, you know."

Though it might sound funny to anyone else, it was actually music to my ears to hear Aunt Garnet nag again. She sounded more like the Aunt Garnet I knew and loved, one who *wasn't* possibly dying of some incurable disease.

"We'll have you over for a big ole supper before you go back to Sugartree," Emory promised. "You'll see what a marvelous cook my Elvia is."

"No hurry," she said, flipping her hand. "I plan on being here a good little while."

Emory and I exchanged a quick glance. That was news to us and would really be news to Dove.

Now I was beginning to wonder if something *else* was going on. Like between her and Uncle WW. Had they broken up? Oh, my stars. That would be the talk of the family for the next fifty years if Aunt Garnet and Uncle WW got a divorce. Still, it was starting to make sense. His reluctance to say why she was out here; her stubbornness in telling anyone why she was visiting; her fatigue and sadness. I'd been through marriage problems not that long ago with Gabe. There was nothing more exhausting; it hurt in a whole different way than being widowed.

At the Cattlemen's Lunch, because of my longtime membership in the Cattlewomen's Association, we were waved through the VIP line, usually reserved for folks who had an event to attend or a booth to work.

"Huh," said Diane, who sat behind me in ninth-grade algebra and whose steers beat mine for first place three years in a row back in our 4-H days. She was in charge of appetizers. "Look who's too good to waitress this year." Her eyes twinkled as she offered Aunt Garnet and me a plate of barbecued Portuguese linguiça sausage. She and her daughter owned a bed-and-breakfast in Pismo Beach.

I popped a piece of spicy sausage in my mouth. "It's my first year off in thirty years!"

"Give her a break," said Susan, Diane's best friend and also an old 4-H buddy of mine. She now raised floppy-eared rabbits in Templeton. "Can't you see she's got company?" She spooned ranch beans on my and Aunt Garnet's divided plates.

I introduced Aunt Garnet who complimented the women on how organized everything was. Though we were in the VIP line and receiving our tri-tip steak, beans, green salad, salsa and garlic bread in minutes, even the regular line was moving along with admirable speed.

"Actually, we have more help than we need this year,"

Diane said. "There are quite a few new members in the Cattlewomen's Association, which you'd know if you ever came to a meeting."

I'd missed the last two, though I kept abreast of things because Dove never missed a meeting. "I know, I know. I promise I'll be there next month. It's this being married thing. Takes up so much of my spare time."

"I hear you," Susan said. She slipped an extra piece of garlic bread on my plate. "Enjoy."

Aunt Garnet and I looked over the round tables arranged under the white canvas tent. They were cheerfully decorated with red-checkered tablecloths and centerpieces made of old cowboy boots filled with artificial daisies and sunflowers. They were also mostly occupied.

"There're some seats," I said, pointing at a table near the back.

"Just a minute," she replied, her gaze roving over the crowd.

I inhaled impatiently, anxious to dig into my steak. Then I chastised myself. Maybe those tables were too far to walk for her. Maybe she was afraid she'd drop her plate. Maybe I should offer to take her tray . . .

"Follow me," she commanded.

Confused, I tagged behind her until I realized where she was heading. I felt a vein in my temple start to throb.

"Hello, Mrs. Piebald," Aunt Garnet said, walking right up to the table where Juliette Piebald sat with Milt. "Mr. Piebald." He chugged a beer, not even stopping to acknowledge her greeting.

"Uh, hi," Juliette said, tilting her head, her expression uncertain.

"Mrs. Wilcox," Aunt Garnet offered. "Garnet Wilcox. Benni's great-aunt. We never actually met the other day during that tragic . . ." Aunt Garnet let her voice trail off.

"Oh, oh, yes," Juliette said. "I . . . that was a .·. . not a good day for me."

Not to mention Cal, I wanted to say.

"How are you, my dear?"

"She's fine," Milt said, setting down his beer bottle. "Bad deal what happened. Juliette did a wonderful job on that exhibit. Shame people won't be able to enjoy it."

A sympathetic noise rumbled from Aunt Garnet's throat.

What in the world did my aunt have up her polyester sleeve?

She fixed her eyes on Juliette. "Any news on who killed that unfortunate young man?"

Juliette glanced at Milt, her expression a little agitated. He kept his eyes on Aunt Garnet.

"Miz Wilcox," he drawled, "all we know is what we read in the paper. Seems to me that you'd have better luck obtaining information from your own niece seeing as she's married to the police chief."

Aunt Garnet jumped in before I could answer. "It is not Chief Ortiz's jurisdiction."

Milt studied the label on his beer. "Well, we were just innocent bystanders."

"Of course you were," Aunt Garnet said, her voice as chipper as if she were talking about planting spring peas rather than a homicide. "I do hope you are able to sleep at night."

"What?" Juliette said.

"We sleep fine," Milt said. "Enjoy your steak, Miz Wilcox. We killed some of our best steers for that lunch you're holding. Excuse my crassness." He sawed at his steak, jiggling the table and splattering reddish brown juice on the checkered table cloth.

"Careful," Juliette said, gripping the edge of the table.

Aunt Garnet studied him a moment. "I grew up on a farm, Mr. Piebald. I've seen my share of killing. Come along, Benni. Let's leave the Piebalds to enjoy their lunch."

I followed my aunt, speechless for the time it took her to

choose a vacant table in the back. The minute we sat down
I blurted, "What in the heck was that about?"

She gave a serene smile. "Just priming the pump. They
might not have killed Cal, but I have a suspicion that they
know more about his death than they're saying. Or at least
one of them does. Maybe my inquiries will make the guilty
one give up the goods." She gazed over her plate of steak,
beans, salad and garlic bread. "Detecting is hard work. I'm
hungry as a farmhand."

I truly did not know what to say, so I just started eating.
Though challenging the Piebalds might not be the wisest
move, she had a point. Sometimes poking at the badger
will force it out of its hole. Then again, the badger could
also spring out baring its sharp teeth.

By the time we finished our lunch, Aunt Garnet was already getting that tautness around her eyes again. It was
only three o'clock, but the temperature had soared to over
a hundred degrees.

I crumpled my paper napkin. "Would you like to call it
a day?"

"You know, a nap does sound good. You don't mind taking me home?"

"Not at all." I picked up my plate and stacked it on top
of hers. "Gabe's down in Santa Maria until late tonight
working with their chief on this rash of stolen cars they've
been having. After I drop you off, I may go back to the museum and tackle some long overdue paperwork."

I dumped our plates in the trash bins with a quick glance
over the lunch crowd, searching for Juliette and Milt. But
they'd already left. Had Aunt Garnet's questioning rattled
them? I guess we'd find out sooner or later.

Aunt Garnet dozed on the way home, rousing only
when we bumped down the Ramsey ranch driveway. Both
Daddy's full-sized white truck and Dove's red Ford Ranger
were parked in front of the house. They'd either skipped
the fair today or had gone and come back already.

The minute we were inside the cool living room, Aunt Garnet disappeared into the guest room. "We'll rendezvous later and discuss our case," she said over her shoulder.

I wandered into the kitchen looking for Dove. Her purse was on its hook next to the door, so I knew she was home. I opened the refrigerator and studied the contents. I wasn't really hungry after our tri-tip steak lunch; it was avoidance. I knew I had to confront Dove about this situation between her and Garnet. I picked an edge of crust off a half-eaten peach pie and enjoyed the refrigerated air on my face until I couldn't put off talking to my gramma any longer.

She was inside the dim barn sorting vegetables that she'd probably picked earlier this morning.

"Hey, Gramma." My voice echoed through the rafters.

"Fetch me some of those paper sacks near the door."

I grabbed a handful and walked across the old wooden floor. "Wow, bountiful year."

She gave a disgusted grunt. "Too many zucchini, not enough friends."

"That could be a book title," I said, shaking open a bag and handing it to her. "Or a folk song. And you have plenty of friends."

"Not enough who want zucchini!"

I watched her load the paper sacks with the slightly risqué-looking vegetables. There'd be a mountain of zucchini bread over the next few months at every San Celina club and philanthropic society meeting.

"Aunt Garnet's taking a nap," I said.

No reply.

"We had a good time at the fair. We saw the Great Kansas Pig Races. She won thirty bucks. We ate at the Cattlemen's Lunch." Possibly irritated some potential killers, I mentally added. "Oh, and I showed her the quilts at the museum. Just a quick tour. We'll probably go back after the fair is over."

Dove continued loading the bags with zucchini, adding

tomatoes to the top of each one. "They could probably use these down at the food bank."

I decided to just dive in. "Dove, I think you need to have a talk with Aunt Garnet. Something is wrong and I think—"

Dove whipped around and held up her hand. Like a well-trained cattle dog, I stopped. A minute passed. Then she went back to dividing vegetables, murmuring softly to herself.

"Did you call Uncle WW again?" I persisted. "Did he tell you *anything*? Just answer me that and I'll shut up."

She turned slowly to look at me. She held a knobby heirloom tomato in one hand. The other went instinctively to her long white braid, which she habitually touched when she was in distress. Her lupine blue eyes were blank and unemotional. "He said she needs to tell me. That was their deal. He apologized, said he knew how stubborn she could be, but that it was up to her." She looked down at the tomato in her hand, let loose of her braid and flicked a piece of dirt off the mottled yellow skin. "Sister has chosen to keep her own counsel. So I'm waitin' on her. I suggest you do the same." She turned back to the bag of vegetables. "I'm leavin' for the food bank in a few moments to drop these off, then I have a historical society meeting. Reckon I'll give them your regrets tonight."

"Yes, ma'am," I said quietly. "I have some work to do at the museum, and then I need to catch up on chores at home. Is there *anything* I can do to help you?"

She rubbed her hands down the front of her calico apron, the pockets bulging with tomatoes. "I need a smog certificate for my truck."

"No problem. We'll switch trucks and I'll take it to the shop near the museum first thing in the morning to be checked. Won't take long."

"Thank you, honeybun," she said, sighing deeply. "I've got to send for the car tags but can't do it until I get that slip of paper sayin' I'm not smogging up the air."

I walked over and put my arms around her shoulders. It seemed for a moment that they trembled, but then I felt the iron return.

"Get along with you," she said, pushing me away. "We can trade back trucks tomorrow."

"I'll put my keys in your purse. I love you, Gramma."

She made an impatient noise at the back of her throat. "If you really loved me, you'd take some of these zucchini."

Armed with a bag of zucchini to pawn off on my unsuspecting neighbors, I walked out to her red Ford Ranger. When I turned the ignition, the low fuel light blinked.

"Dang," I said out loud. She'd obviously been so busy she didn't have time to buy gas. Well, this was one more thing I could do for her since I clearly wasn't any help with the Aunt Garnet problem.

Twenty minutes later I was pumping gas into her truck at the Union 76 station near the freeway when I looked across the islands and spotted Dodge Burnside doing the same thing. His back was to me so, thankfully, we didn't make eye contact. I was tired and didn't feel like enduring one of his threatening scowls. He was talking on a cell phone making dramatic gestures with his free hand. Whoever was on the other end was getting an earful.

We finished at almost the same time. I slipped on my sunglasses and a Farm Supply ball cap and waited until he pulled out of the gas station. Then, crazy as I knew it was, I decided to follow him. I'd never have attempted it in my own purple truck, but I was counting on the fact that he wouldn't recognize Dove's truck. I kept a car length between us as I followed him onto the 101 freeway north. We went over Rosita pass and I held my breath until we passed the Santa Margarita exit. At least he wasn't on his way to Maggie and Katsy's ranch. That would have made me call Hud. He kept at a steady seventy-five miles an hour until he reached the first off-ramp for the town of Atascadero. He exited without signaling, but I was far enough behind that it was no problem to follow.

Once we started driving down El Camino Real, Atascadero's main drag, I had to be more careful. It didn't appear he suspected anyone was following him, but I tried to keep a car or two between us. We drove past the county park and the old Carnegie library, an almost exact copy of the building that held San Celina's historical museum. He made a right turn into a neighborhood of older homes with huge oak trees shading the bumpy street. It was the type of neighborhood duplicated all over the United States with neat front yards filled with bicycles, scooters, rosebushes and decorative house flags.

He stopped in front of a blue and gray bungalow with a deep front porch. Again, I was fortunate that he was so intent on his destination that the small red truck driving past didn't even rate a glance. I drove to the end of the street, straining to see in my rearview mirror who came out of the house. No luck. The wooden screen door blocked the person from view. I turned right and circled the block. Did I dare drive past again? I shoved my braid underneath my cap. The disguise was lame, but it was all I had.

I turned the corner, making a note of the street name—Warner—and drove past the house again. Except for an ancient blue El Camino in the driveway and a child's tricycle on the front porch, there was nothing that distinguished this house from the others. Like many of the houses, an American flag flew from the front porch. With a pen I found clipped to the sun visor, I wrote the address on my palm. I couldn't risk driving by the house again. Posted at the street's entrance was a Neighborhood Watch sign. Some concerned citizen might call the cops if I continued cruising the neighborhood.

"That was a great big waste of time," I said out loud, driving back to the interstate. A half hour later I arrived home greeted by my hungry dog. Scout's expression was definitely baleful.

"Sorry, boy," I said, making his dinner. "It won't happen again. Well, it probably will, but you'll forgive me, right?"

In the living room, I took off my boots and socks, then phoned Hud. No answer at his home phone, so I tried his cell.

"Ford Hudson," he said, his breathing labored. Music tinkled in the background.

"You sound like you've been trying to move a mountain."

"At . . . the . . . gym. Tread . . . mill. What's up?"

I propped my feet up on the coffee table. "I followed Dodge Burnside this evening."

There was a long pause. "Why?"

"We were getting gas at the same time and, well, it seems dumb now, but I thought maybe I could find out something."

I swear I could hear him shaking his head. "You'd really like it to be this dude, wouldn't you?"

"Wouldn't you?"

"This may be hard to believe, but I honestly don't care *who* did it. I just want them caught."

I wiggled my toes, considering his words. "I don't believe that. I think you have a preference about who will go down for this crime."

His laugh filled my ear. "Go down for the crime? Ranch girl, you and your aunt are really a twosome. So you followed your *perp*. Where did it lead you?"

"Okay, nowhere. I mean, he went somewhere, but it was a perfectly nice neighborhood in Atascadero. There was a tricycle on the front porch. A normal, everyday house. I did write down the address. Do you want it?"

"Why not?" he said, giving a dramatic sigh. In the background I could hear the music more clearly now— "Can't Touch This." Maybe somebody was trying to tell me something.

"Call me if it pans out."

"Don't even think about turning in an expense report," he replied, and hung up.

"Nyah, nyah," I said to the phone just as Gabe walked into the living room.

"Who's the lucky recipient of that razor sharp wit?" Gabe asked, setting down his brief case.

I hesitated just long enough for a small frown to appear on his face.

"Benni, what's going on?"

I placed the phone in its base. "Detective Hudson. And before you go all Ricky Ricardo on me, hear me out."

He loosened his tie and took off his jacket, his expression suspicious.

"Sit." I pointed to his leather chair. "Don't say one word until I finish."

He'd been married to me long enough now to heed that command, though I could feel his urge to argue.

I told him what I'd done the last hour. "Then I gave Hud the address. He said he'd look into it."

Gabe was silent a moment. During my explanation he'd been methodically stroking Scout's head. He inhaled, then let it out slowly. "I'm not happy about this."

I shrugged. What else was new?

"Tell me this. Why do you insist on doing things that could possibly bring harm to you? Or people you love?"

"How could my following Dodge Burnside cause my family any harm?"

He raised his eyebrows. "Dove's truck?"

I shook my head. "Even if Dodge had noticed me, *which he didn't*, he wouldn't associate the truck with Dove."

"Except for her personalized license plate."

Oh. Yeah. That.

"Okay, you're right. It was stupid and thoughtless. But nothing happened. He didn't notice me and it was basically a waste of my time."

He gave a half smile and pulled his off his tie. "What progress we are making in our marriage. You actually agree with me."

I pointed a finger at him, giving him a full-on smile. "And you didn't lose your cool. Good boy. Double biscuits."

Scout's ears perked at the last word.

Gabe laughed, balled up his tie and threw it at me. It fell short and I chucked a throw pillow in his direction. He was getting ready to return it when the phone rang.

"I hate this," Hud said before I could say hello.

"Hate what?" I said.

"You being somewhat right."

"About what?"

"That address you gave me? It just so happens to be the residence of the unofficial leader of our very own little North County white supremacist group. You know, that one I told you about. Well, apparently they've recently even given themselves a name—WBU—White Boys United."

"Say that again. I just want to enjoy it for a moment."

"White Boys United?"

"No, the part about me being right."

CHAPTER 12

$\mathcal{G}$ABE AND I ARGUED OFF AND ON THE REST OF THE evening about the possible consequences of my impulsive surveillance. Well, not argue, since neither of us were actually mad. We had come a long way in our relationship.

"I'll say it one last time. I don't feel good about you being so involved," Gabe said, slipping between the bedsheets.

I folded back our summer quilt, draping it over the footboard. "And I'll repeat again that I can't help but be involved. I found Cal's body. I'm friends with Jazz, Katsy, Maggie and Levi. You're involved too. You adore Maggie."

"Yes, I do, but I also understand when something is my job and isn't." He turned on his side to look at me.

I climbed into bed, picking up the book on my bedside table. "How about I promise not to follow Dodge or anyone else suspected in this case ever again?"

He turned back over and turned off his bed lamp. "That's a start."

I leaned across the bed and kissed the snarling USMC bulldog tattoo on his upper back. "I love you, Friday."

"*Querida,* you'll drive me to the whiskey bottle, but I love you too."

The next morning while drinking my first cup of coffee, I called Katsy and Maggie. I'd thought about calling them last night to tell them about Dodge's visit to his nefarious friend, but Gabe and I agreed that it would not make them any safer by knowing that information right before they went to bed.

"They are about as hyperalert as they're going to be," he'd pointed out.

He was right, but I still worried about them.

Katsy answered the phone on the second ring, her voice sounding tired. "Morrison ranch."

"Hey, Katsy. You sound as exhausted as I feel." In the background I could hear Maggie singing to the dogs.

"Bad night?" she asked.

"Just restless."

"I hear you. Even Bess and Harry never settled down last night, kept barking at every little noise."

"Actually, I'm glad they were so vigilant." I told her about following Dodge and what Hud found out. "I was going to call you last night, but Gabe thought it might make you all more nervous and, really, I'm not sure what it proves."

Katsy make a disgusted sound through the phone. "Proves what we already knew, that Dodge Burnside is cow manure and so are his friends."

"At least it's one more piece of information Hud knows."

"Jazz left early this morning."

"What? You mean to work at the fair?"

"I mean she went back home. She didn't want to stay so far away from her friends or her dad. She said she'd be fine." Levi and Jazz lived only a short distance from the fairgrounds, in an older section of Paso Robles.

"Maybe she will. At least the police can get there fast if there is trouble. I assume that Levi and Jazz are getting extra patrols."

"I think she'd be safer out here, but like Maggie says, I don't always understand why people find it isolating out here. I guess I'm a bit of a loner, but I feel better when there aren't so many people around."

I wondered about her and Levi. He was a pretty gregarious guy, loved being around people. That was one of the things that made him such a great fair manager. But opposites were often attracted to each other and managed to thrive. Gabe and I were a perfect example. People gave odds of our marriage lasting about a thousand to one. And here we still were, still married and happy. At least most of the time.

"Anything I can do for you?" I asked.

"Just be there when we need you, girlfriend. Preferably with a loaded shotgun." We both laughed, but knew she was only half joking.

I poured myself a second cup of coffee and called my gramma.

"What?" Dove answered the phone with a bark. She was always a little grouchy during fair time when, like a freshman Cal Poly student, she never failed to over-schedule herself. Her moodiness became worse as the fair wobbled its way toward the final day.

"Dove, it's your favorite granddaughter."

"Sally? How are things up north in Cody? You comin' for a visit, sweetie pie?"

"Ha-ha. I know you're busy so I won't keep you. Just checking to see what Aunt Garnet wants to do today."

"She's staying home. Says she's tired."

"Oh." That certainly freed up my day. I should feel relieved, but I'd gotten sort of used to Aunt Garnet tagging along. "*Is* she sick?"

"She *said* tired." Dove's tone informed me there'd be no

more discussion of the subject. "You're free. Do whatever it is you do."

"Okay," I said carefully, recognizing I was on shaky ground. "Is there anything I can do for you besides take your truck in to get the smog certificate?"

"That's it, honeybun," Dove said, her voice softening.

"We'll connect today sometime and exchange trucks."

"I'll be at the fair all afternoon."

I hung up and stared out the kitchen window until Gabe walked in dressed for work.

"We're out of coffee," he said, pulling on his suit jacket. "Want me to pick up some on the way home from work?"

"We need butter too." I continued staring out the window.

"Dog food?" he asked.

"I buy that at the Farm Supply. We're okay until the weekend."

"Are you all right?" he asked, picking up his briefcase.

I looked over at him. "Do you think the Paso police have a special watch out for Levi and Jazz's house?"

"They're likely patrolling it more. Probably aren't staking it out. At this point, it doesn't seem warranted."

I nodded, knowing that it was really all anyone could do.

He came over to me, brushed a strand of wild, morning hair from my face. "Sweetheart, I know you're worried, but until something actually happens, you know the police can't do anything."

I touched his freshly shaved cheek. He looked like he hadn't slept well either. "Is everything okay at work?"

"Fine. This stolen car situation has got the mayors and city councils of every town in San Celina and Santa Barbara counties with their panties in a wad. Says that it's hurting tourism. Guess it was reported on the major news networks down in LA. Not helpful. Now we have to placate the powers that be *again*."

"Any good leads?"

He stroked my cheek. "We're working with the sheriff's department and highway patrol." His face seemed stretched with fatigue. "We've got some ideas about who's behind it, but no proof."

Gabe loved his job, but I often wondered how long it would be before it either emotionally or physically took its toll on him. "Friday, have you thought about finishing your master's thesis? Teaching has to be easier than chasing car thieves."

He took my hand and kissed the palm. "I'll need a skip loader to clear away the accumulated dust. But rumor is that academia is more stressful than police work. And a lot more treacherous."

A GARAGE THAT PERFORMED SMOG CHECKS WAS ONLY two blocks from the folk art museum. They promised me Dove's truck would be ready in a couple of hours. The first thing I did at the museum was call the store downtown to check on the supply of black cloth dolls. Their stock was down to three. My next call was to Flory Jackson.

"Greetings, Mrs. Jackson. It's Benni Ramsey Harper Ortiz."

"Good morning to you, Mrs. Chief Ortiz." She loved teasing me about being the wife of a police chief. "Whatever you got to say, better say it quick because I'm already late for a Women's Missionary Union meeting at the church and it can't start without me 'cause I got the coffee cake. Our Botswana missionaries are coming to visit us six days after the fair is over and I need three . . . no make that six . . . more hands."

"I hear you. I'd loan you mine if I weren't so attached to them."

Flory groaned loudly into the phone. "If I weren't so

busy, I'd come over there and pull your ear for using that tattered old joke."

"I'll be quick about it. Apparently we are almost completely out of black cloth dolls and people are clamoring for them. Do you have any hiding somewhere?"

"Oh, sugar, I'm sorry, but we gave you all we made. We have ten or so cut out and ready to sew, but they are nowhere near finished."

I picked up a paper clip on my desk and started bending it in crazy shapes. "What if we had an emergency marathon doll-making session? I just hate losing this opportunity for the museum and for the artists to miss out on making money."

"Benni, you know you are preaching to the converted, but I honestly don't know when I can squeeze in one more project."

"There's got to be a few hours we could find. Don't forget, every person who buys a doll receives a booklet and it tells a story that people need to hear about African American history."

My last remark was a blatant and deliberate attempt to persuade her. Oral history, especially of African American women, was Flory's soft spot. She was sixty-seven years old and had spent most of her life sewing for other people. She retired two years ago and, with the encouragement of her Ebony Quilt Guild Sisters, had applied at Cal Poly to study history. She'd not only been accepted, but she qualified for a special senior scholarship too. She started her junior year in September. We were all looking forward to her graduation party.

"Little girl," she said, chuckling. "When you want something, you are as persistent as that grandmamma of yours. You know I can't resist that challenge. Let me check my calendar."

I waited while she hummed "Bringing in the Sheaves" and checked her schedule.

"Okay, Mrs. Chief, I have a four-hour time slot open tomorrow night from five until nine. Now go use some of that manure-scented rhetoric you just spread on me on some other folks and we might get us some workers. We should be able to whip up a good plenty of those dolls. Might have to half paint, half embroider the faces, but that still makes them historically accurate. I'll call Arnell Mason. She's a real quick embroiderer. She can start on some faces tonight."

"Flory, you're the queen. Thank you. If you'll put patterns in a bag on your porch, I'll pick them up and start cutting out dresses and pants tonight."

"No need. They're in our cubby right there at the co-op."

"Perfect! I'll get on the phone and round up as many of the people as I can. Maybe Dove and Aunt Garnet can help. I'd ask Elvia, but you know she's all thumbs when it comes to needlework."

"Honey, when you're as pretty and smart as she is, all you need is thumbs. I doubt I would have got my scholarship without her telling me how to fill out all those application papers."

"Don't you worry about snacks. I'll bring them."

"And I'll let you. I'll provide drinks. See you tomorrow."

I pulled out my Rolodex—I was still old-fashioned enough to not have put all my contacts on the computer—and started calling. In an hour I'd gotten a yes from eight Ebony Sisters who were experienced at making the dolls. That was pretty good considering it was fair time when everyone was crazy busy.

When I called Dove at home and asked for her help, she gave a disappointed squawk. "Shoot, you know I'd fly to the ends of the earth for Flory Jackson. But I'm going to some fancy-pants dinner for Isaac over in Cambria."

"It's okay. There's ten of us coming now, counting me and Flory. We knew it would be a crapshoot during the fair. Do you think Aunt Garnet might be interested?"

Dove's voice went low. "It'd be good for her. She's been acting nuttier than usual today. On the phone so much I'm thinking about starting a tab. She times it so she's talking when I'm out in the yard or the garden, then hangs up when I walk in."

I cradled the receiver against my shoulder, bent another paper clip into a circle then looked through it like a monocle. "Can I talk to her?"

"Garnet Louise!" Dove yelled, practically fracturing one of my eardrums.

"Honestly, Dove, I'm right here in the same county," I heard Aunt Garnet say. "There is no need to bellow like a bull."

"Hey, Aunt Garnet. Benni here. Think you'd be up to a doll-making session tomorrow night?" I explained the situation.

"I'd love to. With all the inspiration at the fair, I've been itching to put a needle to fabric."

"Great, so that's tomorrow. Are you sure you don't want to do anything today?"

"I'm letting you off the hook today. I want to catch up on my stories." Aunt Garnet had been watching *General Hospital* and *All My Children* since they started, something she rarely admitted openly. "Oh, Dove just said to tell you she's on her way back to the fair."

"Okay, tell her I'll find her so we can trade trucks. I'll call you tomorrow morning."

It was almost 11 a.m. before I settled down to my overflowing in basket. Two hours later, I'd finished two grant requests, sent brochures to twenty chambers of commerce, filled out my monthly expense report and finished a month's accumulation of filing. Feeling proud of myself, I walked into the great room rubbing my aching neck. Deb, one of the quilters, was packing a plastic bag with paperback book covers, pillowcases, eyeglass cases and cell phone covers.

"Where's that going?" I asked.

She looked up, startled. Her harried expression was typical during fair time. "Got a call from the gals at the museum booth. The tables are looking bare." She glanced at the big black-and-white schoolhouse clock. "I have to drop these off and be back in time to pick up my girls at ballet practice in an hour."

"Give it to me. I'm heading up there."

"Thank you from the bottom of my overextended heart."

"That's a lot of folks' problem during fair time," I said, picking up the bag. "Is there an inventory sheet?"

"Yes, inside. Just hand it to whoever's working."

I called Gabe and found out that Father Mark called and wanted to have dinner with him tonight.

"No problem. I'll just hang out at the fair and catch some of the events."

It would be the first time since it opened that I could wander around on my own with no agenda or goal.

"Have a shaved ice for me," he said.

By the time I picked up Dove's truck at the garage and drove to Paso, it was almost three o'clock. At the entrance, I begged one of the maintenance guys to give me and my bulky plastic bag of craft items a ride to the booth. Tonight would be one of the fair's busiest nights. We were right in the middle of the fair's run and something was happening in practically every venue. People were still excited yet the fair didn't have that first day frenetic buzz. And no one yet had the zombie look common to the last few days. I dropped off the crafts to two very grateful workers and wandered over to the Bears Quilt Shop booth next door.

"Hey, Russ. How's business?" He wore a red and blue tie-dyed T-shirt that said: "Hold me, thrill me, make me buy fat quarters."

"Better than we thought it would be. We might even make a profit this year. Those fabrics for the Harriet Powers replica quilts are flying off the tables. You sell the book and we sell the fabric. What a team!"

"Glad it's working out. They've run out of dolls, though. We're going to have a doll-making session tomorrow night. Any of you guys free?"

"Wish we were, but we're all here until midnight."

"I thought so. Anyway, we'll do the best we can. I have quite a few people lined up."

"You'll get 'em made, Miss B. Oh, there's something I thought you should know." Russ's voice became serious.

"What is it?"

"You know that Dodge Burnside, the one who was hassling Jazz?" It didn't surprise me that our booth neighbors knew about the incident. During the time that the county fair was in session, it was akin to living in a very small town.

"Yes," I replied slowly, hoping he would tell me Dodge had confessed to murdering Cal and that he was now in custody.

"He came by last night looking for Jazz. Vivs and William saw it all."

"What happened?"

Vivs was over at the fabric measuring table. Russ gestured at him to come over. "Tell Benni what you and William saw last night."

Vivs's dark eyes were solemn. "He was mad and, frankly, a little drunk. Bonnie and Virginia were working. He didn't get a thing off them. They just gave him the runaround." He gave a wide, mischievous grin. "Said that they'd heard she'd left town, maybe even the state."

William walked up holding a bolt of coffee brown fabric printed with silver spurs. "I went over and told him that I heard she went to Missouri."

"Missouri? Why in the world . . ."

William laughed. "First state that popped in my head. Probably because my friend, Laura, just sent me some Jack Stack barbecue. Mr. Dodge stomped off cussing to beat the band."

"What time was that?"

Vivs thought for a moment. "Right before the fair closed. I'd say around eleven p.m."

Long after I'd followed Dodge to his friend's house in Atascadero.

"Thanks, you guys. I'm not sure what that was all about, but it's good to know."

"You take care, Benni," Vivs said, resting his solid hand on my shoulder. "Watch your back."

"Believe me, I will."

Though I still needed to find Dove, I wandered through the midway, savoring the familiar smells of popcorn, cotton candy and America's favorite scent—deep-fried everything. Jack and I had spent so much of our young lives enjoying these rides, playing these impossible games. In a trunk somewhere I had a baby blue teddy bear he won climbing the rope ladder. It took almost every penny he had, but he was determined to win it. In his honor, I took a chance on one of the games he especially loved, the milk can toss. I *almost* got the softball in six times. The giant stuffed pink panthers grinned at me in the same cunning way the carnie did when he took my dollar bills.

"C'mon, honey, one more time," the carnie said. He was gaunt and tanned, his eyes the spooky blue of an Australian shepherd. "You'll win yourself a kitty this time."

I gave him a skeptical smile.

"Let me give it a try," a male voice said behind me.

The carnie snatched the dollar bill extended to him before I could turn around.

Hud grinned at me. "Want a pink panther, little girl?"

I held out my arm and stepped to the side. "Good luck."

"Piece of Yankee cake." He took the three softballs, eyed the milk cans and threw one, two, three—each one landing perfectly inside the milk can.

The carnie gave him an annoyed but respectful look. "You worked the circuit?"

"Nah," Hud said. "Just lucky." He handed the man a ten-dollar bill. "Have lunch on me."

"Thanks, dude." The carnie handed me a stuffed pink panther half my size and then instantly started his patter on other customers.

"How'd you do that?" I asked, shifting the unwieldy toy from one arm to the other. Like a lot of things in life, wanting it was more appealing than actually getting it.

He grabbed the toy from me and stuck it under his arm. "It's all in the toss. The milk can's hole is only one-sixteenth of an inch bigger than the softball. You gotta throw underhanded and give it a little spin." He demonstrated with an imaginary ball. "Not so hard once you figure it out. Took me some practice, but I conquered it."

"You really need to get a life, Clouseau."

He threw his free arm around my shoulders. "You know I had a lonely childhood. Not much to do but practice at things like that."

His voice was flippant, but there was an edge to it. I did know his story. Hud had grown up on a huge ranch in Texas, the only child of a rich, abusive father who'd died a long time ago, leaving Hud a fortune in oil wells, an institutionalized schizophrenic mother and a broken psyche. My heart hurt for the sad young boy I imagined he'd been, setting up replicas of carnival games and working for hours at winning them.

I patted the cat's fuzzy pink head. "Well, Detective Hudson, I'm very impressed with your skills and I think we should donate Mr. Panther to the Sheriff's Department Lost Child booth."

"Good idea. Maisie has so many stuffed animals on her bed at my house I can barely find her in the morning."

On our way to the booth, I told him what the Bears Quilt guys said about Dodge looking for Jazz last night. It didn't seem to faze him.

"He's a jerk, Benni, but so far we don't have any tangible reason to connect him to Calvin Jones's homicide."

"His murder investigation didn't even make the front page of the *Tribune* today. I bet if it had been Juliette Piebald—or one of a city council member's family—the news and the police would still be all over it."

He turned his head away from me. "I resent that. We give all our cases equal importance."

"Yeah, right." I was married to a police chief and knew the score. It was an unspoken but well-known fact that cases were not treated equally. There was no doubt that if Cal had come from a prominent family or was a pretty girl or a young child, his homicide would have garnered more attention. The unfairness of it rankled me.

We passed by the entrance to the Bull Pen. A group of ranchers—friends of my father—lingered at the door shooting the breeze.

"Hey, Benni," one of them called. "What's up?"

"Not much," I called back. "Anyone see Dove?"

"Saw her over at the petting zoo," another rancher said.

I nodded my thanks.

"I have to go exchange keys with Dove," I told Hud. "See you later."

"Later," he replied curtly, obviously annoyed by my accusation.

"Whatever," I muttered as I passed the antique John Deere tractor display. If my words irritated him enough to work harder on Cal's case just to prove me wrong, it was worth his anger.

Dove was right in the middle of the petting zoo, encouraging the young children inside to be slow and careful while petting the lambs, goats and rabbits. The exhibit was sponsored by the San Celina Farm Bureau. Though some of the ranchers didn't like the idea of food animals being treated like pets at the fair, Dove thought it helped teach kids to respect animals, to treat them kindly and humanely. "Children, especially those not raised around farm animals, need to know that even though they might be our supper some day, it's our responsibility to treat them with dignity and compassion while they are in our care."

I walked through the sawdust to where Dove was demonstrating to two little girls how to hold pellets in the flats of their palms. When a pair of hungry little goats nibbled at their palms, the girls shrieked with delight.

"Hey, Gramma," I said, dangling her car keys with the horsehair-braided key chain. "Got your smog certification done. Your truck's parked over by the oak tree in the back of the preferred lot."

She pulled my keys out of her jeans pocket. "Thank you, honeybun. That saves me a good bit of time. Yours is toward the front."

"Yeah, I saw it. What're you doing tonight?"

She stretched, her hands massaging her lower back. "Heading home after this. Garnet wants to fix dinner tonight, so I'm letting her." She looked up at me, sucking in her finely wrinkled cheeks. A large straw sun hat shadowed her eyes. "What're you up to?"

"No specific plans. Just hanging out at the fair."

"Have you seen Isaac's pictures yet?"

"No, I haven't. That's a good idea. He's showing some new ones, right?"

She nodded. "Took 'em when we went to Yosemite last January."

"I'll check them out."

There was an awkward silence. Then she grabbed my hand and squeezed it. Though she didn't say a word, I could feel her fear as surely as if she'd written it on a chalkboard. I squeezed back, knowing that any attempt at words would only annoy her.

On the way to the fine arts building to see Isaac's photos, I decided to drop by Levi's office and see how he was doing. Today there was only the older woman and the snoozing dog at the administration office counter.

"Is Levi in?" I asked.

The woman looked up from her computer and nodded. "Back in his office." The dog yawned and flopped over on its side.

I started down the hallway when Jazz burst out of Levi's office, tears streaming down her face. She rushed past me, her head down.

"Jazz, what's wrong?"

"Nothing," she wailed without looking back.

I hesitated, then walked into Levi's office. He sat behind his desk with the phone in one hand and his walkie-talkie in the other. He nodded at me to take a seat. I watched as he deftly solved a mix-up between two groups who'd somehow scheduled the Wild West Stage at overlapping times.

After a few minutes, he hung up the phone, then turned down his walkie-talkie's volume. He leaned back in his chair and stretched his long arms above his head. "Please tell me you aren't here with a problem that needs my attention."

I held up my hands, showing front and back, like a magician. "Nothing, I swear. I just wanted to see how you are doing."

He sat forward, folding his hands in front of him. Above us, I could hear the air-conditioning cycle and switch on. A cool wash of refrigerated air snaked around the small room. He inhaled deeply. "I'm assuming you encountered my agitated daughter on your way into my office."

I nodded and didn't elaborate. If he wanted to pursue this conversation, that was okay, but if he didn't, no problem.

He rested his chin on one hand. "I'm a horrible father."

"No, you are not."

"She's mad at me."

"She's nineteen."

"No, it's more than that. She has good reason. This

morning"—he turned to stare out his small office window overlooking the fairgrounds—"I told her I was thinking about moving away from the Central Coast."

That caught me completely by surprise. "Levi, you've lived here for twenty-five, thirty years? Where would you go?"

"Thirty-one years," he said softly. "And in all that time I can count on two hands how many times my race was a problem. Maybe it was the people we hung around, but I never felt . . . threatened."

"Levi, has something else happened?"

"Our back door. Someone spray painted swastikas on it last night."

I felt my stomach churn. "Oh, Levi, I'm sorry . . ."

He shook his head. "If it was just me, they couldn't pry me away from my home. They could paint a thousand swastikas, call me every name in the book. I grew up in Alabama. I've seen this, experienced this." His eyes shined with agony. "But my little girl. Benni, I have to protect my little girl."

I waited, not certain what to say.

"I told her after the fair ended, I might resign, look for a job in a bigger city. Atlanta, maybe. Or Los Angeles. I want to go . . ." He looked away. "This might be hard for you to understand, but I want to blend in. Ever since I came to Cal Poly, married Ruth, then settled down here, I've stood out. When I was younger, I didn't mind as much. But now . . ."

I wished that he was revealing this to Gabe . . . or Jim . . . or Oneeda . . . anyone but me. What could I say to him? I was a small-town white woman who'd never come close to experiencing his feelings of alienation.

But I was sure of one thing. "Levi, you're right, I can't even begin to understand what you are going through, but I know this. This fair . . . this county . . . so *many* of us who live here, would miss you. I don't want you to leave."

In the heat of emotion, remembering the times my husband had been disrespected because of his skin color, I added, "Besides, you can't let them win. If you want to live somewhere else, that's fine. But you shouldn't let *them* decide if or when you leave. That gives these terrible people power they shouldn't have."

My voice faltered. Who was I to tell this man what he should or shouldn't do? Right at that moment, I wished that someone could beam me up and deposit me on some other planet. "Oh, Levi, I'm so sorry. That was so embarrassingly condescending of me . . . "

He held up his hand. "You're right. I swear, for a moment there I think my darling Ruth inhabited your body. It's just that when you think your child is in danger, the first thing you want to do is get her away."

"I'm sure Jazz understands that. She's just very emotional right now."

"I hope she does."

"Have you told Hud about the graffiti on your back door?"

He shook his head. "I didn't have time. There's been one crisis after another since I woke up this morning."

"You need to let him know."

He ran his hand down his face. "I'll put it on my list. Really, I promise."

I was worried it would take a backseat to other problems and started to say so when his phone rang and a second later, a voice came over the walkie-talkie. He stared at both of them like they were snakes he'd like to kill with a shovel.

I stood up. "You're busy. I'll catch you later."

He mouthed "thanks" and answered the phone. "Levi here. Can you hold a second?" He flipped on the walkie-talkie and was speaking into it when I slipped out of his office.

Would he tell Hud about the vandalism? I wasn't sure, but I knew it was something that had to be reported. Once outside, I tried Hud's cell phone and got his voice mail.

"Benni here. Call me back right away," I said.

Being married to a cop, I knew how important it was to photograph a crime scene as soon as possible. But, except for telling Hud, it wasn't my place to contact the authorities. So I decided to do what I did feel comfortable with, telling my husband. I tried his cell phone and after four rings it went to voice mail. So I tried his office, surprised when Maggie answered.

"He's not here," she said. "Didn't he tell you he was going to dinner with Father Mark?"

"Yes, he did. Maybe they're in a noisy restaurant and he can't hear his phone. What are you doing there so late?" It was past six o'clock.

"I'm just finishing up a couple of things. Want me to try and reach him? He still wears his pager."

"No hurry, I'll catch him later at home."

"Is there something I can help you with?"

Should I tell Maggie? In for a penny, I thought. "Just talked to Levi."

"What about?"

For a split second, I contemplated not telling her *everything* I'd said to Levi. I was still embarrassed by my presumption. But Maggie and I were good friends, had bonded over the joint responsibility we shared in dealing with my complicated husband. I hoped I wouldn't insult her when I told her what I said to Levi.

"I totally agree with you," she said. "I didn't know his wife, Ruth, very well—I was a kid when she died—but from what I remember Mama saying about Ruth, she would have told him the exact same thing. And I bet she wouldn't have let anyone run them out of town, especially the kind of coward who would spray paint someone's back door."

"That's pretty close to what Levi said. I know I spouted off to him without thinking and that my experience and Levi's is about as opposite as two people's could be. But I was raised that you don't let anyone bully you."

Her laugh over the phone relieved my embarrassment. "Sometimes a man, no matter *what* color his skin is, needs a woman to knock some common sense into him. I know Jazz and she obviously has her mama's stubborn streak. That's probably why she's mad. She feels like someone is trying to force her from her home, the only home she's ever known. I know how she feels. If anyone ever tried to run me off my land, they'd have a fight on their hands."

I leaned against the wall of the administration building. It felt like a heating pad turned on high. "Thanks for not making me feel like an idiot, Maggie."

"You are by no means an idiot, girl. Has Levi told anyone else about the vandalism?"

"I don't know. He said he'd put it on his list of things to do, but between you and me, I have a feeling he's going to ignore it."

"Someone needs to know about it right away."

"I agree, but Hud's phone went to voice mail. I can't get ahold of my husband. I don't feel right about telling anyone else."

"Jim's here. Want to talk to him?"

"That would be great. I know Levi might get annoyed, but if I don't tell someone in authority and something happens to him or Jazz, I'd never forgive myself. I'd like to tell Jim in person, though. I can be there in thirty minutes."

"I'll let him know you're coming."

There was no one Gabe trusted more than Jim to take charge whenever he was out of the office. He once said to me that had Jim's life been less complicated with Oneeda's MS and the town a little more progressive, Jim probably would have gotten the police chief position years ago. I wondered if he and Jim ever talked about that.

Jim's office door was open, so I called out, "Knock, knock."

He stood up behind his wide, oak desk, a twin to Gabe's. "Come on in and sit yourself down." He was dressed in his

usual tweedy jacket, dark slacks, white shirt and colorful
tie. His short, curly hair was more salt than pepper these
days, something that had occurred in the last two years.

I gave him a hug. He smelled faintly of Old Spice, the
same aftershave my dad used. "How's things, Captain
Cleary?"

"Pretty fine. Oneeda says y'all have a doll crisis on your
hands. I went home for lunch and she's been working like
a madwoman instructing our granddaughter Danisha the
proper way to cut out these tiny pants and dresses. And
those little bodies. Looks creepy if you ask me."

I laughed, thinking about all the truly creepy things he'd
seen in his years as a law enforcement officer. He'd worked
the most gang-ridden sections of East LA when he was a
younger man, which was why he spoke Spanish like he
was born in Tijuana. "I'm glad you reminded me. I have a
bunch of dresses to cut out myself tonight."

He gestured to one of his visitor's chairs. "Maggie says
you have something serious you need to discuss." He sat
back down behind his desk, his face relaxed and curious.

I sat down, took a deep breath and told him everything.
Though I'd been a little embarrassed telling Maggie, not
certain of her reaction, I didn't have those qualms with Jim.
Maybe it was his fatherly appearance or because he and
I had talked intimately many times about race issues and
my relationship with Gabe. If I was out of line, he'd gently
tell me so without making me feel stupid. He'd been an
ordained deacon at St. Stephen's Baptist Church for years
and took his spiritual position seriously. There was no
one I knew who lived the Bible more completely than Jim
Cleary. I trusted his opinion as much as Dove's.

He leaned back in his chair when I was through, his
dark brown face troubled. "The sheriff's department and
the Paso police should know about this."

"I don't want Levi to be mad at me. He said he was

going to report it, but I was afraid he wouldn't. I left a message for Hud, but he never called me back."

Jim sat forward, started drumming the square fingers of one hand on the desktop. I could hear laughter coming from the outer office where someone had brought in donuts and was complaining that the icing was smashed. "I'll call Levi first, talk to him. Don't worry, I'll take care of it."

"Thank you so much," I said, relieved. "I have a sort of personal question for you. Feel free not to answer, but have you and Oneeda ever considered leaving the Central Coast?"

They'd lived here for over twenty-five years, had raised the last three of their five children here. Oneeda and he were quilted into the fabric of this community more than anyone I knew. Still, there had to be times when they longed for a larger community of people who understood what it was like to be people of color. That had to be why they belonged to a church that was primarily black and why Oneeda helped form the Ebony Sisters Quilt group.

He scratched the side of his nose. "I think most people who are in the minority sometimes long to be where they don't stand out. But Oneeda and I love the Central Coast. We've never considered leaving for long."

"I think that's how Gabe feels. But, you know, we've never talked about it."

Was Gabe happy living here? When we got married, it was an unspoken agreement that we'd live in San Celina. He had a good job, one he loved, and I . . . well, my whole life was here. Still, had he ever thought that he might be happier somewhere else? He grew up in Kansas, but had spent most of his adult life in Southern California. I thought about how relaxed Gabe became when we visited his Uncle Tony down in Santa Ana. When he and his dad's side of the family got together, the Spanish flew around me like darting swallows. I understood a word here or there, but mostly it was like an Italian opera where I enjoyed the music and the general story line without actually understanding exactly what was going on every minute. I was used to it from weekends visiting Elvia and her family. During those visits, Gabe was transported to his childhood, to familiar days with his father in his Kansas garage, repairing cars and talking to his *tios* visiting from Mexico.

Maybe it was similar to the way I felt when I was with Emory, drinking the sweet tea that people not raised in the South found so cloying, eating boiled peanuts and Aunt Sally's pralines he had shipped in from New Orleans, arguing about which soda pop was more Southern—Coca-Cola or RC. Everyone longed for a place where people spoke their cultural language.

I stood up, hitched my backpack over my shoulder. "Thanks for taking care of this, Jim. And for not making me feel like an idiot for what I said."

Jim came around his desk, pulling me into another hug. "I have no doubt about one thing, Benni. Your heart is always in the right place."

I felt my eyes sting a little, my cheek touching the rough tweed of his jacket. "Tell Oneeda I'll see her tomorrow evening. We've got dolls to make."

"Praise the Lord there's a deacon's meeting otherwise she'd have *me* sewing doll clothes."

"And you'd do it with a smile, mister."

He gave one of his wonderful belly laughs. "You know it, Sister Ortiz."

I stopped back by Maggie's office to say good-bye and found her on the phone. I contemplated just waving, but the agitated look on her face compelled me to wait. She practically threw the phone receiver back in its holder.

"What's wrong?"

"My car needed a new water pump and they promised it would be done today. Of course, they lied. Katsy is probably working at the fair and since she refuses to get a cell phone, I have no way home."

A ride home. That was a fixable problem. I was afraid that something else had happened like the vandalism at Levi's house. "Shoot, I can take you home."

Her face relaxed, the furrows between her eyes softened. "Benni, you're a lifesaver. I know it's really out of your way, but I do appreciate it."

"I'll call Beebs and Millee and ask them to feed Scout. He's the only one in my family whose meals are actually on a schedule. They have a key to our house."

After calling the twins, Maggie and I walked out to my truck. While we drove over Rosita Pass to the Santa Margarita turnoff, I told her about my conversation with Jim. "I'm so relieved to dump it all in his lap. It's horrible having information like that and feeling responsible." I slowed down as we hit what we in San Celina County called a traffic jam—that is, being forced to go from seventy miles an hour to fifty. It usually lasted about ten minutes. When I dared to grumble about it in front of Gabe I was always rewarded with scorn.

"You wouldn't know traffic if it bit you in the tailpipe," he always said with that superior tone that Southern Californians always took when comparing traffic stories.

In a few minutes, we were back to our normal ten miles above the speed limit and soon were traveling down the two-lane highway that led to the Morrison ranch. When we drove up, Katsy was outside the house watering the bright red and orange geraniums blooming in their brick flower beds.

"I was certain she was at the fair!" Maggie said. "I guess I should have called home. I'm so sorry."

"Forget it. I didn't have anything planned for tonight. Honestly, you got me out of doing laundry. Big thrill." Katsy turned off her hose and waved.

Maggie opened her car door. "Sister, what are you doing home? I thought you were going to be at the fair."

"I traded shifts with Pat. Chores were getting behind here. I'll do double on Sunday. She's got family visiting on that day. Where's your car?"

"Still in the shop. Benni was nice enough to give me a ride home."

I came around the truck and leaned against the front fender. "Gabe's out painting the town a pale pink with Father Mark."

"Then how about staying for supper?" Katsy asked. "We have potato salad, fresh tomatoes picked only ten minutes ago and some rib eyes that are tender enough to make your gramma weep."

"You're on, Miz Katsy. Let me just leave a message for *mi esposo* so he doesn't worry about me."

In a half hour we were sitting on their back patio devouring those rib eyes. While we ate we talked about how their new heifers were doing, the mini-roundup they had planned for October and a possible trip they were taking to Alaska. It was a relief to discuss mundane subjects.

I told them about the emergency doll-making marathon at Flory's. "It's tomorrow night. Do you think you can make it?" I asked.

"I'll be there," Katsy said.

"Me too," Maggie said.

"Katsy," I said, "have you talked to Levi today?" I wasn't sure if she'd heard about the vandalism at Levi's house.

She chewed a bite of steak, her face thoughtful. "I went by his office about a half hour after you left. He told me everything."

"Jim Cleary's looking into it." It suddenly occurred to me that Hud never called me back. That bonehead. Apparently he was still annoyed at me.

"Good." Katsy took a last bite of pink beans, then stood

up. "I told Levi he needed to tell the police, but honestly, I think he's got his head in the sand. All he can think about is that dang fair." She picked up my empty plate and stacked it on top of hers.

"He does have a lot on the line," Maggie said, grabbing the bowl of salsa and our drinking glasses. "You know how opinionated people are about the fair. They'll be doubly judgmental of Levi."

"I know," Katsy said, opening the wooden screen door with her foot. "I wish that he worried half as much about our relationship as he does his job."

I chuckled, following her through the back door. "You're preaching to the choir, Sister K."

Maggie called after us, "You two make me want to remain a spinster forever."

"Spinster, my foot," I called back. "You are an independent woman. I think the word *spinster* should be struck from the English dictionary."

After a refusal for my help with the dishes, I said I'd better get home. "Gabe might actually start to miss me though I think there might be a Dodgers game on tonight so I bet he and Father Mark will watch it to the bitter end."

It was around nine o'clock when I finally left their ranch. I'd given Gabe a call from their house and I'd been right about the ball game.

"Dodgers just won and Father Mark just left," he said. "He sends his greetings. I'll make you a chocolate sundae when you get home."

"You're on, Friday. I'll be there in twenty minutes."

"You'd better not be. That road from the Morrison ranch alone *should* take you thirty minutes. Take your time. The ice cream isn't going anywhere."

When I passed the Frio Saloon, the small parking lot was jammed with pickup trucks and cars. That was unusual for a night during the fair. Most people who frequented this out-of-the-way bar would be at the fair. Maybe there was a

special musical group playing tonight or some group meeting for dinner.

Three trucks passed me on the winding road. Yep, there
had to be some kind of event at the Frio. On the radio,
Angus Andy, one of our local DJs on KCOW, was taking
requests. A deep male voice asked for "Ring of Fire," dedi-
cating it to his ex-wife. Because the two-lane highway was
abnormally busy, I didn't think twice about the vehicle behind me. Until the jolt.

"Hey!" I yelped in surprise.

In the rearview mirror a large white truck hovered inches
from my bumper. Before I could react, another bump threw
my head back against the padded headrest. My foot moved
to the brake pedal, but then a thought flashed: *Don't brake!*
I pushed down on the accelerator. The truck behind me fell
back, sped up and bumped me again.

"No!" My voice reverberated in the cab.

A curve up ahead forced me to slow down. The third
bump pushed me into the other lane. Up ahead, headlights
appeared, like twin trains approaching. I whipped the steering wheel to the right, back into my lane, sending up a frantic prayer for help. The car whizzed by, its horn blaring.

I glanced in my mirror in time to see the white truck
pull around me. It barreled past, the engine roaring so loud
it seemed to rattle my truck windows. The windows were
tinted dark, the driver indiscernible. It left me in a puff of
exhaust. I strained to see a license plate, but something
white covered it. Paper? Paint? I could only make out a
shiny flash on the bumper. A sticker of some kind? Pointy
at the bottom, like part of a star. Then it was gone.

I was tempted to pull over to catch my breath, but I knew
it would be dangerous to stop on this road where the traffic
was sporadic. The truck might come back. I forced myself
to keep driving, my hands shaking so badly I could barely
grip the steering wheel. When I reached the tiny town of
Santa Margarita, I again resisted the urge to stop despite

the open café and grocery store. It was still too far from law enforcement help. Only a few more miles over the grade and I'd be back in San Celina. Every few seconds my eyes darted to my rearview mirror. All the headlights behind me stayed at a safe distance. In twenty minutes, I pulled into my driveway. Yellow light glowed from our front window. I could see Gabe sitting in his leather chair. I turned off my engine and rested my head on the steering wheel. It felt cool and solid.

After a few seconds, I straightened. I was thankful to be home, but now I had another problem—telling Gabe what happened. He would go ballistic.

I was wrong.

"I'd tell you to stay out of this case," he said, sitting next to me on the sofa and kneading my tight shoulders with his strong hands, "but I'd be talking to myself. So, my next suggestion is keep your eyes open, don't be alone *anywhere* and call your buddy Hud and tell him what happened. We all know it's probably related to the Calvin Jones case."

I twisted around to look at him. "You're sounding amazingly calm."

He lifted one eyebrow. "Would my getting angry change anything about what you are doing?"

I gave him a half smile. "Probably not."

"There you go."

It sounds crazy, but a part of me was kind of sad. His getting angry at my getting involved in criminal cases was, well, part of our relationship. Did this mean he didn't love me as much as he once did?

"I love you as much as I always have," he said, startling me.

He laughed at my expression, cupped my face in his hands and kissed my lips. "I'm not a mind reader, but your face has about a million tells. Don't ever bet your cattle on a poker hand."

"No chance, Friday. Believe it or not, I'm actually not

doing much to provoke this person. I think it might be Aunt Garnet who caused this, though I'd never tell her that in a million years."

"Aunt Garnet?" He dropped his hands to my upper arms, rubbing them up and down as if I were chilled.

He frowned when I told him what she said to Milt and Juliette Piebald today at the Cattlemen's Lunch.

"You might want to casually ask your aunt to spend more time looking at the fair exhibits and less time antagonizing potential homicide suspects."

"Yeah, right. Maybe *you* want to tell her that."

He stood up, pulling me up with him. "Right now, I say we lock up and go to bed."

I breathed deeply, relieved to be home. "That's the best suggestion I've heard all day."

We made love that night. There was nothing wild or desperate or unusual about it. We were just two people who'd come to know each other well, both physically and, it was appearing, emotionally. The fair had stirred up so many old memories for me, memories of my childhood, my adolescence, my years married to Jack. As I felt Gabe's familiar body under my hands, his weight on me, the deep gingery scent of him surrounding me, a part of me detached and drifted back to the past, remembering another man's scent, another man's weight. Jack had been my first lover, my first *love*.

Two men in one lifetime. Two men who'd loved me. That seemed so unfair. My mind flashed to Cal. He'd grown up with such a small amount of love. Then he finally found someone who cared about him, maybe even loved him, and then he was killed. Not fair. Jack died way too young. Certainly not fair. But without Jack dying, I'd not be here in this moment. Love at the fair. Death at the fair. Fair. Unfair. All the meanings of fair sizzled through my brain, like sparks of electricity.

"Come back." Gabe's deep voice broke into my thoughts.

I opened my eyes. His blue eyes stared down at me. They seemed to glow in the semidark.

"Come back to me," he whispered. "Now. Come back to *me*."

So I did. I concentrated on his scent and feel and taste. Fair or not, all anyone really owned was each single moment.

Later, while my husband murmured in his sleep and my dog snored in his fancy monogrammed dog bed in the corner of the room, I lay wide awake thinking again how unfair it was—Gabe so relaxed, Scout snoozing away and me as full of energy as if I'd drunk a six-pack of Coke.

Who killed Calvin Jones? Trying to lull myself to sleep, I listed the suspects in my head—Milt, Juliette, Dodge, Lloyd, the skinheads in Atascadero, Justin.

Justin? Where did *that* come from? He was a cop, he wouldn't have killed Cal. Would he? I shivered under the sheets, the air-conditioning suddenly making me clammy and cold. I resisted the picture of Justin committing such an act, the antithesis of what he'd sworn to do, uphold the law, protect the innocent.

Maybe that's what he thought he'd been doing, protecting Jazz. Protecting her from a man that no one thought was good for her. Protecting her from a man with the potential to hurt her.

I pulled the thin quilt over me and fit myself around Gabe's body. It would break his heart if Justin was Cal's killer. I tried to force my mind into blankness, searching for sleep, but it would be a long time before I found it.

CHAPTER 13

"*I* WISH I WEREN'T GOING TO SACRAMENTO TODAY," Gabe said the next morning. He had a management seminar that the city had already paid for. His flight left at 8 a.m. and he wouldn't be home until tomorrow afternoon.

"I'll be fine," I said, pouring corn flakes into a ceramic bowl. "Whoever bumped my truck last night was just being annoying more than anything. If they'd really wanted to hurt me, that road from the Frio Saloon would have been the perfect place. They *could've* easily run me into a ditch." I wished now I hadn't told him. But in the past we'd fought about hiding things from each other, so the new rule in our marriage, which I was trying to faithfully follow, was complete transparency.

He scowled across the table. "Exactly."

"Exactly," I repeated. "But they didn't. Which means it was probably kids screwing around. The Frio Saloon was packed. That truck was probably just some drunk Cal Poly students acting out."

He didn't look convinced.

"I promise I'll be careful."

"I'll have extra patrols cruise by the house while I'm gone," he said, draining his coffee cup. Scout let loose a loud, squeaky yawn and thumped his tail on the linoleum floor.

"Whatever you say." Since I wouldn't be sitting inside the house all day it wouldn't protect me much, but if it made him feel better, let him do it.

"What are your plans today?" he asked, pushing back his half-finished oatmeal.

"My paperwork at the museum is caught up, thank goodness, so I'll see if Dove needs me to chauffeur Aunt Garnet around. The situation between them had better come to a head soon or someone—probably me—is going to burst a blood vessel."

Mentioning Dove and Aunt Garnet made Gabe smile. "Those two really do love each other to death."

"*To death* being the key words in that sentence."

After he left for the airport, I called the ranch.

Aunt Garnet answered. "Dove's gone to the fair already. She's a judge for the pickle-eating contest."

"Better her than me." I tried not to imagine what might be the end result of that competition. "Hope they have the fire hoses ready. How are you feeling today?"

"Much more rested. What's on our agenda?"

"Until the doll-making session tonight at Flory Jackson's, I don't have a thing planned. What do you want to do?"

"Pastor Mac came by last night and said they were having a sewing day at the church. They're making and stuffing personal hygiene bags for the homeless shelter." Personal hygiene bags were made by stitching together twelve-inch-square denim fabric with a top that closed with pull cords. We stuffed them with toothpaste, deodorant, toothbrush, dental floss, soap, washcloth, nutrition bars and bottled water. "I thought I'd do that this morning. It will give me a chance to get to know the other ladies in the church better. And maybe see what programs I'd like to . . ." She paused a moment. "I'd just like to help out is all."

I pretended to ignore her slip of the tongue. "How about I pick you up when you're through and we can have lunch?"

"They're providing lunch. Why not come at two p.m. and we can hang out until we go to Mrs. Jackson's house."

Hearing the words *hang out* come from Aunt Garnet's lips made me smile. She was getting downright hip. "Two p.m. it is."

"You have a wonderful day, niece."

"You, too, Aunt Garnet."

Since Hud never called me back, I decided to hunt him down. I guessed he'd be at the fairgrounds so the first place I tried was the administration office. Three people were working and four others lingered in the reception area. The older woman behind the counter now recognized me.

"Levi's got someone in his office and others waiting," she told me.

"Actually, I'm here to see Ford Hudson. With the sheriff's department."

She pointed with her thumb. "Go on back. No one wants to see him."

From behind Levi's door a male voice rumbled. The owner of the voice didn't sound happy. It sounded like someone was giving Levi the business. I sent peaceful vibes through the door, hoping this crisis and the others waiting were small ones.

I knocked on the half-open door to Hud's temporary office. "Hey, Clouseau! You decent?"

"Have rarely been accused of that," he answered.

He sat behind his desk with a *San Celina Tribune* spread out in front of him. It was opened to the sports page. A large mug of coffee and a white box labeled Chewy's Donuts shared the desk top.

"Fried food at the fair not good enough for you?" I commented, peering down into the box before sitting down.

He took a sip from his mug. "Got here too early this morning. Nothing was open."

"Not even the Kiwanis booth?"

He shook his head.

"That *is* early. Any reason why?"

"None I want to tell you."

"So," I said, "why did you ignore my message yesterday?"

He looked back down at the paper. "I was going to get to it."

"Quit being so pissy. You know, it really was something important. You heard about what someone did to Levi's back door?"

"Yes, Levi called me. We've checked it out. Took some photos. Not much to go on."

"I was trying to call to tell you about it."

"So, I found out eventually. That it?"

He was really starting to annoy me. "Something happened to me last night. Gabe is convinced it has to do with Cal's murder."

"So, talk."

I told him about the white truck bumping me and just in the spirit of full disclosure, what Aunt Garnet said to the Piebalds at the Cattlemen's Lunch yesterday.

"She's a nervy one," he said, his voice admiring. "Between her and Dove you didn't stand a chance at being shy and retiring."

"I don't really think the Piebalds killed Cal, do you? Though, heaven knows, seeing Milt Piebald in an orange jumpsuit would give more than one person in this town some satisfaction. And now that we're on the subject, just exactly who do you suspect?" I looked through the box of doughnuts and chose one that looked like a jelly. I took a bite. Jackpot. The raspberry filling was almost as good as Dove's homemade jam.

"Thanks for the information, now run along and have a good time at the fair. I hear the husband-calling contest is looking for participants. Use that screechy voice of yours for good, not evil."

"You are a cad."

"I've been called worse."

I took another bite, then put my partially-eaten doughnut down right on top of his newspaper. Raspberry jam leaked down onto the face of a goofy-looking baseball player.

"Hey!" Hud said.

"I deserve to know what's going on since my life was in danger. Kind of."

He picked up my donut with a napkin and tossed it in the trash. "I've been given strict orders to keep you out of this. In fact, I was told by someone in very high authority to subtly, artfully, and very cleverly discourage you from being involved."

"Who told you that? Your boss? How does she even know . . . ?"

He grinned at me.

I realized then who he meant. "*Gabe* called you?"

He held out his hands. "Sorry, my little crab apple. I wanted to keep his identity from you, but shoot, I figure *our* relationship has always been based on complete truth. Not like, apparently, your marriage."

I narrowed my eyes. "That's not funny."

He looked down at his jam-stained paper. "Seriously, he's probably right this time, Benni. I hate admitting this, but we don't have a clue about who killed Calvin Jones. You or your aunt stirring up the waters might help us, but Gabe's right, it could be putting both of you in danger."

I bit my bottom lip, tasting the sweet remnants of the raspberry jam. "I don't want Aunt Garnet to get hurt."

He folded up the paper and pushed it aside. "Let's go for a walk. I want you to tell me every detail you remember about the incident last night. Who knows, maybe we'll get lucky. Even if it turns out to be just college kids, they need to be talked to about using trucks as lethal weapons."

I followed him down the hallway. Levi's office door was still closed, but no voices could be heard. Outside, the bright sun instantly caused me to squint. I kept forgetting my hat in my truck.

"Here," Hud said, pulling his sheriff's department cap off and putting on my head. "Don't want to wreck that pretty redhead's complexion." He smiled down at me. "Tell me what you remember."

As we walked through the crowd I mentally tried to relive the few terrifying moments. My description of the truck wasn't especially helpful. "It was white. Like about a million ranchers' trucks in this county. The back license plate was blocked out, with something white."

"Paint? Paper?"

"I don't know. It happened so fast. You know how that is. I remember thinking that I needed to remember everything. But it's crazy. *That's* what I remember, wanting to remember." I was frustrated with myself. I should have been better at this, yet I couldn't give enough of a description to eliminate anyone who owned a white full-size pickup truck.

We walked past a row of Footsie Wootsies, those twenty-five-cent foot massaging machines that I hadn't been able to resist since I was five years old.

"Got a quarter?" I asked Hud, sitting down on one painted with a black-and-white cow pattern.

"You are as bad as Maisie," he said, rummaging through his pocket. He put one in mine, then sat in the pink one next to me.

My machine started vibrating. "You can't just sit there. It's against the rules. You have to pay or step off the Footsie Wootsie." The last few words came out sounding like I was a cartoon robot.

He put a quarter in his. "What else do you remember?"

I closed my eyes and concentrated. My feet buzzed, sending vibrations through my body. Around me, the sounds of the fair seemed to meld into one loud hum. Then it stopped. I opened my eyes to find Hud staring at me, his machine still going, his expression patient.

"There was a sticker," I said. "On the bumper. An odd-shaped one. Pointy at the bottom, like a star. When the truck pulled around me, it sparkled in my headlights."

"Sparkling pointy starlike sticker. Great work, Trixie Belden." He stood up, his machine still running, wasting a perfectly good foot massage. "Now, run along and enjoy the fair. You could *try* to stay out of trouble."

The ground underneath my feet seemed to still be buzzing. "*You* could try to sound a little less condescending." I took off his hat and tossed it at him like a Frisbee.

He slipped it back on his head, his laughter following me as I walked away. My thoughts turned to ways I could get back at him. Maybe his daughter would receive a nice anonymous present—a cute little bunny, a cute little *pregnant* bunny. At the entrance to the Bull Pen, I nixed the bunny plan. I liked his ex-wife, Laura Lee. I'd never do that to her.

Before punching the code to enter the hospitality suite, I pulled out my cell phone, moving from ways I could torture Hud to a verbal smack down with my own husband. Of course my call went directly to voice mail. Either he was out of range or he'd turned his phone off. I left a terse message.

"You are in *mucho grande* trouble, Chief. Be forewarned." I pressed the end button.

Upstairs the hospitality suite was busy. After the usual bantering with people I knew, I went over to the bar, bought a Coke and wandered out on the balcony to see what was happening in the arena.

It was my good luck to catch the barrel racers practice. When I was a teenager I'd competed a few years at local high school rodeos, where I'd learned just enough to appreciate that the sport was much more difficult than people realized.

There were four girls in the arena waiting their turn at taking their horses through the clover-leaf pattern around the fifty-five-gallon steel barrels. I could see Maggie across the arena talking to one of the girls, giving her some pointers. Maggie had competed in college rodeo and had been good enough to go pro if she'd wanted. But she always claimed she was too much of a homebody to live on the road like so many rodeo athletes did. "I'd miss my garden," she'd said. "And my cows."

A lanky young man walked up next to her, took off his red cap and slipped it on her head. She turned and smiled up at him, smacking him lightly in the chest. From here, I could see it was my stepson, Sam. I laughed to myself. Leave it to Sam to be wherever there were cute girls congregated.

I watched the girls practice their runs, my mind relaxed for the first time in days. I didn't even hear someone come up beside me.

"That Katie Seaver is probably going to win," Milt Piebald said, leaning on the rail next to me.

I glanced over, trying not to look surprised, irritated or any of the negative emotions flowing through me right then.

"She's good," I agreed, looking back at the arena. The last thing I wanted to do was engage in conversation with Milt.

"So, what's the chief up to today?" he asked.

I continued watching the barrel racers practice. "Working."

"If you call it that." He laughed and bumped my shoulder with his. "I heard he's going to be out of town."

I moved over a foot. "Where'd you hear that?"

He grinned and sucked on a toothpick hanging from his lips. "I get around."

"I need to pick up my aunt," I said, turning to go back inside.

"That the same aunt who was so snippy to me and Juliette yesterday?" he asked, his voice light, but mocking. "You might need to reel Miss Marple in a little or she could irritate the wrong people someday."

A flame lit in my chest and I turned slowly around. It was one thing to try to scare me. I could walk away from that. But you start messing with my family and I'm going to start shooting. "She's elderly and isn't always diplomatic with her words. But I'm warning you. Stay away from her."

He gave me an unhurried grin and pushed back the rim of his gray cowboy hat so I could see the full expanse of his wide, tanned face. His blue eyes flashed bright against his skin. "What in John Wayne are you talking about? Juliette and I were tickled to death by your aunt. She gave us a good old laugh. I've got a couple of loony aunts myself who feel like they need to tell everyone how to run their lives. That's all I was trying to say."

He ran his tongue over the top of his shiny teeth, then smacked his lips. "You seem a tad jumpy. Tell your gramma I'll make her a good trade for that little red truck of hers whenever she wants."

I tried to keep my face calm when I went back into the air-conditioned suite. His laughter followed me until the glass door closed. In less than five minutes, he'd managed to threaten me, my aunt and my gramma, letting me know that he knew exactly what was going on. Now I was convinced that he had to know something about Cal's death.

I wove my way through the crowd and down the stairs. I pushed open the door and practically head-butted Justin Piebald.

"Hey," he said, grabbing my shoulders. "You okay?"

I stopped, blinked my eyes rapidly, trying to hide my angry tears. "Yeah, fine. Just allergies. Dust, you know. Crazy. All the animals. Alfalfa and . . . you know, allergies." I realized I was babbling, so I clamped my mouth shut.

"Uh, yeah," he said, his expression confused. "Right. What . . . well . . . you know it's . . ." He stuttered like a teenage boy.

I stared at him, wondering what he thought about his father. Now that he was a cop, did it embarrass him to have a father who it was rumored was slightly crooked? What would it do to Justin if his father actually was involved with Cal's homicide?

"Have you seen Jazz?" I said, without exactly knowing why.

Just the mention of her name caused his cheeks to turn pink. "Not today. Why?"

"Just wondering if she's doing okay." I inspected the toes of my boots. This exchange was awkward and I wasn't sure how to maneuver out of it.

"Sure you're okay?" he repeated.

"Yes, I'm fine. Thank you." I went around him and melted into the crowd. When I got about fifty feet away, I turned around. He was still standing in the Bull Pen's entryway, watching me. The suspicious thoughts I'd had last night came back to me.

Stop it, I told myself. There is absolutely no reason for you to mistrust Justin. Even if Milt was involved with Cal's death, there's no reason to believe Justin was. Except what if he knew something and was torn between his sworn duty as a police officer and his emotional duty as a son? Which would win out? I didn't know Justin well enough to guess. But I knew somebody who might.

Sam was still in the arena shooting the breeze with the barrel-racing girls. From the bleachers he yelled comments that were a combination of encouragement and harassment. The girls called back with good-natured hoots.

"Hey, Sam," I said, sliding in next to him. "I have a question about a friend of yours."

His darkly tanned face was half shaded by the rim of his red cap. "Whatever they did, I swear I wasn't involved."

"As far as I know, none of your friends have done anything. I just want to know what you think about Justin Piebald."

He turned his head back to the arena to watch a pretty dark-haired young woman run the barrels. "He's cool . . . for a cop. Why?"

"I know this is awkward, what with him being your friend and also working for your dad, but his dad . . ."

"His dad's a dickhead."

"I agree. But what I was wondering was . . ."

"If Justin is like his dad? About as much as I'm like *my* dad. Does that answer your question?"

"Sort of. It's just that . . . okay, what if . . . what if there was something about his dad he knew, something his dad had done that wasn't legal . . ." Up here in the bleachers, the midday sun felt like scalding water on the back of my neck. I undid my ponytail, feeling instant relief when my damp hair covered my neck.

Sam's face remained neutral, but his chocolate eyes were troubled. "I don't want to be between my friend and you and dad."

I chewed the inside of my cheek. "I have a bad feeling about his dad and I'm afraid that maybe Justin might know something." Around us the cacophony sounds of the fair seemed to ebb and flow like a stormy ocean.

"Look, I know that some weird ass stuff is going down between Justin and his dad. I don't know if it has anything to do with Cal. I don't think so. I *hope* not. But Justin's my friend."

"If you knew . . ."

He looked me directly in the eyes. "If I knew for sure that Justin or his dad had anything to do with Cal's death, you know I'd tell you. Dad might think I have completely whacked out morals, but I don't."

I touched his forearm. It was hot and slightly damp. "Sam, I'm sorry. I didn't mean to imply anything like that. And I'm sure Gabe doesn't think you have whacked out morals. It's just I know what it's like to feel like you need to protect a friend."

"If Justin helped cover up his dad murdering Cal, then he isn't my friend." He shifted on the bench, the wood creaking under his weight. "You know, Cal was my friend too."

"One last question?"

"Sure."

"Do you think the relationship between Jazz and Cal was serious? I mean, like marriage serious?"

He shook his head without hesitation. "Doubt it. Jazz told me she liked him, but she was also kind of confused about how she felt. She felt sorry for him too and that's never cool. If a guy figures something like that out it would make him feel totally lame. Second rate."

"You think Cal knew she felt sorry for him?" It seemed this young man didn't catch any breaks in his short life.

Sam considered my words. "He was so into her that I doubt he noticed. He was just glad she was hanging with him. And even if he did find out, he probably wouldn't have been surprised or maybe even cared. Cal didn't expect much in life."

"That's sad."

Sam shrugged one shoulder. "Yeah, it's messed up. But,

you know, Cal was one of the most righteous guys I ever met. When he believed something, he was totally into it. He was all about doing what was right and treating people with respect. And that dude wasn't afraid of anything. I always got the feeling that was because he felt like he had nothing to lose, you know?"

I leaned down and gave him a hug. "Thanks, Sam. Every time I hear a little more about Cal I think that I would have liked him."

"You would have. He thought you were pretty cool."

"Me?" Why was I even on this young man's radar?

"He got onto me once when I was ragging on you. He said that I should cut you some slack because the person who had to change the most when you and dad got married was you, that you had to figure out how to be a second wife, a cop's wife *and* a stepmom."

"That was very perceptive of him." I tapped the rim of his ball cap. "You were ragging on me? I've always been an excellent stepmother."

"It was when I wanted to buy my truck, remember?"

"Yes, and I was smart not to take sides." Sam had wanted Gabe to loan him the down payment and Gabe wanted him to earn the money himself. Despite being tempted when Sam begged me to intervene, I'd stayed out of it. They'd compromised. What Sam saved for a down payment, Gabe matched and they both felt satisfied. And neither was angry at me.

"Thanks for your insight," I said. "I just hope that the sheriff's department solves this soon. Cal deserves justice."

"For sure."

I was walking past the Australian Battered Potatoes stand when I heard my name called. One of the members of the San Celina Quilt Guild hurried toward me, holding an ice-cream cone the size of a baseball mitt.

"Wow, for me? Thanks!" I said, holding out my hand.

"You wish. This is my lunch and dinner. I've taken a

double shift at the fair booth so Retha can help make dolls tonight. I'm glad I caught you. Maria embroidered some doll faces."

"Thanks for taking a double shift. Like you probably heard, the dolls are selling incredibly well. Are the doll faces at the booth?"

"No, she's finishing them up over at the Family Campground. Said you could come on by anytime. If she's not there, ask Bobby Joe where they are. Nothing gets past him."

I laughed. "Some things never change. I'll head over right now."

The Family Campground was in back of the midway. The noisy, dusty campground was an adult's nightmare and a kid's dream. Many of the kids competing lived in the Central Valley or Shandon or San Miguel. Commuting every day could be a real pain so many 4-H and FFA leaders brought their RVs, tent trailers, campers, canvas tents and plain old canopies and during the fair, the vacant lot behind the midway became "Kidville."

Kidville's unofficial mayor was Bobby Joe Gomez, an ex–bull rider and San Celina High School football star most notorious for being voted prom king three years in a row. That was a good fifteen years before my time in high school, but his reputation was school legend. Bobby Joe was not only as handsome as a movie star with his thick, wavy mahogany hair and rugged jawline; he was as easy-going and good-natured as a department store Santa.

For the last thirty or so years, Bobby Joe had held the position of Kidville's snack and soft drink guard, squabble mediator, Band-Aid dispenser, soother of broken hearts and king of the oak wood barbecue. From his perch on his electric wheelchair, he ruled his temporary kingdom with a Solomon-like benevolence. An unfortunate ride on a bull in Reno named Whiskey Pete ended his rodeo career and permanently injured his spine, but started a whole new career that probably ended up paying him much better than rodeo every would. His insurance agency carried the personal, ranch and car insurance for almost all the ag people in San Celina County.

I'd stayed overnight at the campground myself a few times when I was a kid. Walking into the crowded maze of tents and sleeping bags brought back some wonderful memories of late nights in Kidville eating Frito pie, s'mores and singing chorus after chorus of "Row, Row, Row Your Boat" or "Ninety-nine Bottles of Beer on the Wall."

Maria was nowhere to be seen, but Bobby Joe was inside his fancy RV enjoying a blue and red tinted shaved ice and watching *General Hospital* on a tiny television. He wore a colorful Hawaiian shirt and a dark blue ball cap that said Don't Even Think About It. It was his favorite admonition to any kid who came up to him with a questioning look on his or her face.

"Caught you," I said, climbing up the ramp.

"Nothing to catch," he said, licking a bit of red ice from his bottom lip. "My addiction to *General Hospital* is a known fact. It's my only vice."

"No comment," I heard his wife, Janet, say.

I glanced down the short hallway. She was lying on the king-sized bed with an ice pack on her head.

"What happened?" I said.

"Sinus headache," Bobby Joe said.

"Man, I'm sorry."

"It's the dust. She took some decongestant. What can I do for you?" he asked, putting the soap opera tape on hold.

"I think you have some doll faces Maria embroidered?"

"In the top drawer under the stove."

I found them and stuffed them in my backpack.

"Get yourself a Coke while you're up," he said.

"That sounds great." I pulled a bottled Coke from the refrigerator.

"So, how's the fair going for you?"

I sat down on the captain's chair across from him. "I suppose you heard about Calvin Jones."

"What is it with you and homicides? Trying to keep your husband in a job?"

I grimaced. "Not hardly."

"Sorry, bad joke. Did you know the young man? The paper didn't say much and everyone in fair management's been pretty tight-lipped."

"That's understandable. It's not exactly the family-friendly image the fair is looking to promote." I took a long drink of my soda. "I didn't actually know Calvin Jones, but he sounds like he was a nice young man."

"That's too bad. I imagine this has been rough for Levi too. There are those in this county who'd pay extra admission just to see things go wrong on his watch." He set his cup of shaved ice down on the table next to him.

"Like who?" I said, my ears almost twitching. Metaphorically speaking, Bobby Joe Gomez knew where a good many bodies were buried in our county.

He gave me one of his famous James Dean, bad-boy grins. "Now, I don't like to talk out of school . . ."

"Don't let him kid you, Benni," Janet called from the bedroom. "He's a bigger gossip than the *National Enquirer*."

He feigned shock. "Whatever is she talking about?" He crooked his finger at me. I leaned closer.

"Milt Piebald's got political ambitions," he said in a low voice. "Mayor of Paso and then, some say, he has eyes on being a senator or governor."

That was his big piece of gossip? I leaned back, a little disappointed. Milt Piebald wouldn't be the first slightly off-plumb businessperson who had political aspirations. "So?"

"Finding a body in his Family Farm exhibit isn't exactly the type of free publicity that he was angling for."

Now I was really disappointed because what Bobby Joe

suggested meant that someone else was behind Cal's murder, someone who had it in for Milt Piebald. "Any idea who might have it in for Milt?"

"Maybe only every other person who bought a car from him."

"That's no help."

"Sorry, it's all I got, Inspector Ortiz."

I stood up, drained my bottle and set it down on the counter. "Thanks, Bobby Joe. You've given me some food for thought."

"Wish I could tell you more. Hey, on your way out could you take my granddaughter's gym bag and throw it with the others?" He pointed to a pink and white Hello Kitty canvas bag.

"Sure." I reached down and picked it up, groaning at its weight. "Geeze, Louise, what does she have in here, rocks?"

"It's her dance clothes, believe it or not. They're going to be performing tonight at seven p.m."

"Where do you want it?" I asked, heaving it over my shoulder.

"Outside by the red cooler, next to the others. Thanks."

I walked down the ramp and carried the bulky bag over to the cooler, setting it next to the other girly bags. Just as I was walking away sunlight through a space in the canopies caused something to flash, catching my eye. I bent down to look at the jumble of colorful duffels and backpacks. A sparkly heart-shaped sticker decorated one light blue bag. I covered the top half of it with my hand. The bottom was pointy, like a star. It might have been the sticker I'd seen on the white pickup truck who'd played bumper cars with me.

I glanced over the rest of bags. Four others had similar stickers. In black Old English lettering they said Road to Queen. I picked up the blue bag and went back up the ramp. Bobby Joe was back to watching his soap opera.

"Quick question," I said, holding out the bag. "Do you know what this sticker is for?"

He glanced up. "It's the beauty queen classes that Juliette Piebald teaches over at the Paso Robles community center. My little granddaughter has a ball at them. The kids just adore Juliette."

CHAPTER 14

I WALKED THROUGH THE FAIRGROUNDS CONTEMPLAT-
ing this new piece of information. Did Juliette Piebald
have a white truck? Could she be the person who tried
to run me off the road the other night? For what possible
reason? She'd been a tentative suspect because of Aunt
Garnet's suggestion about her and Dodge Burnside, but I
honestly couldn't imagine her smashing Calvin Jones over
the head, rolling his body in the Harriet Powers quilt and
then planting it in her own exhibit.

Though what Bobby Joe said about Milt's political aspirations might give her motivation. If he ran for office,
an affair might be discovered by some newspaper reporter
looking for a juicy story. But would Juliette actually *kill*
someone to conceal a love affair? She might not alone, but
if the affair was with Dodge Burnside, maybe she talked
him into helping her. Maybe his dad helped them both.
Maybe she and Lloyd Burnside were having an affair. Possibilities caused my brain to buzz like one of those Footsie

Wootsie machines. How would Cal have found out about this alleged affair and why would he care? It didn't make any sense.

Once I reached the parking lot, I couldn't resist taking a quick stroll through the vehicles looking for the sparkly sticker advertising Juliette Piebald's rodeo queen classes. Since I needed to pick up Aunt Garnet at 2 p.m., I only had time for the rows of cars and trucks in preferred parking. That seemed easy enough. Though looking for a white full-size pickup eliminated many vehicles, I had a lot of bumpers to check. White pickups in a California ranching community were the color of choice mostly for the safety factor (easier to see in the gold and green hills and, especially, at intersections), but also because they were often fleet vehicles and cheaper.

After fifteen minutes in hundred-degree heat, I gave up. There were just too many white full-size pickups. Disappointed, I drove back to San Celina.

At First Baptist, I found Aunt Garnet sitting in the front row of the sanctuary. Her head was bent and it appeared she was praying so I decided to go to the church office and shoot the breeze with Pastor Mac.

His assistant, Trudy, was chewing a wad of gum whose cinnamon flavor was apparent when I walked through the doorway. "He's at the fair," she said.

"I'm actually here for my aunt Garnet, but she's in the sanctuary. If she comes looking for me, I'll be waiting for her on the bench outside."

"She said she needed time alone with Jesus," Trudy said. "I told her to just take as much time as she wants. She was a real big help with the hygiene bags. I think she might become a regular."

I almost asked Trudy what she meant by that because it sounded like she had more information about Aunt Garnet's intentions than any of us. But, bless her heart, Trudy was a bit of a gabber and I didn't want it to get around church that Dove and I had no idea what was going on with Aunt Garnet.

Ten minutes later my aunt caught me sitting on the bench in the church's garden gazebo chewing on a hangnail.

"Sorry," I said, my hand dropping like I'd been caught stealing a Milky Way bar. But my bright pink cuticle announced my sin. All my life Aunt Garnet had nagged me about using cuticle cream. I braced myself for her lecture.

She just smiled. "I hope you haven't been waiting long."

"Uh, no," I said, standing up. "Everything . . . okay?"

"A couple of the men cooked us ladies a real nice brunch," she said as we walked toward my truck. "Ham and cheese quiche, tiny cinnamon rolls and fresh papaya and pineapple. And the strawberries! They were picked this morning. Delicious."

I opened the passenger door, surprised yet again by her unpredictable new persona. "We do have wonderfully fresh fruit here in California." Once we were settled inside the truck, I decided to go for it.

"Aunt Garnet, I have a question."

"What is it?" Her face was placid and friendly. Her Jean Naté cologne smelled like lemon icebox pie.

"Uh . . . you know, I've noticed that . . . I was wondering . . . Is everything . . ."

Oh, for cryin' out loud, I told myself, just say it. "What's going on with you? Are you sick? Are you and Uncle WW breaking up?"

Her expression registered a moment of surprise, then went neutral again. "Why, Benni, I'm just fine. And William Wiley and I are most certainly not, as you put it, breaking up." She folded her hands neatly in her lap and stared straight ahead. "I do believe I'll try one of those churros at the fair today. They looked delicious."

And that was that. I pitied any attorney who ever had to cross-examine Garnet Louise Wilcox on the witness stand.

I got right back on Interstate 101 and headed up to Paso Robles. We talked about what we'd do the two hours until we were due at Flory Jackson's house.

"There's the Mission Beach Cloggers at three p.m. or we could watch the pig races again or go look at the photography and art displays. There's also a local wildflower exhibit I thought you might like." Aunt Garnet loved her wildflowers.

Aunt Garnet didn't react to any of my suggestions. "What's going on with our case?"

I pretended to concentrate on the road. "You know how the police are. Hud keeps me in the dark. So like Gabe. Two of a kind. That's cops for you. Honestly, it drives me nuts." Why did I always prattle on and on like a teenager at their first driving test every time I wanted to appear cool and nonchalant?

"Can the chatter," Aunt Garnet said.

"Huh?"

I swear on a stack of poker chips she giggled.

"I know you've found out something. Give up the goods."

"Give up the goods? Who are you and what have you done with Aunt Garnet?"

"She's right here," she said, her voice soft. "Battle fatigued, but here."

It was the perfect opportunity for me to pump her again for information about her visit. But she blocked my play. "Give an old broad a break. What's the scoop on Mr. Jones's homicide?"

I couldn't disappoint her despite Hud and Gabe's warnings. This ersatz criminal investigation seemed to be the only thing that made her forget her problems, whatever they were. So I clued her in on everything that had happened since I left the Morrison ranch last night.

She settled back in her seat, satisfied. We passed the off-ramp to the Templeton Stock Auction. Only a few more miles to Paso. It was silent on her side of the cab and I hoped that my information had satisfied her curiosity.

I should have known better.

"Didn't you say that Milt Piebald owns a car lot?" Her thin, white eyebrows moved inward. She twisted the hankie she held in a knot.

"Actually he owns five."

"What's the closest one to us right now?"

"The one in Paso Robles. It's not far from the fairgrounds."

"Does Juliette work for the business?"

"Maybe. I honestly don't know that much about their personal life."

"So, I was thinking . . ."

I felt like swinging my arms helplessly like the robot on *Lost in Space*—Danger, Will Robinson!

"Let's see if we can find her truck. We obviously can't go to all of the lots . . . today. But we could hit the Paso Robles one before we go sew the dolls." She tilted her head and smiled at me, pleased with her plan.

"Uh . . ."

"I could pretend I was in the market for a car while you snoop around."

Aunt Garnet had definitely been watching way too many *Matlock* reruns.

"You know," I said, looking down at my watch. "The time . . ."

"Nonsense," she said, resurrecting her familiar prim voice. "We have plenty of time. What's wrong, are you chicken?"

I turned my head to gape at her. Was I being double-dog-dared by a seventy-five-year-old woman?

"It'll take us a half hour at the longest," she said. "Who knows, we might get lucky."

"Okay," I finally said, not knowing what else to do. I mean, really, what could happen? It was broad daylight in the middle of Paso Robles.

I drove north on Main Street to Piebald's Awesome Autos. The oversized fiberglass pinto horse and the gargantuan American flag were visible from two blocks away.

"There it is!" Aunt Garnet said. She leaned forward, her soft peach face animated; her gnarled hands gripped her pocketbook. "Albenia, I have a good feeling about this."

That made one of us.

I pulled into the newly paved parking lot. My truck was the only one there. So much for blending into the crowd. The sales office was a flat-roofed pink stucco building painted with a garish brown and white pinto pony spots.

It could win the tackiest building in America award. Frankly, I was surprised that Juliette hadn't nagged Milt into tearing it down and building more modern offices. The warehouse behind the car lot was a huge metal building that, thankfully, hadn't been painted to match the office. It was a nondescript dark green.

I turned off the motor. Before we could step out of the truck, a salesman was coming out of the office and ambling toward us.

"Here's our cover," Aunt Garnet whispered. "I'm moving to San Celina from Arkansas and need a reliable vehicle. While I keep the salesman busy trying to sell me one of these lemons, you wander around the lot to see if you can find that sticker. Got it?" Her blue eyes looked downright beady. Honestly, I was getting a little scared—not of anything at the car lot but of my demented aunt.

"Got it," I said weakly.

"Hello, beautiful ladies," the salesman said. He was tall with sharp angles—nose, elbows, chin. His short-sleeved cowboy shirt—bright red with white piping—hung on his thin frame. His jeans looked ready to slip off his nonex-

istent hips and puddle on the ground around his cowboy
boots. The man looked like a two-by-four come to life.
"What can I do you for today?"

Aunt Garnet looked over at me, raised one white eyebrow as if to say, Remember your lines, and replied,
"Young man, I am obviously looking for a car. This is a car
lot, isn't it? That is, unless this place is actually a front for
something else."

He widened his eyes, then gave a hawing laugh that
ended in a wet-sounding cough. Too many unfiltered cigarettes, something that we could smell when he got within a
few feet of us. Aunt Garnet's nose twitched.

He moved into his spiel. "You and me's going to get
along just fine, young lady." He winked at Aunt Garnet,
then turned to me. "And is this your sister?"

"My niece," Aunt Garnet said stiffly. "I do not have time
to waste. I want something economical, easy to drive and that
hasn't been in an accident." She narrowed one eye at him. "I
worked in a body and fender shop in Arkansas, so don't think
about trying to pull one over on me." That was a blatant lie.
Aunt Garnet had never held a paying job in her life.

The man held up his hands. "Wouldn't think of it,
Mrs. . . ."

"Miss Honeycutt," she said. Okay, she was using her
maiden name. Her idea of a disguise. I felt like I was in the
middle of an episode of *Murder, She Wrote.* "This is my
niece . . . Rita."

Rita? I knew she was thinking on the fly, but did she
have to choose my tacky younger cousin's name? Well,
Rita was Aunt Garnet's real granddaughter, so it made
some kind of sense. Okay, I'd be Rita for the next half hour.
This, I kept telling myself, was going to be a really funny
story someday.

She pointedly looked over the salesman's shoulder.
"Is Mr. Piebald here? I really prefer to deal with upper
management."

I almost choked on my spit. What if he was? What in the heck did she plan on saying to him?

The man's face looked slightly panicked. "No, ma'am, he's not here today. He's over to the fair. We got some cars showing there this year."

"That's fine," she said curtly. "I'm sure you can tell me everything I need to know. Rita will be looking around while you show me cars. I hope that's acceptable." She turned to me. "Rita, dear, you know what I'm looking for."

"No problem," he said eagerly, certain he had the sale in the bag. "Just stay a ways back from them repair bays in back, Miss Rita. We do our own body work and detailing. It can get a little dirty sometimes."

"Rita's a smart girl," Aunt Garnet said. "She can take care of herself." Then she boldly walked over to the man and slipped her arm through his. "What did you say your name was?"

"Raymond," he replied, his smile growing as wide as a Boston terrier's.

"Raymond, I believe you and I can do some business today." Aunt Garnet was really piling on the Southern lady bull pucky.

"Yes, ma'am, I believe we can," he replied, thrusting his skinny neck forward. If he'd been a cartoon character there would have been dollar signs in his eyes.

So, off they strolled down the aisles of cars and trucks, Aunt Garnet's voice throwing out phrases like "rack and pinion steering" and "disc brakes." I heard her ask if one of the vehicles had "off-road capabilities." That gave me a crazy mental picture of my great-aunt bumping over a sand dune on Pismo Beach.

I wandered the aisles of used cars, checking the bumpers of any white Ford and Chevy trucks. I was just killing time while Aunt Garnet played detective. The chances of the particular truck that tried to run me off the road being here were pretty slim. On the other hand, this was making

Aunt Garnet happy, not hurting anyone, and it would give us something to laugh about later. The lot was empty of other customers, not surprising since it was midday and midweek.

When I reached the back of the lot, I was far enough away from Aunt Garnet and the salesman to see but not hear them. I gazed idly over the cars and trucks, then thought of something—the employee parking lot. That's where Juliette or Milt's truck would be if it was anywhere. Chances were the employees parked in the back so I headed toward the large metal building. It was a long shot because this truck—if it existed—could just as well be at their ranch. And there was no way I was driving Aunt Garnet out there. No excuse in the world would explain our presence at the Piebald ranch. When I walked closer to the warehouse, I heard male voices, probably the guys detailing or repairing the cars they'd recently bought.

Next to the building I discovered a small parking lot that appeared to be where the workers parked. The beat-up trucks and cars likely belonged to the men working in the warehouse. There were two white trucks, but neither had anything except dirt on their bumpers. Having done my due diligence and investigated, I was sure it would satisfy Aunt Garnet.

Circling back, I passed the warehouse again. I almost jumped out of my boots when a door flew open and a man stepped out.

"What are you doing back here?" he asked in a gravelly voice, slamming the door behind him.

I froze, speechless. He was dressed in black jeans, a tight white T-shirt and red suspenders. His arms and neck were covered with green and black tattoos; a swastika bloomed over his larynx. His shaved pink head shined in the bright sunlight.

"Nothing," I stammered. "I'm uh . . ." *Ladies' room. That's always a good excuse.* "The ladies' room. I'm looking for . . . I have to . . ."

A tiny mole twitched under one aqua eye. I stared at him, mesmerized. It wasn't a mole, but another tiny swastika. It was like I'd stepped into the scene of a B-movie.

"Inside the sales office," he growled.

"Thanks." I turned around and started walking, willing myself to not break out and run.

"I know who you are, Mrs. Ortiz," he called after me.

I felt sweat dampen my breastbone. So he knew who I was. People sometimes recognized me. My and Gabe's photo was occasionally in the *Tribune*. But I had a feeling this guy didn't peruse the society pages.

"You'd better watch yourself." His voice carried across the lot like a flaming arrow.

Don't look, don't look, I kept telling myself.

"You'd better watch your family."

The word *family* hit my ears as I rounded the corner of the office. I leaned against the building for a moment, feeling my head grow fuzzy, my eyes darken around the edges. This was not just Milt Piebald making vague innuendos. This skinhead creep was threatening my family. My mind flashed on Dove and Isaac, Daddy and Aunt Garnet out at the ranch, suddenly realizing how vulnerable they were. How anyone could come up our ranch's long driveway, shoot at them, set the house on fire, put poison out for our animals. So many ways to hurt people. And we'd never know when it might happen. Is this how Jim and Oneeda, Maggie and Katsy, Flory and the Sisters felt all the time? In that moment, I felt an uncomfortable mixture of shame and gratitude. In so many ways my life had been easy. All simply because of a random toss of genetics.

I hurried across the parking lot toward Aunt Garnet who, by this time, had the salesman looking dazed. When I reached them, she was asking about the passing capabilities of a 1992 red and black Camaro.

"I need some get-up-and-go," she was telling him. "And a trunk big enough to carry my walker."

If I wasn't so nervous, I would have laughed out loud. Aunt Garnet didn't *have* a walker. My heart skipped a beat. Did she? Pushing that thought aside, I took her arm. "We gotta go, Aunt Garnet. Emergency at home."

"What is it?" Her face turned grayish white.

I felt cruel, scaring her needlessly, but I didn't have time to think up another reason to leave the car lot. I pulled gently on her arm. It was thin and delicate under my hand.

"Dove needs us." I looked over at the salesman, whose face was a mixture of disappointment and irritation. "She'll be back later."

"We're open until ten p.m.," he said, following us.

I kept Aunt Garnet moving as fast as her Keds would let her.

"My card!" The salesman patted his pockets. "Shoot, I don't have one on me. Wait, I have one in the office . . ."

"No time," I called over my shoulder. "It's Randall, right?"

"Raymond!" he called after us.

"Whatever. Trust me. We gotta boogie, Aunt Garnet."

"Then let's boogie," she said, quickstepping toward my truck.

We were buckled up and driving out of the lot in less than three minutes.

I glanced in my rearview mirror. Raymond was standing in the middle of the lot, his hands on his shrunken hips, wondering what in the world just happened.

"What's the rush?" Aunt Garnet said, pulling a tortoiseshell compact from her purse and patting her shiny nose with the round pad.

"I think we're in trouble. Big trouble."

CHAPTER 15

"*I* FEEL JUST TERRIBLE," AUNT GARNET SAID WHEN I told her about the skinhead-looking guy who caught me snooping. "This is entirely my fault."

"If anyone is at fault, it's me. Gabe's always telling me to keep my nose out of police business and I never listen."

"You went to the car lot because I asked you to. Dove will kill me if she finds out I put you in danger."

"She will not, because we *aren't* going to tell her."

Aunt Garnet and I looked at each other. Then we burst out laughing.

"Yeah, right," I said. "Like we can keep anything from Dove."

"Amen."

"As soon as we get to San Celina, I'm going to call the ranch, warn them that I—"

"We," Aunt Garnet corrected.

"Okay, *we* might have stirred a hornet's nest and to stay on alert. I'm also going to run by and pick up Scout, take him to Emory and Elvia's house. Gabe's gone tonight and you and I will be at Flory's making dolls. I don't want to leave Scout alone."

"Good thinking," Aunt Garnet said.

While her side of the cab grew silent—hopefully she was petitioning the Lord on our behalf—I kept a sharp eye in my rearview mirror. Though I doubted whether that young man was following us, I knew that he and any of his friends could find me or my family whenever they wanted. It was no secret where we lived or where we worked, and like most people, we had predictable habits.

Jesus, please protect my family and my foolish self, I prayed.

We swung by my house to pick up Scout and call Daddy. I explained what had just happened to me and Aunt Garnet, about this guy's vague threats.

"If you were twelve, I swear I'd restrict you," Daddy said. "You call Gabe about this?"

"Not yet," I said, leaving it at that. I'd tell my husband later. "It's probably nothing, you know. I'm probably just being dramatic."

"Not the first time," Daddy said. "Don't worry, we're armed out here. You watch out for you and Garnet."

"I will."

I took Scout over to Emory and Elvia's, explaining what happened. While Aunt Garnet went upstairs with Elvia to meet Sophie Lou, Emory and I stood on his wide front porch and discussed what to do.

"You will stay here tonight," Emory said.

"No argument there. I set the burglar alarm at home. I'm sure everything will be okay."

"Nevertheless, I'm calling Jim Cleary and telling him that they need to keep a close watch on your house tonight." He slipped his arm around my shoulders. For a moment, I rested against his solid body. "Have you called Gabe?"

I looked out over his deep emerald yard at the lavender

blue "Sterling Silver" rosebushes covered with blossoms. "When he's traveling we always talk at ten p.m. because he's usually back in his hotel room by then. I'll tell him tonight."

Emory laughed and rapped his knuckles on the back of my head. "He's gonna kill you."

"You don't have to sound so gleeful. It wasn't *my* idea to go to the car lot. That's my story and I'm sticking to it."

"Good luck with that one, sweetcakes. For the record, our guest room is open for as long as you might need it."

Twenty minutes later, after a quick trip to Stern's Bakery, Aunt Garnet and I were pulling up in front of Flory Jackson's two-story house. So far, we'd seen no suspicious activity, so I was coming to the conclusion that the skinhead's threats were, at least for now, empty words.

Flory Jackson's red and white Victorian home was located in one of San Celina's oldest neighborhoods and was called "the Peppermint Stick House" by the dozens of foster kids that she'd cared for over the last forty years. It was as unique as her African-style crazy quilts. Her baby quilts, a popular item in the folk art museum gift shop, were made in traditional crazy-quilt fashion with velvets and lots of embroidery, but they also incorporated bold-colored batik fabric and symbols from African folk legends. She was an originating member of the Ebony Sisters Quilting Guild. Her school visitations promoting African American quilts and history were a favorite among local teachers.

By the number of cars parked on the street and in her driveway, it appeared that Aunt Garnet and I were the last to arrive.

"Hey, Flory," I said, when she opened her white front door. "I've got the sugar to keep us going." I held up two pink bakery boxes.

"Then, come on in," Flory said. "The ladies are already stuffing and sewing." Her soft black hair was pulled up in a twist, held secure by a hair comb made of tiny, rainbow-colored ribbons. She wore a butter yellow and rust caftan that brought out the gold flecks in her eyes.

I moved to the side to let Aunt Garnet enter first. "Flory, this is my aunt, Garnet Wilcox, from Sugartree, Arkansas."

Flory took Aunt Garnet's hands in hers. "Mrs. Wilcox, it is a pleasure to finally meet Dove's baby sister. I've heard so much about you. All good, of course."

Aunt Garnet's uncomfortable expression relaxed a little with Flory's words. I couldn't help wondering what Dove had really told Flory about Aunt Garnet.

We followed Flory down a long hallway with wood floors buffed to a high shine to a large, airy family room. Eight women, all from the Ebony Sisters quilt guild, were busy with some task pertaining to dollmaking. A huge burst of laughter greeted us when we entered the room. I glanced over at Aunt Garnet who hesitated at the doorway.

"Don't mind them, Mrs. Wilcox," Flory said, drawing Aunt Garnet into the room decorated with quilts, African tribal masks and two impressionistic paintings of black women carrying red baskets on their heads. "May I get you something to drink?"

"Please, call me Garnet," my aunt said. "Yes, that would be lovely."

"Why, I surely will, Garnet." Flory returned her smile. "Ladies, this is Garnet, Benni's aunt. She's Dove's sister, visiting from Arkansas."

The women called out greetings and Flory quickly introduced them—Muriel, D'Arbry, Arnell, Florene, Lizbit and Bettie. Katsy and Maggie sat at two sewing machines in the corner sewing tiny dresses and shirts.

"I promise there will be no pop quiz," Flory said to Aunt Garnet.

"Praise the Lord," my aunt answered, laughing. "I have trouble remembering my own name these days."

"I hear you, Sister Garnet," Arnell said. "You come on over and sit next to me. I've got *all* the good gossip."

"She means she causes all the good gossip," Florene cracked.

Comfortable laugher rippled through the room.

"At least I have a life," Arnell said. "You don't have nothin' interesting enough in your life to cause any gossip." She pointed a blue crochet hook at Florene and gave a dramatic sniff.

"They are sisters by blood," Flory said in a stage whisper to Aunt Garnet.

"And they fight like two polecats in a burlap bag," D'Arbry added.

Aunt Garnet smiled. "I understand. My sister and I have our moments."

Flory nodded knowingly, then turned to me. "Let me help Garnet start on some dolls. Jazz is in the kitchen making lemonade and sweet tea."

I held up the bakery boxes. "I'll take these cookies in and help her get the refreshments ready."

She smiled at me. "Lovely. So, Garnet," I heard her say, "would you prefer working on bodies, clothes or faces?"

Inside her large yellow and white country kitchen decorated in a chicken and egg theme, I found Jazz stirring a pitcher of pale pink lemonade.

"Flory sent me in here to give you a hand." I set the bakery boxes down on the counter. "Do you know where she keeps her platters?"

"On top of the refrigerator," Jazz said. She wore tight blue jeans, a lacy black tank top and five strands of turquoise and black beads. "We have tons to do tonight."

"Yeah, we do," I said, reaching for a platter. "But it's great that the dolls are selling so well."

She opened the bakery box. "Chocolate macaroons and lemon squares! My favorites!" She took a macaroon and bit into it. "I love the fair, but I'll be glad when it's over. Dad's a train wreck."

I placed the large yellow Fiestaware platter on the

butcher-block counter. "Did the police check out the graffiti on your back door?"

She started arranging cookies on the platter. "That sheriff friend of yours came by with some other cops. Took
some pictures and stuff. Dad paid the kid next door to
paint over it. The police asked us some questions, like if
we heard anything. It's probably those freaks Cal hung out
with when he was younger. I think they killed him, but your
friend is totally ignoring me." She shrugged, acting blasé,
but her bottom lip trembled.

I started helping her arrange cookies on the platter. I seriously doubted that Hud was ignoring her information. He
just didn't like giving away his suspicions. "Be careful."

"Like, duh, Benni. Of course I'm careful."

"I know it sounds lame, but I just couldn't think of what
else to say."

She flattened the empty box, then opened the second
one. "No worries. I know you're only trying to help."

We took the platter of cookies, some glasses and the
pitchers of lemonade and sweet tea to the family room. We
set the snacks on the square glass coffee table bisecting two
seven-foot brown leather sofas.

"Ladies, help yourselves whenever you need a break,"
Flory said. She indicated a place next to Muriel. "Benni,
would you like to stuff bodies?"

"Sounds a little weird," I said, laughing, "but sure."

She handed me a stack of doll bodies, a red crochet needle and a big bag of stuffing. "Pack them firm, but not tight,
then pass them to Arnell. She's stitching them up."

Flory had everything organized, with people stuffing
bodies, sewing up their backs, sewing on buttons for eyes,
finishing dresses and pants or stitching on hair. "If we finish everything we've brought tonight," she announced,
"we'll have thirty more dolls to sell."

We set to work, stopping only momentarily to use the
bathroom, nibble at a cookie or sip a drink. It seemed the

faster everyone worked, the faster they talked. Aunt Garnet and I listened while the Sisters covered everything from fried chicken to church revivals, chubby babies to the definition of "good" hair.

"Did you see Ruthie Lee's hair last Sunday?" Florene asked, shaking her head. "She ought not to press it herself. There she was sitting in front of me at church and I watched the kinks exploding like popcorn all over her head. Someone needs to hide that hot comb and tell that girl to get herself to a professional hairdresser."

"Now, Florene," Arnell said. "You know she's been having hard times. Probably can't afford to go to the beauty parlor."

"Still and all," Florene said. "I wouldn't be caught dead in a coffin wearing hair that was tryin' to get back home."

"I know that's right," Reba said.

"A beauty shop don't always do the trick," Muriel said, touching her smooth, pecan-colored bob. "There's days when my hair looks good for about five minutes after I leave Bobbi's Coiffures, but then"—she snapped her fingers—"my kitchen goes right on back home."

The women in the room roared with laughter. Aunt Garnet and I smiled, not understanding the joke. But never one to be shy when I didn't understand something, I turned to Muriel. "I don't get it."

She patted my knee with her warm hand. "You wouldn't, sweet pea. The kitchen is what us black ladies call the nape of the neck. On many of us, the hair there curls in little balls and depending on how kinky your hair is it can be a big pain in the patootie, especially when it's hot and humid."

"Thank the good Lord for San Celina weather," Florene said. "My hair's a dream here. But when I go back home to Alabama . . ." She shook her head. "Don't miss that humid air one little bit."

"I'm a witness," Bettie said. "It's the same in Georgia." The other women murmured in agreement.

I glanced over at Aunt Garnet, whose expression was thoughtful but interested. The only time I'd seen her around any black people in all the years I'd visited Arkansas with Dove was when she talked to Miss DeLora, the housekeeper who'd raised Emory, and that was usually to ask for a recipe or a way to get a stubborn stain out of Uncle WW's gray Dickies work clothes.

"Did you see Rolanda's hair at the Parker wedding last Saturday?" said Muriel. "Oh my, but she's got a beautiful head of hair. Thick as three ropes and smooth as a baby's bottom."

Arnell gave a cynical snort. "She might have good hair, but that woman needs some makeup lessons. She wears that orange lipstick like it's going out of style on a westbound train."

The women laughed again, with me and Aunt Garnet joining in this time. All women understood about someone wearing too much makeup.

Jazz, silent during the conversation, suddenly blurted out, "Why *do* you all talk so much about hair? What's the big deal?"

The room went silent for a moment, the women looking at each other, furrowed eyebrows communicating their discomfort. Jazz's light brown hair was as smooth as Malibu Barbie's.

Flory was the first one to answer her. "Well, Jazz, I guess you could say it's a cultural thing with African American women. Something that binds us together because it's a common dilemma." She tilted her head, considering her words. "No, *dilemma* is not the correct word, because there's nothing *wrong* with our hair. It's just that it's one of the things we can commiserate about with each other that others . . ." She glanced at me and smiled. "Those who don't have our type of hair just don't have the same problems. It would be a little like you talking with your friends about how we older folks don't understand your music."

Arnell picked up one of my stuffed dolls and proceeded to finish off the opening in the back with tiny perfect stitches. "Speaking of music. What's with that Vanilla Ice fella? Is he a white boy trying to act black or a black boy who just happens to be white?"

"Arnell," Florene said, laughing behind her hand. "You are a caution."

"Seriously," Jazz said. "This hair thing bugs me sometimes. I've heard you all talk about me having 'good' hair. Why do you say that—good hair? Hair is hair. I think it's ridiculous to judge people by what is really just dead cells growing out of your head." Her statement caused a few of the ladies to touch their hairdos, some of which were straightened, some left natural.

"You know, Cal and I talked about stuff like this a lot," she continued. The mention of the murdered boy's name caused the room to go quiet. "People judge other people by such stupid things like who your parents are, what color your skin is, what your hair is like. Our hair shouldn't matter. Our skin color shouldn't matter." She looked down at the doll she was stuffing. The fabric was three shades darker than her coffee-with-cream skin. "He was probably killed because he was dating someone with skin a few shades darker than his and I think that sucks. And I think everyone contributes to that. Both sides are . . . they should . . ." Her words faltered.

All the women's eyes were on her, their faces such a mix of emotions that I couldn't tell what was going to happen. It was like watching a movie scene, observing this young girl confront the black side of her heritage, call them out on a cultural habit she found troubling and confusing. How would these ladies react?

Flory walked over to Jazz and sat down next to her on the sofa. Like all of the women in this room, Flory was an adult during the civil rights era of the sixties. These women had likely experienced prejudice in ways that Jazz would never encounter. But I didn't see resentment on Flory's face, no bitterness toward this young girl who didn't completely understand what the generation before her suffered for her father and mother's right to marry and create her.

She put her arm around Jazz's shoulders. "You're a lucky girl to have had your beautiful mother and your handsome father, who both love you so much, who made you the lovely girl you are today. And you're lucky to have known your friend, Cal, who was obviously a good boy . . . man . . . who was trying to change his life. No one's perfect; no one knows all the answers. But it's people like you who have a foot in each world—you're the ones who will change things. It is getting better, I promise. I'm just sorry your young man might have been killed because things haven't changed fast enough."

Jazz wiped a hand across her now wet cheek. "Sometimes I don't feel like I fit anywhere."

"I'm sorry," Flory said, stroking her hair. "It's hard being first, but somebody's got to do it. You have to be strong." She kissed Jazz's temple. "You are our future, baby."

Flory's optimism was heartening, but I couldn't help thinking about the angry young man with the Nazi tattoos who confronted me at the car lot today. He was around the same age as Jazz. The hatred was still out there.

We worked for another two hours, but the conversation stayed neutral with the usual chitchat about local politics, what movies people were seeing and who might run for mayor next year. It was almost 10 p.m. when we agreed to call it a night. We did manage to completely finish twenty-eight dolls.

"I don't care if I ever see another one of these dolls again in my lifetime," Katsy grumbled, packing away her sewing machine.

On the ride back to the ranch, Aunt Garnet was quiet. I wondered what she thought of tonight and the direction the dialogue took. When we turned down the long driveway to the ranch, she finally spoke. "That was . . . enlightening."

"Yes, it was."

"I hope Jazz will be all right."

"I think she will be. It's not easy being biracial, but she has lots of people supporting her." I pulled up in front of the ranch house. The porch light was on and Dove was sitting on the front porch swing.

Aunt Garnet's face was shadowed in the truck's cab. "You know, we never did get the churches merged in Sugartree."

I nodded, remembering how hard some of the people in Sugartree had tried to combine a local black Baptist Church with the all-white Sugartree First Baptist that Aunt Garnet had attended almost her entire life.

"We couldn't figure out a way to make everyone happy in how they worship the Lord." Her voice sounded sad. "But there are some of us who started a Bible study—five black women and five white women. We're still meeting every other Wednesday night. It's a start."

I leaned over and hugged her, wondering if my gramma knew how her sister was changing. "It sure is, Aunt Garnet. It sure is."

CHAPTER 16

$\mathcal{J}$T TOOK ME TWENTY MINUTES TO CONVINCE DOVE and Daddy that it was safe for me to drive alone back to town.

"I have my cell phone," I said. "And nothing's happened yet, so I think this guy was just talking through his hat. I'll be safe with Emory and Elvia." Finally I convinced them. Just to make her happy, I called Dove once I stepped over the threshold of Emory and Elvia's house.

"Safe and sound," I told my gramma.

"I could just wring Garnet's neck for getting you in such a bind."

"Cut her some slack, Gramma," I said, thinking those were words I never thought I'd ever say in my life regarding Aunt Garnet. "I think she was just trying to forget her problems for a while. You know, this thing between you two has gotten way out of hand. If she's willing to get involved in something dangerous to avoid talking to you, then—"

"Stop right there, little missy," Dove said. "My sister and I have been dealing with each other twice as long as you've been alive. We'll do this in our own time."

"Honeycutt time," I mumbled, repeating what Uncle WW always called it when the sisters took their own slow-as-cold-molasses time.

"What was that?" Dove's voice held the same warning it did when I would smart off as a kid.

"I said *Honeycutt time.* You two always do things whenever you feel like it despite the fact that it affects other people. I'm tired of it. I'm tired of being in the middle. I'm . . ." Before I could prevent it, a sob tumbled from my lips.

"Honeybun," Dove said, her voice became gentle. "Are you sure you're going to be okay? Have you called Gabe about this?"

"I will as soon as I get off the phone with you. I'm sorry. I'm just scared for you all. I'm so afraid you or Daddy or Aunt Garnet will get hurt or killed because of something I . . ."

"Pshaw. The only person who's going to have the privilege of killing my sister is me. I'm not about to let someone take that pleasure from me. I've been waiting too long."

I couldn't help laughing. "I'll call you tomorrow."

"Trust in our Lord. He's got the whole world in his hands."

"Love you, Dove."

"Right back at you."

My next phone call was much harder. I decided to go upstairs to the guest room. This would take a little more privacy. After a bit of hemming and hawing, I told Gabe everything.

"I'm coming home right now."

"That's ridiculous," I replied, rubbing my bare foot across Scout's silky rib cage. He was lying on his side, peacefully asleep. "There's no plane to San Celina this time of night."

"I'll rent a car. I can make it in three hours."

"That is at least a four-and-a-half-hour drive! And I'll feel guilty for the rest of my life if you kill yourself coming back here to save me from nothing."

"It's not nothing."

Downstairs I could hear Emory and Elvia's voices. It was past 11 p.m., but Sophie Lou had been feverish and cranky. No doubt it would be a long night for everyone.

"I know it's not, Friday, but there's really nothing you can do. I'm safe. Aunt Garnet's safe. Scout is safe. The house is alarmed and you can have a patrol car check it every hour. There's not much more you could do even if you were here."

"Thanks for the vote of confidence."

"I just meant that you'd have to sleep too. Really, Gabe, I think this guy was just mouthing off."

"Have you called Detective Hudson?"

"Actually, it didn't even occur to me." That had to make him a little happy.

I could hear his breathing over the phone line. It reminded me of when we first started dating and we'd spent hours on the phone, neither of us wanting to hang up.

"Call him. It's his case."

"I will. Seriously, the only thing that will likely disturb our sleep will be Sophie Lou. She's a little colicky tonight."

Hud picked up on the first ring.

"You really shouldn't give into peer pressure so easily," he said, after hearing my story. "If your aunt jumped off a cliff—"

"My great-aunt is not a peer. And I've been taught to mind my elders."

"Nevertheless—"

"Stop. I've been lectured enough tonight."

"Then step back." There was no humor in his voice. "There's more to this than you know. I need you to step back from it before someone gets hurt."

"What do you mean there's more to this than I know?"

"Just do what I ask, okay? You're my best friend in the world. I don't want to lose you."

I was surprised silent. I was his best friend in the world?

"Okay, I will." Then I couldn't help giving a small laugh.

"My favorite sound. Stay safe, ranch girl."

"Likewise, Clouseau."

The next morning at seven thirty I was sitting with Elvia and Sophie at the kitchen table drinking my first cup of coffee when Emory burst into the room.

"Benni, you have to come see this!"

His unshaved morning face was frantic. He was dressed in wrinkled khakis and a sweatshirt, clothes he'd thrown on to step outside and pick up the newspaper. We'd noticed he'd been gone a little too long but assumed some talkative neighbor had accosted him.

I jumped up, jiggling the table. Hot coffee sloshed into my cup's thick white saucer. "What is it?"

"Your house." He gestured at me to follow him. I started after him, wearing a pair of Elvia's shorts and an Arkansas Razorback T-shirt I'd borrowed from Emory. I didn't even bother with shoes.

"Darlin', you and Sophie stay on the porch," he told Elvia who'd grabbed the baby from her carrier.

"Is it dangerous?" she asked.

He hesitated. "No, but . . . I'd feel better if you stayed here."

I ran my hand over Sophie's downy hair. "You can see us from the porch."

Scout followed me, but I told him to stay with Elvia while I followed my cousin down the street. A small crowd had gathered in front of my and Gabe's California bungalow. I was relieved to see it was still there. From the horrified look on Emory's face when he burst into the kitchen, I was afraid that someone had burned our house to the ground.

A few seconds later we were standing in front of my yard, gawking at the lawn. Swastikas and obscene words had been spray-painted on our grass, our mailbox, our paneled garage, and our front door. Acid burned the back of my throat. I gulped back the bitter-sweet taste, willing myself to not be sick. I felt my cousin's hand rubbing comforting circles on my back.

"It's gonna be okay," he murmured. "It's gonna be okay."

A black-and-white patrol car pulled up, dispersing the rubberneckers on the street. They moved back to the sidewalk. Our neighbors, Beebs and Millee, pushed through and came over to me, pulling me into magnolia-scented hugs.

"Oh, sweetie pie," Beebs said. "It's terrible, terrible. We didn't hear a thing. We must have slept right through it."

"Those pinheads," Millee said. "Good thing for them we did. I'd've knocked their blocks off." She stepped back, poised her hands in karate chops.

"Thanks," I said. "But I'm glad you didn't hear them. I would have hated it if either of you had been hurt."

"What happened?" Beebs asked. "Why did they do this to you? Where's Gabe?"

Before I could answer her questions, one of the officers walked over, slipping his nightstick into his belt loop. He must have been new because I didn't recognize him. A tall young woman with curly chestnut hair pulled back in a tight, low ponytail followed him. I remembered her. Last year at the annual San Celina Police and Fire Charity Basketball tournament she'd scored more points than any of the men, a feat gleefully reported on the front page of the *Tribune*.

"Are you all right, Mrs. Ortiz?" the young woman said. Her badge said T. Caldwell. Tina. That was her name. The guys called her Tee.

"I'm fine. I wasn't even here. I spent the night at my

cousin's house down the street. But I think I know who might have done this."

She nodded, communicating something to the other officer who had black hair and a square, handsome face. He was shorter than her by a good three inches but outweighed her by thirty muscled pounds.

"Everyone stay back, please," the male officer said.

The crowd, even larger now since our neighborhood had many older folks who rose early and took walks, obeyed the officer and inched back a few steps. Officer Tee took me aside and asked me to explain who I thought might have done this. While we talked, police started cordoning off a large swath of sidewalk in front of our house and Jim Cleary arrived.

"Benni, are you okay?" Jim asked.

"Yes, but Gabe . . ."

"I called him, but he must be in the air because his phone went directly to voice mail. He apparently caught an early flight. There's a message for him to call me as soon as he turns his phone back on. Let me catch up on what's going on." He went over to Officer Tee and started talking to her.

Minutes later photographers and reporters from the local media arrived. Hud arrived right behind the KSCC news truck, his scruffy face telling me that he'd just rolled out of bed. He brushed past the perky blond newscaster.

"Are you all right?" he asked me.

"Yes, you realize it's probably that guy I told you about. Or his friends." A thought suddenly occurred to me. "Flory! You need to send someone to Flory Jackson's house on Mill Street. We were there last night. They might have followed us! And our ranch . . . what if Dove and Daddy . . . What about Maggie and Katsy?" Panic overcame me and I felt my knees buckle slightly. Hud reached over to grab me, but Emory was quicker. His arm tightened around my shoulders.

"Everyone at the ranch is fine," Emory said. "I called

Dove. This Ms. Jackson. What's her number? And your friends Maggie and . . ."

"Katsy," I said, shaking my head. "I don't know their numbers by heart, but they're in my purse at . . ."

Hud waved his hand—no matter.

Before he could call, Jim came over. "What's wrong?"

I grabbed his arm. "Jim! Flory Jackson . . . we were at her house last night with the Ebony Sisters and the people who did this . . . Maggie and Katsy . . ."

He patted my hand. "I know Flory and I have Maggie's number on my phone. I'll give them a call." He pulled a cell phone from his pocket and walked a small distance away. A few minutes later he returned. "Everyone's fine. No sign of any vandalism. I'm afraid it's just your and Gabe's house." He frowned. "So far. Do you have your house keys? The bomb dog has arrived."

"Bomb dog?" I said. "Do you think . . . ?"

"It's just a precaution," Jim said.

I went back to Elvia and Emory's for my house key. In less than a half hour, the dog had cleared our house.

"Scout's going to feel so violated having another dog's scent in his house," I murmured. Emory sympathetically squeezed my shoulder.

Jim, Emory and I entered the house. Since our alarm had never sounded, it appeared that the damage was only to the exterior. Everything looked exactly like it did when I left for the fair yesterday. It felt like a week ago instead of less than twenty-four hours.

Normally I'm a pretty neat person. Gabe is still half-Marine. Between the two of us, the inside of our house is usually fit to be seen. But it had been a busy week and with the fair and all, so things were a little messy. It embarrassed me that the officer with the bomb dog and some of his detectives had seen my and Gabe's unmade bed, the breakfast dishes in the sink, our overflowing laundry basket.

But there were more pressing things for me to worry

about, specifically that whoever vandalized our house was watching close enough to know exactly when they would be least likely caught.

One of the detectives found Jim and me in the backyard, where we were inspecting for damage.

"One of the neighbors . . ." He looked down at his small leather notebook. "Mrs. Soto?"

"She lives catty-corner from us in the lavender and gray Victorian," I said. "She grows African violets in a greenhouse in the back." I didn't know why I felt the need to tell that.

The detective, who had deep brown basset hound eyes and a habit of sniffing after each sentence, nodded like the information meant something. "She said she got up about one a.m. to . . . umm . . . you know . . . use the john and she thought she heard the screech of tires. She said she didn't think anything about it because it's happened so much with the Cal Poly kids . . ."

"Except that it's summer," I said.

He nodded. "Yes, she said that occurred to her so she looked out the window. Said she saw something, possibly a light-colored vehicle. She heard male voices. Then they drove on so she went back to bed. Said she didn't bother calling because by the time the police got there, they'd've been gone." He stuck the notebook inside his jacket. "None of your other close neighbors heard a thing."

After Jim and I ascertained that only the front of the house had been vandalized, we went back into the living room. One of the detectives came to inform us that they'd taken pictures of the scene and gathered what evidence they could.

"Thanks, Stu," Jim said. His cell phone rang. "Hey, Chief."

While Jim informed Gabe about what happened and what was being done, I looked through the living room window at the crowd still gathered across the street. I watched people point a finger, then comment to each other. It felt like our house was a zoo exhibit.

"Benni?" Jim held his phone out to me.

"*Querida?*"

"Gabe."

"My plane just landed. I'll be there in twenty minutes."

I handed the phone back to Jim. "I'd better start cleaning it up."

"I'll stay and help."

I shook my head. "You go on back home to Oneeda. Tell her what's going on. I didn't tell the ladies all the details last night because I didn't want to scare anyone needlessly. Everyone should be aware that we have these kinds of people here in San Celina."

Jim's dark brown eyes turned down at the corners. "Benni, people like that have always been out there. I'll talk to Flory and she'll tell the others, but don't worry. We have all spent our lives looking behind us for people like that."

I leaned my head back against the fireplace mantel. "Oh, Jim, I'm so sorry. Because of Gabe, I thought I understood a little . . . but I didn't, not really."

"There's no way you could. Unless you're a person of color, chances are you've never had someone pull their purse or package a little closer when you walk by. Or start a sentence, 'I'm not a racist' but then proceed to tell you some blatantly racist joke. Or ask me if I sunburn!" He smiled and shook his head, taking ten years off his face. "As my grandkids would say, duh! Sure I do, if I sit in the sun long enough." He patted my shoulder. "We know that it can happen anywhere, anytime. And it's usually when we don't expect it, which is why we always unconsciously *do* expect it. Once they see Gabe's back, I doubt they'll be bothering you again."

"I hope not. But, I'm wondering . . ." I chewed my bottom lip.

"Wondering what?"

"What if there is something that is connected with Calvin Jones's death? Maybe . . ."

"Maybe you ought to let the sheriff's department handle it," Hud said, coming up behind me.

Jim's eyebrows went up and he didn't say anything. But his expression confirmed he was in complete agreement with Hud.

"Okay, okay," I said, holding up my hands. "Honestly, I never thought I'd get into so much hot water just trying to do something my prim and proper great-aunt asked me to do."

"On that loaded emotional note, I think I'll head on home," Jim said. "Tell Gabe I'll call him later and let him know if we've found out anything more from the neighbors. We've still got detectives canvassing all the houses in a three-block perimeter."

Then Hud and I were alone.

"I do think this is connected to Calvin Jones," I said.

His face was blank. For the first time I noticed that his hair, a little long and shaggy, had streaks of gray in it. There was even a shadow of gray in his day old beard.

"I know you can't tell me anything," I said, "but—"

"But nothing," Gabe's voice said behind me. Honestly, I was going to start wearing one of those bike helmets with the tiny rearview mirrors. "He won't tell you anything because you're not going to be involved in this any longer."

Hud smiled, held up a hand. "Thanks for the save, Chief. She's all yours."

"Let me know what's going on," I called after him. He didn't even acknowledge me. I turned back to my husband, who, surprisingly, didn't look mad.

"Are you all right?" he asked, putting his arms around me.

"Yes, yes, yes," I said into his chest. "Your detectives are through with photos and all. I was just getting ready to go outside and attempt a cleanup."

"There's turpentine in the garage. And, fortunately, there's lots of trim and house paint left. Let's get started."

Emory stayed to help us, as did Beebs and Millee. A half hour later, thanks to Elvia, we had her father, Hector, two of her brothers, Miguel and Ramon, D-Daddy and Gabe's son, Sam. When Sam drove up, Justin Piebald rode with him. For some reason I couldn't look Justin in the eye. I doubted that he had anything to do with this, but I couldn't help wondering if he knew that one of the young men I suspected was involved with the vandalism worked for his dad.

It wasn't long before our house was almost back to normal. The only remnants we couldn't completely clean away or paint over were the swastikas painted on the lawn. We tried mowing it and that helped a little. But we'd just have to let the grass grow long enough to cut off the paint on the thick St. Augustine blades.

"Maybe we can paint over it," Sam suggested. "Let me find some spray paint."

WHILE EVERYONE ELSE LOLLED AROUND THE FRONT yard and porch eating the doughnuts, muffins and coffee Gabe bought, I sat on the porch swing and talked to Dove on the phone.

"Garnet's just sick about this," Dove said. "Says she's thinking about going back to Arkansas tomorrow. Said she brought this on y'all."

"That's ridiculous. Let me speak to her."

"I dare you to talk sense into that woman," said Dove before handing the phone to her sister.

"I'm sorry," Aunt Garnet said. "I was being a foolish old woman and look what happened. Life is not a television show. I don't know what I was thinking."

"You weren't being silly. Look at it this way. We obviously did *something* to make these people nervous. You know there is something going on and, sometimes a little push is just what bad guys need to make that mistake that will get them caught. We have probably helped the cops." Actually, what I was saying was a bunch of bull, which is exactly what my husband's exasperated expression was saying to me. I shot him an apologetic look. All I wanted to do was make my aunt feel better.

"I suppose," she said.

"You can't go home yet because you haven't taken care of business. You *know* that. I don't know why you're here, but I do know that you and Dove have got to talk. You can't leave until that happens."

Dead silence. "I think Dove is calling me." Then she hung up.

I held out the cordless phone and stared at it, openmouthed.

"What's wrong?" Gabe said.

"My aunt hung up on me! And I was trying to make her feel better about what she—"

Gabe cleared his throat.

"Okay, what *we* did yesterday. But the minute I mention why she is visiting, she's gone."

Gabe rocked the swing with one foot. "Perhaps you ought to keep a low profile for a few days."

"You're absolutely right," I said, putting the phone on the side table. "I'm totally minding my own business and not doing a thing to help anyone."

And I did. For almost a day and a half.

CHAPTER 17

$\mathcal{A}$ PHOTO OF OUR VANDALIZED HOUSE WAS ABOVE THE fold on the front page of Friday's *Tribune*. When the chief of police is a minority and there is racist graffiti painted all over his house and lawn, that's news in any town. San Celina didn't have many incidents involving race relations, so here it was a major story. By the bare-bones reporting, the writer revealed he didn't know the backstory about why we'd been targeted. The article suggested it was because of Gabe's Latino heritage.

I didn't go to the fair despite the fact that Katsy was giving a talk today. As much as I wanted to see her, I agreed with Gabe that it might be wiser to not make myself a target.

I spent most of the day doing household chores. In the afternoon; I sat on the porch with Scout and visited with Elvia who came by with some books I'd ordered. Just seeing my goddaughter's plump velvety cheeks and shiny dark eyes made me smile. Beebs and Millee made a smoked chicken, wild rice casserole and banana cupcakes for my lunch.

"Oh, girls, I'm not sick," I said, taking the white and blue CorningWare dish from Beebs.

"We know that," Millee said. "We just didn't know what else to do."

"*We're* sick," Beebs said, carrying the plate of six cupcakes. "Sick that something like that can happen right here in our lovely town."

I was sitting on the front porch when Gabe called at 4 p.m. "I have to work late tonight. Won't be home until after nine. Maybe later."

"Oh, man, I wanted us to go to the country rodeo tonight. I'm going stir crazy."

He surprised me by not immediately arguing about why I should stay home. "You should be safe enough at the fair as long as you're with other people. What about Scout?"

"I'll ask the twins to watch him. I don't feel good about leaving him here alone just yet."

"I agree. Is there anyone you can ride with to the fair?"

The only people I could think of were Beebs and Millee, but I needed them to watch Scout. "I could go by the ranch and ride in with Dove and Daddy."

"But you'd still be driving by yourself to the ranch."

That's when I really got angry. Not at Gabe, but at the people whose actions had made my driving the thirty miles to Paso Robles a major problem. "Those people . . . whoever they were . . . I hate it that they have that kind of power."

"Yes," Gabe agreed, but didn't elaborate.

From my perch on the porch I, unfortunately, had a bird's-eye view of the remnants of the swastika on our grass. Or rather the odd, flowerlike shape that Sam tried to change it into using a can of spray paint. We should just dig up the grass and plant flowers. "When they invaded our house, they took away our sanctuary."

"I know. Just watch your back. I mean that literally."

"I promise that I will stay in large groups of people at all times. I'll be as vigilant as a . . ." I tried to think of an apt metaphor, but failed. "I'll be careful."

"*Te amo.*"

"Love you too, Friday."

Before I left, I decided to call the ranch.

"How's Aunt Garnet?" I asked Dove.

Dove's deep sigh sounded like a wind swooshing down a canyon. "She's moping around here like a teenage girl who's lost her first beau. I just don't know what I'm going to do."

This time Dove actually sounded concerned rather than irritated. That really worried me.

"Here's a novel concept. Why not just ask her what's wrong?"

No response.

"I truly don't understand you, Gramma. You have never, in all my life, ever had trouble asking anyone anything! What's the big dang problem?"

"Because that's *not* how we do things."

I held out the phone, tempted to pound it on the porch railing. "I think how y'all do things is not working out so great and maybe, just *maybe* you should try something new."

"See you at the rodeo," she said, and hung up.

I considered throwing the phone into the front yard, but I knew my dramatic gesture would send the twins flying over here to see what was wrong. They were monitoring my house like Columbos in broom skirts.

"That's it," I said to Scout, who reclined on his side with one eye open. He'd been nervous since our house had been vandalized and had slept as poorly as I last night. "I wash my hands of them. I do, I truly do."

His tail thumped twice.

"You, sir, are a true gentleman." I scratched his soft belly.

The rodeo didn't start until seven thirty, so I puttered around the house until a little after six. I called the twins, told them what both Gabe and I were doing and asked if they'd dog-sit.

"No problem," Beebs said. "Bring him over. We'll keep a sharp eye on Scout and your house."

"We have the cops on speed dial," Millee said on the other line.

When I arrived at the fair there were no parking spaces left near the grounds so I was forced to find a spot in an off-site parking lot two blocks away. But plenty of people were walking toward the fairgrounds so there was little chance of me getting attacked. When I left tonight, I'd simply catch a ride back to my truck with Dove and Daddy. Gabe couldn't fault my diligence.

The Bull Pen was beyond crowded tonight. The country rodeo was one of our most popular events because almost everyone had a family member or a friend or a child or a friend's child competing. It was truly a local gathering, all the contestants competing either from San Celina or Monterey County. It was an old-fashioned rodeo, existing more for fun and bragging rights than paying a large purse. But though the purses were small, the silver-plated belt buckles were big and much coveted. The bulls and broncs were spirited, but not crazy. The events were ones that most ag people could relate to—team penning, team roping, barrel racing, breakaway roping and double mugging, a combination steer wrestling and roping that originated in Hawaii.

A performance by the Wranglerettes Drill Team opened the rodeo. It was always a crowd pleaser watching the lithe young girls move in and out of formation on their precisely trained horses, their red, white and blue American flags fluttering in the wind, the horses galloping in time to the

patriotic music. We all rose for the National Anthem sung
in a wispy soprano by this year's Miss Mid-State Fair.

Dove, Daddy and Aunt Garnet arrived right after the
first go-round of barrel racers. Dove chattered like a par-
rot on crack, Aunt Garnet looked calm and thoughtful and
Daddy appeared a little tight around his eyes.

I sidled up to him at the bar. "Hey, Daddy, what's happening with the *hermanas y Sugartree*?"

He ordered a bottle of Budweiser, something he rarely
did. Daddy just wasn't a drinker. "Pumpkin, those two
women are about ready to drive me to drink." The bar-
tender slid the icy bottle across to him.

"Apparently they already have." I laughed.

He didn't. I'd never seen him look so miserable.

"Where's Isaac?" I asked.

"He went down to Santa Barbara for some kind of lecture. Comes back Sunday. I'll sure be glad to see him."

I put a hand on my dad's forearm. "I'll come over tomorrow and force them to get this all out in the open."

He gave me a look that said—good luck—then took a
long swig of beer.

The evening flew by watching the local young and not-
so-young people compete. I joked and talked with people
I'd known my whole life, cheered their kids to victory, la-
mented their defeats, ate three of Emory's delicious minia-
ture smoked chicken sandwiches and enough cheese grits
to embarrass myself. In true addict fashion, I swigged three
bottles of non-diet Coke. And I deliberately stayed away
from Dove and Aunt Garnet. They sat next to each other all
evening out on the balcony chairs watching the rodeo but,
from what I could tell, didn't say one word to each other.
Tomorrow, this whole business was coming to a head if I
had to handcuff those two together and throw them in the
pokey.

They were announcing the last go-round of bullriders
when I wandered back into the hospitality suite. After the

last ride, a sluggish river of sweaty, slightly tipsy people would flow from the stadium seats either into the arena or back to the fairgrounds, which were open until midnight. In the arena there was the traditional dance after the rodeo, but I hadn't gone to one since my late twenties. It used to be one of the highlights of the fair for me back when my eyes didn't start fluttering at 11 p.m.

I searched the crowd for Daddy and the sisters. Dang it, I should have told him when we were at the bar that I'd need a ride back to my truck. I finally spotted him and Dove over by the exit. Dove's face was flushed pink, not, I suspected, from the warm room. I pushed through the crowd toward them.

"Hey, are you getting ready to head home?" I glanced around. "Where's Aunt Garnet?"

"She's hiding out in the bathroom," Dove snapped. "Just like when she was a child. She used to do that to Mama all the time."

"What?" Even I was becoming weary of that being my unoriginal response to everything in the last few days.

Daddy shuffled his feet and looked at the ground. "Garnet and Dove had a little set-to."

I placed my hands on my hips, feeling like I was refereeing between two five-year-olds. "Oh, for Pete's sake, what happened?"

Dove looked as guilty as a chicken-chasing puppy. "Nothing."

Daddy cleared his throat and continued to study the brown commercial carpet.

"Okay, we quarreled," Dove said. "Big deal. She'll get over it once she admits I'm right."

"About what?" I asked.

"Gramma Honeycutt's teapot."

"Her what?"

She enunciated slowly. "Gram-ma Hon-ey-cutt's tea-pot."

"What about it?"

"I said it had pink flowers. She said they were green."

"Lord help us, you are both crazy as rabid dogs."

"They're pink! I'd swear it on Gramma's grave."

"Where is this teapot?"

She waved her hand dismissively. "Broke when we were six. That's not the point."

Daddy looked helplessly at me. I swear his eyes were starting to tear up.

"I'm stopping at the liquor store on the way back to the ranch," he declared.

"You do realize you are displacing acute anxiety with irrational anger," I said to Dove.

"Don't start on me with that psychic mumbo-jumbo."

"Psychological."

"She'll be fine. Said she's going back to Arkansas tomorrow. I'll drive her to the train station myself. Throw her bags after her."

Not, I thought, until this was all resolved. "Why doesn't she come home with me tonight? Give you both some time to cool off."

Daddy looked like he would collapse from relief. "Thanks, pumpkin. We all need a night off."

I started to hug my gramma, but she pushed me aside and started down the steps. When I hugged my dad, I whispered in his ear. "This *will* be resolved tomorrow."

"It better," he whispered back, "or I'm moving out to the bunkhouse with Sam."

Once they left, I called Gabe's cell phone to warn him we would be having company tonight. It went directly to voice mail, which meant he'd either turned it off or was out of range. Where *was* he that he couldn't have his cell phone on? He was so intent on me not being alone so no one could hurt me and here I couldn't even reach him.

The Bull Pen had grown hot and sticky and I was tired. All I wanted to do was find Aunt Garnet and go home. I'd

keep my promise to Gabe and ask one of the security guys
to drive us to my truck.

The three-stall bathroom was hip deep in teased hair,
fringed cowboy shirts tied under boobs and the chemical
fog of multiple varieties of hairspray. Teenage and twenty-
something girls maneuvered for a section of the two long
mirrors trying to repair rodeo queen curls that had wilted in
the heat. Aunt Garnet wasn't among them.

"Was an older lady with short white hair just in here?"
I asked a friendly-looking young woman wearing a sleeve-
less red T-shirt and a matching cowboy hat.

"Not in the last ten minutes." We were so close I could
smell her grape-flavored gum. "That's how long I've been
waiting to pee."

"Thanks," I said, backing out.

I scanned the crowd, but I didn't see her anywhere.
I checked the coat room, which doubled as a child-care
area. A bored-looking girl in her early teens sat on the
floor entertaining a toddler with LEGOs.

Now I was starting to worry. Where could she have gone?
The only answer was out to the fairgrounds. Worry was quickly
overtaken by annoyance. It could take me hours to find her.
I suddenly regretted my intervention in the Honeycutt girls'
lifelong feud. Since when was it *my* job to play diplomat?

I went down the stairs, getting more irritated with each
step. I was tired, hot and wanted more than anything just
to go home and take a cool shower. I reached the bottom of
the stairs, shoved the door open and ran right into the rock-
hard chest of Detective Ford Hudson.

"Whoa!" he said, grabbing my shoulders. "Any particular reason you are imitating a battering ram?"

"My crazy aunt," I said, pulling away. "She got in a
huge, ridiculously petty fight with Dove and is wandering
around the fairgrounds somewhere. It's going to take me
hours to find her."

He cleared his throat. "Unfortunately, ranch girl, it isn't."

CHAPTER 18

*H*IS EXPRESSION WASN'T TEASING AND I FELT MY chest constrict. Around me the mock-terror screams from the midway, giggling packs of girls, crying babies, became muted, like someone abruptly stuck cotton in my ears.

"Hud, what's happened to my aunt?"

"Don't panic . . ."

I grabbed the lapels of his denim jacket. "Tell me."

He placed his hands over mine. "You need to come with me. I'll explain while we drive." He flagged down a security cart, flashed his badge and told them to take us to the fairground entrance.

"What is going on?" I asked.

He placed a finger on his lips, glanced over at our driver.

Minutes later we were inside his Dodge Ram truck and I repeated, "Tell me."

"Just a minute." He flipped open his phone and dialed. "Hud here. What's going on?" He listened a moment, then said, "We're on our way. Yeah, she's with me." He stuck the phone in his shirt pocket, then started the truck. "First off, for the moment, your aunt is fine."

I inhaled. The air smelled like vanilla and motor oil. "For the moment? Where is she?"

He turned on the ignition and shifted into drive. "Like a certain someone related to her who will remain unnamed, she has wandered into something she shouldn't have wandered into."

"What in the heck are you babbling about?"

He concentrated on the dark road. "You know if it weren't so dang important, I'd find it hilarious. But multiple law enforcment agencies have been working on this sting operation for almost six months and there's a good possibility that your—as you so aptly put it—crazy aunt might have flushed all that down the toilet."

Frustration made my eyes burn. "I'm totally lost."

"Condensed soup version. Milt Piebald. Stolen cars. Chop shop. Hot parts. Car parts these days are apparently more profitable than selling whole cars. Milt's got a whole string of people on his unofficial payroll. Most of White Boys United, actually. Why, Mr. Piebald's the Donald Trump of bumpers, side mirrors and alternators. Calvin Jones probably knew about it, maybe even worked for Milt when he was hanging around his skinhead buddies. We're guessing he, for reasons as yet unknown, threatened to go to the police. Maybe he was into blackmail or wanted to make a little spending money to impress his new girlfriend. Maybe he hated what they were doing. Shoot, maybe the guy actually had a conscience. Those details aren't clear yet. He was killed. It was made to look like it was a racially motivated incident to throw us off."

"All the stuff with Levi was fake?"

"Well, not exactly fake. The crimes committed were real—the letters, the quilt theft, the graffiti on his house and yours. Still can probably classify them as hate crimes. It's just that the actual motivation wasn't because Levi was black."

"It was to fool the police."

"Brilliant plan actually, what with Cal dating Jazz and her daddy being the fair's first African American manager. I'll admit it did fool us initially. When race is involved, people get nervous, don't think straight, get tunnel vision, which is exactly what Mr. Piebald hoped would happen. However, he didn't count on one of his little skinhead worker bees getting caught driving drunk, violating probation and on top of that having child-support payments in arrears to the tune of eight thousand dollars. To avoid jail time and possibly lose all visiting rights to his kids, he made a deal with the district attorney's office to give up the goods on his boss." Hud turned down Main Street in Paso heading north. "So much for loyalty among thieves."

His words tangled in my head like a crazy alphabet soup. "Okay, that explains what happened with Calvin Jones, but what does my aunt have to do with any of this?"

He turned off Main Street onto a side street where he pulled up behind a strip mall that supported a grocery store, a dry cleaner, a day spa, a used book store and a Subway sandwich shop. A half-dozen police cars and a SWAT van were parked in a haphazard pattern with SWAT team members and cops wearing dark windbreakers milled around with Styrofoam cups in their hands.

"What's going on?"

He turned off the ignition and got out of the truck.

I unbuckled my seat belt and jumped out, running to catch him. "That explains what happened with Calvin Jones. But my aunt, what . . . ?"

He pointed to an unmarked car. "Ask him." The car door opened and Gabe stepped out.

"What in the heck is going on?" I asked Gabe.

Hud walked up behind me. "I told her a smidgen, but I left the family part for you."

Gabe put his hands on my shoulders. "What do you know?"

"That all the things directed at Levi and Jazz were red herrings. That Milt Piebald is behind it. Where's Aunt Garnet?"

Gabe and Hud exchanged looks.

"Sweetheart," Gabe said. "She's sitting in the Piebald's sales office chatting with Juliette Piebald. We've got the SWAT team, dozens of officers and a stack of arrest warrants ready to take down this gang except that we can't because your aunt is discussing corn bread recipes with Juliette Piebald."

I couldn't have been more surprised than if you had told me that Aunt Garnet had been accepted as a running back by the NFL. I looked at Gabe, then at Hud, then back at Gabe. "Uh . . . well . . . I . . ."

"Exactly our reaction. The reason I sent Hud for you is we need your help."

"Is she in danger?"

"Hopefully not. That's where you come in. I need you to casually go in the office and *get her out of there.*"

"Is Juliette in on the stolen car parts ring? Did she know about Cal's murder?"

Hud piped in, "Who knows? That's always the sixty-four-million-dollar question when it comes to wives, isn't it? How much of Gabe's work life are you privy to?"

Gabe frowned at him. "Hudson, shut up."

Hud held up his hands. "Just an observation by an impartial third party."

Apparently I didn't know *enough* about my husband's work life. I knew he'd been working on this stolen car case with other agencies. Not once had he hinted that Milt Piebald was possibly involved.

Gabe looked into my eyes. "Forget him. You know I'm

only doing this because we can't think of any other logical, safe way to remove her from the premises. Do you think you can do it?"

"Of course I can. She's my aunt."

"Just walk in there, make up some kind of excuse and get her out of there," Hud said. "Leave the rest to us. No heroics."

"I have no intention of being any kind of hero."

Gabe squeezed my shoulders. "*Querida*, you know how much I hate using you like this, but there's no one else."

"I know. I'll be careful. I won't do anything rash."

"We'll be watching everything you do and we've got the place wired for sound. We'll hear everything that is going on. Don't worry, sweetheart, you've got the best backup in the country."

"I've always known that."

"You ready?" Gabe asked. "We'll have you drive Hudson's truck."

I nodded, swallowing salty water.

Hud handed me the truck keys. His keychain was black and tan braided horsehair. "Once you get your aunt into the truck, drive out of the parking lot and back across the street to this parking lot."

"Got it."

Gabe kissed me quickly on the lips. "Be safe," he murmured.

I climbed into Hud's truck and started the engine. Five minutes later I pulled up in front of the car lot office. I could see Juliette and Aunt Garnet through the plate-glass window. The rumble from his V8 engine rattled the windows, causing both of them to look up, surprised.

I pocketed Hud's keys and opened the office door. "Hey, Aunt Garnet! I've been looking for you everywhere. Dove needs you at home right away. She's having stomach problems. She thinks it's her ulcer acting up. She's asking for you." Stop babbling, I told myself. Too much information.

Aunt Garnet stood up, touching her chest bone. "Oh, dear, her ulcer? I must . . ." She reached for her handbag sitting on the desk.

"Wait," Juliette said, standing up, obviously flustered. "She can't go yet. Garnet and I aren't through with our conversation."

"You'll have to finish later," I said, attempting a relaxed smile. "Really, her sister is sick and wants to see her. Aunt Garnet can come back tomorrow." Or, better yet, never.

Juliette's face turned pale and glanced behind her at a closed office door. "But she can't leave. I need to . . ." Her clear, modulated voice rose an octave. I got the distinct feeling she wasn't talking to us. "I can't do this. It's wrong . . ." She groaned and leaned forward, covering her face with her hands. "Just go. I don't care anymore."

Relieved, I grabbed Aunt Garnet's arm. We were almost out the door when a loud voice commanded, "Stop right there."

We turned to see Milt Piebald stepping through the now open office door. "You two can just sit yourselves back down so we can have ourselves a little chat. I've been told you've been playing a little game of cat and mouse with my sales force."

"I wouldn't exactly call that ill-dressed gentleman a sales force," Aunt Garnet said.

I squeezed her arm in an effort to quiet her.

"Mr. Piebald," Aunt Garnet said. "I came by to simply check out your fleet to see if there was a vehicle that I might purchase for a reasonable price to putter around town in. I must say I'm not impressed with your selection. I have absolutely no interest in whatever else it is you people do here."

I squeezed her arm again. *Too much info, Aunt Garnet.*

She reached over and lightly smacked my hand. "Quit pinching me, Benni. I know exactly what I'm doing."

I pictured Gabe having a heart attack in the van where

they were listening to all this. Was he regretting ever marrying into my totally nutso family?

Milt turned to Juliette, his face turning the color of a pomegranate. "What did you tell her?"

"Nothing! She doesn't know anything." Juliette started to stand. Milt made a lowering gesture with his hand and, like a well-trained cow dog, she obeyed.

The wooden desk chair squeaked from her weight.

"Look," I said. "I don't know what you two are doing and I don't care. I just need to take my aunt home." With a death grip on Aunt Garnet's arm, I started pulling her toward the door.

"Stop," he bellowed again.

I stopped. My mind tallied the facts of our situation. He wasn't going to let us go until he found out what we knew. Chances were he wouldn't kill us. That would be stupid. He knew he'd never get away with that. Then again, he might be desperate. Did he have any idea what was waiting for him outside?

All I had to do was talk our way out of this. Give him what he thinks we have . . . information.

I stepped in front of Aunt Garnet. "Okay, we'll tell you what we found out."

I could only imagine that Gabe and the other police officers were having conniption fits right about now. Hold off, I thought, sending a mental message to my husband. Don't send in the cavalry yet.

"We know everything," I said. "We know that Juliette and Lloyd Burnside are having an affair . . ."

Juliette gasped, sat back in her chair. Milt watched us with wary eyes, his wide mouth partially open.

"We realize that you're both trying to cover it up to save your budding political career. And you know what? We don't care. These days, I'd say that no one does. We certainly have no intention of telling anyone. So, that's what we know, and frankly, whatever deal you two have made about having an open marriage, that's no skin off my—our—noses." *Please, please fall for this.* I felt Aunt Garnet's hand come up and rest on my shoulder.

"She's right," Aunt Garnet said. "I find it utterly despicable and biblically immoral, but it is not our business."

Milt locked eyes with me. Juliette emitted little moans from where she sat, but I didn't look at her. What Milt saw on my face right now was crucial to whether he believed my words. *Please*, I prayed, *for once in my life let me have a poker face.* Everything sounded magnified—Juliette's distressed cries, the buzz from the fluorescent lights, the sound of Aunt Garnet's breathing behind me.

Milt rubbed a hand over his face, glanced over at Juliette, then back at us.

"Get out of here, you dumb broads. And if I hear of you telling anyone about this I'll make that Mex husband of yours suffer. I have the power to do it and I will. And I'll sue you both for defamation of character. You got that?"

"Loud and clear," I said, turning to Aunt Garnet. "Let's go." My heart pounded while I walked Aunt Garnet out, helped her up into Hud's pickup truck and drove slowly out of the lot.

"That was close," Aunt Garnet said.

Once we left the car lot, we drove across the street to the strip mall. As we were pulling into the parking lot, dozens of police cars and cops on foot swarmed past us into the Piebald offices and surrounded the warehouse. I turned off the truck engine and we watched, a front row seat to the whole scenario.

"For heaven's sakes," Aunt Garnet said, leaning forward to see better. "I wonder what that's all about."

There was a rap on my window. I turned to see the face of my husband.

I flung open the door and practically jumped in his arms.

"Good work, Ortiz," he said, burying his face in my hair.

"Likewise, Ortiz."

Aunt Garnet's voice echoed from the depths of the cab. "Does someone want to give me the four-one-one on what just happened?"

CHAPTER 19

"*I*'LL EXPLAIN WHEN I DRIVE YOU HOME," I TOLD HER.

"Your truck's behind the strip mall," Gabe said, handing me my keys. I gave him Hud's. "I'll come by the ranch later." He kissed me on the lips. "I'll call Levi and let him know what happened. He can call Maggie and Katsy."

"Good. They'll be beyond relieved, I'm sure."

After calling the twins and telling them we'd be a little later than I expected, I drove Aunt Garnet back to the ranch.

"Before I explain what just happened, tell me how you ended up going with Juliette Piebald. Are you crazy?" I shouldn't have added that last remark, but it came out before I could stop it.

"I know it was foolish to go with her," Aunt Garnet said contritely. "But I was so mad at Dove that I told her I'd find my own way home. Then realized that I'd spoken myself into a corner. Juliette saw me sitting on a bench in front of the giant pumpkin exhibit and I guess I looked a little flustered. We got to talking about sisters and before I knew it, I told her the whole story. She offered to take me home. She excused herself and I heard her call her husband on her cell phone, but I thought she was just telling him that she was taking me home. I didn't know it was a trap. I wasn't ever really worried. I had pepper spray in my purse . . ."

"You do?"

She sat up straighter and pursed her thin lips. "I was going to use it on that Mr. Piebald if he came at you. I am not without resources, Benni."

Apparently not.

"It didn't occur to you that maybe going off with someone who was a suspect in a murder investigation wasn't too . . . uh . . . wise?"

She took a hankie out of her purse and dabbed her hairline. "You know, in any new endeavor there is always a learning curve. Cut me some slack. Besides, I thought I could take her down if I had to."

Okay, I had to admit, her comment shut me up for a moment.

"So," I finally said. "What *were* you two talking about when I drove up?"

"Corn bread recipes. But, of course, now we know it was just a ruse and she was trying to find out what I knew about the car theft ring. We never got past corn bread, though, and then you showed up."

I gave a little laugh. Gabe hadn't been kidding. She and Juliette were exchanging corn bread recipes.

"I was telling her that Dove's was the best I'd ever eaten. It's that fourth cheese she uses. Smoked white cheddar from this family dairy in Wisconsin and a touch of cayenne pepper."

"You know her secret ingredients?"

She patted my forearm. "Oh, Benni, I've known for years. I just like to rattle Dove's cage. Why, our squabbles are what keep our blood moving."

During our drive home, I filled her in on the details.

"So, all this time Mr. Jones's homicide and the vandalism actually had nothing to do with Levi being fair manager."

"Isn't that something?"

From the road the lights of the Ramsey ranch glowed yellow and inviting. The familiar scrape of my truck tires on the gravel driveway was the most comforting sound in the world.

Inside the house, Dove, Daddy and Isaac had just sat down in the living room, getting ready to eat popcorn and watch a Pink Panther movie.

When Aunt Garnet sank into the sofa next to Dove, she said, "This feels heavenly."

"You look exhausted, sister," Dove said.

"I am, sister. Catching killers is exhausting business."

Dove sat straight up. "Doing what?"

Aunt Garnet laughed and winked at me. "Turn off the TV. Have we got a story for y'all."

I LET AUNT GARNET TELL THE STORY. I DON'T THINK I'D ever seen her so animated. When she was finished, satisfied with everyone's exclamations, she leaned back and gave a deep sigh. "I'm glad it's over."

Dove, who'd remained surprisingly positive during Aunt Garnet's tale, said, "I'm glad you're okay. God was really looking out for you both."

"Yes, he was," Aunt Garnet said. "He certainly gave Benni the gift of gab in the exact moment we needed it. Her story about Juliette and Lloyd Burnside having an affair was inspired."

"And true," Gabe said, walking into the living room.

"I knew it!" I said.

Gabe sat down next to me on the sofa. "When they got everyone down to the sheriff's department, Juliette broke down and confessed everything, including the Milky Way bar she stole when she was twelve years old. I think the district attorney's office won't have any trouble convincing her to cut a deal and testify against Milt, which would make the stolen cars case against him stronger."

"But the real question is, did he really have Calvin Jones killed?" I asked.

"Looks like it. We don't know yet which of the WBU boys actually killed Mr. Jones. Our snitch only knew it went down, not who did it, though he gave us his best guess. We've picked up the guy he suspected killed Cal and he's being questioned now. No doubt once he hears the words death penalty, he'll roll over and give us Milt. From what the snitch said, Calvin Jones stumbled into the operation when one of his old pals offered to sell him some hot parts for his truck. Cal must have gone to Milt with the intention of asking him to stop." Gabe shook his head. "Did he really think Milt would just up and stop?"

I nodded. "Cal mentioned to Jazz that he was going to try to talk someone out of doing something illegal. Why didn't Cal just go to the police?"

Gabe shrugged. "Apparently Cal worked for Milt for a few months when he was still in high school. My best guess is maybe he felt like he owed him the chance to turn over a new leaf. You know, kind of like when someone gets sober or stops smoking. They want others to join them in their new straight and honest life. Why he went to Milt will always remain a mystery unless Milt chooses to tell us. And I doubt that will ever happen."

"Maybe Cal's feelings about Jazz made him want to do the right thing. To impress her, maybe," I said. "To show her he really had changed."

"Could be," Gabe said. "A good woman can often do that to a man."

"I hate asking this, but what about Justin?" I asked.

"Do you think he knew about any of this? I mean, it's his father . . ."

"I talked to him long before we planned the sting," Gabe said. "He wasn't aware of anything. He hadn't lived with or worked for his father for years. His dad's quickie marriage to Juliette never sat well with Justin. He was willing to work with us to stop his father, but we couldn't use him. Too risky. Especially when we suspected Milt might be behind Cal's death."

"Poor kid," I said. "That must have been hard."

"He's a tough young man. He'll survive this."

"Well, it's over now," Aunt Garnet said. "We can finally get back to normal."

"Whatever that is in this family," Gabe said.

Isaac, who'd been quiet up until then, touched Dove gently on the shoulder. "Don't you have something you need to tell Garnet?"

Dove looked over at her sister, her face suddenly serious. "William Wiley called."

Aunt Garnet jumped up, her face panicked. "When? Is he all right? Oh, my, I didn't call him today . . ."

Dove went over to her, taking her hand. "He's just fine. But he left a message."

Aunt Garnet looked like she was going to be sick. In the background, the mantel clock Gabe and I bought Dove last year for her birthday ticked unbearably loud.

Dove said. "He said to tell you it's time."

"Time?" Aunt Garnet whispered.

"What is it?" I said, going to her, slipping my arms around her trembling shoulders. "Aunt Garnet, what's wrong?"

"It's WW," she said in a small, scared voice. "He has Parkinson's. I think we might need to move to California."

CHAPTER 20

"*O*F COURSE YOU WILL!" DOVE EXCLAIMED, PULLING her sister into a hug. Both women started crying. "Don't you worry at all. We'll take care of you both."

"Thank you, sister," Garnet said, hugging Dove so hard I thought she'd break a rib. "I just didn't know how to tell everyone."

Tears stung my eyes. How hard it must have been for Aunt Garnet to admit that she couldn't take care of Uncle WW. After the sisters were through crying, Garnet gave us more details. Uncle WW had been diagnosed a year ago, but she'd kept it from everyone. Both she and Uncle WW had a lot of pride, something that the rest of us couldn't really call them out on. It was a family trait.

"I'd stay there except we don't have much family left in Sugartree any longer. I'll miss the old house, of course, but William Wiley's having a real difficult time going up and down those steep stairs. He has to use the wheelchair more and more."

"Who's taking care of him now?" I asked.

"Jake and Neba Jean." Jake was Aunt Garnet and Uncle WW's only child; he and Neba Jean were my cousin Rita's parents. "But I didn't tell you this. Jake has decided to take a job in Vermont." Jake was an accountant. From what I heard, a really good one.

"Vermont?" Dove exclaimed. "What the heck is in Vermont?"

"A job that pays a lot more than the job he has now. And they need the money," Aunt Garnet said, her voice a little apologetic. "Neba Jean's gotten them into a little financial bind . . . again."

It was an unspoken fact that everyone knew that Neba Jean loved her blackjack. Hopefully, there weren't many casinos around Vermont. Though it was a little too close to Atlantic City. Was there anyplace anymore where there wasn't a casino? Guess that was Uncle Jake's problem.

"Don't you worry about a thing," Dove said, rocking her sister back and forth. "We're going to be with you every step of the way."

With those words, Garnet started bawling again and Dove joined her.

I got up and fetched them a box of tissues.

While they pulled handfuls of tissues from the box, I asked, "Anyone want a piece of pie?"

"I do!" Daddy, Isaac and Gabe said simultaneously. All of them sounded relieved. There was just too much emotion flowing through the room right now.

That made us women laugh. Thank the good Lord for pie.

Dove and Aunt Garnet's loving truce lasted about eighteen hours. The next afternoon, Aunt Garnet made some snarky remark about Dove's potato salad needing a smidge more mustard and a tad less mayonnaise. Dove said that Aunt Garnet's sour cream biscuits tasted like sawdust, and

they were off and running again, each one calling me practically every hour to complain about the other.

But there was a difference now. It didn't feel as . . .
mean-spirited. It was more like a longtime married couple
sniping at each other because they trusted the love of the
other one so completely that they knew they could let off
steam.

Uncle WW had contacted a realtor while Aunt Garnet
was away and their house already had two offers. I promised to fly back to Sugartree to help my aunt and uncle
pack up a lifetime of possessions, help them decide what
would come to California, what they'd give away, what
they'd discard. I knew Dove would be right there next to
me, helping her sister every step of the way. Emory was
going to contact a specialist in Santa Barbara to look into
transferring Uncle WW's insurance and medical records.
We'd get them out here, and then, like families do, we'd
deal with my uncle's illness as it progressed. We'd just take
it one day at a time. That tired old saying was a cliché for
a very good reason.

Another surprise happened after Aunt Garnet revealed
the reason she'd come to San Celina. Emory's dad, my
uncle Boone, decided to sell *his* house and move to San
Celina. He said he'd been thinking about it since Emory
and Elvia had gotten married, but now that Sophie Lou
was here, there was nothing keeping him in Sugartree. The
home office would stay in Arkansas under the watchful eye
of Uncle Boone's longtime plant manager.

"What is going on here?" Gabe said when I told him
the news. It was Sunday afternoon, the last day of the Mid-
State Fair. We stood on our front porch watching Beebs
and Millee flirt with our new neighbor. He was half their
age and had fine-looking, muscular legs. "Half the state of
Arkansas is moving to San Celina."

"Hey, your family is welcome too. Do you think we'd
be able to convince your mom to come out here to live?"

His face was thoughtful and for a minute I panicked. I loved Kathryn Ortiz, but I wasn't *serious*.

"Nah," he finally said. "She might like coming out for a few months in the winter, but her heart is in Kansas." He gave me a mischievous smile. "You'd have a handful if Dove, Garnet and my mom all lived here."

"Oh, pshaw," I said, waving a hand. "I can handle three old ladies. I'll put them to work at the museum."

He pulled me into his arms and hugged me. "You are okay Aunt Garnet is moving out?"

"Yeah, I am. She and I actually had fun together. She's . . . different. More mellow. This might be the start of a whole new era in her life."

"She's got a hard road ahead of her," he said, resting his chin on my head.

"They both do. But she and Uncle WW have all of us."

"*La familia*," he said.

"Yes, *la familia*."

We were quiet for a moment, each lost in our own thoughts of what the word *family* meant. With Aunt Garnet, Uncle WW and Uncle Boone all moving to San Celina, my extended family was growing.

I sighed, rubbed my face against the front of Gabe's shirt, inhaling the sweet scent of clean cotton.

"Quarter for your thoughts." His lips were warm on the top of my head.

I laughed and slipped my hands into the back pockets of his jeans. He still felt fine, real fine. "Inflation strikes the Ortiz household."

"Well?" he said.

"Just thinking about Calvin Jones and how he didn't have any family at all. What will happen to his body?"

"Once they establish he has no next of kin, the state will bury him."

"Paupers' field," I said softly.

"Unfortunately, yes."

"We can't let that happen. I want to pay for his funeral and for a decent burial. And a proper headstone. He deserves that." I waited for Gabe to protest.

"I agree. I'll talk to the sheriff's department about it tomorrow."

I looked up at him. "Want to go to the fair tonight? It's the last time you'll get a chance to taste raspberry wine ice cream."

"Wine ice cream. Sounds wonderful."

I wrinkled my nose. "Not to me. But there is something I want to see. The deep-fried-food contest. I hear that one of the entries is a deep-fried jelly doughnut."

"Isn't that redundant?"

"Seriously, they take a jelly doughnut, dip it in a batter and deep fry it. It's supposed to be doubly delicious."

"Only you could possibly think that."

So that's what we did. We went to the fair, ate some raspberry wine ice cream (wasn't as bad as it sounds), laughed at the fried-food contest (deep-fried bacon won) and congratulated Levi on the fair's successful run.

"Now that it's over, Katsy has talked me into that Alaska cruise," he said, sitting with us in the wine gardens. The sound of a blues band playing in the arena floated through the warm air and surrounded the misty gardens with a melancholy vibe. "Maggie and Jazz are coming too."

"Good for them," I said. "You all need a family vacation."

After dark, Gabe and I walked through the midway holding hands talking about what the rest of the year might bring. The air had cooled and the bright, colorful lights of the carnival rides flashed and pulsated. When we reached the Ferris wheel, Gabe turned to me.

"How about a ride, Mrs. Ortiz?"

"Only if you pay."

He bought our tickets at the booth and gave them to the carnie, slipping him some bills.

"I saw that little maneuver, Chief," I said, stepping into the ride's rocking seat. "Why are you bribing the operator?"

He smiled and pulled the lock bar across our laps. When the Ferris wheel started, we circled a few times, exclaiming like the other riders, at the incredible nighttime view of the fair and the city of Paso Robles. After a few rotations, the Ferris wheel stopped with our car at the very top.

"Very smooth," I said, tucking my arm into his. "And how much did this cost you?"

"I'm trying to be romantic."

I smiled at him, thinking how lucky I was to have this man. The thought flashed through my head—the last time I'd been on a Ferris wheel was with Jack.

But I wasn't sad. That was another time, another life. It had been a good ride with him. And it was a good ride now.

"Here." He reached into his pocket and handed me a small box.

"What is this?" For a moment my mind thrashed around frantically. Had I forgotten an important date?

"Relax, you didn't forget an anniversary. I just bought you a gift. No reason."

Relieved, I opened the box. It was a ring. A pear-shaped diamond set in a plain gold band. I slipped it on my finger next to my gold wedding band. "It's gorgeous, Friday."

"I know you're not the jewelry type. And it won't hurt my feelings if you only wear it occasionally. But I never bought you an engagement ring and . . ." He leaned over and kissed me hard, causing our seat to rock.

"Whoa," I said, gripping his arm. "No more sudden moves until we touch planet earth."

"I love you, *querida*," he said.

"I love you back, Sergeant Friday."

The operator gave us another minute before starting the Ferris wheel moving again. As we slowly descended, we watched the carnival lights flicker, neon firecrackers against the purple-black sky. Around us people screamed and laughed and cried and kissed, making memories that would last for the rest of their lives. We stepped off the Ferris wheel, taking a moment for our legs to get used to solid ground again and started walking toward the rest of our lives.

An excellent source for the history of black cloth dolls is "No Longer Hidden—A Catalogue of the Exhibit of Black Cloth Dolls 1870–1930," by Roben Campbell. For more information about black cloth dolls, please check out the website www.blackclothdolls.com.

FROM NATIONAL BESTSELLING AUTHOR

Earlene Fowler

THE NEW BOOK IN THE AGATHA AWARD–WINNING
BENNI HARPER MYSTERIES

SPIDER WEB

Benni and the ladies of her Coffin Star Quilt Guild are excited to display their Graveyard Quilt at the first ever San Celina Memory Festival. But when a local cop is wounded by a mysterious sharpshooter who seems to have a vendetta against the police, Benni fears for her own loved ones—especially her police chief husband, Gabe, who now suffers from post-traumatic stress disorder.

Troubled by her husband's emotional trauma and a mysterious new San Celina resident—a woman who knows too much about Gabe's past—Benni is drawn into the search for the sniper, determined to make her hometown safe again . . . before their peaceful street fair becomes a shooter's deadly target range.

PRAISE FOR
EARLENE FOWLER'S BENNI HARPER MYSTERIES

"Breezy [and] humorous."
—*Chicago Sun-Times*

"Fowler's charm as a storyteller derives from the way she unpredictably sews all these other disparate plots together, just like one of those quilts in Benni's museum."
—*The Washington Post*

penguin.com

THE
SADDLEMAKER'S WIFE

By National Bestselling Author

Earlene Fowler

After the death of her husband, Cole, Ruby McGavin arrives in Cardinal, California, where she has inherited part of a cattle ranch. But she is shocked to discover that Cole's family, despite what he told her, is still very much alive.

Though intent on selling out to the McGavins and starting a new life, she cannot help but be drawn to them—particularly handsome saddlemaker Lucas McGavin. And the more she learns about them, the more she wonders if she ever really knew Cole…

"[A] sweetly told narrative."
—*The New York Times*

"Emotionally powerful."
—*Publishers Weekly* (starred review)

penguin.com

EARLENE FOWLER

Don't miss any of the Agatha Award–winning
series featuring Benni Harper, curator of San
Celina's folk art museum and amateur sleuth.

Fool's Puzzle
Irish Chain
Kansas Troubles
Goose in the Pond
Dove in the Window
Mariner's Compass
Seven Sisters
Arkansas Traveler
Steps to the Altar
Sunshine and Shadow
Broken Dishes
Delectable Mountains
Tumbling Blocks
State Fair

BERKLEY PRIME CRIME

penguin.com

WELL-CRAFTED MYSTERIES
FROM BERKLEY PRIME CRIME

- **Earlene Fowler** Don't miss these Agatha Award–winning quilting mysteries featuring Benni Harper.

- **Monica Ferris** These *USA Today* bestselling Needlecraft Mysteries include free knitting patterns.

- **Laura Childs** Her Scrapbooking Mysteries offer tips to satisfy the most die-hard crafters.

- **Maggie Sefton** These popular Knitting Mysteries come with knitting patterns and recipes.

- **Lucy Lawrence** These brilliant Decoupage Mysteries involve cutouts, glue, and varnish.

- **Elizabeth Lynn Casey** The Southern Sewing Circle Mysteries are filled with friends, southern charm—and murder.

M5G0610